"Angela?"

The sound of Blade's voice startled Angel, and she jumped up to find him standing only a few feet behind her. "What are you doing here?" she demanded.

"It's not safe out here alone at night, Angela. There can be danger anywhere . . ."

"Danger? But there's no one around." She spoke softly, mesmerized by the way the moonlight softened his features.

"Things can happen when you're alone in the wilderness, and . . ." Blade lifted one hand to touch her cheek.

Angel took a step closer to him. Her eyelids drifted downward as she savored the sweetness of his touch. She wanted him to kiss her.

"Ah . . . Angel . . ." Blade's voice was barely a whisper as he used her nickname for the first time. He bent to her, seeking her lips with his own. It was a tentative kiss at first, a soft exploration, but it soon exploded into something far more powerful and wonderful than she had ever imagined possible . . .

Books by Bobbi Smith

DREAM WARRIOR

PIRATE'S PROMISE

TEXAS SPLENDOR

CAPTURE MY HEART

DESERT HEART

THE GUNFIGHTER

Published by Zebra Books

The Gunfighter

BOBBI SMITH

ZEBRA BOOKS
Kensington Publishing Corp.
http://www.kensingtonbooks.com

ZEBRA BOOKS are published by

Kensington Publishing Corp.
119 West 40th Street
New York, NY 10018

All Kensington titles, imprints, and distributed lines are available at special quantity discounts for bulk purchases for sales promotion, premiums, fund-raising, educational, or institutional use.

Special book excerpts or customized printings can also be created to fit specific needs. For details, write or phone the office of the Kensington Special Sales Manager: Attn. Special Sales Department. Kensington Publishing Corp., 119 West 40th Street, New York, NY 10018. Phone: 1-800-221-2647.

Zebra and the Z logo Reg. U.S. Pat. & TM Off.

ISBN-13: 978-1-4201-0531-5
ISBN-10: 1-4201-0531-0

First Printing: April 1993
10 9 8 7 6 5 4 3

Previously published under the title *Beneath Passion's Skies*.

Printed in the United States of America

In memory of my mother—Miss you, Mom. . . .

Prologue

Tall, blond-haired Lee Jackson, his handsome features set in rigid lines of self-control, his brown-eyed gaze hard and angry, stood beside his beloved sister Helene's coffin staring down at her lifeless form. In life, she had been light-hearted and loving, full of fun and adventure. Many were the times when, in their childhood, she'd led him on a merry chase. She'd been so willful and headstrong that he, the older brother by five years who was supposed to protect her, had been run ragged trying to keep her out of harm's way.

Memories of Helene as a little girl besieged him. His eyes burned, and Lee closed them to still the tears that threatened. When he opened them again and looked down at his sister, he tried to tell himself that this couldn't be Helene, but there was no denying it. The dead woman before him was his cherished sibling, and he would never hug her or hear the lilting sounds of her laughter again.

Bitterness filled Lee. When their parents had died four years before, Helene had only been fifteen and he'd become her guardian. She'd grown into a beautiful young woman and had had an army of suitors intent on winning her hand. She'd enjoyed them all, but had fallen in love with Michael Marsden, a man Lee had disliked intensely from the very start. He'd tried to warn her about this stranger to their city. He had attempted to show her the less than glowing information he'd learned about the man, but she'd been too stubborn and "too much in love" to listen. And now . . .

Lee's hands clenched into fists at his sides as he struggled to control the savage fury that filled him. *Marsden . . .* The man's name was a curse on his soul. He would not rest until he saw his sister's death avenged. The authorities had ruled her death an accident from a fall from her horse, but Lee knew differently. Helene had been an expert horsewoman. Her death had been no accident. There were strange bruises on her body, bruises that could not have been caused in a fall. He'd known then that Marsden had been responsible, but there had been no way to prove it.

Lee had confronted his brother-in-law, but Marsden had been unflinching in the face of his accusations. Lee was sorry now that he'd threatened him, for right afterward he'd left town and taken all of Helene's considerable inheritance with him. The man's cowardly flight only convinced Lee all the more of his guilt. Lee vowed somehow, some way, no matter what the cost, he was going to find the bastard and make him pay for what he'd done.

A violent, searing hatred filled Lee. Had he not been forced to stay in town and see to Helene's funeral, he would have gone after Marsden as soon as he'd discovered him missing. Now the murderer had a head start on him, but Lee would follow; and when he caught him, Helene would be avenged. He would see to it.

Chapter One

Philadelphia
One Year Later

"Oh, Michael . . ." Celia Maguire sighed. "You're wonderful."

"And so are you, my dear." Michael Marsden smiled down at the dark-haired, dark-eyed young beauty lying naked beneath him. It wasn't a smile of affection that curved his handsome mouth, though, but one of immense self-satisfaction. Michael never ceased to be amazed at how naive and stupid women were and how easily they fell prey to his calculated advances. This seventeen-year-old maid from the Windsor household had come to him like a ripe plum, tumbling into his bed with an eager willingness that had surprised even him. He had never guessed he would meet with such unhampered success, but he wasn't about to complain. His plan was progressing at a rate he hadn't dreamed possible—and with very

9

little effort. Soon. . . . very soon, he would win that which he sought and claim the ultimate prize.

Celia believed Michael truly desired her for herself, and she gazed up at him adoringly. Michael Marsden was the most attractive man she'd ever seen. Desire blossomed anew within her as she studied his classically perfect features, blue eyes, and blond hair. He was so rich and so powerful! Her heartbeat quickened, and she shivered with the knowledge that she was here in his arms. Being a lowly servant far removed from his social circle, Celia didn't know what she'd done to merit his attentions, but she wasn't about to question her good fortune. The moment was too perfect. Wanting to make love with him again before she had to leave, she moved sinuously against him.

"You're an eager little thing," Michael remarked with a chuckle. He responded to her enticing movements by caressing her ample curves.

"Only for you," she whispered breathlessly.

Michael silenced her declarations of devotion with a harsh kiss. He felt no emotion for Celia, and he despised the fact that she was trying to romanticize what was a purely physical act for him. It suited his purpose to have her, so he took her. She was a means to an end, nothing more.

They coupled in heated silence, the quiet broken only by their ragged breathing and by Celia's cry of final ecstasy as she attained her pleasure. The act finished, Michael moved away from her clinging presence.

"Dawn is nearly upon us, sweet," he told her in a tone he hoped conveyed regret.

"I know. I have to go," she sighed. "I can't afford to be late."

"Even now that Windsor's dead?"

"It's worse now. His older spinster-sister, Blanche, has moved in and taken over. She gave Mrs. Delaney, the housekeeper, a free hand with us, and there'll be hell to pay if I'm not there on time." Celia pressed one last kiss on his lips and then rose from the bed. She was very conscious of Michael's eyes on her as she began to dress, and she longed to climb back into the wide, comfortable bed with him and forget the dull drudgery of her life. "Things are really different with the old man gone."

"Why?" Michael asked, taking care not to show how pleased he was that she was finally talking about her employer. He'd been waiting all night for a chance to bring up the subject of the Windsor family, and now she had done it for him.

"Well, they had the reading of the will yesterday afternoon . . ."

"Oh?" Michael pretended ignorance of the matter, while in truth he was very much aware of it. It had been for that reason, and that reason alone, that he'd brought Celia to his bed last night. Household servants always knew the details of what was going on in their employers' lives, and he hoped to glean some important information from her.

"Yes, Mr. Windsor left each of his daughters very well off, of course, but there was a real interesting clause in the will."

"There was? You mean he didn't divide everything equally?" Michael had to force himself not to sound eager.

"No. Mr. Windsor had always wanted a son, and, evidently, he was still so upset about never having had one that he put a clause in the will that leaves the bulk of his business interests to his first-born grandson."

"He what?" Michael was astounded. *This was almost too good to be true!*

Celia mistook his excitement for disbelief. "It's crazy. His business associates are in control until the boy turns ten, then he'll inherit everything. It's strange, isn't it? What if his daughters never have a son?"

"It's very strange," Michael agreed, but he couldn't have been more delighted. A sense of euphoria gripped him. His family had a history of siring only males. There hadn't been a female Marsden born for three generations.

"Mary, the other kitchen maid, and me were wondering which of the girls would get married first to try to claim the money. Seems it's not much of a contest, though, since Elizabeth is eighteen and the other two, Sarah and Angela, are only eleven and nine. Of course, the oldest one might have only daughters and that would give the other two a chance. We were laughing about that when Mrs. Delaney walked in and caught us." Celia grimaced as she remembered their run-in with the formidable, white-haired battle-ax. "Mrs. Delaney said we were crude to think that everyone else was as greedy as we were. She said the

Windsor girls love each other and that the money doesn't matter to them."

"She's probably right," Michael said thoughtfully. Everything he'd learned about the three daughters since coming to Philadelphia earlier that month seemed to indicate that the housekeeper's assessment was true.

"Well, if that's true, then they're stupid. If I were one of them, I'd be marrying a man today and bedding him tonight just to get my hands on the rest of that money ten years down the road!" she announced as she pulled on her dress and fastened the buttons.

As Celia spoke, Michael saw the gleam of jealousy and avarice in her eyes, and he knew he'd have to be careful how he handled her once he put his plan into action. Rising from the bed, he went to take her in his arms. She'd just given him the bit of information he'd been hoping for, and he was not ungrateful. He kissed her.

"Will I see you again?" Celia asked anxiously.

"Of course. I'll send for you," he promised.

Celia left him then, slipping from his room at the fancy hotel without anyone taking notice. She felt as if she were walking on air as she headed back to her job at the Windsor mansion. Michael Marsden desired her and he wanted to see her again! Fantasies of her new lover filled her head, and she wondered how soon he would send for her. She hoped it would be that very next night.

Celia would have been devastated had she known that Michael never gave her another thought after she'd gone. As soon as he'd closed the door behind her, Michael began planning his seduction of and wedding to another woman—Elizabeth Windsor. He would turn on all his charm and claim the oldest heiress for his own. He'd heard she was a quiet girl, and if that proved to be true, he was certain she would be no match for his ardent courtship. She would be his.

Michael gave a triumphant laugh as he vowed to himself to marry the wench in less than six months time. He would have preferred a quicker trip to the altar, but he knew there would be resistance because of her state of mourning. Anxious though he was, it didn't pay to flaunt every rule of society. He would console Elizabeth, and he would offer her a strong shoulder to lean on in this, her time of need. By the time he proposed, she'd be so smitten, she'd never even think of saying 'no.'

Ignoring the triviality of getting her with child, Michael mused on his goal of taking control of the Windsor inheritance. It didn't even occur to him that Elizabeth might not give birth to a boy. He wanted one; therefore, she would have one. The fortune would be his.

Four months later at the Windsor home

"Do you really think it's all right, Aunt Blanche?" blonde-haired, brown-eyed Elizabeth Windsor asked her aunt as the maid helped her don the dark blue satin gown. Her cheeks were flushed with excitement, but her expression was a bit worried as she awaited her aunt's answer. Tonight was the night she'd been longing for! In just a few moments, Michael Marsden would be coming for her to escort her to the Uttersons' ball. Elizabeth wanted desperately to attend with the handsome, dashing Marsden who'd been so kind and attentive since her father's death, but it had been only four months since the funeral, and she feared gossip would result.

"Of course, it's all right, Elizabeth," the grayhaired, bird-like spinster responded from where she perched on the edge of her oldest niece's bed. Though initially she'd hesitated at the thought of Elizabeth going to a social gathering so soon, Michael had completely won her over. Charmer that he was, Blanche had been completely powerless before the force of his personality. She had given in to his wishes like a willow bending before a hurricane wind. "Michael's a perfect gentleman. He would never compromise you in any way."

"You're right, of course," Elizabeth agreed, thoughts of the debonair young man bringing a smile to her lovely features. She was a pretty young woman, but growing up knowing that her father had wanted a son had rendered her less than sure of her own self-worth. She found being the center of Michael's attentions dazzling and flattering.

"There's no need to worry about anyone talking about you. If they do, it will be because they're envious," Blanche confided, thinking how lucky her niece was to be going out with Marsden. Though Michael was relatively new in town, it was well-known that he was very successful. Why, the suite of rooms he'd taken at one of the best hotels in town was costing him a small fortune. He gained entrée wherever he went and was seen only with the most influential members of Philadelphia society. He was a man with class and breeding, and he would make an excellent husband for Elizabeth. Blanche only hoped things progressed in that direction.

"Thank you." Elizabeth gave her elderly guardian a hug. "Do you think this gown is appropriate?" she asked as she smoothed the demure, full-skirted dress.

"Yes, darling, it's just the thing. Since this is your first outing since the funeral, it's best to keep—"

Their conversation was interrupted as eleven-year-old Sarah, the middle sister, came running into the room. A little bit heavy for her age, she was of average height, with medium brown hair and brown eyes. Yet, while there was nothing extraordinary about her physical appearance, she exuded an inner happiness that no one could ignore. Sarah always looked for the good in everyone and always credited them with the best of intentions. She was a delight to be around, and everyone who knew her loved her.

"He's here! Michael's here!" Sarah announced, her dark eyes aglow. She thought Michael Marsden the most wonderful man in the whole wide world, and she was as thrilled by Elizabeth's date with him as Elizabeth was. "His carriage just pulled up!"

"Oh, good." Michael had arrived! Elizabeth paused only long enough to give her sister a quick kiss on the cheek, then hurried for the door. She couldn't wait for him to see her dressed up. In the months he'd been coming to call, she'd had to wear

16

mourning clothes, but tonight would be different. At last, she could dress for him as a woman should. She wanted to please him, to win his heart as he had already won hers. Elizabeth hoped tonight would be the beginning of a true and real courtship for them.

Michael was more than pleased with himself as he mounted the front steps to the palatial Windsor home. Since that day, months ago, when he'd made his first call to the family to pay his respects, he'd been resolute in bestowing his attentions on the young, impressionable Elizabeth. Tonight he would reap the rewards of his efforts.

Michael was glad that he'd managed to overcome senile Aunt Blanche's initial objections to her niece's appearing in public so soon. It had annoyed him to have to play the fool to the doddering, old woman but he'd done it. With flattery and pure force of will, he'd won her over. Elizabeth would attend the ball with him.

Elizabeth. A fleeting image of her crossed his mind as he raised the solid brass doorknocker and let it fall. She was a passably pretty girl, and she was certainly malleable enough. In fact, the truth be known, she was much too eager to please him for his own tastes. He liked more sophisticated women, women who knew how to play love's games. The promise of all that Windsor money, however, kept his interest in the virginal heiress very much alive. After they'd married and she'd borne him the required son, he would return to indulging his own jaded desires.

Until then, he would bide his time and do whatever was necessary to achieve his goal. Michael's musings were interrupted as Robert, the Windsor's butler, opened the door.

"Good evening, Mr. Marsden. Come in," the tall, distinguished, gray-haired servant greeted him warmly as he held the door wide.

"Good evening, Robert," he returned as he stepped into the spacious marble-tiled, two-story foyer.

"If you'll make yourself comfortable in the parlor, sir, I'll inform Miss Elizabeth that you've arrived."

"Thank you." Michael moved with familiar ease into the parlor. He smiled to himself with confidence as he settled in on the sofa to await Elizabeth's entrance.

"Hello, Michael." Elizabeth spoke as she appeared in the doorway.

"Elizabeth." With all the gallantry of an ardent suitor, he came to his feet and crossed the room to take her hand as she moved forward. "You look lovely." Raising her hand to his lips, he pressed a soft kiss upon it.

Elizabeth nearly swooned at his display. Before her father's death she'd been courted by a few young men, but none had had the intensity of Michael. She lifted her gaze to his and was spellbound by the heated look in his blue eyes. Her heart skipped a beat and her breath caught in her throat.

Blanche and Sarah joined them then, shattering the spell Michael had been weaving around her.

"Good evening, ladies." He charmed them both with a wide smile.

Blanche returned his smile with a flustered one of her own and Sarah blushed prettily.

"It's good to see you again, Michael. I trust you'll take good care of my niece tonight?"

"Have no doubts, Miss Windsor. No harm will ever come to Elizabeth as long as she's with me," he vowed in all honesty. He couldn't afford to let anything happen to her. "Shall we go?"

"Yes, I'm quite ready. All I need is my wrap."

Robert appeared with the necessary garment, and Michael took it from him and slipped it around her shoulders. Elizabeth couldn't suppress the excitement that shivered through her at his touch. They bid everyone good night, and Blanche and Sarah watched from the doorway as the couple climbed into the carriage and drove away. It was only after they turned back inside that they noticed nine-year-old Angela, nicknamed Angel because of her angelic appearance with her pale gold hair and perfect features, standing by herself watching them from the far end of the hall.

"Angel? What's the matter?" Sarah asked, realizing for the first time that she hadn't come to see Elizabeth leave on her date. "Why didn't you come see Elizabeth in her new dress? She looked so pretty!"

Angel was generally a happy child, always ready for fun and excitement, but tonight as she came forward for the first time, she was frowning darkly and her green eyes, usually sparkling with merriment and mischief, were stormy with turbulent emotion.

"I didn't come out, because I don't like Michael Marsden. I didn't want to be around him," Angel declared belligerently. In the way of young children, she didn't know why she despised her sister's suitor, she just knew that she did.

"You don't like Michael?" Sarah repeated, staring at her aghast. Michael was handsome and rich. She could find no flaw in his character for he had been nothing but kind to them from his very first visit.

"Angel, I can't believe you said that," Blanche agreed, distressed by the child's reaction. "Michael is considerate and thoughtful, and he obviously cares a great deal for Elizabeth."

"I don't care. I don't like him, and I don't trust him," Angel persisted, a stubborn tilt to her chin.

"But why?" Sarah pressed, knowing it was unusual for her little sister to be so outspoken in her dislike of someone.

"I don't know why. There's just something about him. He's not nice, and I don't like the way he looks at Elizabeth." At nine, there was no way Angel could put into words the feelings she had about Michael. She only knew that she saw a strange hunger in his gaze and sometimes a shadow of meanness there, too. She wanted to stay as far away from him as she could.

"Michael looks at your sister that way because he finds her attractive," Blanche lectured. "It could be he's falling in love with her, and I can't think of anything that would please me more."

"But—" The thought of his marrying her sister frightened Angel. She loved Elizabeth. Elizabeth had raised her since their mother died six years ago, and she didn't want to see her big sister hurt by a man she instinctively knew wasn't what he appeared to be.

"Hush, now. I'll hear no more disparaging things about him." Blanche defended the man she thought to be perfect. "You see to it that you behave when he's around."

"Yes, ma'am," Angel replied, realizing it was useless to argue. Chastened, but not convinced, she disappeared upstairs to her room without another word.

The evening passed in what seemed the blink of an eye to Elizabeth. She had never had such a wonderful time. With Michael by her side, she felt beautiful. He was attentive to her every need, anticipating her desires even before she knew what they might be. When they danced, the feel of his strong arms about her made her feel feminine and cherished. She was in heaven. If there were whispers of disapproval over her having returned to the social scene too soon, Elizabeth was unaware of them. She was too enthralled with her escort to pay attention to anything else.

Michael knew his victory was within reach as he escorted Elizabeth out to his carriage at the end of the evening. There was no doubt in his mind that she was totally captivated, and he knew the time had come to declare himself. He could see no reason to wait. The sooner he took her to bed, the sooner she'd be carrying his son. As he helped her into the waiting conveyance, his hands lingered possessively at her waist. After giving directions to the driver to take the long way home, Michael climbed inside and sat down beside her.

"Did you enjoy yourself?" he asked as he boldly took her hand in his and drew her near.

Elizabeth sighed, "Oh, yes! I had a wonderful time. Thank you." Michael was everything she'd ever dreamed of in a man, and she knew in that moment that she would love only him for the rest of her life.

Michael read her emotions as easily as he would read a child's primer.

"Oh, my darling," he murmured, taking her in his arms. "You're so beautiful. I've wanted to do this all night long." As the carriage rumbled off into the night, he held her close and kissed her. His mouth covered hers with expert precision as he deliberately sought to rouse her to a fever pitch. Parting her lips, he deepened the kiss as his hand moved to caress the soft swell of her breast.

Elizabeth stiffened at this unexpected intimacy, but then relaxed as shivers of delight coursed through her. This was Michael, the man she'd been waiting for all of her life. She loved him. Looping her arms about his neck, she returned his kiss full measure. She wanted to be close to him. She'd wanted this for ever so long. When Michael drew back, Elizabeth blinked up at him through passion-dazed eyes.

"Michael?"

"Ah, sweetheart," Michael told her huskily, playing the tortured lover. "I've waited so long to hold you and kiss you as a man who loves a woman should. But I don't want to press you . . ."

At his use of the word "love," she smiled up at him. "Do you, Michael? Do you love me?" she asked eagerly in all innocence.

"What do you think, my darling?" he returned, allowing her to believe that he did. He pulled her back against him and claimed her mouth once more to further convince her. If he had to act like a besotted suitor to get his hands on her fortune, he would.

Happiness surged through Elizabeth. Michael loved her and she loved him! When they finally broke apart many heated kisses later, Elizabeth knew she had to tell him that she felt the same way.

"I love you, too, Michael."

"Elizabeth, I've waited so long to hear you say that. Marry me and make me the happiest man in the world." His words were no lie. He would be the happiest man in the world if she married him—especially if she got pregnant right away.

"Yes, yes! Oh, yes! I'll marry you! There's nothing I want more than to be your wife."

Michael kissed her deeply and with great feeling. His victory was complete! She was his! He exalted in her surrender to him. The knowledge that she was his for the taking filled him with a great sense of power. It had all been so easy. Now, all he needed was a son . . .

When he ended the embrace some time later, he continued to hold her close as he said, "I'll have to speak to your aunt, of course."

"Soon, I hope," Elizabeth said without reserve as

she nestled in his arms. She was ecstatic. This was the man she was going to spend the rest of her life with. This was the man who would take care of her, love her, cherish her and make her happy for all eternity. Her life couldn't have been more perfect at that moment.

"I'll wake her tonight, if you like," Michael teased, "but I think tomorrow morning might be better, don't you?"

"Tomorrow will be perfect," she agreed, pressing a kiss to his lips. She felt warm and safe with him. This was love as she'd always known it would be.

The following day, Blanche, of course, offered no objection to Michael's proposal; and, at his insistence, the wedding was scheduled to take place a scant three months later. It was to be a lavish affair. Blanche and Sarah were caught up in the excitement of the planning. The arrangements were made, and a white satin gown beaded with pearls and suitable for a princess was ordered for Elizabeth. Blanche was determined to give her niece everything that she, herself, had never had. Elizabeth would be the prettiest bride Philadelphia had ever seen.

Only Angel remained distant and aloof from the preparations for the coming celebration. She could find no joy in the thought of Elizabeth marrying Michael Marsden. Her hatred of the man was reinforced late one afternoon just three weeks before the wedding when she started downstairs unexpectedly and came upon Celia, the maid, in the front foyer with Michael. Angel stopped where she was and remained unseen in the shadows. It was obvious that Celia thought she and Michael were alone for she smiled up at him quite brazenly.

"Michael," Celia cooed. "It's so good to see you."

Angel frowned at the servant's familiarity with her sister's fiancé. Robert always referred to Michael as Mr. Marsden whenever he addressed them. She grew even more worried when he responded to Celia with a smile.

"Hello, Celia."

"Everyone's upstairs right now," she told him, giving him a coy look.

"Oh?" Without another word, Michael drew the maid into a corner where he thought no one could see them and kissed her.

Angel was outraged. She turned and rushed back to her sister's room wanting to tell her what she'd seen.

"Elizabeth!" Angel hurried into the bedroom to find her sister sitting at her dressing table brushing out her hair.

"What is it, sweetie?" she asked. Elizabeth adored Angel, and she knew she was going to miss her after she married and went to live in the big, new house Michael had bought for them.

"It's Michael—"

"Michael? Yes, I know, he's here already. I was just finishing my hair before I went down to see him."

"No—you don't understand." Angel was upset and it showed in her distressed manner.

Elizabeth put her hairbrush aside and turned to

regard her little sister with concern. "What's happened? What don't I understand?"

"I just saw him downstairs with Celia, and they were talking and . . ."

Elizabeth frowned, wondering why Angel thought this was so important. "And?"

"And . . . and he was . . . !"

"Angela!" Aunt Blanche's voice had rung out from the doorway behind her, cutting through the conversation. "What did I tell you before?"

Angel cringed. "I was just—"

"I know what you 'were just.' You were just trying to cause trouble, that's what you 'were just'! Michael has never been anything but the perfect gentleman. If he was talking with Celia, then I'm sure there was a reason for it."

"But, Aunt Blanche, Michael was—"

"I never thought I'd see the day when you'd act like this, trying to spoil things for your sister," Blanche said scathingly. "If you can't be nice, then go to your room! I've half a mind now not to let you attend the wedding at all."

"Oh, I don't think that's necessary," Elizabeth put in soothingly. Angel was so young, and, having just lost their father, Elizabeth figured she was worried about losing her, too. Wanting to reassure Angel, she rose from the dressing table to go to her. "I love you, Angel, very much."

"I know. That's why I had to tell you about Michael. He's not nice."

Elizabeth stiffened at her continued protests. Trying to be understanding, she said, "I'm sorry you

26

don't like Michael. I wish you did. He means the world to me and we are going to be married. I'd like you to be happy for me—for us."

Confused, Angel could only stare at Elizabeth in silence. Elizabeth waited a moment hoping for a warm response, but when there was none, she pressed a soft kiss on her sister's cheek and left the room to go to her fiancé. Angel watched her go, wondering why she hadn't wanted to hear the truth.

"Since you didn't see fit to apologize, young lady," Blanche stated firmly, "I want you to go to your room and stay there until you're ready to tell your sister you're sorry."

Angel fought back the hot tears of anger and frustration as she ran out of the bedroom. She didn't know if she could ever apologize for trying to tell Elizabeth the truth.

Chapter Two

Resplendent in her beautiful pearl-studded, lace-trimmed, white satin gown, Elizabeth truly looked like a royal princess on her wedding day. The ceremony was held in the early evening in the parlor of the Windsor mansion and a reception followed immediately thereafter. Elizabeth positively glowed with love for her new husband. Michael, too, appeared to be madly in love. He showered his bride with attention, affection, and extravagant gifts, convincing everyone that it was indeed a love match for them. Everyone, that is, except Angel.

While Blanche and Sarah were swept along in the excitement of the fairy-tale perfect wedding, Angel shared none of their joy. It was true that Angel had never seen her sister so happy, but she was still repelled by Michael. She despised him, and no matter what others might think or say, she would never forget or forgive the kiss she'd witnessed between him and Celia.

Though the reception seemed a joyful celebration, Angel couldn't keep from worrying about Elizabeth. Michael acted like he loved her, but Angel knew better. Upset, she slipped away from the party unnoticed and ran away from the house.

The moon shone brightly, lighting Angel's way; and without difficulty, she found the cemetery where her parents were buried. Most people would have been afraid to enter a graveyard at night, but not Angel. She had known only kindness and love from her parents, and she felt completely safe in the serenity of the park-like setting. Troubled and desperate, she dropped to her knees before their headstones and began to cry.

"Oh, Mama . . . Papa . . . I don't know what to do," Angel sobbed. "I don't like him! I don't like him at all! He's going to hurt Elizabeth, I just know he is!"

Angel wept inconsolably before her parents' graves, wanting to help her sister, yet not knowing how. It was late when she finally returned to the house. The reception was still going on. No one had missed her, and she was glad. She looked around hoping to see Elizabeth again.

"Sarah, where's Elizabeth?" Angel asked as she sought out her sister.

"Didn't you see them leave? They've gone on their honeymoon. Isn't that romantic?" Sarah sighed dreamily, imagining the day when she would be carried off by a handsome husband of her own.

Angel struggled not to let Sarah see how deeply the news that Elizabeth was already departed upset her.

There was nothing more she could do. It really was too late.

Elizabeth donned a seductive, white-lace nightgown and wrapper and dabbed her favorite perfume at her wrists and throat as she readied herself for her wedding night. She had a general idea of what went on between a man and a woman, and she was looking forward to making love with Michael. She wanted so badly to be with him that her heart actually ached. He'd been so wonderful all night that she couldn't wait to be in his arms, kissing him and . . .

"My darling, are you ready?" Michael asked as he knocked lightly on the door that led to the sitting room of their honeymoon suite.

"Oh, yes," she answered eagerly, her eyes shining in eager anticipation of the night to come.

Michael had no such romantic illusions. At last they were married. All that remained was getting her pregnant. He knew Elizabeth was a virgin, and the prospect of initiating her to carnal delights did not appeal to him. He liked his women to be experienced. *Still,* Michael mused, *it will not be too unsavory a duty, and then there is the matter of the money* . . . He supposed a man could do anything as long as the price was right. He entered the bedroom wearing only a heavy, silk dressing gown to find his bride standing in the middle of the room.

"You look beautiful, Elizabeth," Michael murmured as he turned down the lamp and moved to take her in his arms.

"I wanted to be . . . for you."

Michael lifted her easily and laid her upon the bed, then stretched out beside her. He dispensed with the small talk and immediately began to kiss her and caress her.

Elizabeth wanted to be wooed, to be caught up in the excitement of the moment, but Michael gave her no time to relax and enjoy his touch. He had one thing and one thing only on his mind and that was to get her with child.

Elizabeth felt the initial stirrings of desire and grew anxious to know love's full pleasure. Michael, however, was unconcerned with satisfying her. He stripped away the precious garments she'd chosen with such care and then shed his own dressing gown. Despite the look of slight distress on her face, he did not pause.

"Don't worry, I'll try not to hurt you."

"I trust you, Michael," she told him, believing that he would be gentle with her. "You would never hurt me."

Michael moved over her trembling body and nudged his way between her thighs. Elizabeth grew nervous as he probed at her, seeking to breach her innocence. When he positioned himself and thrust forward, destroying the proof of her chastity, she was stunned by the almost painful invasion. Tensing, Elizabeth held herself stiffly as she tried to adjust to the foreignness of having him deep within her. She wanted to enjoy this new intimacy, but it was impossible for Michael was no longer kissing or caressing her. He seemed totally unaware of her discomfort and confusion as he moved against her seeking his own pleasure. Elizabeth concluded that it was her own fault she wasn't enjoying her husband's lovemaking. In an effort to once again feel the excitement she'd known before in his embrace, she wrapped her arms around him and held him close.

"I love you, Michael," she whispered as he thrust against her with ever-increasing intensity.

Michael didn't answer, but continued his pace, building to his own satisfaction. As pleasure heaved through him, he groaned and collapsed on top of her.

Elizabeth believed she should be thrilled. Michael had just made love to her. This was the moment she'd dreamed of, the moment she'd waited so breathlessly for, and yet all she felt was empty. When he abruptly moved away from her to rest on his own side of the bed with his eyes closed, she was hurt. Tears welled up in her eyes. Weren't there supposed to be tender touches and loving kisses at moments like this? Bewildered, her soul chilled, she drew a blanket up over her and huddled beneath it.

It surprised Elizabeth when Michael turned to her again a short time later. He murmured only a few words of affection before possessing her body once more. Through the long, dark hours of the night, he took her over and over again, until finally just before dawn he withdrew from her and fell into an exhausted sleep.

Elizabeth lay stiff and sore beside him in their marriage bed. The blood of her lost innocence stained the sheet, but she had lost more than just her physical innocence. As she stared out the window at the first

32

pale light of dawn, a single tear escaped and traced down her cheek. It was a new day . . . the beginning of her life with Michael. She'd thought she'd feel beautiful and loved this morning; instead, she felt alone, so very alone.

Unbidden, Angel's words from that night so long ago slipped into her thoughts. *He's not nice.* Elizabeth banished the memory as quickly as she could. She told herself firmly that things would get better, that it was her fault she had not enjoyed the night. They were married now, and when you were married you cared about each other and took care of each other. You put each other's happiness before your own. She loved Michael, and he loved her. Everything would be fine.

In the Windsor mansion, Angel awoke after a night of fitful rest. Her first thought was of Elizabeth, and she prayed her sister was all right.

Ten Months Later

It was late, well past midnight. The spacious Marsden abode was dark except for the light shining from the window of the master bedroom on the second floor. Though in daylight, one could see that the lawns of the manse were perfectly tended and the house itself was in perfect condition, there was an eeriness about the place at night. It seemed to have no warmth . . . no love . . . no soul.

Sitting alone in the master bedroom, her hands resting on the swollen mound of her stomach, Elizabeth wiped away the tears that refused to stop. *Where was Michael?* She felt abandoned.

A dull ache in her lower back tormented her, and she shifted uncomfortably in the upholstered wing chair, trying to alleviate the misery. Nothing seemed to work, though, and she sighed her vexation.

When the mantel clock chimed the hour of two, Elizabeth glared at the offending timepiece. She knew it was late! She didn't have to be so sorely and regularly reminded of the hour and of her husband's absence!

Pushing awkwardly to her feet, Elizabeth moved to the window to look down at the street below. It was deserted. There was no sign of horse or carriage. She was still alone.

Elizabeth rubbed the small of her back as she wandered to the bed to lie down. Thoughts of Michael filled her as she settled in. She missed him desperately. He'd been gone since before she'd wakened this morning, and he had left no note for her telling her of his plans for the day. Not that that was unusual anymore. Ever since she'd told him she was expecting the baby, he'd changed. Before her pregnancy, he had come to her bed and made love to her almost every night. For the past six months, though, he'd rarely touched her. In fact, once her pregnancy had begun to show he'd moved out of the master bedroom completely. He'd told her that it was in deference to her delicate condition. She would have accepted that, if he'd continued to spend time with her, but with each passing day he'd grown more and more distant and spent more and more time away from home.

Elizabeth could only conclude that it was her fault he didn't want to be with her anymore. She had driven him away from her somehow, but just as soon as she'd had the baby and her slender figure returned she intended to win him back. Rolling to her side, Elizabeth pulled the covers over her and silently prayed that Michael would come home soon.

It was nearly nine the next morning when a knock sounded at her door and Rose, her maid, peeked inside.

"Miss Elizabeth? Your aunt and your sisters are downstairs. They said you were expecting them. Oh, my . . ." Rose stopped abruptly as she saw her mistress lying pale and terrified in the bed.

"Rose. . . . I think I'm having the baby. You'd best send for the doctor."

"Yes, ma'am."

She rushed from the room to do as she'd been instructed, pausing only long enough to tell Aunt Blanche, Sarah, and Angel of her mistress' condition. Moments later the three of them came hurrying into the bedroom to be with Elizabeth.

"Elizabeth! Are you all right?" Angel asked as she ran to her side.

"I think so."

"Are you in pain?" Sarah worried.

"It's not too bad yet. It comes and goes. That's why I wasn't sure for a long time that I was really in labor." As a contraction seized her, Elizabeth grimaced and bit down on her lip.

"Oh, dear . . ." Blanche swooned weakly and staggered across the room to collapse in the wing chair.

"Where's Michael?" Angel asked.

"Does he know?" Sarah put in.

"No, not yet. He's at work."

"Shouldn't we send for him?" Sarah encouraged.

"Yes, please. I'd feel better if he were here. I need him."

Angel didn't like the idea of seeing Michael, but she was anxious to do whatever she could to make Elizabeth feel better. Hurrying off, she told the maid to summon her hated brother-in-law home.

When the doctor arrived, Angel, Sarah, and Blanche were ushered from the bedroom. They waited excitedly in the study downstairs for news that the babe had been born.

Michael finally arrived a little past eleven. He greeted them all with a kiss on the cheek and a celebratory hug. Sarah and Blanche were thrilled to see him, blinded as they always were by his charming demeanor. Angel, however, had the strangest urge to wipe off her cheek where he'd kissed her; and she did, the first time nobody was looking, scrubbing at the spot as if something vile had touched her there. She kept her distance from the man, taking the chair farthest from him and staying quiet as a mouse to avoid drawing his attention.

It was just past noon when the physician finally came downstairs to tell them the good news. Elizabeth had had a boy and the child was in perfect health. They were all ecstatic. No one more so than Michael.

"Thank God!" he practically shouted, pouring himself a double-shot of whiskey and downing it with gusto. In just a few years, the Windsor fortune would be his! Life was wonderful! He'd known this was going to work!

"How's Elizabeth?" Angel was the first to ask.

"She's fine. A little weak and tired, of course, but fine."

Recovering himself, Michael spoke up, "Yes, I must see my wife."

He set his tumbler aside and followed the physician from the room. He looked to all to be the delighted new father, and, in fact, he was. Elizabeth had given him the son he'd needed, and he was thrilled at the thought of the money that would be his in just ten short years. He entered the bedroom and fawned dramatically over her.

As desperate as Elizabeth was to reclaim Michael's attentions, she allowed herself to believe his tender declarations. She convinced herself that he did love her and that he would soon return to her bed.

After watching Michael and Elizabeth together with their son, Blanche and Sarah were certain that their marriage had been made in heaven.

Elizabeth's recovery was an easy one; yet, days passed and Michael made no move to return to their bedroom or her bed. The christening was held six weeks later, and the boy was named Christopher. He was a beautiful, happy infant, and Elizabeth's life would have been perfect if only she'd had her husband's complete devotion. She couldn't bear to let her family know that all the love seemed to have gone out of her marriage. Insecure as she was, she believed she was to blame for the fact that Michael seldom came home at night and that, when he did, he sometimes carried the scent of another woman's perfume on his clothing. Once Elizabeth had stopped at the bank to withdraw some funds and had found her account balance to be far lower than it should have been. Michael was spending the money her father had left her, but on what . . . on whom?

Again the memory of Angel's words had returned to haunt Elizabeth, but she'd refused to admit she'd made a mistake. She still believed she loved Michael. She worked twice as hard at trying to please him, but met with little success. He came to her bed occasionally, but his lovemaking was almost mechanical. He was so coldly indifferent that she became more and more desperate to be loved.

Filled with so much love to give, Elizabeth sought fulfillment in loving her son. She devoted herself to the tiny babe, lavishing on him all the attention she longed to give her husband, all the love he didn't want. Christopher became the center of her life. He meant the world to her. There was no one alive she cared about more. She would do anything for her child.

Nine Years Later
April, 1858

It was three in the morning. Unable to sleep, Elizabeth sat before the mirror on her vanity table staring at her reflection as she waited for her husband to come home. Her mood was somber as she studied her features. Lingering shadows of sadness haunted her eyes, and she knew why.

Elizabeth had long realized that Michael was not faithful to her. Recently, she'd heard the rumor that he was having a passionate affair with Mary Ann Warner, a woman she'd considered her best friend. The gossip hurt and reinforced what she'd already known—Michael was not the gentle, loving man she'd believed him to be when she'd married him.

At the thought of her dashingly handsome husband, bitter bile rose in Elizabeth's throat. She'd learned through the years that he was heartless and vicious and totally self-serving. Though in public he played the part of the adoring husband and father, in private, he never showed any warmth or affection.

Elizabeth thought of his lovemaking and wondered what Mary Ann saw in him. Their marital encounters had been nothing more than cold, clinical matings. There was no tenderness involved when he came to her, and Michael always left her immediately after achieving his own satisfaction. He'd never cared about pleasing her. Many was the night that she'd cried hot, frustrated tears into her pillow.

Elizabeth had remained with Michael for the past ten years because she'd always hoped things would improve. It had taken her until now to realize that they never would. During the first few years of their marriage whenever she'd accidentally annoyed him, he'd actually been brutal in his response. Frightened, she'd tried even harder to make him happy, but she'd never succeeded. It seemed she could do nothing right.

Caught up in this vortex of misery and spinning ever downward and out of control, Elizabeth had seen no chance for escape. She had lived her life one day at a time, always striving to please, but always failing. Michael dominated her with savagery. His constant browbeating and belittling left her in a state of complete subjugation. She lost herself to his brutality, both physical and mental. She lived in fear, cowed by blows that were carefully placed so they would never show. Only her love for Christopher kept her sane. He was her life and her one joy.

Elizabeth stared at her mirror-image and, seeing the fire of determination burning in her eyes for the first time, knew that today had been the turning point in her life. What had happened that morning had been the final straw—the breaking point—the moment that forced her out of her prison of terror and into action. Until now, she'd been the only one physically hurt by Michael's cruelty. But today, for no reason, he'd hit Christopher. Seeing her precious child abused cracked the pitiful, numbing shell she'd erected around herself. No one was going to harm her son. No one. She'd made up her mind then and there that Michael would never have another chance to hit him.

Firm unwavering resolve shone in Elizabeth's eyes.

She was going to break free of Michael's strangling web of terror. She was going to take Christopher and they were going to leave him. They would walk away and never look back.

Righteous anger filled Elizabeth, and she clung to it for strength. The battered shreds of what little self-respect she had left filled her with an inner power she'd never experienced before. She hadn't had the strength to save herself from Michael, but she would save Christopher. When Michael returned tonight, she was going to tell him that it was over, that they were leaving. She was going to insure her son's happiness. In less than a year, Christopher would have his inheritance and everything would be fine.

The sound of someone coming up the walk brought Elizabeth to her feet. *Michael! He was back!* Taking a deep, steadying breath, she turned toward the bedroom door. She stood frozen with fear for an instant. Terror quaked through her. It took her a moment to get a grip on her emotions, but she finally did. Drawing heavily on her inner resolve, she prepared to face her misery and put an end to it. Terrified but determined, she went forth to save her son.

Michael was more than pleased with himself as he entered the house. He had won handily gaming at his club tonight, but the few hundred dollars he'd gleaned were nothing compared to the fortune he was going to come into in less than twelve months when Christopher turned ten. With the Windsor inheritance under his control, he would have everything he'd ever dreamed of—untold riches and a young, beautiful, passionate mistress. Michael smiled.

Thoughts of Mary Ann, his latest conquest, sent heat surging through him. She was a firebrand in bed, and he'd just spent the evening buried in the molten depths of her lithe body. It didn't bother him in the least that she was his wife's best friend. He thought women were put on Earth to be used by men as men saw fit, and he took great pleasure in doing just that. When he tired of them, he discarded them, and it was going to please him immensely to be rid of his bothersome wife as soon as the money situation was resolved. The past nearly ten years of marriage to her had been tedious in the extreme.

Michael considered that he might have enjoyed married life more if he'd waited and married Angel. She'd grown into one very beautiful young woman, and he would have greatly enjoyed tasting of her long-legged, full-breasted charms. She'd always been standoffish with him, too, and her attitude intrigued him. He liked a challenge in his carnal pursuits and she certainly presented one. Money, however, had always been his main goal, and while Angel might stir his blood, he hadn't had the time to wait for her to grow up. He'd made do with Elizabeth; and she had, of course, provided him with the male heir he'd desired.

Michael let himself into the house and moved silently across the foyer into the study. After lighting the lamp on his desk top, he opened the liquor cabinet and poured himself a tumbler of his favorite whiskey. He still felt invigorated from his hours with

Mary Ann and he knew sleep would be long in coming. He'd had only enough time to take one drink of the potent liquor when he heard someone at the doorway. Michael glanced up, frowning slightly at the intrusion. He was surprised to find Elizabeth standing there watching him, a strange look upon her face.

"You're up awfully late, aren't you?" Michael asked curtly.

"I've been waiting up so I could talk to you." Elizabeth was so nervous that she kept her hands hidden within the folds of her dressing gown so he couldn't see how badly they were trembling.

"Why didn't you go to bed? You certainly look like you could use the rest. Besides, anything we have to say to each other could be said over breakfast." He had no desire to speak with her—now or later.

"That's true enough—if you were ever here at breakfast. But since you're never around, either at breakfast or any other meal . . ."

"Don't start that again."

"You don't have to worry, Michael. You won't be putting up with me for much longer."

Michael glanced up, his eyes narrowing in suspicion. "What are you talking about?"

"The reason I stayed up half the night waiting for you is because I wanted to be face-to-face with you when I told you—"

"Told me what?"

The white-hot memory of his striking Christopher gave Elizabeth the courage to go on.

"I'm leaving you, Michael," she declared, boldly overcoming her own personal terror.

He stared at her in disbelief for a second and then laughed. It was a chilling sound that echoed evilly through the stillness of the house. "No, I don't think so."

"Christopher and I are moving back home with my family in the morning. I refuse to live this way any longer."

"And what way is that?" Michael asked softly as he slowly placed his glass on the desktop, then took a menacing step toward her. He expected to see her flinch before him as she always did, and he was surprised when she held her ground.

"In fear and terror, but not any more. You've hurt me and Christopher for the last time. I'm not the same naive little girl you married. I've learned a lot."

"Obviously you haven't learned enough," he said in a deadly tone. "Perhaps it's time I remind you of the lessons you seem to have forgotten. The first one being that you are my wife and you will do exactly what I say."

Fear filled Elizabeth. Her instincts told her to run, but she knew there was no backing down . . . not now, not ever again. She fought against the strangling grip of terror and lifted her head a little higher in defiance.

"No. Never again. The fact that I'm still your wife is a mere technicality. There was a time when I thought you were the most wonderful man in the world, but not any more. You've killed any love I ever had for you. I've made an appointment with John Hayden, my father's attorney, and—"

"You've what?!" Michael reached out and grabbed her by the arm, his fingers digging painfully into that tender flesh.

"I'm going to see Mr. Hayden tomorrow and direct him to take whatever steps are necessary to obtain a divorce from you."

Her announcement stunned and enraged him. "There will be no divorce!" he snarled, snaring her other arm and giving her a vicious shake.

Elizabeth fought back, twisting with all her might. The fact that she actually resisted him caught Michael off-guard, and she managed to jerk free of his bruising hold.

"I'm leaving you, Michael!"

"Like hell you are!"

"You can't stop me!" She saw the ugly look in his eyes and started to back toward the door.

"Oh, yes I can. You're not going anywhere!"

"You don't love me, and you don't love Christopher! The only thing you've ever cared about was my money! Well, you're not going to get your hands on it! I won't let you!" Elizabeth was afraid to take her eyes off him now. She realized, too late, that confronting him had been foolish. She should have left him without a word of warning. If she had, she would have been safely in the circle of her family's love and protection before he'd discovered what she was doing. Now . . .

"Elizabeth. . . . come here!" he seethed, his expression growing even more savage.

The look on his face broke what little control she had, and Elizabeth pivoted, ready to flee the room. Michael anticipated her move, though; and in a rage, he lunged at her and caught her. He jerked her back to him.

"I've invested too much time and effort in you. You're not going anywhere!"

"Let me go!"

"Never!" Michael hit her, a violent blow that sent her head reeling.

"No! No!" Elizabeth was wracked with pain. He'd never hit her this hard before, and panic unlike anything she'd ever known filled her. "Don't!" She struggled to break free, to get away, but it was too late.

Michael was livid. She would obey him or else! Too much was at stake here! He drew back to strike again; and, in that moment, Elizabeth realized she was fighting for her life. In desperation, she kicked out at him, making contact but not kicking him hard enough to escape.

Outraged that she would dare strike at him, Michael backhanded her with all his might. Elizabeth tumbled backward and fell, striking her head with a sickening thud on the sharp edge of the bookcase behind her. With a groan, she slid to the floor.

Michael waited, staring at her limp form, slumped against the bookcase. There was no remorse in the pitiless gaze, only unbridled fury.

How dare she think she could leave him? How dare she? As she lay unmoving, a cold realization dawned on him. She might be dead . . . His eyes suddenly shone with amoral excitement. Dead . . .

A cruel, almost satanic smile lifted his snarling mouth. If she were dead, all of his problems would be solved. *Yes,* he concluded, *his darling wife could leave him, but only through death.*

Michael's lethal logic drove him on. With his darling wife deceased, he would gain sole custody of Christopher and so have a free hand with the Windsor money when the time came. Kneeling beside her, he felt her pulse and discovered that it was erratic, but still beating. It annoyed him that she wasn't already dead, but there would be no stopping him now. He knew exactly what he had to do.

After checking the darkened main hall to make sure no one was around, Michael gathered his unconscious wife in his arms and silently carried her from the study. Never before had he been so glad that the servants' quarters were located in a separate building at the rear of the house. Christopher was the only other person home, and Michael knew he did not awaken easily.

Pausing at the foot of the staircase, Michael studied its steep angle with satisfaction. It didn't take him long to make his decision. His wife was going to suffer a terrible, tragic accident on the steps. In the morning, when her body was found at the foot of the stairs, everyone would think she'd fallen. No one would suspect foul play, for no one but Elizabeth knew that he'd come home tonight.

The stairs seemed endless to Michael as he climbed them carrying Elizabeth's dead weight. He had to stop twice to catch his breath before he finally reached the top. After steadying himself, Michael turned and surveyed the foyer below. It was a long way down and that suited him just fine. With all the strength he could muster, he lifted Elizabeth as high as he could and then threw her violently down the stairs.

Michael was filled with perverse pleasure as he watched her body career down the steep steps. Tumbling like a broken ragdoll, Elizabeth crashed heavily against the railing and then continued her deadly descent until she landed at the bottom.

Michael stood silently at the top of the staircase watching Elizabeth for signs of life. Quietly descending to the entryway, he once again knelt beside her to check her pulse. This time there was none. She was dead, her neck broken during the fall. His deadly plan had worked. A distant memory of Helene came to Michael then, and arrogance filled him. He'd gotten away with murder twice now. His smile broadened with self-confidence at the thought.

Returning to the study, he silently toasted his handling of the situation then tossed off the rest of the liquor. Ever cautious, he wiped out the glass and put it away, then extinguished the light. After taking one last look around to make sure there was no trace of his presence remaining to incriminate him, he left the house.

As he made the trek back to his office, Michael practiced what he would say when he was finally informed of his wife's tragic accident. He knew he had to be convincing. He could not risk bringing any suspicion upon himself. He would make it a point to mourn his beloved's death openly for there could be no leaving this time. Like it or not, he had to stay in Philadelphia until Christopher inherited. After that, he would find a way to rid himself of the child so he could enjoy the fortune that would be his.

The thought was a pleasant one, and Michael was still smiling as he settled in at his office to await the terrible news he knew would come in the morning. The night had been a long one, but it had been very profitable indeed.

Chapter Three

Evening shadows were deepening as yet another carriage drew up before the Marsden house. The traffic of friends and acquaintances had been steady that day as all came to offer their heartfelt condolences to the family and express their shock and horror over Elizabeth's untimely passing.

Such an immense outpouring of sympathy and caring would have impressed most families; and Angel, Sarah, and Blanche were touched and deeply appreciative of those who'd cared enough to come. Michael, however, could hardly wait for the day to end. Though he'd remained faithfully beside his wife's coffin in the parlor playing the grieving husband to the hilt, his thoughts were far from mourning and misery. While outwardly he appeared sad, in actuality he'd spent most of his time watching Angel and planning a strategy to get the blonde beauty into his bed. He found the fantasy quite a pleasant pastime in the midst of all the tears and irritating sympathetic small talk.

"Michael?"

At the sound of Angel softly calling his name, Michael excused himself from the elderly couple he'd been speaking with. He hurried to join her where she stood in the parlor doorway with Christopher, one arm protectively around the boy's shoulders.

Christopher had been the one to discover his mother lying dead at the foot of the stairs the day before; and when Angel had arrived on the scene, he'd been distraught. It had taken her hours to quiet him, and she'd been hovering over him ever since, wanting to ease his sorrow.

"What is it?" Michael asked, coming to put a seemingly loving hand on his son's shoulder, too. In the process he oh-so-accidentally brushed Angel's hand with his.

"Christopher's tired, so I'm going to take him upstairs and put him to bed." At Michael's "accidental" touch, Angel quickly dropped her arm away from the boy.

Angel's shifting away from him had not gone unnoticed, and it piqued Michael's desire for her even more. He was not a man who took "no" for an answer. He glanced down at his son, letting his gaze drift innocently over the swell of Angel's breasts beneath the dreary black of her mourning gown as he did so. "It's been rough for you, hasn't it, son?"

"Yes, sir," Christopher answered numbly. He did not look up at his father, but actually stepped just a little bit closer to the protective warmth of his aunt.

"Well, you go on upstairs now. A night's rest might do you a world of good," Michael agreed, glad that the miserable, crying brat would be out of his way for a while. It didn't matter one bit to him that Christopher had made the grizzly discovery. Concern for his son's happiness had never been a priority with him.

"Yes, sir."

"Angel . . ." Michael spoke again, when she started to turn away. "I want to thank you for all you've done for us. You've been so helpful. I don't know what I would have done without you." Michael lifted his hand to her shoulder in what looked to be a gesture of simple affection.

His touch sent a wave of revulsion through Angel, and she could hardly wait to get away from him. "There's no way I could have done any less for my sister and her son."

"Well, I appreciate your being here for us more than you'll ever know," he replied, his gaze trapping hers.

Angel detested this man, and she had to fight to keep from shuddering at the look he was giving her. She wanted to scream at him that she wasn't there for him, that she was there for Christopher—the boy was the only one who mattered to her now. But she didn't. She nodded and moved away, ushering the boy toward the stairs.

Michael paused there in the doorway long enough to enjoy the view of Angel's gently swaying hips as she mounted the steps. He felt a familiar tightening in his loins and wished he were the one she was taking up to bed instead of his son. He had a heated vision of her body beneath his, her long, slender legs locked around his waist as he . . . With an effort, Michael tore his thoughts away from that exciting image. He told himself to bide his time for all good things come to those who wait.

Michael was feeling nearly invincible as he returned to the parlor. Not one hint of suspicion had been cast his way over his wife's tragic "accident," and he was firmly convinced that no one could stop him now. No one! All he had to do was keep Christopher happy for a few more months, and the money would be his!

It sounded easy enough, but Michael couldn't help but grimace inwardly as he remembered how hysterical the boy had been when he'd returned home to the death scene the previous morning. It had been a relief to have Angel, Sarah, and Blanche already there, for they'd saved him from the tiresome duty of having to comfort the crying child. He'd had a hard enough time pretending to be distraught himself without having to worry about Christopher, too.

There was a knock at the front door and the servant answered it.

"Good evening, Miss Warner. Come in."

"Thank you."

At the sound of that very familiar voice, Michael looked up to see Mary Ann entering the house. He returned to his place near the coffin and watched as she went first to Blanche and Sarah to offer her sympathies. After a few minutes, she left them and came straight to him.

Michael found himself mentally comparing Mary Ann's dark-haired beauty to Angel's pale loveliness and decided that Mary Ann was definitely lacking. If it came down to a choice between the two women, he had no doubt about which one he'd choose. The thought surprised him, for a little over twenty-four hours before he'd been looking forward to continuing his affair with Mary Ann. Now. . . . he mentally shrugged his indifference to the idea. It didn't bother him at all that his wife was not yet in her grave. He'd never allowed Elizabeth to interfere with his more carnal pleasures after Christopher had been born.

"Michael." Mary Ann said his name in a whisper. "I'm so sorry. I know how devastating this must be for you. . . . Elizabeth was such a good friend to me."

"Thank you," he replied. He knew she had no idea of what had really happened, and he wanted to keep it that way.

"If there's anything I can do for you . . ." She lifted her gaze to his, her double meaning clear.

"I appreciate your thoughtfulness, Mary Ann, but there's really nothing anyone can do. It'll just be a matter of time."

"I understand." She pressed his hand. "Take care."

"We'll try."

Mary Ann started to leave, but encountered Angel on her way back from putting Christopher to bed.

"Angel, I'm glad I got the chance to see you before I left. I'm so sorry about Elizabeth."

"Thank you, Mary Ann. It was good of you to come."

"I couldn't stay away. It's all so tragic. How's Christopher?"

"It's been very difficult for him," she replied. "You know how close they were. He loved her dearly."

When they had finished speaking and Mary Ann had departed, Angel moved across the parlor to join her sister and aunt. She felt someone watching her and glanced around to find Michael's eyes upon her, his expression unreadable. Angel felt uncomfortable, so she quickly sat down beside Sarah on the sofa and angled her back toward her brother-in-law so she wouldn't have to look at him.

Damn, but Angel is lovely! Michael mused. He knew the man who won her was going to be very lucky, and he planned to be that man. Though she pretended to dislike him, he knew that animosity added passion to a relationship. Michael contemplated the tempting possibilities as he greeted yet another acquaintance.

"Have any trouble with Christopher?" Sarah asked Angel, her brown eyes dark with concern.

"I got him in bed, but when I closed his door he started crying again." Great sadness showed in Angel's face, and her heart ached. "How could this have happened? Why did he have to be the one to find Elizabeth?"

"I don't know. What's terrible is there's nothing we can do except be there for him."

"I know." Angel sighed heavily. She knew she hadn't yet felt the full magnitude of the pain of her sister's death. Since rushing to the house yesterday morning and arriving in time to see the doctor pronounce Elizabeth dead, she'd felt as if her entire being were encased in ice. Angel knew one day she'd have to face the agony, but right now she was glad for the numbing protection.

More visitors arrived, and Sarah and Blanche went to speak with them. Angel was glad for the distraction and took a moment longer on the sofa to pull herself together.

"Miss Windsor . . ."

Angel looked up to find George Martin, the undertaker, standing beside her. She rose to speak with him. "Mr. Martin, how kind of you to come."

"I just wanted you to know how very sorry I am about your loss. Your sister's death is such a shock. It always saddens me when someone young dies senselessly."

"Perhaps it's true what they say—that only the good die young," Angel observed, feeling old beyond her years.

"Indeed. Elizabeth was a lovely young woman."

"She was very special."

George looked sad. "It's such a shame, and she was so badly bruised. Why, if I hadn't known about the fall, I would have wondered how that had all happened."

"What do you mean?"

"Well, some of the marks on her body even looked a little like hand marks, but then . . ."

At his words, Angel went even colder inside. What little color she'd had in her face drained away.

Seeing her distress, George immediately apologized. "I'm sorry, Angela. I shouldn't have mentioned these things to you. I didn't mean to upset you."

"No. . . . no, it's all right." Angel let her gaze slide to where Michael was standing, deep in conversation with a business acquaintance. *Could he have hurt Elizabeth? Would he have dared to harm her?* Her mind was racing at the horrifying possibility, and she paid little notice when George took his leave of her.

"If you'll excuse me, Angela. I must offer my condolences to Michael."

"Of course."

"Angel?" Sarah appeared beside her after speaking with another visitor. "I just learned the strangest thing."

"What?" Angel forced herself to pay attention to what her sister was saying.

"I was talking to Mr. Hayden, and he told me that Elizabeth had made an appointment to see him today."

"She wanted to see father's lawyer?" Angel was startled by this news. "What for?"

"She told him it was important, but that she didn't want to say any more until she was in his office."

"That's strange."

"I know, but I can't help but think that it couldn't have been too important or she would have mentioned it to us."

"That's true enough," she agreed.

Even as she acknowledged that Elizabeth always confided in them, Angel couldn't help but wonder if it were possible that she'd harbored some secrets too terrible to share. Coupled with what she'd learned from George Martin, Angel knew she was going to have to pay Mr. Hayden a visit as soon as possible.

It was almost nine o'clock that evening when the last of the grievers departed and the family was finally alone. Unable to sleep, Christopher had come back downstairs about an hour before. He'd sought out Angel and had stayed with her the whole time.

"I suppose we'd better be going," Aunt Blanche said wearily.

"Please don't go!" Christopher blurted out. Almost in a panic, he threw his arms around Angel and hung on tight.

"Sweetheart, we'll be back early in the morning," Angel tried to explain in a soothing tone, but he just tightened his grip.

"Don't leave me. Not tonight," he begged. "Please."

His whining annoyed Michael. He almost wished the women would take the miserable brat with them and get him out of his sight, but he didn't want to sound heartless. No loving father would send his child away on a night like this.

"Why don't you ladies spend the night here? There's plenty of room."

"Oh, no . . ." Aunt Blanche began, but Michael refused to take "no" for an answer.

"Christopher obviously needs you and wants you here. I really would appreciate it." He sounded humble, but the truth was he would have appreciated anything that would shut the boy up.

Angel and Sarah needed no further encouragement. Christopher had been traumatized enough.

Angel's arms tightened around him. "All right. We'll stay. Won't we, Aunt Blanche? Christopher needs us."

"All right," the old woman agreed. "But we'll need to send one of the servants to get some of our things."

"That's no problem," Michael responded, satisfied that his whimpering offspring would be out of sight and out of mind for at least the rest of the night. The thought of Angel sleeping under his roof pleased him, too.

"Thank you."

"Oh, good," he sighed, reassured.

As soon as the servant returned with their clothes and necessities, the women and Christopher retired for the night.

Christopher had begged for Angel to sleep with him in his room, and so she had, gathering his sweet little body close to hers as they curled up together in his bed. She was surprised when he'd quickly fallen asleep in her arms. She'd expected him to be restless. The emotional strain of the day had obviously taken its toll on him, and he slept soundly, an innocent babe.

Once she was sure Christopher was asleep, Angel inched away, moving to her own side of the bed without disturbing him. She lay awake long into the night. Her emotions were in turmoil as she tried to decide what to do. Why had Elizabeth made that appointment with the lawyer? Were the bruises George Martin had mentioned related to the fall or had they been caused by something or *someone* else?

It didn't take Angel long to make a decision about what she needed to do, but she knew she couldn't act upon it until Michael had come upstairs for the night.

It was the wee morning hours before Angel finally heard her brother-in-law ascend the staircase and enter his own bedroom down the hall. She waited until she was sure he'd retired, then rose from Christopher's bed with steely determination. Drawing on her wrapper, she lit a lamp; and, keeping it turned down low, she crept from the room.

The house was quiet and dark. Even the servants had gone to their quarters. Angel was relieved for she needed privacy. Reaching the top of the steps, she paused. The flickering lamplight cast shadows and added a ghostly feel to the oppressive stillness.

Angel trembled as she tried to imagine what had happened there at the top of the steps the night Elizabeth fell. Had she been sleepy and just lost her footing on the steep staircase or had something else caused her to take that deadly tumble? Clutching the bannister, Angel bravely descended, the need to find the answers to her questions driving her ever onward.

She reached the foyer, then silently entered the parlor. After placing the lamp on a table near the coffin, she moved nearer to gaze down at her sister. In life, Elizabeth had been a vibrant, loving woman. In death she looked pallid and grim. The lips that had laughed and smiled so often were dour and sullen. While Angel knew it was her sister, the dead woman bore little real resemblance to the delightful woman Elizabeth had really been.

Sorrow filled Angel, but it was soon thrust aside by

the barely contained rage that threatened to overwhelm her. She had to know the truth about what had happened. She had to!

Angel stared at her sister for a moment longer, searching her memory for any indication Elizabeth might have given, however subtly, that her life had been less than perfect after she'd married. Their times together had always been happy ones, though, and Angel could not recall any instance where her sister had been unusually worried about anything. She wondered if her oldest sibling had been that good an actress or if Elizabeth really had been content. Angel wondered briefly, too, if she were just letting her hatred of Michael cloud her thinking; and she knew at that moment that she had to discover the truth.

Girding herself, Angel reached out with unsteady hands and unbuttoned the cuff on the sleeve of Elizabeth's dress. After one last nervous glance back over her shoulder to make sure she was still alone, she carefully began to push the material up her sister's arm.

Angel was glad the garment was loose-fitting as she slipped the sleeve slowly upward, looking for the bruises George Martin had mentioned. There were no marks on Elizabeth's forearm, but Angel kept going. When she checked up higher, past her elbow on her upper arm, the sight of the ugly discolorations caused her to gasp out loud.

"Oh my God!!" The words were torn from her as she realized what she'd discovered.

The bruises marring the soft flesh of her sister's upper arm were in the form of a perfect hand print.

It was obvious to Angel that someone had grabbed her there and with a great deal of force. There was no way that that particular bruise could have been made in a fall down the stairs.

Angel staggered backward a step, her hand at her throat as she swallowed reflexively in revulsion. All her doubts were gone, washed away in her sister's blood. Angel *knew* what had happened.

Leaving the lamp in the parlor, Angel hurried back upstairs and slipped into the room where Sarah was sleeping. She shook her sister awake.

"Sarah." Her whisper was urgent.

"Angel?" Sarah asked sleepily. "What's the matter?"

"Shhh. . . . keep your voice down."

"Why?" She was only barely awake, staring at Angel in confusion.

"I need you to come with me. There's something you have to see."

"See? In the middle of the night?" Sarah protested, but did manage to keep her voice hushed.

"Here, put on your wrapper and I'll show you!" Angel had no time for arguing as she shoved the robe at her.

Sarah was fully awake now, and she quickly donned the wrapper. "Where are you taking me?"

"Just downstairs. Now, be quiet. We can't let anybody know what we're doing."

Sarah followed her downstairs and into the parlor. She was surprised that there was a lamp already burning there.

"What are you doing?" she asked, hanging back when Angel went straight to the coffin.

"Look at this," Angel demanded.

"Look at what?" Sarah edged forward, trying to ignore the shivers that were skittering up and down her spine. At the sight of the black and blue marks on Elizabeth's arm, she too was shocked.

"But what? How?" She lifted horror-filled dark eyes to Angel's emerald ones, and she saw the truth reflected in her sister's hard, accusing expression. "You think that . . . no." Sarah shook her head, trying to deny that which couldn't be denied.

"Sarah, listen to me! George Martin told me earlier this evening that there had been some unusual bruises on her body. I just had to see for myself. I couldn't believe that she'd just fallen like that."

"And you think Michael? . . ."

Angel's gaze didn't waver. "You told me yourself that Elizabeth had made an appointment with a lawyer. Why do you suppose she did that?"

Their gazes met and locked in nervous understanding of what they'd just discovered.

"What are we going to do?" Sarah asked, stricken. Between the two of them, Sarah had always been the calming, more mature influence, but now she was at a loss to deal with their gruesome discovery. She had trusted Michael.

Before Angel could reply, Christopher's soft voice sliced through the silence of the night like a scream, startling both women.

"Aunt Angel? Aunt Sarah?"

They turned to see the solitary little figure of their

nephew standing in the doorway, his hair mussed I from sleep, his loose-fitting pajamas making him look even more pitifully waif-like.

"Christopher! What are you doing up at this hour?" Angel was worried. The last thing they needed was for Michael to hear them and come downstairs and find them.

"I woke up, Aunt Angel, and you were gone. I was lonely, so I came down to see my mother again," he said in a tortured voice, lifting his brown eyes to hers.

"Oh, honey, I'm so sorry. I didn't mean to upset you by leaving you alone." Angel could see the pain in his gaze, and she held out her arms to him.

Christopher went into her arms and accepted her hug. He then moved to look at his mother and saw that her sleeve had been pushed up and the bruises exposed.

"You weren't supposed to know," he mumbled sadly, tears welling up in his eyes.

"Know what?"

The boy looked nervous and upset. He shifted his gaze guiltily away. "Mother told me not to tell anybody, ever, especially not you." He bit his lip as he realized that the truth was now out.

"Why not?"

"Mama didn't want you to know that Papa hit her sometimes—and me, too—when we didn't make him happy," he blurted out miserably, believing he'd broken his mother's trust.

"Oh, sweetheart." Sarah embraced the child, holding him to her bosom as she exchanged horrified looks with Angel over the top of his head.

"How long ago did you make that promise to your mother?" Angel prompted.

"A long time ago," he confessed. "She said it had to be our secret, but now that she's dead I don't want to stay here any more. Please don't make me stay here."

At his words, Angel knew pain so vicious that it might as well have been a knife in her heart. She'd been right all along! Michael was a fiend! He had killed her sister and beaten his son!

"Don't worry, Christopher. We'll take care of you, but you mustn't say a word about tonight to anyone else. All right?"

He nodded.

"What do you think we ought to do?" Sarah asked in a trembling voice.

"Right now, nothing. Tomorrow, after the funeral, we'll make sure Christopher comes home with us for a visit, and then I'm going to pay Mr. Hayden a visit," Angel told her with conviction. She knew they had to take quick action if they were to save Christopher.

"I'm going with you," Sarah declared staunchly. Though she was a gentle person, she would not tolerate anyone hurting her loved ones. Now that she knew the whole, terrible truth, she was filled with as much spirit and determination as Angel was.

"Thanks." Angel felt better knowing Sarah would be at her side.

Angel adjusted Elizabeth's sleeve once more so no one would learn of their horrible discovery. Picking up the lamp, she led the way back up to their bedrooms. Angel was firmly resolved that she was going to see Michael pay for what he'd done and make certain that he would never have the opportunity to lay a hand on Christopher again. As long as she had a breath in her body, Angel was going to insure no harm ever came to her nephew.

The following morning found the skies leaden and a steady, miserable drizzle soaking the land and all who ventured out upon it. As Angel stood at Elizabeth's gravesite listening to Reverend Jacob's solemn prayers, she thought it almost seemed as if the heavens were weeping. Today, she could no longer hold back her tears. This was the end of it. She would never see Elizabeth again.

Sarah, too, was crying. The bruises on Elizabeth's body had at first shocked, then sickened her. She glanced up, and through the veil of her tears she saw Michael, looking much the grieving husband as he stood nearby.

Sarah realized that she'd been under Michael's spell from the start, but she would not let him affect her any longer. What troubled her was the knowledge that Elizabeth had stayed with him so long, even though he had treated her so brutally. Had she loved him so much that she would tolerate such cruelties from him? Sarah had always thought love was a kind and gentle thing. She'd thought it meant giving your mate all of yourself with nothing held back. She'd thought it meant sharing the good times and the bad times without recriminations and with the total trust that the other person would always be there for you no matter what. Her sister had supposedly married for love, and yet her life had ended in violence at her husband's hand. Sarah's troubled thoughts were interrupted as the minister completed his prayers.

"Amen," Reverend Jacobs intoned, and those gathered in the cemetery responded in kind. He closed his Bible with a thump and moved through the small group of mourners, expressing his sympathies. He stopped to speak at length with Michael.

Angel and Sarah were filled with loathing as they watched them talk, but somehow, they managed to keep that telltale emotion from showing. It wouldn't do to let on that they knew the truth about him. That would come later.

"What are we going to do now, Aunt Angel?" Christopher asked as he huddled near her. He had hardly ventured an inch from her side all morning.

"We're going to see if your father will let you spend a few days with us."

"Good."

"Why don't you take Aunt Blanche and go wait for us in the carriage? We'll only be a few minutes," Sarah suggested, and she was pleased when the boy complied, accompanying their elderly, weeping aunt to the shelter of the conveyance.

Michael looked up as Angel and Sarah joined him. "Well, it's over."

He sounded so sincerely upset that the women realized if they hadn't known the truth about him, they would have been convinced that he was honestly grieving for his dead wife.

67

"Ladies, you have my deepest sympathies," Reverend Jacobs told them as he prepared to leave. "Michael, I'll stop by and see you later."

"Thank you, Reverend Jacobs."

When the preacher had gone, Angel spoke first.

"Michael, Christopher's so upset we were wondering if you'd mind if he came to stay with us for a few days. It's hard for him to be in your house right now after what happened."

"Of course it's all right. It will probably do him a world of good to get away for a while."

"Good. We have been very worried about him."

"I appreciate your concern." He was glad they were taking the boy. He wanted to celebrate his newfound freedom. He didn't want to be playing nanny to a crying nine-year-old.

"We love Christopher."

"We all love Christopher." Michael boldly moved to hug both Angel and Sarah.

Both women had to fight to keep their real emotions from showing when he embraced them. They bid him good-bye and promised that he would be hearing from them soon.

It was much later that afternoon when Angel and Sarah sat across the desk from John Hayden, the lawyer. Their faces reflected the outrage they were feeling over what he'd just told them.

"But Michael killed Elizabeth just as sure as if he'd taken a gun and shot her!" Angel insisted.

"Angela, you've known me for many years. You

know I will always be completely honest and forthright with you; and, while I agree that what you've told me is shocking, you still have no solid evidence to prove your case. No matter what you might think, Michael's innocent unless you can prove otherwise. You have only bruises on your sister's arm and a child's word that his father occasionally hit his mother to back up your story. It's not enough to convict him."

"Why not? Why can't we have him arrested?"

"As horrible as it is, I'm afraid it's not against the law for a man to strike his wife. In the eyes of the law, she's considered his property, you know."

"You mean there really is nothing we can do?" They spoke in unison.

"I'm sorry," Mr. Hayden answered with finality. He felt deeply troubled denying them hope; but, without some tangible proof, a conviction would be impossible. "I wish there were something more positive I could tell you or something I could do to help you."

"We're sorry, too." Angel and Sarah rose to go. They didn't speak again until they were safely inside their carriage.

"Now what?" Sarah asked. "We can't let Christopher go back home to Michael. We just can't."

"I know. If he killed Elizabeth, there's no telling what he might do to Christopher, although I doubt he'd do him any serious harm before he claims his inheritance."

"You're right. The money . . ."

"I know. It could be that's all he's ever been after,"

Angel remarked bitterly. She thought for a moment, then lifted her gaze to her sister's. "There's only one thing left for us to do."

"What?"

"We've got to get Christopher as far away from Michael as possible."

They looked at each other solemnly, understanding the danger they would face in such a risky venture. Still, there was no alternative. They loved their nephew and would do everything they could to protect him.

Chapter Four

St. Louis—Ten Days Later

Sarah opened the hotel room door to Angel's soft call.

"Come on in," Sarah urged, closing the door quickly behind her. "Is Christopher sleeping?"

"Yes, he was asleep almost before his head hit the pillow."

"All this traveling's been hard on him," Sarah said sympathetically.

"It's been hard on all of us, and it's not over yet," Angel agreed wearily. They'd fled Philadelphia to escape Michael nine days ago, and they hadn't stopped running since.

"You're right about that."

Angel paced to the window, then turned to her sibling. "Do you remember Anne Taylor?"

"Your friend from school?"

"Yes. Well, her family moved to California several

years ago, and though we don't keep in regular touch, I did just get a letter from her not too long ago."

"So?"

"So I think we should head for California," she announced.

"California?"

"San Francisco to be more specific. Anne's newly married and living there."

"But it's so far."

"Precisely. San Francisco's a boom town, and I can't think of a better place to hide. Anne's always been a good friend to me. She'll help us find a safe place to stay. Then, all we'll have to do is bide our time. Once Christopher's old enough to stand up to Michael, we can go back home."

"Are you sure you want to do this? As vicious as Michael is, there's no telling what he might do." Sarah was worried about involving Anne in their trouble.

"What other choice do we have? Aunt Blanche only met Anne once, and Michael never did. He's probably never even heard me mention her." Angel fell silent for a moment, then lifted her troubled emerald gaze to Sarah's dark, equally worried one. "Besides," she said in a small voice. "I can't think of anyone else. He knows all of our close friends and relatives. Anne's our only hope."

They both stared at each other for a moment, thinking about the magnitude of their actions. They could just imagine the uproar that had occurred the day their disappearance was discovered.

Though John Hayden had discouraged them in their attempts to prosecute Michael, he had been very sympathetic to their cause. It was his carefully worded advice given the following morning when Angel had returned to speak with him once more that had helped her decide to take Christopher and run. It was their intention to keep the boy safely out of his father's clutches until he was old enough to take care of himself. It didn't matter to Sarah or to Angel that their own lives were being completely disrupted. They only cared about protecting Christopher. They had lost Elizabeth. They would not lose Christopher.

Mr. Hayden had willingly agreed to help them in every legal way he could, and they had taken him up on his offer of support with great relief. At his suggestion and through his efforts, they would have access to the money they'd put in a special, secret account away from their regular bank. The lawyer had also promised to begin a check into Michael's background to see if there was anything revealing or unsavory in his past. Hayden had warned Angel that he probably wouldn't discover anything but had promised that if he did, he would do everything in his power to get them awarded custody of the boy. Hayden had also agreed to handle any and all of the necessary work connected with Christopher's claiming his inheritance when the time came. Angel had known they had a true friend in their late father's attorney when she'd left his office that day.

"All right," Sarah consented, "but how are we going to get to California?"

"I've been thinking about that," Angel told her,

"and the most important thing we need to do is to make things as hard as we possibly can for Michael. He's going to expect us to take the easiest route, and from what I've been able to find out, the most comfortable way is by ship to Panama, where you cross the isthmus there and then sail the rest of the way up the west coast. We have to do the unexpected. We have to keep him off-balance."

"You're right." Sarah smiled. In the past, Angel's antics had sometimes landed them in trouble, but this time her quick-thinking had helped them escape from Michael unnoticed. They had a head start on him, but God only knew how long that would last. "Your idea to buy the tickets to New York and then have us head west instead was very clever. If you hadn't thought of that, he would have caught up with us by now."

"It did work, didn't it?" Angel remarked, feeling a little proud of how well they'd managed so far. "I just hated leaving without telling Aunt Blanche, but if she didn't know anything, she couldn't give us away."

"I hope she's not too upset with us."

"Oh, I'm sure she is, but we did leave her the note." They'd told her in the missive of their suspicions about Michael and how they were taking Christopher away to keep him safe. They had promised to be in touch when they could and told her not to worry.

"I'm sure that wasn't much consolation to her, being left in the dark like that."

"Now don't go feeling guilty, Sarah. We didn't have a choice. If we'd stayed, who knows if Christopher would have been alive the day after his tenth birthday?"

"I know, but it's still so hard to believe. I thought Michael was wonderful for so long."

"So did Elizabeth, and now she's dead," Angel said with fervent emotion. "He's charming and handsome and as deadly as a snake. That's why we have to be careful."

"You're right."

Dragging her thoughts back to their current situation, she concentrated on the need to move and move quickly. "That's why I think it would be best if we split up and go in different directions."

"Split up?" Sarah stared at her sister aghast. "Are you crazy?"

"Michael's not going to let us go without a fight. He's not going to give up." A tingle of fear frissoned down her spine as she said the words, but Angel ignored it as best she could.

"But that's all the more reason why we should stick together. We'll be stronger together!" Sarah argued.

"How strong could we be if he sends some big, mean men after us? There's no way we could win in a showdown. We've got to outsmart him."

"But we don't have to—"

"If we separate," Angel interrupted, "he'll lose our trail. At best, we've got a week's head start. At worst, he could show up here tomorrow! Sarah, think about it! The more false leads we leave, the harder it will be for him to find the real one that takes him to Christopher."

"I know, I just want us to be together."

"I do, too, and we will be just as soon as we all reach San Francisco. Trust me, this is the safest way for Christopher."

"All right. What do you want me to do?"

"I'll buy three tickets and go on to New Orleans so it will look like we're taking the Panama route, but you and Christopher are going to go overland."

"By wagon train?" Sarah had read accounts of the rigors of crossing the country that way and knew it wouldn't be easy. She would be a woman alone.

"Yes. It'd be too easy for Michael if we all went on to New Orleans. Once he found out our destination, all he'd have to do is wire someone there and have us intercepted. If he's close on our trail now, they might even be waiting at the dock for us when we make port. You've got to go by land."

"All right."

"Good, and I want Christopher to travel with you."

"With me?" This really surprised her. She and Christopher were close, but it was no secret that Angel was his favorite.

"Michael knows how Christopher and I feel about each other. He'd never dream I'd agree to be parted from him. He'll be looking for us. You, on the other hand, can dress like a widow for the trip and tell everyone that he's your son. They should believe you."

"Christopher isn't going to like this. He's come to depend on you so much since Elizabeth died."

"I know." Angel's eyes filled with tears, but she

blinked them away. There was no time for sentiment. She had to think clearly. "It's going to be hard on both of us, but I want him safe, Sarah."

"If we go by wagon train, what are you going to do? How are you going to get to San Francisco?"

"Don't worry about me. I'll think of something. We need to concentrate on getting you and Christopher out of town as fast as we can. I heard someone talking down in the lobby when we checked in, and they said that since the new railroad went through to Jefferson City, the trip up to Kansas City has been cut down to about fifty hours now. Most of the wagon trains leave from a town called Independence near there."

"How soon do you want us to leave?"

"Tomorrow morning."

"We'd better start getting ready, then. I'll need to buy some mourning clothes."

At the thought, Sarah lifted emotion-filled dark eyes to her sister's. In that quiet, poignant moment, they thought of Elizabeth's funeral and remembered the way they'd deliberately decided to leave their mourning things behind on the day they'd fled. They had wanted to throw Michael off when he attempted to follow them from Philadelphia and had known that the mourning clothes there would draw attention to them and make them stand out. Now, however, nearly a thousand miles from home, Sarah could pass as a widow with a son without fear.

"And we have to come up with a believable story about why you're traveling to California with your 'son.' "

"Angel?"

"What?"

"You'll be careful, won't you? I mean, I'll have Christopher with me, but you're going to be all by yourself."

"Don't worry." Angel managed a grin that made her look like a mischievous little girl again. "I'll be fine. Didn't I always manage to get out of trouble when I was younger?"

"As I remember it, you always managed to get into trouble, not out of it."

"Well, I'm older now."

Sarah couldn't help but laugh, and they fell into each other's arms and embraced lovingly. The next few months were going to be dangerous, but they believed in what they were doing. No matter what hardships befell them along the way, they firmly believed that love would give them the strength they needed to see it through.

At mid-morning the following day, the train carrying Sarah and Christopher away from St. Louis moved off down the track on its way west. Angel lingered on the platform watching until it was out of sight.

It was good to know that her sister and nephew were safely away, but a sudden sense of loneliness and unease gripped her. Fear hovered at the edges of her consciousness, and she glanced at the people standing nearby. Nothing seemed amiss. Everyone seemed to have a reason for being here.

Fighting against the terror that threatened, Angel

forced the panic away. She scolded herself in annoyance, for this was no time to be weak. She prided herself on being the kind of person who took action when it was needed, and there was still much she had to do. She had to make a plan of her own for getting to California. Gritting her teeth, Angel gave a lift of her chin and started back to the hotel.

Angel's path from the station took her down Veranda Row past all the fancy stores. She was lost in thought as she moved along the crowded sidewalks. The shoppers were out in full force this morning, and even Angel found herself glancing occasionally into the store windows as she passed by to see what was on display. At the sight of a particularly attractive bonnet, she stopped abruptly to look at it, and it was then that she felt the slight tug on her drawstring purse.

"What? ! . . ."

Reacting on pure instinct, she snared the hand of the young boy who was trying to reach into her purse.

"Damn it, lady! What the hell are you trying to do! Let go of me!" He gave a violent yank trying to free his hand from her iron hold.

Angel stared down into the brash, aggressive youth's dirty, belligerent face, and her first thought was that he reminded her of Christopher. He was approximately the same height and build as her nephew, and he had brown eyes like his, too, but that was where the resemblance ended. Where Christopher's eyes were full of love, warmth, and trust, this boy's were filled with fury and a sullen wariness as he glowered up at her.

"What did you think you were doing?" she demanded, refusing to let him go.

"I wasn't doin' a damn thing!" The boy continued to fight her, twisting and trying to break loose. Every line of his small body was tense as he tried to get free of her.

"Why don't I believe you?" For all his defiance and fury, Angel could see that he was really scared, and she understood why. He was obviously a street urchin who made his living by picking pockets, and if she turned him in he'd get into big trouble. It angered her that a boy so young, a boy who needed a home, a good meal, and someone to care for him, could be reduced to thievery just to survive. It was no life for a grown-up, let alone a child.

"C'mon, lady. You got no reason to hold me!"

"We'll see about that."

Angel wondered distantly how Christopher would have fared if he'd been forced to fend for himself. The thought troubled her as she tried to control the hostile, struggling boy before her. As Angel considered that this boy was probably alone in the world a wild idea came to her. A conspiratorial half-smile curved her lips as she realized the perfection of her plan. This boy needed help, and she was just the one who could provide it. Of course in helping him she would be indirectly helping herself, but what did it matter as long as they both benefited from the arrangement? Without another word, Angel started to walk toward her hotel, forcing him in step with her.

"Wait a minute! Who the hell do you think you are, trying to drag me along? I ain't goin' anywhere with you!"

"Do you want to bet?"

The fact that the woman was smiling at him, yet sounding so dead serious left Lucky completely off-balance. He wasn't sure what she was going to do, but he figured she was probably taking him to the sheriff's office to turn him in. Lucky grimaced at the thought and increased his resistance. If the sheriff got his hands on him, Lucky knew he'd end up back at the horrible orphanage he'd run away from several years ago. Living on the streets wasn't easy, but it was far better than the orphan's home had been. Digging in his heels, he kept trying to break away, but the lady's grip was strong and he hadn't eaten in a couple of days.

"Where d'ya think you're takin' me?" he demanded of his captor.

"You'll find out in a few minutes." Angel's answer was cryptic as she kept walking.

"Like hell I will!" the boy cursed out loud. He gave another violent, but futile jerk of his arm. Of all the rotten luck! Out of all the women on the streets this morning he could have robbed, he'd had to go and pick on this one! He'd chosen her to steal from because she'd looked so pretty and dainty. He figured she'd be an easy mark and wouldn't give him much trouble. He'd had no idea at the time that she had a grip like a blacksmith and the disposition of a jail guard or he never would have tried.

As they drew near the cross street that led to the

sheriff's office, Lucky began to fight her in earnest. It shocked him when she came to a complete stop and turned on him, her expression serious.

"You can come quietly with me into my hotel or we can go straight to the sheriff's office. What's it going to be?"

"The hotel?" Lucky repeated in surprise. He'd thought his fate sealed, but here she hadn't been taking him to the law at all. She was taking him to her hotel. He frowned, wondering why.

"Well?" Angel asked.

The choice wasn't really a choice. Lucky certainly didn't want to go to the sheriff's office. He nodded his agreement and followed her into the luxurious lobby of the Planter's House Hotel.

Until that moment, Lucky had only managed to catch peeks of the inside of this famous hotel. Now, seeing the sumptuously appointed lobby for the first time up close with its chandeliers and plush carpets, he was greatly impressed. He gawked openly at his surroundings as his captor led him across the wide room to the stairs.

As they started up the main staircase, Lucky glanced up at the woman who still held his hand in a death-grip and saw how she held her head high and moved with confident elegance before the stares of the other hotel guests. He wondered how he could ever have mistakenly thought she was delicate. She was as strong-willed as she was beautiful, and as she led him to her room on the third floor, Lucky began to think that maybe he should just play along with her and see what happened. He knew he'd have to be careful, though, for he had a feeling she would know instantly if he were trying to pull something fast on her.

Angel paid no attention to the questioning looks of the other guests as she took the unkempt, poorly-dressed boy directly to her room. She didn't let go of him until they were inside with the door closed and locked behind them. Only then did she turn her full attention to him, studying him seriously in an attempt to see through the layers of grime he sported from head to toe. His hair was so filthy and greasy that there was no telling the color. It could have been anything from blond to brown. His clothes were little better than rags and hung loosely on his thin, wiry body. It was his eyes, though, that caught and held her attention. A clear, warm brown, they fairly sparkled with a keen, challenging intelligence as they returned her regard with tempered hostility. Angel was so intent upon finalizing her plans in her mind before speaking to the boy about them, that she failed to realize just how frightened the poor child was.

"Why'd ya lock the door? You think I'm gonna run away?"

"You might, but I'm hoping you're smarter than that. Now, allow me to introduce myself, my name is Angela Roberts."

"So? What d'ya want with me?"

"First, I'd like to know your name."

"What's it to you?"

"I just want to know, that's all. By the way, you look hungry. When was the last time you had something to eat—or took a bath?" Her nose wrinkled a little in distaste.

"What's any of that got to do with knowin' my name? Why don't you just let me go? I didn't take anything from you." His chin took on a mutinous tilt as he clung to his fragile pride.

"Only because I caught you before you could. Don't you realize the trouble you can get yourself into by stealing?"

"I can take care of myself."

"Of course you can," she said with no small amount of sarcasm. "You'll be safe and happy living a life of crime. If you're stealing out of ladies' purses for a living now, what are you going to be doing in five or ten years?"

"That ain't none of your damned business!"

"You have a nasty mouth for one so young," she pointed out, unruffled by his use of profanity.

"My mouth ain't none of your concern! If you hadn't gone and yanked me off the street, you wouldn't have to be worrying about it now, would ya?" he snarled angrily.

"If I may point out, I didn't 'yank you off the street.' You decided to come with me, remember? The choice was yours." Tenderness tugged at her heart. Angel had spent enough time with Christopher to know all about little boys and their bravado, and she decided to call his bluff then and there. She didn't want to fight with him. She wanted to help him.

Caught up short by her logic, he turned even more defensive. "Why are you buttin' your nose into my affairs, anyhow? What's it to you what I say or do?"

"Would you like something to eat?" Angel deliberately changed the topic.

Lucky blinked in confusion, then looked cynical. "What's the catch? What d'ya want?" He knew that nobody gave anything away without expecting something in return.

"I want to make a deal with you."

"Oh, yeah?" He didn't trust her one little bit.

"Yes. You tell me your name and I'll get you some food."

Lucky eyed her cautiously, trying to understand exactly what she was after. Any other woman would have been raising Cain by now over his trying to steal from her; yet this one was acting just as calm as you please, offering to get him food in exchange for his telling her his name. She'd been looking at him kind of funny, and nothing she was doing made much sense, but he was real hungry.

"My name's Lucky," he replied slowly.

"Lucky? That's an unusual name. Is that your birth name?"

"Lucas is my given name, but the other boys on the street have been callin' me Lucky ever since the time I managed to get away from the sheriff and his boys." His chin lifted again and the defiance returned to his brown-eyed gaze.

"Interesting," Angel murmured, thinking of what a harrowing experience that had to have been for the boy. "Now, what's your last name?"

"I don't have no last name."

"We both know you do, Lucky. How can I take

you home to your parents if I don't know what your real name is?"

"Who asked you to take me home?" He balked almost in a panic. If she told anybody who he was, he was as good as back in the orphanage, and he couldn't let that happen again.

"Don't you want to go home?" She was surprised by the vehemence of his protest.

"I don't want nothin' from you!"

"Not even a hot meal?" she asked. "You need a bath, too, and you could certainly use some new clothes as well."

"Right, lady. I'll just eat my stomach full, take a nice bath, and then run on down to the store and buy some new clothes," he sneered. "Course that'll be right after I get some money out of the bank."

"I can get you all three," Angel told him calmly.

"Why would ya want to?"

"I told you before, I want to make a deal with you."

"You're crazy."

"Am I?" she challenged. "Why don't you try me and see? What have you got to lose? Unless, of course, you're afraid . . ."

Lucky had far too much pride to let her think he was scared, even though he was. "What do you really want?"

"I want the truth from you. I want to know where your parents are."

"I ain't got no parents. They died three years ago from cholera," he confessed flatly.

"I see. I'm sorry." The news didn't surprise her. "Then you're living with relatives?"

"No, I ain't got nobody else. Some preacher put me in an orphanage, but I got out of there as fast as I could," he explained, trying not to let his feelings show. He'd buried the pain of his loss deep inside, and he wanted to keep it there. He wasn't about to let this lady or anyone else know the hopelessness and fear he'd lived with since that day when, at six, he'd been abandoned in the cold, cruel world. His innocence had been torn from him then, and he now knew more about the ugliness of the world than many adults.

"You got out of the orphanage?"

"I ran away." He suppressed the feeling of desperation that surged forth at the memory of his escape from the mean-spirited women who'd run the children's home.

"Was it that bad?" Angel asked gently. She'd seen a darkening in his expression and wondered what terrible things had happened to him there.

"It wasn't pretty. At least on the streets, there ain't nobody beatin' on me all the time. I'm my own man. I can do whatever I want, and there ain't nobody to tell me different." Lucky was filled with a sense of self-satisfaction that went far beyond his years. No one had cared about him when he'd first arrived at the children's home. He'd been lost and forlorn; and when he'd dared cry over his dead parents, he'd been beaten and starved. When he'd decided to run away, no one had helped him. He'd made it by himself.

"So, you're your own man, are you?" Angel was

more perceptive than he gave her credit for. She realized that life in the orphanage must have been hell for him and that he'd run away just to stay alive. She admired his courage and spunk and understood why he didn't want to tell her his real name. He probably thought she would turn him in.

"That's right."

"Well, I have an idea you just might find interesting. I'd like to offer you a job."

"Yeah?" The boy gave her a measuring look, not trusting her.

"I'd like to hire you to accompany me to California."

Lucky stared at her, dumbfounded. "You serious? You want me to go with you to California? Why?"

"Suffice it to say that I have to make the trip and having you along will just make it all the more memorable." The fear that she might be placing him in harm's way haunted her, but she dismissed it. Even if Michael did find them, he wouldn't harm Lucky. Christopher was the boy he was after. Lucky would be safe with her, far safer than if he stayed here and lived on the streets.

"But why are you askin' me to go after I tried to rob you?"

"You're perfect for what I need, and I think you're intelligent enough to handle it."

"What do you 'need' and what do I have 'to handle'?" he asked warily. It sounded too good to be true.

"I'll tell you all that if and when you agree to go."

"And if I don't, you'll turn me over to the sheriff, right?" He wasn't completely naive and gullible.

Angel remained silent, letting him believe that she would, even though she never would have had the heart.

"All right. I'll go." There was no need to think about it.

"I knew you were smart."

"You said this was a job. How much are you gonna pay me?"

Angel had to fight to keep from smiling at his brashness, but she knew he wouldn't be alive today if he were the quiet sort.

"I'll pay you $500 when we reach San Francisco—providing you do exactly what I say until we get there. Does that sound fair to you?"

Lucky had never known that much money existed, and his eyes widened in appreciation of the amount. "What exactly is it that you want me to do?"

"I need for you to pretend to be my brother. What we will tell people is that I was to be married in the fall to my fiancé who lives in San Francisco, but because our parents met an untimely demise back in Pittsburgh, we're going west early. My fiancé is expecting us, and he and I will be married as soon as we arrive."

"Is that all true? Are your folks dead, too?"

"Yes, both my parents are dead." They looked at each other in mutual understanding of the sorrow they had each faced and conquered in their own ways.

"What about the rest of it? Are you really gettin' married when we get there?"

"Yes, and that's why I'm in such a hurry. I miss Christopher desperately, and I can't wait to see him again." She managed to get by with only a partial lie and wondered if that improved things with God.

"I still don't understand why you need me with you," Lucky said thoughtfully, "but it doesn't matter as long as you pay me."

"That's right." Angel nodded. The boy only needed to know what he had to do.

"I'm gonna be real good at this, Sis," he told her with a wide, cocky grin. The fear that had gripped him earlier had eased. He still thought this Angela Roberts was crazy, but he wasn't about to look a gift horse in the mouth. He would take her money and enjoy the trip. *California.* It sounded good to him. "I'm gonna fool everybody. I'm gonna be the best little brother you ever had."

"I'm sure you will be, but I find 'Sis' a trifle obnoxious. People who know me call me Angel."

"Angel?" Gazing up at her, he suddenly realized that the name fit her. She was beautiful, the most beautiful woman he'd ever seen—outside of his mother, of course.

"Yes. Now, Lucky, there is one other thing . . ."

"What?" he asked guardedly.

"You really do need a bath."

"No! I ain't takin' no damned bath!"

"Lucky, I'm only going to say this once. If you use that kind of language in my company again, I will personally wash your mouth out with the strongest soap I can find. Do I make myself clear?"

The determined look in her green eyes and the unyielding tone of her voice convinced him that she meant business. He knew he would have to clean up his mouth before she so kindly obliged and did it for him. "Yeah," he admitted grudgingly.

"Fine. We're coming to understand each other. Now, if you're going to pass for a relative of mine, you must look the part. You have another choice here. You can bathe yourself, and I do mean bathe; or I can help you with your bath and make sure, personally, that the job is done throroughly and correctly. Which will it be?"

He shot her a black look as he muttered. "I'll do it myself."

"Good." Satisfied that things were going to work out between them, she gathered up her purse and started for the door.

"Where ya goin'?"

"I have a few errands to run, and I thought you might like some privacy while you bathe."

"How do you know I'll still be here when you get back? How do you know I won't steal all your stuff and run off."

Angel stopped and looked him straight in the eye. "You could do that if you wanted to, but I'm hoping you realize the job I'm offering you is worth a lot more than the little bit of money you'd make off selling the things I have in this room."

He returned her assessing gaze, but didn't respond.

"I'd like to think that I can trust you. What will it be, Lucky? Will you be here when I get back?"

"Yeah." He was still reluctant to completely believe what was happening.

Angel sensed his doubts and decided it was time to convince him of her sincerity. "Good. I'll be back in a little while. In the meantime, I'll be sure to have some food sent up with your bath. How's that?"

"All right."

"Fine. Enjoy a good soak," she teased as she left the room.

He scowled at the thought. Then she was gone, closing the door, but not locking it behind her.

Lucky stood in the middle of the plushly appointed room, staring about in disbelief. He asked himself if he'd been dreaming, but he knew the answer just by his surroundings. As reality sank in on him, his thoughts became a riotous, joyous tumble. He really was going to California!

Lucky let out a loud whoop of excitement. He didn't want to question his good fortune. He just wanted to enjoy it. Unmindful of his filthy condition, he threw himself upon the double bed and lay spread-eagled on its inviting softness, laughing. He hadn't lain in a real bed since his parents died; and, after a moment of enjoying its comfort, the child in him finally came out. Sitting up, Lucky began to bounce. He was still laughing and bouncing and having quite a good time when a knock at the door a few minutes later brought him up short.

Sobering, Lucky looked around at the mess he'd made. The covers and pillows were all over the floor.

For a minute, he feared it was Angel returning to tell him she'd changed her mind, and he was tense as he called out.

"Who is it?"

"We're the maids. We've got the food that was ordered, and we're here to prepare the bath."

Lucky jumped up and hastily threw the covers back on the bed. He opened the door, then stood back as the two maids entered the room carrying clean towels and a covered tray of delicious-smelling food. They were young, not more than eighteen, and they eyed him with barely concealed, and hastily disguised, distaste. It was only a quick glance on their part, but it was enough to make Lucky self-conscious. He stared down at his bare, dirty feet and suddenly realized how he must look to these two. It embarrassed him.

"Miss Roberts has ordered an extra bed brought in, so we'll be back with a trundle later," one maid informed him as they set the tray of food on the nightstand and began preparing the bath. When they'd finished their duties, they left the room.

Lucky shut the door after them; and, alone once again, he eyed the tub and its steaming contents with less than affection. He couldn't really remember the last time he'd had a real scrubbing. Since he'd left the orphanage, he'd had to make do with just washing off whenever he got the chance. Now, faced with the chance to sit in a real bathtub in clean hot water, he decided it might not be so bad after all. The tantalizing aroma of the hot food on the tray enticed him and he considered eating first, but the memory of the look the maids had given him sent him straight into the tub.

Lucky shed his filthy clothing and stepped into the bathtub and sat down. The heat of the water embraced him, and he relaxed a little as he leaned back. It had never occurred to him that it would be so nice to bathe. He was surprised when a sigh escaped him.

Vague memories of a time, long ago, when his mother had bathed him stirred in the back of Lucky's mind, but they were so distant that it almost seemed as if that had happened to another person in another lifetime. He sat quietly for a while, enjoying the luxury, until the temperature of the water started to drop dramatically. It was then that he knew he had to start scrubbing. Dunking beneath the surface to wet his hair, Lucky washed from top to bottom as Angel had instructed him to do. Then, just to make sure he'd done a good enough job, he repeated the procedure. He told himself that he wasn't doing it to please her. He told himself he was doing it because it was a part of their deal and because he certainly didn't want her finding a spot he might have missed and washing him herself.

Angel left the Planter's House and headed back toward the shopping district. She was glad Lucky had agreed to accompany her, but to make their charade believable, she was going to have to make a few changes in the boy. New clothing came first, then a haircut. Those two things would be the easiest to deal with. Once his outward appearance was polished, it was time for the hard part—teaching him manners. She was also going to have to work on his speech. The boy definitely needed help there. The way he talked now, he would never convince anyone that he came from a genteel background. She hoped he proved to be a quick study.

Angel smiled as she thought of the youngster. He had lived through rougher times than she could even imagine, and she respected him for it. She was determined to help him in any way she could and to try to make his life a little happier.

Angel entered a store that carried boys' things and enlisted a clerk's help in making her selections. It took quite a while to choose a wardrobe for her new 'little brother,' but when she was done, she was pleased.

"Miss Roberts, would you like us to deliver these to your room at the hotel?" the clerk asked as she paid in cash.

"Yes, thank you, but I will need to take a few things with me now." Angel picked out an outfit Lucky could wear while they were in town, along with underthings and shoes.

"Yes, ma'am. Thank you for coming in."

The first part of her task accomplished, Angel began to think about her situation again. Now that the boy was going with her, everything changed. On the way back to the hotel, Angel made it a point to stop at the office of one of the best steamboat lines to book their passage for New Orleans. When she'd thought she was traveling alone, she'd planned to leave town quietly. Now, however, she decided to draw attention to herself, so that if Michael or his men did come looking for her, she would be remembered. Angel wanted Michael's men to follow her. She wanted them to think that she had Christopher with her. She had to give Sarah time to get their nephew to safety.

Chapter Five

Three Days Later in New Orleans

Cyril Davis, the diminutive, balding, bespectacled clerk at the front desk of the hotel, looked up as the tall, lean, dark-haired man descended the staircase and crossed the lobby toward him.

"Good evening, Mr. Masters," Cyril greeted him with a quick ingratiating smile. He'd heard the talk about this man, Blade Masters, for his name had been on a lot of lips since he'd arrived in town the day before. Rumor had it that he was one of the fastest gunfighters around, and though he was a half-breed—his mother had been an Indian, his father white—he had garnered much respect for his talents through the years. The story went that he'd killed his first man at age fourteen, avenging his mother's death, and, after that, had begun hiring out his gun for a living. From the gossip Cyril had heard, Masters had put the last twenty men who'd dared to challenge him in their graves. It was said that he never backed down from a fight, and the clerk believed every word of it as he stared into Masters' hard, silvery eyes across the width of the desk. Cyril saw no warmth or humor in the depths of his gaze, only coldness. Being big on survival, the little clerk had no intention of upsetting this particular hotel guest in any way.

"Hello, Davis," Blade replied. "Are there any messages for me?"

"No, sir."

Blade frowned, and Cyril quaked in his shoes as he waited for the gunfighter to say more.

"Thanks." Blade gave him a curt, dismissing nod.

Cyril was relieved when Masters turned and walked away. Without being too obvious, Cyril studied him as he headed from the lobby. The man moved with a predatory grace that marked him as dangerous even though he appeared a normal businessman in dark trousers and coat and white shirt and tie. The clerk wondered if he were carrying a gun and then had his answer when he saw the slight, telltale bulge beneath his coat, low on his right side. A man like Masters didn't dare go anywhere unarmed. With a reputation like his, there was always a young hothead out there wanting to prove himself against him.

For a moment, Cyril almost felt sorry for the gunman, imagining how it would feel to have to always be on guard, but the clerk quickly shoved the ridiculous emotion away. Masters had to like what he was doing or he wouldn't be doing it. A man like him could quit any time he wanted. As another hotel guest approached, Cyril's thoughts were torn from the intriguing gunfighter and forced back to the work at hand.

Blade left the hotel and stepped outside into the cool darkness of the New Orleans night. Again he was struck by the size of the city. He was not a fan of civilization, and a part of him longed to be back in Texas where it was wild, open, and free. He loved that wide beautiful country, and if his negotiations with his old boss, Clancy Barrett, went as well as he hoped they would, he'd soon be back there, calling Texas home permanently.

At the thought of Barrett and the ranch, the Rocking B, that he wanted to buy from him, Blade smiled. He'd heard that Clancy had left Texas and put the Rocking B up for sale, so he'd followed him here to New Orleans to make him an offer. Clancy was registered at the St. Louis Hotel, and Blade had left a message for him there earlier that afternoon. Blade had hoped they could meet right away, but since it was getting late he doubted he would hear from him that night.

At loose ends, Blade decided to try a bit of the wild side of New Orleans' night life. He headed for the riverfront to find the kind of entertainment he was looking for—a fast game of poker and a fast, good-looking woman.

"Honey, I'm gonna bring you all the luck you need tonight!" Molly, a red-haired, big-bosomed saloon girl, crowed delightedly as she sidled up to the darkly handsome stranger who'd just joined the poker game in the back corner of the saloon where she plied her trade.

Blade chuckled as he glanced up at her. "You're feeling lucky tonight, are you?"

"Ever since I saw you walk through that door," she told him truthfully, her brightly painted lips parting in a smile as she rubbed her hip intimately against his shoulder. She'd seen a lot of men in her time, but there was something so compelling about this one that he'd caught her eye the moment he'd entered the bar. She'd been waiting for the chance to speak to him, and she was glad now that she'd been brazen enough to approach him. "I'm Molly."

Blade smiled back in invitation. "Then join me, Molly. I think I could use a little extra luck tonight."

"My pleasure," she responded happily. Even as experienced as Molly was, this man was so handsome that her heart skipped a beat just looking at him. His overlong black hair brushed his collar, and when he smiled, his white teeth flashed brilliantly against his dark tan. Vivid gray eyes met hers knowingly, and she returned his regard without hesitation.

"I'll need another whiskey before we get serious about playing this hand."

"I'll be right back, honey."

Molly hurried off to get his drink. When she returned with the whiskey, she didn't wait to be invited, but sat right down on his lap. Looping one arm about his shoulders, she leaned toward him giving him an unobstructed view of her bosom in the low-cut, seductive, red-satin gown.

"Anything else you need?" Molly purred.

The other men at the table chuckled knowingly.

"Just luck for right now. Hmm, let's see about these cards . . ."

With Molly cuddling close, Blade played for several hours. Her promise of bringing him good fortune held true, for he won far more than he lost. When he was victorious, she rewarded him with a kiss, and soon the other men were wishing that they'd had sense enough to grab her for their own when they'd first come in. After a time, Molly realized that she still hadn't learned his name.

"Sugar, I've been your good luck charm for hours, but I don't know who you are." She rubbed against him suggestively.

"The name's Masters. Blade Masters."

"Well, Blade Masters, if you like what I'm doing for you down here, why don't you come upstairs with me and get real lucky?" Her breath was hot and heavy in his ear. She was tired of the poker game and ready for more exciting action.

"We're doing so well here, I hate to leave just yet. Maybe in another few hands we'll go," he told her as he caressed her boldly.

The others at the table shared a stunned look of surprise at learning his identity. Several onlookers who'd gathered to watch the game moved away to spread the news among the other patrons that there was a gunfighter in their midst.

"You're Blade Masters?" one man at the table asked. He was regarding him differently now. A touch of fear shone in his eyes.

"Is that a problem?" Blade asked tersely.

"No . . . no problem."

The game continued uninterrupted.

Across the room, a dark-haired young man stood with his back to the bar, a glass of whiskey in his hand. When the news that Blade Masters was in the saloon came to him, he took a deep drink. He was a tall, lanky boy, anxious to make a name for himself as a quick draw, and he knew the man who beat Masters in a gunfight would be instantly famous across the country. Tense with excitement, he walked slowly toward the table where Blade sat facing him, playing poker.

Blade glanced up and immediately recognized the boy's grim, determined look. Just like all the others he'd faced, this kid was too young and stupid to be afraid of him. Blade knew what was coming, and he was filled with a helpless anger. He didn't want to face another man in a senseless gunfight, but sometimes he didn't have a choice.

"Masters!"

A hush fell over the room, and even the piano player quit pounding out his raucous melodies. Molly and the card players at the table rose and backed away into the crowd, leaving Blade and the boy facing each other. All attention was riveted on the two men.

"Stand up, Masters."

"Just who am I standing up for?" Blade laughed, hoping to turn the situation to his advantage.

"Name's Cal Moore, and I think your reputation as being the fastest gun alive is one big lie."

Blade shrugged. "So? Think what you want. It makes no difference to me."

Cal was disappointed by his lack of response and pressed further. "In fact, I think you're a damned coward. All those men you killed. . . . I think you probably shot 'em in the back."

Blade's gray-eyed gaze hardened, but he still did not get up. Instead, he spoke slowly and softly, "Get out of here, boy, before you start something you're going to regret."

Cal licked his lips and his hand dropped to hover near his sidearm. "I'll bet that's exactly what you did! You shot 'em all in the back. A half-breed would do a thing like that."

Blade's smile faded as he slowly laid down his cards. He rose to his feet in a deceptively smooth move, hoping to intimidate the boy into leaving. "Don't push this," he warned.

Cal knew he'd touched on a sensitive spot, a spot that would make Masters go for his gun. He believed he was ready for him. He thought he could beat him.

Blade read his thoughts. "Dying's not a pretty thing, boy."

"I ain't gonna be the one dying."

"Maybe you oughta have another drink and forget about this."

"You don't think I can beat you," the foolish young man challenged.

"I know you can't." Blade's voice was like velvet over steel and his eyes met Cal's.

For one moment, the boy was shaken by the lethal look in the gunfighter's silvery gaze. But he knew he was being watched by everyone in the saloon and he couldn't back down, not now. He swallowed tightly.

"Don't make this mistake, Cal. Go on back to the bar and leave it alone."

Coldness coiled within Blade like a rattler getting ready to strike. His body seemed to relax as he let his hand drop down close to his gun, a gun he did not want to use if he could possibly avoid it.

"So, the famous Blade Masters is trying to weasel out of a fight. Maybe it's true what they say about breeds," he taunted. "I heard they ain't nothing but a bunch of thieving cowards."

Cal didn't recognize the resignation in Blade's eyes nor the steadiness in his hand. He continued to verbally attack him.

"I understand you had a squaw for a mother and some fly-by-night for a father. Tell me, was Masters really your pa or did you just pick some white man—maybe one of the bunch who mounted your mother that month?"

Blade could clearly see the face of his beautiful loving mother in his mind, and he knew this was one taunt he could never walk away from.

"Little boys with big mouths don't know when to shut up," he said with a harsh laugh. "You shouldn't judge a good woman by your own mother, and you shouldn't try to do a man's job when you should still be getting your pants changed. You going to talk all night?"

The boy stiffened, but Blade seemed to relax even more. Only his eyes revealed the deadly threat. It was too late now for Cal to even think of backing down.

For the first time, Cal knew uncertainty and fear. He would have glanced nervously away, but the gun-fighter's gaze held his. Cal trembled, then knowing there was nothing more to say, he went for his gun.

Blade read his movement perfectly; and, with lightning speed, he drew his own gun and fired. The speed of his hand made everyone gasp for Cal's gun had barely cleared leather when Blade's bullet found its mark.

Cal looked up, shocked. *This couldn't be happening to him! He was fast! He knew he was!* Suddenly, his strength left him and he crumpled to the floor, his life's blood draining away.

Blade stared down at him feeling the same pity, anger, and bitterness that always filled him at a time like this. It had happened too often in his life, and he was tired of it . . . so tired.

All those watching needed no further proof that the rumors being spread about Masters were true. Blade Masters was every bit as fast as they'd heard.

Roscoe Topps, the bartender, hurried to check the fallen man, but it didn't take a genius to figure out he was dead.

"He's dead," the bartender announced. "Somebody go for the law!"

"Oh, Blade," Molly broke the silence as she rushed to his side. "Are you all right?"

"I'm fine," he responded, slowly holstering his gun and turning away from the sight of the carnage.

The crowd in the saloon started talking, milling about. They closed in around Roscoe, trying to get a look at Cal where he lay sprawled on the floor.

"There ain't nothin' to see here! Go get another drink!" Roscoe barked, annoyed by their morbid curiosity.

A deputy came rushing in a few moments later and quickly knelt with the bartender beside the body.

"What happened, Roscoe?" Lester Straub demanded.

"Gunfight. This damned fool kept agitatin' until he went and got himself killed. It was a fair fight."

"Who did it?"

"I did." Blade had seen the lawman enter the saloon, and he came forward, knowing there would an interrogation.

"Who are you?"

"Blade Masters."

Straub recognized the name, and he straightened a little as he regarded Blade. "I'm sorry about this, but I'm afraid I'm going to have to ask you to come with me down to the sheriff's office. He's going to want to ask you a few questions."

The last thing Blade wanted or needed was trouble with the law. Though he was innocent of any wrongdoing, he gave the deputy a curt nod of agreement.

"Let's go," Straub directed.

"Wait." Molly hurried forth to grab Blade's arm, not wanting the evening to end this way. "Will you be back?"

Blade gently withdrew from her touch. "Not tonight, Molly."

"But what about your winnings?"

"You keep them."

"But Blade . . ." Her eyes implored him to return

to her, but she saw no answering interest in his gaze.

He turned from her and led the way out of the saloon with the deputy close behind him. He remained silent as they walked through the streets of town. When they reached the office, Sheriff Tannen was sitting at his desk. He looked up as the door opened.

"What's the problem, Straub?"

"There was a shooting in the Backwater Saloon. Witnesses all said it was a fair fight."

"The other man dead?" Tannen studied the man his deputy had brought in.

"Yes, sir."

"What's your name?" he asked Blade, noticing how easily he wore his gun and how calm he seemed.

"Masters."

"You Blade Masters?"

"I am," he answered flatly.

"Well, Masters, I don't doubt for a minute what the witnesses said about the gunfight. I know your reputation. The thing is, trouble seems to follow your kind wherever you go, and I don't want that kind of trouble in my town."

"I'm here on business. I'll only be here a few more days."

"A few days isn't good enough. I'll give you one more day, and then I want you out of here."

"I didn't do anything wrong."

"So I heard, but I have this thing about men dying." He pinned Blade with a steady look. "I don't like it."

"Neither do I, sheriff."

"Good. But just to make sure that you know I'm serious, I think I'd like you to be my guest and spend the night here with us. It might help you see the wisdom of riding out right on time."

It wasn't the first time he'd been jailed unfairly, and though he wanted to rage at the injustice of it, Blade knew better.

"So I'm to accept the hospitality of your jail for the night?" he asked sarcastically.

"That's right, and first thing in the morning you'll be free to go and finish up your business. Now, I'd like your gun, please."

"When do I get it back?"

"I'll personally see it returned to you when you leave in the morning. But I don't want to get word of your using it again while you're here. Do you understand me?"

Deputy Straub tensed at the sheriff's words. He was expecting trouble. He was surprised when Blade only nodded and turned over his sidearm without further comment.

"Show Mr. Masters where he's going to spend the night, Straub," Tannen ordered, never taking his eyes off his 'guest.'

The deputy opened the door that led to the block of jail cells, and Blade walked straight on in ahead of him. He entered the cell Straub indicated and sat down on the hard bunk. When the door was slammed shut and locked behind him, he swore under his breath.

Blade lay back and folded his arms beneath his head. He stared up at the dirty ceiling. He'd had about all the civilization he could stand and was more eager than ever to get away from New Orleans as fast as he could. Tomorrow, he decided, he would find Clancy and work out a deal with him for the ranch. When that was done, he was going to head straight back to Texas and stay there. It would feel good to be alone out on the range again.

It was late in the evening when the steamer Angel and Lucky had booked passage on from St. Louis readied itself to dock in New Orleans. Standing on deck at the rail, they watched the lights of the city as they put into port. They had been together for almost four full days, and Angel was sure he could pass for her younger brother with no difficulty. He'd cleaned up nicely. His hair had turned out to be light brown, and he had a cute smattering of freckles across the bridge of his nose. There was a healthy glow in his cheeks that had been missing when they'd first met, and she thought he was already filling out nicely.

Angel had been pleasantly surprised to discover that Lucky was as bright as she'd hoped. She smiled to herself as she thought of their first meal together in the hotel dining room. It had been a disaster. She'd been horrified as she'd watched him use his fingers to eat, wolfing down the food and chewing loudly with his mouth open. While not condemning his manners publicly, she'd shown him by example the proper way to use the utensils and napkin and the correct way to chew in polite company. Thus had begun Lucky's intensive training in etiquette, and he'd come quite far in just a few days. As for as his "language," he had suffered only minor slips since she'd threatened him with washing out his mouth, and she was proud of him.

Sometimes, Angel would catch him watching her with a wary look in his eyes, but as soon as he realized she'd noticed, he'd mask his expression. She wasn't quite sure what he was thinking, but she was glad that fate had thrown them together. Despite his rough edges, Lucky had an irrepressible good humor that kept her spirits up in spite of her worries about Sarah and Christopher.

Angel thought of Michael and wondered if his men were close behind them. She had no doubt that he'd sent someone after them, and she turned her attention to the riverfront to keep watch, just in case they'd somehow managed to beat them to New Orleans.

"So now what are we going to do?" Lucky asked as the steamer tied up and the gangplank was lowered.

"It's too late to see about our passage to California now, so we'll have to get a hotel room for the night. In the morning, I'll check with the steamship lines and find out when the next departure is for Panama."

Lucky noticed then how tense Angel had gotten since the boat had pulled into port and how closely she watched the crowd on the levee. "What's the matter?"

His perceptiveness surprised her, and she forced herself to relax. "Nothing. Why?" she answered him

110

as casually as she could, but she still kept an eye out for any sign of trouble.

"You looked—oh, I don't know—funny."

"Funny?"

"Yeah, like you're worried 'bout something."

Reasonably sure that there was no one on the landing looking for them, Angel turned a bright smile on him. "I'm not worried. I'm just nervous about making our connections. That's all."

Lucky accepted her explanation at face value, and they began their preparations to leave the steamer. Once in the city, they took a room at one of the better hotels and, after eating in the hotel's dining room, they settled in for the night.

Angel didn't know why, but a sense of disquiet filled her as she tried to rest. Troubled, she finally gave up her quest for slumber and rose from the bed to pace the room. She took great care to move quietly, for she didn't want to disturb Lucky. He was sleeping peacefully in his own bed, looking so young and innocent that she couldn't bear to wake him. He was totally oblivious of the deception and danger swirling around him, and she wanted it to stay that way.

As she gazed down at the boy, Angel again felt a moment of regret over having drawn him into her intrigue. But then she remembered how desperate he'd looked that first day in St. Louis and how hungry he'd been, and she knew she'd done the right thing. With her, he was clean, well-fed, and off the streets. She meant to keep him that way.

Lucky had won a place in her heart that first afternoon when she'd returned to the hotel with his clothes and found him scrubbed clean and waiting for her. He had donned his old clothes in a defensive move and stood before her, daring her to say anything. She'd been smart enough not to. Instead, she'd complimented him on his cleanliness and had merely handed him the new things she'd purchased. He hadn't said a word, but had taken them and disappeared behind the dressing screen. Moments later, he'd reappeared looking so handsome that she'd truly been impressed and told him so. For a moment, he'd beamed, but then had guarded his expression, afraid of revealing too much to her too soon.

It had been that way ever since between them. Lucky wasn't one to trust completely, and Angel didn't blame him. It would take time to win him over, but she didn't mind. Trust was something that had to be earned, and she intended to earn his.

Moving to the window, Angel stared out over the darkened city. The haunting worry that had plagued her earlier had eased a bit, and she was relieved. Feeling more in control, she returned to bed and finally slept.

Chapter Six

Meanwhile in Philadelphia . . .

Michael was furious as he sat at his desk in his office. It had been two weeks since Angel and Sarah had disappeared with Christopher—two weeks of frustration and anger.

Michael swore out loud as he remembered his confrontation with Aunt Blanche the day he'd discovered they were gone. The old woman had all but thrown him out of the house when he'd come to claim Christopher and take him home. It had been then that he'd discovered that Angel and Sarah had fled with the boy. Outrage had filled him, but there'd been little he could do. He'd tried to sweet-talk Blanche, but this time she'd proven immune to his charm. There had been hatred and loathing in her eyes as she'd accused him of hurting Elizabeth.

Michael was unsure exactly what had caused Angel and Sarah to suspect him, but ultimately it didn't matter. What mattered was that no charges had been filed with the authorities and that meant they had no solid proof of his guilt. They couldn't prove a thing!

Michael had considered going to the law and accusing them of kidnapping but had decided it would be far wiser and more expedient to take matters into his own hands. Though they had a head start on him, he'd hired four of the best men he could find and told them to track the trio down and bring them back no matter what the expense.

"Mr. Marsden?" His clerk's voice was accompanied by a knock at the door.

"Yes, what it is?" He looked up, wondering at the interruption.

"A telegram, sir. I thought you'd want to see it right away." The clerk entered the room and handed him the missive.

"Thank you."

When the man had gone, Michael quickly opened and read the contents. For the first time since Christopher had disappeared, he smiled. After a slow start, it looked like his men were finally on to something. A woman fitting Angel's description accompanied by a small boy had left St. Louis for New Orleans and two of his men had followed her there. The remaining two men were still in St. Louis checking on other possibilities. Finally! A solid lead!

Michael felt in control once again. Soon, Christopher would be back where he belonged, and as for the women. . . . Sarah, he dismissed summarily, but not Angel, not his defiant little Angel. Michael leaned back in his chair and steepled his fingers thoughtfully before him as he considered how much he was going to enjoy punishing her for her audacity in thinking she could escape him. She'd dared to defy him, but in doing so, had only increased the challenge to him to make her his own. He chuckled evilly to himself. The day was coming when she would be his in every way.

Totally confident, Michael returned his full attention to his business interests.

After a light breakfast at the hotel, Angel took Lucky back to their room and told him to stay there while she went to the shipping lines' office to book their passage to California. She was about to enter the building when she heard the sound of men's voices.

"The woman's name is Windsor, though she may be using another name. I have this small portrait of her. Have you seen her? Has she been in? She'd be booking passage for at least two, maybe three people."

Angel began to tremble. *They were here! They'd almost found her! Dear God! What would have happened if she'd walked in without pausing to listen?!*

"No, sir, I can't say as how I've seen her. As good-looking as she is, I sure would have remembered."

"Let me know if she comes in, will you? My name's Brad Watkins and I'm staying at the Delta Hotel."

"I sure will. What do you want her for, anyway? What did she do?"

"It's a family matter," Watkins told him in a confidential tone. "Her husband's the one who sent me."

"Oh."

"There'll be a goodly sum for you if you're the one who brings me the information."

"Well, I'll be sure to keep a watch, then."

Angel's breath caught in her throat as she listened to the man who was hunting her. She wished she could see him, but there was no way she could look into the office without being seen herself. Carefully, she retreated from the doorway and hurried back the way she'd come. There were some shops ahead, and she knew she could dart inside and watch for him. She would get a glimpse or better and know exactly what he looked like.

Angel entered the first store she came to. It was a fabric emporium, and she browsed near the window until she saw Michael's man, Watkins, emerge from the office. Of average height and build, he had sandy hair and a mustache and didn't appear dangerous. But Angel knew looks could be deceiving, and he was wearing a gun.

Angel realized she was going to have to act quickly. If Michael's men found her now, they'd discover right away that Lucky was not Christopher and know to look elsewhere; and her sister hadn't had the time she needed yet to make her escape.

Watching through the window, Angel waited until Watkins had sauntered toward the levee before drawing a deep breath. As the tension drained out of her, her knees almost buckled in relief. She remained in the store a moment longer, regrouping, trying to think straight. Just because she'd eluded him this time, didn't mean her luck would hold. He was ac-

116

tively searching for her; and, since he was checking all the shipping offices, there was no way they could continue with their plan to sail to California. She had to find another way to get there, and she had no time to lose.

"Can I help you with anything today, miss?" the proprietor inquired, approaching her.

"No, thank you. I'm just looking." Angel managed a weak smile and left.

Outside, she fell into step behind two middle-aged ladies as she made her way back to the hotel. She didn't pay attention to their conversation as they moved in front of her until one of them began to whisper in hushed, excited tones.

"Look, Thelma! That's him!" One woman elbowed the other, indicating without subtlety a man walking down the other side of the street.

"That's who, Rose?" the heavy-set Thelma asked.

"Blade Masters, you idiot!" Rose whispered as she grabbed her friend's arm and slowed her pace so they could get a better look at the black-haired, unshaven, dangerous-looking man opposite them.

"Blade Masters—the gunfighter?" she gasped, her eyes widening.

"The same! I know, because Warren pointed him out to me last night at dinner. Can you imagine? He was actually dining at the St. Louis Hotel."

Thelma's gaze turned even more avid. "He certainly looks the part. Is he really as fast with his gun as they say?"

"From what I hear, they've lost count of the number of men he's killed."

Thelma shivered at the thought. "He's a half-breed, isn't he?"

"Yes. His mother was an Indian, but other than that no one seems to know much else about him. The only story I heard was that he avenged some wrong to his family when he was just a boy, and supposedly he's been making his living as a hired gun ever since."

"How exciting!"

"Thelma! I'm shocked!" Rose gave her friend a surprised look.

"Oh, Rose, you know you're just as curious about him as I am. At least, I've got enough nerve to admit it. You just hide your interest behind gossip."

Rose was pensive for a moment as she considered her friend's critical words, then confessed, "You're right, but I'll never admit that to anyone else. He was one handsome man, though, in a devilish sort of way, wasn't he?"

Thelma giggled in a schoolgirlish sort of way as she answered, "Yes."

The rest of their conversation drifted off as they turned into a shop. They'd been completely unaware of Angel behind them.

Angel hadn't meant to listen, but their gossip had intrigued her. Curious, she'd glanced at the man and had been mesmerized by the sight of him, unable to look away. Rose had been right—he was devilishly handsome . . . tall, lean, and darkly tan. His hair was as black as a raven's wing, and he wore his gun as if it were a part of him. There was an aura of confidence and power in the way he carried himself and in the way he moved. He looked like a man in complete control, a man who had faced his worst fears and defeated them.

Angel thought about what the women had said about his prowess with a gun, and she wondered how brave Michael would be if he had to do battle with a man like Masters. The thought made her smile, but her smile faded quickly as the reality of her situation returned. She had no time to think about gunfighters. The only thing she had time for was figuring out a new way to California—and she had to come up with it fast.

After passing a sleepless night, Blade had left the jail with repeated instructions from the sheriff that he be out of New Orleans by the following day. The prospect suited him just fine, but first he had to have his meeting with Clancy Barrett. After that, he would be more than happy to oblige.

Blade was in less than a pleasant temperament as he headed back to his hotel. He was aware that some people were staring at him as he made his way down the streets, but he paid no attention to their interest. All he cared about was getting back to his room so he could get cleaned up and rest. No matter how clean a jail cell was, Blade always felt dirty after spending time in one. When he arrived at the hotel to find that Clancy had sent a note requesting he join him that evening for dinner at the St. Charles Hotel, his humor vastly improved. Blade went up to his room, eager for the day to pass.

* * *

When Angel and Lucky came down to the hotel dining room to eat that evening, she deliberately requested an out-of-the-way table. She knew Watkins could show up at any time, and she wanted to stay out of sight as much as possible. They were given a table near the back of the room, and that pleased her greatly. There was only one other guest nearby, a gray-haired, heavy-set man who looked about fifty, and he was definitely not Watkins. Angel felt relatively safe as they settled down to eat.

They were about half-way through their meal and involved in a deep discussion about the merits of Lucky's method of eating peas with his fingers when Angel stopped in mid-sentence. Out of the corner of her eye she caught sight of a man standing at the entrance to the dining room, looking around for someone. For a moment she feared it might be one of Michael's men, but when she glanced in that direction she was surprised to find that the man was Blade Masters.

The gunfighter was clean-shaven and attractively dressed now, and Angel found him even more appealing than she had earlier that day. The dark material of his coat fit his wide shoulders flawlessly, and the white of his shirt emphasized his tan. His trousers clung to his long, muscular legs like a second skin. His was a commanding figure, and the rugged arrogance of his features fascinated her. She allowed herself the pleasure of looking at him until his searching gaze fell upon her and he started to move in her direction.

Panic filled Angel. *Why would Blade Masters be coming toward her? She knew Watkins was after them, but had Michael somehow managed to hire Masters, too? Was he coming for them now?* She was like a moth before a flame. She couldn't tear her gaze away from him as he drew ever nearer, and yet she knew that she should probably grab Lucky and run from the room as fast as she could.

Lucky noticed her distraction and looked over his shoulder to see Blade coming their way. "Who's that?"

"What?" she responded distractedly, her eyes still on the gunfighter, her mind racing to find possible ways to escape. Every step brought him closer and took her nearer to fleeing the restaurant in blind fear.

"Who is he?" he repeated. "Why are you starin' at him?"

At his words, Angel finally dragged her gaze away. She kept her voice down as she remarked, "You're absolutely right, it's impolite to stare."

Masters was heading on a collision course with them, and Angel clasped her hands in her lap as she tried desperately to think of how to get away. Finally, when he was closing on the table, she decided to brazen it out. She raised her gaze in challenge and looked him straight in the eye.

Angel didn't know what she expected would happen, but she found herself breathless when her emerald gaze collided with and was held captive by

Blade's silver one. She could only stare at him, entranced, as he continued to approach.

"So, I've finally caught up with you!"

His deep voice sent terror surging through Angel. She felt hot and cold. The end was here. She'd failed. . . . Michael had won.

As quickly as the panic seized Angel, it was gone. Blade strode past their table, his gaze locked on the older, heavy-set gentleman sitting alone in the back of the dining room.

"Blade! It's great to see you!" The man rose to greet him. "I was glad to get your message."

Profound relief flooded through Angel. *They were safe. They were safe.*

"Who is he?" Lucky persisted. "Do you know him?"

"No. I don't know him," she answered, composed once again and wondering why she'd let her imagination run away with her. "Now, about your peas . . ."

"Yeah, peas. I hate 'em." The boy scowled.

She shot him an exasperated look. "They're good for you."

"They're green," he declared firmly as if no one had ever noticed before. "I make it a point not to eat anything green."

"Eat or no dessert," she blackmailed, indulging her own appetite as she turned her attention back to her meal.

Lucky was chafing under yet another restriction. "I don't really have to do anything you say."

"If you want to get paid you do," Angel countered

cooly, not the least bit put-off by his show of defiance.

He glared at her but then, thinking of the money involved, decided against further protest and downed the offending vegetables.

Blade clasped Clancy's hand and settled into the chair opposite him at the table. He was glad Clancy was already there, for he was eager to talk to his old friend and make his offer for his ranch. Blade had noticed the pretty blonde woman sitting with the young boy at a table nearby as he'd crossed the room to join Clancy. She looked a little young to have a son his age, but she had the most beautiful green eyes he'd ever seen; and, had he not been so intent on business, he might have been tempted to speak to her. As it was, he had a ranch to buy and that was more important. Women could wait.

"I was beginning to think I was going to miss you here in New Orleans."

"No, I'll be in town for the rest of the month."

They settled in and ordered, then spent time renewing their friendship. As Clancy polished off his second helping of the fancy dessert, Blade turned the conversation to his reason for being there. He made his offer to buy the Rocking B, then fell silent, waiting anxiously for his reply.

"Blade, I'm sorry," Clancy replied with an earnestness he truly felt. "I appreciate your offer. I know you're a man of your word and that you'd eventually pay off the balance you'd owe me, but my circumstances are such that I must have the full amount up front."

"I see." Though Blade had saved a substantial amount for a down payment, he was still $5,000 short of Clancy's asking price. His dream of settling in Texas was shattered.

The ranch owner was completely sympathetic to his situation, but business was business. "You know there's no one else I'd rather sell to, but I can't accept your offer as it is. If you find a way to come up with the money, get back in touch with me. I won't be travelling on to Savannah to join my family until the first."

Blade's face was an emotionless mask. He knew it would be next to impossible for him to come up with the necessary amount of money any time soon. "I'll do that. If you change your mind, I'll be at the St. Louis Hotel until tomorrow morning."

Blade stood to go and Clancy did, too, extending his hand in friendship. "You're my friend. I'm sorry we can't come to terms."

"So am I. I'll see what I can do about coming up with the extra money."

Clancy nodded in response.

"I'll be in touch." Blade strode from the dining room, his mood black.

The men's deep voices carried to Angel and Lucky's table as they negotiated. When Masters' offer to buy the ranch was turned down and he left the dining room, Angel could see that he was disappointed. Having heard most of what was said, Angel calculated that the ranch owner was in dire need of cash up front; and, as she watched Masters leave, it dawned on her that her problem had been solved. Masters was a hired gun. She needed someone to help her escape from Michael's men. Masters needed money. She had money. It was an arrangement made in heaven, and she offered up a prayer of thanks.

Angel knew she would have to act quickly. She couldn't risk letting Masters get away. She'd heard him say he was staying at the St. Louis Hotel, so she would seek him out and make him an offer he couldn't refuse. She would hire him to escort them to California for the sum of $5000, the exact amount he needed to complete the deal on the ranch.

"Are you finished eating, Lucky? It's about time to go back upstairs," Angel asked, eager to get him safely tucked in bed for the night so she could carry out her bold plan.

"Yeah." Lucky had one big bite of cake left, so he stuffed it all in his mouth at once and then pushed away from the table.

Angel sighed and cast a glance heavenward. "The cake must be very good," she observed drolly.

"Um, yeah, it is," he mumbled, crumbs escaping as he grinned at her. In the way of boys, he wiped his mouth with the back of his arm.

"That's what napkins are for," she instructed in low tones as they started from the table.

"Oh," was all Lucky replied.

When they reached their room, Angel informed him that she had to go out again for a while. She stayed only long enough to put the boy to bed, then donned a dark cloak. A quick glance in the mirror told her she looked suitably demure in the nondescript garment, so she left the room with the promise to return soon.

Lucky waited until he'd heard Angel move off down the hall before he got up out of bed again. He knew ladies didn't go out unescorted in the evening, and he wondered what was so important that she would have to go out alone. He remembered her nervousness when they'd first reached port the day before, and today she'd been upset when she'd returned from checking on their passage to California. She hadn't told him much, only that their departure had been delayed for a few days. He'd assumed at the time that she was upset because it would take them longer to get to her fiancé. Now, he doubted that that was the cause. Something was wrong, but he didn't know what.

Lucky began to dress. He couldn't admit to himself that he was worried about Angel. He told himself he was following her because he wanted to see what she was doing and because if anything happened to her he wouldn't get paid.

Lucky hurried from the room and reached the landing overlooking the lobby just as Angel went outside. He continued his pursuit as casually as he could, glad that no one noticed him. Lucky reached the door as she entered a hired carriage, but he heard her direct the driver to take her to the St. Louis Hotel. The vehicle sped off, and he followed on foot. Angel had pointed the hotel out to him when they'd first arrived in town, and he was sure he could find it again. A city was a city, and he was no stranger to the streets.

Angel was nervous as she rode in the hired conveyance on the short trip to Masters' hotel. She knew her scheme would outrage polite society, but it was far too late to worry about propriety. Her situation was serious, and it called for action.

If the gossip she'd heard proved right, Blade Masters was a mercenary man. He hired himself out for a fee, and she was willing to pay that fee. Angel thought of the handsome gunman and realized she was going to have to be very careful. Attractive though he might be, he was still a hired gun who sold himself to the highest bidder. She could never trust him, for his allegiance was only to money. Knowing that ahead-of-time helped, and she was determined that, should he take the job, their relationship would be strictly business.

The carriage drew to a stop before Masters' hotel, and Angel descended with the driver's help. She paid him, then went inside. Thoughts of Christopher gave her the strength she needed as she bravely walked up to the front desk.

"Excuse me, but could you tell me Mr. Masters' room number please?" Angel asked the clerk.

Surprised, Cyril glanced up quickly to find himself staring at a lovely, young woman of obvious breeding and culture. She was the prettiest female he'd seen in quite a while, with her pale hair and green eyes; and he couldn't help but wonder what a woman of her quality wanted with Masters. "Um . . . well, yes.

Mr. Masters' room is on the top floor, but I'm afraid he isn't in."

"Oh." Angel was disappointed, and it showed in her expression. "I see." She considered leaving a message, but decided against it.

Seeing her distress, Cyril quickly offered, "Mr. Masters isn't in his room, but he is in the bar. Would you like me to get him for you?"

Angel graced the little man with her brightest smile. "Yes, thank you."

"Who shall I tell him is calling?" he inquired with authority. He found something vaguely familiar about her, but he couldn't say what it was.

"Tell him Miss Angela Roberts is here, and that I have an important business offer for him."

"If you'll have a seat, I'll be right back." There were no other guests at the desk needing his help right then, so Cyril went to get Masters for her himself.

Angel glanced around the spacious lobby and spied a loveseat nestled in a quiet area to one side of the staircase. As tense as she was about propositioning Masters, she was also concerned about running into Watkins again. The loveseat's location afforded her a good view of the lobby so she'd be able to see trouble coming if the situation arose. She wasn't about to take any unnecessary chances.

Blade's mood had been black as he'd returned to his hotel. He'd been about to enter the lobby when he'd heard a man call out to him. Recognizing immediately the voice of the sheriff, he'd sworn silently to himself as he'd stopped and turned to face the man who'd provided him with such wonderful accomodations the night before.

"Good evening, Sheriff Tannen."

"Evening, Masters. I see you're still in town."

Blade's anger and frustration had suddenly changed into a great and heavy weariness. "I've just been finishing up my business."

"So you'll be gone in the morning." It hadn't been a question, but a statement.

"I said I would, and I'm a man of my word."

"I know that, and I'm sorry things have to be this way." Tannen's respect for Masters had grown since he'd had dealings with him. Masters had a cool head and common sense, and Tannen wished him a long life—as long as he lived it far away from New Orleans.

"You don't have to explain. I understand." Blade had gone on into the hotel.

Tannen had watched him go, thinking it was a shame that the man would probably never find any peace.

Once inside the hotel, Blade had headed straight for the bar and ordered a double bourbon. When the bartender had set it before him, he'd taken a deep drink and savored its searing warmth. He'd been draining the last remnants from the glass when it finally began to take effect. His frustration over losing the ranch hadn't lessened any, but his mood mellowed and the tightness in his shoulders eased. He was on his third bourbon when the hotel's desk clerk approached him.

"Mr. Masters? There's someone at the desk asking to see you."

For a moment, Blade brightened. He thought Clancy had changed his mind and had come to accept his offer. "Is it a Mr. Barrett?"

Cyril looked puzzled. "No, sir. This is a lady, a Miss Angela Roberts."

"I don't know any Angela Roberts." He scowled.

"She's blonde and quite pretty, if I may say so, sir. She mentioned that she had a business matter to discuss with you." Cyril related all he knew with great eagerness. Busybody that he was, his beady little eyes were bright with interest.

"And she's alone?" he asked in growing disgust. This wasn't the first time a woman had heard about his reputation and brazenly sought him out, and he knew it wouldn't be the last.

"Yes, sir. Shall I tell her you'll be right out?"

"No, Cyril. Tell her I'm not interested in any kind of offer she has to make. Just tell her to go away."

The clerk was clearly shocked. "Go away, sir?" He would have gladly met with that young woman any place, any time.

"That's what I said."

The firmness of his tone sent the clerk scurrying back to the lobby. Angel saw him emerge from the bar alone; it suddenly dawned on her that the gunfighter might refuse to meet with her. Angel hadn't considered that possibility before, and she began to worry.

"Umm, Miss Roberts," Cyril began nervously, "Mr. Masters sent a message for you."

"Yes?"

"He said that he wasn't interested in your 'offer' and that you should go away."

"He said what?" Angel stared at the clerk in annoyance.

"I'm sorry. He made it perfectly clear that he doesn't want to talk to you. Perhaps you'd better go?" he suggested.

"I'll go all right," she seethed under her breath, realizing in anger what Masters thought she was 'offering.' She stood up and, assuming her most dignified manner, strode straight for the entrance to the bar.

"But Miss Roberts, ladies aren't allowed in there," Cyril protested, chasing after her. His voice trailed off as she turned and pinned him with a frosty glare.

Angel continued her march into the men's sanctuary unopposed; but Cyril, unable to control his curiosity, raced to the doorway to watch.

Chapter Seven

Angel took several bold steps into the bar and then paused to let her gaze sweep the room in search of Blade Masters. She was conscious of men staring at her, shocked, but she didn't care. She was looking for Masters, and she wasn't leaving until she'd talked to him. It took her only a second to recognize him. Tall, lean, and magnetically attractive, he was unmistakable even though he stood at the bar with his back to her. No other man in the room exuded the same sense of power—only Masters. Knowing there could be no turning back now, Angel took a deep breath and walked straight toward him.

As soon as Blade had sent the desk clerk away, he'd put all thoughts of the woman from his mind. He'd expected his cold dismissing message to discourage even the most ardent of 'admirers.' Ordering another bourbon, Blade was about to take a drink when he noticed that the room had gone very quiet.

Sam, the bartender, stared past him, a look of shock on his florid features.

"Ma'am, you're going to have to go back out into the lobby," Sam announced sternly. "Ladies are not permitted in here."

Startled at such brazenness—a men's only room, the hotel bar was off-limits to women—Blade turned to see who the insolent female could be. He froze. The woman behind him was the same woman he'd seen at dinner. The one fleeting glimpse he'd had of her in the dining room had told him she was pretty; but now, up close, there was no mistaking the loveliness of her features. Though her hair was pulled back in a severe bun at the nape of her neck, its color was a glorious blonde that looked as if it were spun of gold and sunlight. How would it look, Blade wondered, if he pulled the pins from it and let it fall loosely around her shoulders in a pale shimmering cape? Or, better yet, how would it look spread out on a pillow in bed? He thought her mouth infinitely kissable. She was a feast for any man's eyes. Suddenly, the idea of being with a woman didn't seem like such a bad one after all.

"I have no intention of leaving," Angel replied as she slanted Blade a challenging look. "I'm here to speak with Mr. Masters, and I intend to stay until I do."

"You're here to see Masters?" Sam repeated in amazement. He glanced at Blade questioningly.

"That's right," she affirmed, looking Blade squarely in the eye now. "Well, Mr. Masters?"

A slow, knowing smile carved its way across

Blade's darkly handsome face. She was making no secret of the fact that she wanted him, and she was gorgeous. Perhaps a little brazenness in a woman wasn't such a bad thing either. Her aggressiveness might prove interesting in bed. His smile broadened at the thought, and a flame of desire flickered in his silver gaze as he looked her over once more.

Finally, he spoke. "It's all right, Sam. I'll handle it."

"All right, sir." For Blade Masters the rules could be broken.

"Can I buy you a drink?" Blade offered, still smiling as he thought ahead to the night to come. Maybe this trip to New Orleans wouldn't prove a totally useless endeavor.

"No, thank you," Angel refused primly. The look on Masters' face told her what he was thinking, and she stiffened, anxious to dissuade him of any such notion. She had no amorous interest in him. Her purpose was business.

Her refusal surprised Blade. The women who sought him out ordinarily wanted a good time. "Well, then, what exactly can I do for you, Miss—?"

"Roberts," Angel answered succinctly, fighting the urge to turn on her heel and run. She told herself she'd handled worse than Blade Masters. She'd dealt with Michael. "Miss Angela Roberts." A quick glance told her that all eyes were still eagerly upon them, all ears trying to hear their conversation. With a professional efficiency, Angel continued, "I have a business offer I'd like to present to you, but I think it would be best if we spoke somewhere a little more private."

"I agree with you completely," Blade responded smoothly. He motioned toward a table in the back of the room. "That one looks quite secluded. We should be able to talk there without any interruptions." He lowered his voice to give emphasis to the last word.

His confident, knowing attitude annoyed Angel, and she anticipated great pleasure in disappointing him. He was obviously accustomed to women fawning over him, not that she had to wonder why. He was the best-looking man she'd ever seen; and, as they made their way toward the table, she was extremely conscious of him walking close behind her. It was an unnerving sensation for her to be so physically aware of him. She'd never had this kind of reaction to anyone before. It took an effort to hold herself to a demure pace and not skitter out of his way as she wanted to. This was business, she told herself. He was a man who hired himself out for money, and she had money.

When they reached the table, Blade offered, "Let me help you with your cloak."

Angel would have preferred to keep it on, but to refuse would have shown him her uncertainty, for it was very warm in the bar. She loosened the tie, and Blade slipped the protective garment from her shoulders, his fingers grazing her shoulders as he did so. It was an innocent enough gesture, but at that simple touch, Angel's pulse quickened. When he reached around and drew out a chair for her, she was glad to slip into the seat and distance herself from his overpowering nearness. She graced him with a calm smile that belied the nervousness that gripped her.

Blade was still standing over her, her cloak slung across his arm, when she smiled up at him, and her smile stopped him cold. He'd been with many pretty women in his time, but never before had a simple smile seared through him like a branding iron. He stared down at her, momentarily entranced. She was beautiful, but there was something else about her that captivated him, something in her eyes—an innocence, almost—and it puzzled him. Certainly she was no innocent. She'd come here looking for him; she'd sought him out. Angela Roberts was a woman who knew what she wanted, and Blade planned to see that she got it.

He gave himself a mental shake, breaking the spell that had briefly bound him. He sat down, assessing her. Her figure was as perfect as her face—her breasts, full; her waist, small. He was going to enjoy the night ahead. Reaching out to take her hand, Blade asked, "Now, tell me, Miss Roberts, what exactly did you want from me?"

Angel had intended to set a formal tone, but the moment his hand closed over hers, her heart gave a wild jolt. Startled, her eyes widened in surprise.

"Mr. Masters—" she started to protest.

"Are you sure you wouldn't like something to drink?" he urged. He could sense a tenseness in her and thought a drink would help.

Angel pulled herself together. He was attractive, true, but her interest in him was purely professional.

She had to stop this right now. She had to get control of the situation.

"No, Mr. Masters, I don't want anything to drink," Angel began again, this time more forcefully, "and the first thing you can do for me is to . . ." She had meant to tell him to let her go, but he had begun to caress her palm and the sensitive inside of her wrist with an accomplished touch, and she was temporarily speechless.

"Yes?"

The leer she had detected in his smile had moved to his voice. The suggestiveness immediately brought Angel to her senses. She firmly pulled her hand free.

He looked at her, smiled knowingly, and leaned back in his chair. "Most women like that." He seemed amused.

Angel forced steel into her tone. "I am not most women, and I'm definitely not interested in your amorous intentions."

"You are different," Blade agreed, studying her with a hungry gaze. "You're not wearing a wedding ring, so you're not sneaking out on your husband tonight," he observed thoughtfully, then frowned. "What about your son?"

"My son?"

"You were dining with a boy."

"He's my brother," she supplied with dignity. "Now, about my offer—"

"Tell me, Miss Roberts—" He didn't let her finish. "Does your father know you're out chasing men?"

"I am not chasing you." Angel was thoroughly disgusted. Was there no convincing him that she hadn't come there to bed him? She realized with disappointment that she'd given him too much credit. She'd thought he had a modicum of intelligence. She'd thought he would be interested in making money.

"Perhaps seeking you out wasn't such a good idea, Mr. Masters," she told him, her voice tight. "I was under the impression that you would be interested in a paying job, but I was wrong and you aren't really interested in buying that ranch. I'm sorry to have taken up your time." Angel started to rise. "If you'll excuse me—?"

Caught off-guard, Blade suddenly realized he might have misjudged Miss Angela Roberts. Maybe the innocence he'd seen in her was real. He frowned, perplexed. She intrigued him. "Just how much would this 'job' pay?"

"$5000," Angel answered. For the first time since she'd approached him, he stopped leering and started listening. She sat back down and hurried to explain, "I'm in need of someone with your expertise. I've heard of your reputation, and I believe you're worth that amount."

"To do what?" Blade's gaze hardened. He'd heard that line many times before, but never from a woman. Usually it was some fool with vengeance on his mind who didn't want to do the dirty work himself. Blade prided himself on never having taken one of those jobs. Though she was offering the exact amount he needed for the ranch, he was prepared to turn her down.

"I'd like to hire you to escort my brother and me to California."

Blade stared at her. "You want to pay me $5000 to take you and your brother to California?" he repeated. "Lady, all you have to do is go down to the levee and book passage on a boat. You don't need me."

"I don't want to travel by boat. I want to make the trip overland. It's essential that I get to California as quickly as possible."

He knew desperation when he heard it and grew curious as to her reasons. There was more going on here than a trip to California. "Why?"

"My reasons are none of your business, Mr. Masters."

"That's where you're wrong. Your reasons will be my business if I agree to take you. Is someone chasing you, Miss Roberts?"

"No."

"You refuse to take the easy, safe way by boat. You boldly walk right into a saloon and seek out a man you know only by reputation. You ask this stranger to take you on a cross-country trip, and you say there's no reason other than you just want to travel by land. Somehow, I don't believe you."

"Frankly, Mr. Masters, I don't care whether you believe me or not. All you have to do is take my brother and me to San Francisco. How difficult can that be?"

"You tell me," he came back at her. "Who's after you and what do they want?"

"Look, do you want to buy your ranch or do you

139

want the answers to your questions? I'll tell you this much. The man I love is waiting for me in San Francisco, and I'm going there to meet him so we can be married. Now, the choice is yours. Are you interested in the job or not?"

He could only stare at her. "Your fiancé is in San Francisco, and you want me to take you to him? Why didn't he come for you himself? What about your reputation?"

"He's busy right now and couldn't leave. As far as my reputation goes, Christopher trusts me; and for the considerable fee I'd be paying you, I'd expect you to maintain a strict employee/employer relationship with me. If you take the job, your only concern will be getting us there. Nothing else."

"Your intended, this Christopher, must be a most understanding man." There was no mistaking the sarcasm in his tone.

"He is."

"Look, Miss Roberts, there are no fancy hotels on the way west. It's hot and dry and dirty. There'll be days on end without any sign of other people and long nights sleeping out on the open range."

"It sounds wonderful," she cut him off. "Do you want the job?"

Blade studied her intently as if measuring her worth, then nodded. "All right, you've got yourself a guide. When do you want to leave?"

"Tomorrow. As early as we possibly can."

"Do you have any idea what you're getting yourself into? It would be much easier for you if you sailed," he cautioned.

"I'm not some spoiled little girl who can't stand a few hardships, Mr. Masters. I've ridden for years." Angel wasn't really lying about her equestrian abilities. She'd ridden her first horse when she was five. Of course she'd absolutely hated it and had only been on horseback a handful of times since, but Masters didn't need to know that. She knew the basics of staying on a horse's back and that was all that mattered. She wondered about Lucky, but shrugged away the thought. If he didn't know how to ride now, he was going to learn fast. "Now, what do we need for the trip?"

Preliminaries over, they discussed details and made arrangements. When they'd finished, she opened her purse and handed Blade a packet of bills.

"This should be enough for you to buy the supplies that we need. If you'll accompany me back to the St. Charles, I'll pay you the first half of your fee in advance. I'll give you the other $2500 when we arrive in San Francisco. Does that sound reasonable to you?"

"More than reasonable," Blade agreed, wary, but not about to turn down the money he needed to buy the ranch. For $5000, he'd lead her wherever she wanted to go and, if need be, he'd protect her from the devil himself. "Let's go."

The patrons of the bar watched with avid lust as Blade helped Angel don her cloak again. When he had escorted her from the room, the men exchanged looks with Sam.

"I wish a woman who looked like that would come after me," one man remarked. "I wouldn't even want to talk about it. I'd just go wherever she wanted to take me." His cronies laughed in agreement, envying the gunfighter's luck.

Lucky had made it to the St. Louis Hotel without incident, but hesitated to enter. Assuming his old ways, he lingered by the main entrance trying to catch a glimpse of what was going on within the hotel. With no sign of Angel inside, he decided to make himself as inconspicuous as possible and wait for her to come out.

Lucky was standing in the shadows near the doorway when the sound of young voices caught his attention. Two dirty, poorly-dressed boys of about his age watched him from an alley a short distance away. Less than a week before, he'd been living as they were—in quiet desperation never knowing where a morsel or a meal was coming from. Lucky figured they'd probably been there all night, keeping an eye on the hotel guests and looking for an easy mark—as he used to do in St. Louis. They would have seen Angel if she'd come back out. He didn't think she could have left already, but he wanted to make sure.

"You been here long?" Lucky asked as he walked toward them.

"Yeah, so?" Eli, the taller and older of the two, answered defensively. He eyed Lucky and decided he was rich and might have some money on him. Giving his brother their standard signal, Eli was ready for action.

"Did you see a pretty blonde-haired woman wearing a cloak go into the hotel?"

"Why should we tell you?" Eli challenged, stepping closer as his brother, Joss, moved behind Lucky.

Lucky knew they were setting him up, for he'd done it many times himself in the past. When the bigger boy reached out to shove him backward so he'd fall, he was prepared. Lucky dodged to his right so Eli's blow glanced off his shoulder, and then he countered with a sharp punch to the boy's stomach. He smiled when he heard the boy go "oof" as he knocked the wind out of him.

"Eli!!" Joss couldn't believe that this rich kid had bested his brother. He charged at Lucky, but Lucky, expecting his attack, fended the smaller boy off with no trouble.

"Look, I didn't come over here to fight with you. I asked you a question. There's no reason—"

But Eli had launched himself at him, and they tumbled together to the ground. Rolling and tussling in the damp alley, each boy fought to get the upper hand. Lucky was frustrated and angry. He hadn't wanted to fight, but that didn't matter any more. He had to. A little heavier than Eli, he would have won handily had he not been wearing his new clothes. They restricted his movements and slowed him down. His years on the streets paid off, however; and, even after Joss joined in, he managed to more than hold his own against both of them.

"You done fightin'?" Lucky demanded as they paused in their struggle. Eli finally nodded, and Lucky went on, "I didn't come over here to pick a damned fight with you. I just wanted to ask you a couple of questions, that's all."

Eli was shocked by this boy's fighting abilities. "You sure ain't no snotty rich kid," he breathed.

"Hell no." Lucky spat in disgust as he pushed away from them and stood up. His clothes were messy, but at least there was no mud or blood on them. Wrinkles he could explain, the other would have been impossible. He looked from Eli to Joss. "My name's Lucky."

"I'm Eli, and this is Joss. Where're you from?" They looked at him with new respect.

"St. Louis."

"What are you doin' down here?"

"I came down with my sister, and right now I'm trying to find her. Did you see a pretty, blonde-haired lady go into the hotel?" Thinking of Angel again, his worries returned. He couldn't imagine what had caused her to come here alone.

"She come in a carriage?"

"Yes."

"She went in about twenty minutes ago, and she ain't come out yet," Joss offered.

"If she's your sister, why ain't you with her?" Eli asked, curious.

"She was going out and she told me to go to bed, but I didn't feel like sleeping. I thought I'd follow her and see what was going on," he explained simply, at ease with these two. "Say, you got anything to smoke?"

The one thing Lucky had really missed since coming to live with Angel was smoking. Up until now, she'd been right beside him almost every waking minute. Tonight, however, was different. He was on his own again; and, if these boys had a cigarette, he'd pay almost anything they'd ask for it. After all, Angel might be inside quite a while, so he might as well relax and enjoy himself.

"Ya got any money?" seven-year-old Joss asked.

"Enough." Angel had given him a small amount to carry in case of an emergency. A cigarette, by Lucky's calculations, was definitely an emergency.

"Let's see." Eli stepped closer to get a look at Lucky's money.

Lucky pulled some change out of his pocket and held it out to the older youth.

Eli snatched it up. "Go 'head and give him one, Joss."

Joss dug in his pants' pocket and pulled out a bit of tobacco, a crumpled piece of paper, and a match. He handed them over to Lucky, who quickly and expertly rolled himself a cigarette and lit it. He inhaled deeply. Smoking had been one of his few pleasures when he'd lived on the streets.

"Ya want some more?" Joss asked, hopefully, for they needed all the money they could get.

"Sure. I got enough for two more."

They made the deal, and Lucky stuffed the extra papers and tobacco deep in his pocket where he hoped Angel would never find it.

Waiting in silence with them, enjoying his smoke, Lucky couldn't help but think how fortunate these two were to have each other. He'd been all by himself after he'd left the orphanage. Oh, he'd had friends on the street, but no one he could really count on if things got bad. He was finishing off the cigarette when Joss spoke up.

"Ain't that your sister?"

Lucky turned as Angel emerged from the hotel. At first, thinking she was coming out alone, he was tempted to go to her. But then Lucky saw him—the same man she'd been watching so intensely during dinner. Staying in the shadows, he strained to hear what they were saying. What was she doing with that man? She was engaged to Christopher, and he was in California! Why was she with that stranger? Lucky managed to pick up on a little of their conversation as they waited for a carriage.

"I should be able to get everything we need and be ready before noon tomorrow."

"Good. My brother and I are anxious to be on our way. The sooner we go, the better."

Angel had told him their ship had been delayed. She hadn't said anything about changing their plans—or including anyone else in them. He didn't know why he was upset, but he was.

"The St. Charles Hotel, please," Blade directed when a carriage finally stopped for them.

"I gotta go." Lucky tossed the cigarette stub aside. "Thanks for the smokes."

"Wait a minute! Where are you goin'?" Eli asked.

"I gotta get back to the St. Charles before she does, or there'll be hell to pay!" Lucky panted from half-way down the block.

"We know a faster way."

At top speed, they led him down the dark alleys,

racing through a maze of twists and turns until they came out on a street near his hotel. Lucky was impressed. Their route had cut minutes off the way he'd originally come, and he knew he had a good chance of getting back into their room ahead of Angel.

Lucky paused outside the hotel to look back, but Eli and Joss had already disappeared into the night and the life that had been his. Eating and sleeping in gutters. Never a kind word from anyone. His thoughts were forced back to his present predicament, however, when Angel's carriage turned the corner and headed his way.

Lucky darted inside, crossing the lobby without incident. He charged up the stairs and into their room, throwing off his clothes like a wild man and diving beneath the covers. Nervous, he lay stiff as a board, trying to relax, to pretend to be asleep.

Angel and Blade entered the hotel together, but she had him wait for her in the lobby while she went up to the room to get his money. She was glad that she'd sold some of her jewelry while they were in St. Louis so she had enough cash to pay him. All they had to do, she realized, was to make it through the following morning without being caught by Michael's men. Once they were on their way out of town with Masters, she felt sure that the men hunting her would never be able to locate them.

Angel let herself into their hotel room quietly. She lit a lamp, but kept it low so it wouldn't disturb Lucky. As she got the money ready, a great sense of relief filled her. Their plans were made! They were going to get away!

Smiling in the half-light, Angel moved across the room to check on Lucky, lying asleep on the trundle bed. She was glad he could sleep soundly, for he was going to need all the rest he could get. The next few weeks would be hard on both of them.

He looked sweet and vulnerable as he slept, and Angel felt a surge of love for him. The urge to kiss him filled her. Without a sound, she knelt beside him, gently brushing a lock of hair away from his forehead, and pressed a soft kiss on his brow. She was relieved he didn't waken. He was so young, and she hoped with all her heart that she would be able to care for him and win his trust.

Pushing herself up, Angel noticed a faint smell of cigarette smoke in the air. From the bar, of course. Men and their habits! Quickly, she left the room. She didn't want to keep Masters waiting. He was their salvation, although he didn't know it.

Lucky had kept his eyes shut tight when he'd heard Angel enter the room and come toward him. When she'd knelt down beside him, he'd expected her to call his bluff and tell him she knew he was faking. Instead, she'd kissed him! No one had ever kissed him like that—except, perhaps, his mother. But he'd been a baby then. A little kid.

Behind his closed eyelids, tears prickled and burned. A tightness gripped his throat; and when she moved away, he almost cried out for her to stay. He wanted to throw his arms around her neck and hang on. He wanted to tell her that he loved her and that she should be careful—that she should take care of herself so nothing happened to her. He wanted to tell her that he never wanted to be away from her. But he couldn't. He was afraid that if he told her he loved her, something would happen to her just like it had to his parents. So he remained quiet, pretending to be asleep to fool her and pretending he wasn't crying to fool himself.

It was several hours later when Blade returned to his own hotel. He'd gone straight to Clancy with the $2500 and made him another offer on the ranch. A cash-down offer that Clancy had quickly accepted. Once Blade reached California and wired Clancy the balance due, the Rocking B would be his.

As he settled in for the night, Blade reviewed the events of the day. There wasn't much that made sense about Angela Roberts or her plan, but he wouldn't argue with her. She had the money, and she was the boss. He would take her to California by the safest, fastest route possible, deliver her to her waiting, understanding fiancé, and then retire to Texas and his own quiet ranch.

But as Blade drifted off to sleep, his thoughts drifted from images of the range to the beautiful, mysterious Angela Roberts. What secrets lay hidden behind those enchanting emerald eyes? Before the trip was over, he promised himself, he would find out.

Chapter Eight

St. Louis

Lean, dark-haired Steve Spencer sat at the poker table, his classically-handsome features carefully schooled to reveal nothing about the cards he held in his hand. At thirty-two, he was the consummate gambler. Dressed in a black suit, showy brocade waistcoat, white shirt and tie, with diamond studs winking at his cuffs and an expensive gold watch adorning his vest pocket, he looked every bit the part. He was smooth and confident, steady of hand and nerve. Steve prided himself on being a man in control at all times, and he was definitely so right now.

"And I'll raise you a thousand," Steve announced in a soft low voice that had an edge of steel to it. He let his gaze sweep the table, watching the other men and gauging their reactions to his wager.

A hush fell over the spectators gathered in the backroom of the saloon where the marathon card game had been going on for hours. *A thousand! Spencer had bet a thousand!* A murmur of excitement ran through the crowd as they waited anxiously. They pressed in closer. The tension mounted, and their gazes fixed on the elegant, smooth Steve Spencer.

Gray-haired, fiftyish Hal Jenkins had been gambling for enough years to know when he was beaten. As he stared at Spencer and saw his cool reserve, he knew a pair of sixes wouldn't do it. In disgust, he threw down his hand. "I'm out," he stated flatly.

Skinny, balding, businessman Stewart Warren had been in the game since the beginning, winning some, losing more. But as he studied his hand now, he grew nervous. He glanced at Spencer and back at his cards several times before making his decision. He had two pair, fours and eights, but a thousand dollars was a lot of money. Conservative that he was, Stewart decided to cut his losses. He would fold. "Me, too." He followed Hal's sensible lead.

All eyes turned to the last player, Johnny Dillon. At twenty, the long-limbed, lanky young man was far younger than the others and looked to be barely shaving. Obviously nervous, his hands less than steady, he swallowed as he eyed the stone-faced Spencer. "A thousand?" he repeated in a hoarse voice.

"That's the bet," Steve confirmed. He was a gambler by choice and by trade. His luck coupled with skill, had always been good, and he generally came out on the winning end. Tonight, however, his luck had been not merely good, it had been great. He was five hundred ahead for the night, and if he took this hand, it would be one of his biggest wins ever. "Are you in or out?"

Uncertain, Dillon studied his cards. He held three tens, and he had the thousand dollars. The trouble was the money wasn't his. It belonged to his brothers. He'd come to St. Louis to sell some livestock, and he had the cash receipts in his pocket. He had been using his own funds to play, but that money was now gone. If he folded his hand, he would lose everything. If he stayed in and won, he'd be a hero and they'd all be rich. Dillon eyed the pile in the center of the table, and then with the foolish bravado of the young and inexperienced, he made his decision. "I'm staying." He pulled his bet from his pocket and added it to the pot. "And I call."

A gasp escaped those hovering near the table. They knew Spencer was not given to bluffing. Eagerly, they waited to see what the men held.

"Full house," Steve said as he spread his cards on the table, and Dillon stared in disbelief at the pair of kings and three jacks.

"But . . ." The young man lifted wide, horrified eyes to his opponent.

Steve saw the stricken look on his face, knew he'd won, and started to gather in the pot.

"Wait," Dillon blurted out.

For a minute, Steve actually thought he might have read him wrong and that he might have a better hand. He paused. "Let's see your cards."

He laid them down, and the crowd erupted. Spen-cer had won! His full house had beaten Dillon's three of a kind!

Steve knew desperation when he saw it and had sympathy for the boy. He'd lost some big pots himself in his time and knew exactly how it felt. The humiliation was terrible, not to mention that you'd just lost all your money. Steve remembered how angry he'd been and how stupid he'd felt after one particularly devastating loss, and it had been then that he'd made up his first and most important rule of gambling—if you can't afford to lose it, don't bet it. He'd learned his lesson the hard way, and he hoped Dillon learned his today.

"Sorry, Dillon. Full house wins," Steve told him.

Dillon continued to stare at the money Steve was pocketing. Horror filled him as he realized what he'd done. The color drained from his face. He'd lost everything—not only his money, but his brothers' money, too!

Total embarrassment, along with fear, seared Dillon's soul. His brothers were clean-living men. They'd never understand how he could have gambled away the money they'd worked so long and hard for, and he doubted they'd ever forgive him. He'd convinced them that he was mature enough to come to the city alone, and they'd trusted him. Dillon couldn't bear the shame of his own stupidity. He was visibly trembling as he pushed away from the table and strode from the room without a word.

Steve was immediately enveloped by the horde, bombarded by congratulations on his expert play. It had been an honest game and he'd won fairly, and Steve headed for the bar to have a celebration drink.

It had been a long night. Now it was time to relax and enjoy his winnings.

Steve remained in the bar, drinking and visiting, and it was near three in the morning before he finally made his way back to his hotel room. It seemed he had only just fallen asleep when someone knocked loudly on his door.

"Spencer! Damnit! Wake up!" an urgent voice shouted through the locked portal.

After a groggy minute or two, Steve realized it was growing light outside and dragged himself out of bed, tugged on his pants, and threw the door wide.

"George? What are you doing here?" Steve stared at the bartender from the saloon in confusion as he tried to shake off the remnants of sleep.

"Let me in, will you?" the old man asked, looking over his shoulder at the empty corridor.

Steve stepped aside. The bartender entered, and Steve closed the door. "What is it?"

"Something bad's happened, Steve. You gotta get out of town."

He was immediately wide awake. "What?"

"The Dillon kid? The one you won big from tonight?"

"Yeah?"

"He killed himself. Shot himself dead in his hotel room. I heard it from one of the girls."

Steve was stunned. "For God's sake, why?"

"The money he lost to you belonged to his brothers. The sheriff sent for them, and they're already on their way to town. They're a stiff-necked pair; and,

154

they could come after you." George's expression was serious as he faced his friend.

"It won't be the first time." Steve tried to dismiss the warning.

"Listen to me. I wouldn't have come here if I didn't smell trouble. If you value your hide, get out of St. Louis. Now."

Steve swore. He didn't like running, but he recognized the extent of danger from the very real concern on George's face. "All right. I'll leave today."

"I'll send you a wire. Let you know what happens. Where you plan on going?"

"I'll head up to Kansas City. Now that the train's through to Jefferson City, it's not a bad trip. Besides, if Dillon's brothers do try coming after me, they'll probably check steamers first. If it takes them more than a day, it'll give me enough time to lose myself in Kansas City."

"Where'll you stay?"

"Send the wire to the Bartlett Hotel. I'll be able to pick it up at the desk."

George nodded, then shook Spencer's hand. "You take care of yourself, Steve, and keep a watch out."

"I will. And, George?" He waited until his friend was looking at him. "Thanks for the warning."

Annoyed by the need, Steve dressed in nondescript clothing that would not call attention to him and headed for the railroad station. He arrived in time to make the train; and, after buying his ticket, he boarded and settled in on one of the hard benches.

The car filled up quickly. Heeding George's warning, Steve positioned himself so he could see who came on board. Though he appeared at ease, he was tense, prepared for the worst. Several farmers and a few families migrating west entered the car. A woman in mourning attended by her young son settled in on the seat across the aisle from him. Steve was relieved when the train finally left the depot. Only then was he able to relax.

As the train left the city behind, Steve stared out the window. In the early morning light everything looked green and fresh. The pastoral panorama was a far cry from the tension-filled, smoke-shrouded saloon last night. He thought with sorrow of the Dillon boy. He had been young, and his death senseless.

Steve firmly believed that there was no problem so great that it was worth taking your life. Life could be miserable—and he'd had his own fair share of misery—but there was always hope that it would get better. It took courage to face the truth; but if you did, you generally made out all right. Of course the outcome wasn't always perfect, but time and patience helped. He wished the boy had talked to him. He wished he could turn back the clock and tell the kid not to place that last bet. But it was too late. There could be no changing the past.

Steve drew a deep breath, leaned back in his seat, and closed his eyes. He had to think of a way to cover his tracks once he left the train at Jefferson City and booked passage on the steamer to complete the trip to Kansas City. If the Dillons came after him, as George surmised, they'd be looking for a man traveling alone. Steve needed a new identity. But what? A young voice interrupted his concentration.

"Hi!" The boy who'd boarded the train with his widowed mother was watching him.

"Hello."

"Christopher, it isn't polite to disturb other travelers." Sarah gave the attractive stranger an apologetic smile. She knew Christopher was bored, but the less attention they drew to themselves the better. Besides, there was no telling who this man might be. Good looks didn't mean a thing. She couldn't trust anyone any more.

"I'm sorry," the boy mumbled.

"It's all right, son. You didn't disturb me," Steve replied kindly, his gaze resting upon the boy's mother as he spoke. It surprised him that she was young and pretty, and he thought it a shame that she'd been widowed and left alone with a son to raise so early in her life. He knew things couldn't be easy for her.

Christopher flashed him a wide boyish grin, then turned back in his seat. He didn't want his Aunt Sarah to be angry with him.

Sarah was glad when he settled down. She nodded politely to Steve then returned her attention to the window and the lush Missouri countryside.

An hour passed, and Steve grew restless. He made his way to the men's car, where he was pleased to find a card game in progress, and joined in. The bets were small, and that suited him fine. All he wanted was to pass the time of day.

Christopher, meanwhile, had watched Steve leave and wondered where he was going. Sarah, he noticed, was looking sleepy, and he grew hopeful. If she fell asleep, he would follow the stranger and take a look around the train. He behaved himself, sitting church-mouse still, until Sarah actually did doze off. Grabbing his chance and slipping quietly from their seat, Christopher sneaked down the aisle in search of his new friend. He made it to the men's car without incident and crept inside without detection. The men concentrated on their card-playing, and Christopher peeked over the back of one of the seats to watch.

Steve had the deck, and the boy looked on in amazement as the man shuffled and dealt cards. The boy was awed by his skill and dexterity. He'd never seen anyone handle cards like that before, and he wished he could learn how to do it that well. It looked like fun. Fascinated, he lost track of time.

Sarah lurched awake with the train's change of rhythm after one of its many stops. She stared in confusion, trying to remember where she was, and why. Reality soon intruded and—with it—panic, for Christopher was nowhere in sight. Had someone taken him from the train while she slept? Jumping up, she began a near-frantic search. She had to find him! He had to be there!

Eventually, having checked the rest of the train, Sarah approached the men's car. So far her search had proved futile, and she was growing more and more frightened with each passing mile the train traveled. She knew women weren't welcome in this exclusively male haven, but this was an emergency. Tradition be damned, she had to find Christopher! Desperation prodded her as she reached for the door. She paused long enough to look through the small window, and it was then that she saw him.

Sarah wasn't sure whether to laugh in delight or cry in relief as she threw the door wide and marched inside. Her heart still pounded in her breast, and her hands still shook.

"Christopher! Thank God I've found you!" she said as she hurried toward him.

"Uh-oh," Christopher mumbled, guilt assailing him as he scrambled to his feet to stand before his aunt.

Steve and the other card players looked up at the interruption, and for the first time they noticed the boy. Steve glanced from Christopher to Sarah and would have smiled at the youth's antics if it hadn't been for his mother's strained expression.

"Christopher, do you have any idea what I just went through looking for you?" Sarah demanded, her voice unsteady.

Christopher had never known her to raise her voice before, and he blanched at her scolding, understanding only now what she must have thought when she awoke and found him gone. Tears welled up in his eyes. "I'm sorry, but I . . ."

"You left without telling me, and I thought—"

"Don't be too hard on him, ma'am. He was perfectly safe the whole time," Steve interceded gently as he set his cards aside and stood up to address her. For some reason, he felt the need to reassure her that everything was all right.

Standing as close as they were, Steve was startled to discover how young she really was—and how very pretty. Her beauty was natural and unaffected, and the starkness of her dowdy mourning garb only served to enhance it. Her hair was brown; her complexion was flawless peaches and cream. He realized she couldn't have been much more than a child herself when she'd given birth, and he found himself wondering about her. Suddenly aware of the direction his thoughts had taken, Steve clamped down on them. This delicate young woman had recently lost her husband. She deserved his full sympathy and kindness.

Sarah gazed up at the darkly-handsome man she recognized from their own train car, momentarily chagrined by his defense of Christopher. She managed a weary smile. "I know you're right, but so much has happened to us lately." She gathered Christopher protectively near.

"I understand, Mrs.—?"

"Johnson. Sarah Johnson. And this is Christopher."

"It's a pleasure, ma'am. I'm Steve Spencer." He turned his dark gaze to the boy. "In the future, Christopher, always let your mother know where you're going. It isn't good to worry her. Mothers are special people. You only get one in life, and you're lucky enough to still have yours. She deserves to be treated right." Steve had never known his own mother. She'd died giving birth to him; and, consequently, he held mothers in high regard. But the poignancy of his words eluded him.

"Yes, sir," Christopher answered softly, knowing how true Steve's words were. Pain shown in his brown eyes as regret filled him. He wished his mother were still alive. He wished he'd been older and bigger

160

and stronger. If he had been, he could have helped her when his father was mean and she wouldn't be dead now. They'd be together, home in Philadelphia, and they'd be happy.

Sarah saw the sorrow in Christopher's expression, and her heart ached for him. She understood the effect Steve's words had had. "I think it's time we went back to our car and let these gentlemen resume their play," she said. "Mr. Spencer, it was nice meeting you."

Sarah had started to go when she glanced back and found his gaze intent upon her. Their eyes met, and a shiver tingled through her. Time seemed suspended. Though she didn't know why, she was suddenly very aware of him as a man. He was tall, but not too tall, and he was handsome—very. His hair was dark, his nose was straight. His mouth and jaw were firm and could have been called unyielding, but Sarah instinctively knew he laughed often. His eyes, however, were what held her so rapt. They were a beautiful hazel, and she saw a gentle, abiding kindness mirrored in their depths. Still, even though in the past—with the glaring exception of Michael—her instincts about people had generally proven accurate, she didn't dare to trust them this time. She couldn't take any risks. They would have to remain polite strangers.

"It was nice meeting you, too, Mrs. Johnson," Steve responded. He watched as they left the car, and he found himself wondering what had happened to her husband and what she was going to do now that she was alone.

Sarah and Christopher returned to their seats.

"I am really sorry, Aunt Sarah," he told her miserably.

"Shh. I'm your mother, remember?" She glanced around to make sure nobody was paying attention.

He was upset at having forgotten. "Mother," he said with emphasis, then grinned at her wickedly, his sense of humor regained. "Did you see Mr. Spencer playing cards?"

"No, dear, I didn't. Why?"

"He's good," he told her with undisguised admiration for the man's talent. "You should have seen him. He won and won! He could deal fast, too!"

As Christopher regaled her with stories of Spencer's expertise, Sarah found herself thinking about him. She wondered how he'd come to be so good at cards. He didn't dress like a gambler, but then she'd learned that looks could be deceiving. Staring out the window, Sarah concentrated on the journey and tried to forget about the man. Good-looking and kind though he might be, Steve Spencer could never be more than an acquaintance who'd passed time with a widow and her son on a train in the middle of the Missouri wilds.

As they neared Jefferson City, Steve dropped out of the game and returned to his seat. Most of the passengers were going all the way through to Kansas City and would transfer directly to the steamboat there. But it was in Jeff City that Spencer had to disappear, for if the Dillons managed to track him

162

this far, they'd be looking for a lone man boarding a riverboat.

Steve cast a glance over at the Johnsons. The boy was nestled against his mother's side, sound asleep. It was a peaceful picture. He frowned, a plan occurring to him. There was a risk involved, and, gambler that he was, Steve carefully considered all possibilities before making his decision. If anything went wrong, he courted disaster; but if it worked, it would be well worth the risk. Should he? Yes. He would take the gamble and bluff his way to success.

The train pulled into the depot on schedule, and the passengers disembarked. Sarah and Christopher joined the crowd heading to the shipping office to get their tickets for the final leg of the trip upriver to Kansas City. They were near the back of the group and knew they would have quite a long wait.

Sarah was nervous. She missed having Angel beside her to buoy her spirits and confidence. Now, though, she was totally on her own, and she was afraid. She kept Christopher next to her and kept a close watch on the crowd. She noticed Steve Spencer behind them, and they exchanged casual greetings as it came their turn to step inside.

The office was good-sized, but there were still quite a few people in line ahead of her. She'd only been in the room for a minute when she noticed two men lounging to the side, watching her. She could almost feel their eyes upon her, and her fear increased. Were these Michael's men? She clamped a restraining hand on Christopher's arm as she fought down panic and the urge to flee. Offering up fervent prayers for Christopher's safety, Sarah begged God to make the line move faster so they could get away from the men's scrutiny.

Sarah wasn't the only one who'd noticed the two men. Steve saw them, too, as soon as he walked through the door. He knew it would have been physically impossible for the Dillons to get there ahead of him, but there was always the chance that they'd telegraphed relatives in town. Prepared for the worst, hoping for the best, he positioned himself closer to Sarah and Christopher. In another moment, he would put his plan into action. He hoped it worked, because if it didn't he was going to have a lot of questions to answer to a lot of people.

The clerk looked up as Sarah and Christopher finally made it up to the desk. "Yes, ma'am. What can I do for you?"

"I'd like—" she began, but she never got the chance to finish her sentence because Steve's deep voice broke in from behind her.

"My wife and I would like to book passage for ourselves and our son to Kansas City." Steve slipped a possessive arm about her slender waist and smiled down at the waiting clerk.

Chapter Nine

Sarah stiffened at Spencer's bold touch. She turned on him about to tell him in no uncertain terms to take his hands off of her when again her gaze fell upon the two men across the room. Sarah had never prided herself on being a quick-thinker, that was Angel's specialty, but today, faced with the threat of the unknown from the strangers watching her, she knew immediately what she had to do. Forcing the irritation out of her expression, she gave the card-player her nicest smile.

"I still can't believe we're almost there, can you, dear?" Sarah managed as her eyes sparkled in answering challenge to Spencer's daring. "Our trip's half over."

"It seems like hardly any time has passed since we made the decision to do this, and now here we are." He matched her smile for smile and look for look. "Our next stop is Kansas City."

"Mother?" Christopher looked at the two of them

in confusion. Only the tightening of Sarah's hand on his shoulder stopped him from saying more.

"Are you getting excited, son?" Steve brought the boy into the conversation.

"Yeah," he answered his friend with a grin. "Things just keep getting more exciting all the time." Christopher didn't know what Steve was up to, but he thought it a great adventure and willingly played along. He wasn't sure what his Aunt Sarah was going to have to say about all this once they were alone, but for now he was having fun.

Steve had been expecting an explosion. He'd expected Sarah Johnson to announce that he was no husband of hers and that he had to be suffering some kind of crazy delusion and wasn't playing with a full deck. Instead, she'd gone along with his story and even the boy had joined in! Steve didn't know why, but he was tremendously relieved. Questions and answers would be in order later, but for right now, he would just keep smiling.

The clerk, busy writing, said, "I'll need your names, please."

Sarah answered calmly. "We're the Johnsons."

"Here you are, sir." The clerk handed Steve the tickets, accepting payment. "Have a safe trip."

"Thank you."

The three of them started toward the door. As they passed the two watching, waiting men, Sarah took Steve's arm, and they exited the office very much the happy family. Steve stopped outside only long enough to make arrangements for their things to be taken to the steamer. Sarah and Christopher stood off to the side.

"What's happening?" the boy asked, his eyes alight with mischief and curiosity.

"Shh," she cautioned. The two men had moved to the door of the office, still watching them. Sarah had the distinct feeling that they were predators, waiting for the opportunity to close on their prey. It took more courage than she knew she had to face them.

"Ready?" Steve asked, rejoining their family circle.

Sarah fell silent as she placed her hand on Steve's arm and once more walked at his side. She could feel the hardness of the muscles beneath her fingers, and his solidness reassured her. Still, she wasn't certain whether to thank God for sending him or pray harder for deliverance from him. What did he hope to gain by declaring her his wife and Christopher his son? His demeanor, however, revealed nothing. He looked calm and happy, a picture-perfect family man, as they strolled through the streets. Sarah managed to keep all her churning questions to herself until they were well away from the office. Only then did she let go of his arm and move away.

"All right, Mr. Spencer, what's going on? The first time we ever laid eyes on you was on the train coming up here, and yet there in the office you stepped right up and claimed us as your family. Why?" Her dark eyes narrowed as she tried to discern his motive, but Steve's gambler's expression gave nothing away.

"The question goes both ways," he countered, upping the ante. "Why did you go along with me? You could have kicked up a fuss back there in the office, and yet you didn't say a word. Why did you stay quiet?"

Sarah was cornered. This stranger, this Steve Spencer, would give no information without gaining some in return, knowledge she couldn't reveal. The stakes were too high. She had to brazen her way through.

"It's your game, Mr. Spencer. All I'll tell you is that for right now it suits my purpose to go along with you."

"It does?" he uttered. Sarah was not nearly as adept at hiding her thoughts as Steve, and he'd seen the flicker of fear in her gaze before she'd answered him. Was she glad for his protection? That puzzled him. "Have I rescued a damsel in distress?"

"You might say that," Sarah responded cryptically, refusing to elaborate and piquing his interest even more.

They had reached the levee and were starting up the ramp to the steamer. Steve had no chance to ask anything else, interrupted by a steward who greeted them on deck and showed them to their cabin. Steve held the stateroom door for Sarah and Christopher and then followed them inside.

Hearing the door shut behind her, Sarah was overwhelmingly aware of Steve Spencer, standing close behind her in the small cabin. Although his timely intercession in the shipping office had worked perfectly, she was through with the charade. They were on board the ship. There was no need to continue.

"Well, Mr. Spencer, it's certainly been interesting." She tried to sound dismissive. "And now that we're all safe—"

"Yes?"

"You may go," Sarah finished, moving boldly back to the door and opening it for him.

Her actions made Steve wonder even more about her reasons for wanting him with her at the shipping office. Whatever danger she'd perceived to exist before, she now believed gone.

"You want me to leave?" he asked with a lift of one expressive dark brow.

"Certainly, Mr. Spencer. You didn't really expect to stay in the cabin with us, did you?" she asked with a cool composure she did not feel. When he looked at her, she felt as if he could see into her soul, and she didn't like it. She knew she wasn't a good actress. She'd always told the truth—until now.

"Where else would I go? We're registered as Mr. and Mrs. Johnson."

"I'm sure there must be some place else you can sleep," Sarah insisted. She glanced at the two beds in such close proximity, flustered. Having him pretend to be her husband while they'd booked passage was one thing. Sleeping in such intimate surroundings with him was something else entirely. And while she was glad that the passenger list with the Johnson family name on it would throw off anyone following them, there was certainly no need for them to continue with the pretense. Steve Spencer was a stranger. He was not her husband!

"I see." Steve did not find spending the two nights of travel time on deck an appealing option.

"If you don't mind—" Sarah began again more assertively. He was too overpowering this close.

They were at a stand-off. As Sarah waited for Steve to go, she happened to look outside. She stopped in mid-sentence as the same two men from the steamship office walked by. They glanced at her pointedly, and a hard knot of fear tightened in her stomach. She gripped the doorknob tighter, so no one would see the tremor in her hands. The blush of agitation faded from her cheeks, leaving her suddenly ashen.

"Perhaps I was wrong, dear. I think I'd rather wait until it's a bit cooler before we go for a stroll on the deck. Is that all right with you, darling?" she choked, closing the door quickly.

Steve had seen the two men and automatically tensed, assuming they had found him out. But the Dillons could not have known what he looked like. He was safe. Yet Sarah's reaction told him something was amiss and—whatever it was—the two men were at the root of it. He felt a surge of protectiveness toward his "family."

"What's going on? Do you know those men?"

"I have no idea who they are."

"Then why do you look so frightened and why the change of heart? You did just call me 'darling,' didn't you?"

"I was talking to Christopher," she snapped defensively. She would tell him nothing.

"In that case, I'll guess I'll go ahead and leave." He started toward the door, calling her bluff.

Sarah had lost, and she knew it. If Michael's men thought the family a fake, they would close in on her and Christopher like wolves. In desperation, she blurted out, "No. . . . wait. Don't go. You can stay." But even as she gave in, she questioned her motive—and her sanity.

"Oh, good!" Christopher exclaimed, eager to enjoy more of Steve's company and hoping he would teach him how to play cards.

"You're sure this time?"

"You may share the room with us for the duration of the trip."

"What about those two men?" He returned to the original subject, probing.

"Mr. Spencer," Sarah began in her iciest voice, "I have not pressured you about your actions in the shipping office. I'm sure you had your personal reasons, and I will not attempt to learn what they were. I would appreciate it if you would extend to me the same courtesy. My business shall remain my business. When we reach Kansas City, we will go our separate ways and there will be no need for recriminations on either side. Now, if you can accept things on that level, then you are welcome to remain. Otherwise, sir—" She glanced pointedly at the door.

"I do believe I will take you up on your most generous offer. Thank you."

"Oh, there is one other thing . . ." Sarah was determined not to be beholden to him in any way. She opened her purse and drew out the full amount for their tickets. "Here's the money for our passage. There is absolutely no reason why you should pay for us."

"There's no need," he said. He had used her to cover his tracks. He owed her.

"Mr. Spencer," she said firmly, "I do not want to be indebted to you when we part company."

He saw the determination in her eyes and did not argue. "All right." He took the currency from her and placed it in his billfold. "Now, there is one thing more we should discuss."

"What?" She was instantly cautious.

"Don't you think we'll be more convincing as a married couple if we at least know each other's names? Let's start over. Madam, I'm Steve Spencer, a cowboy en route to Kansas City and points west."

It irked Sarah to accept a total stranger as her savior, but she had no alternative. "I'm Sarah," she murmured with little friendliness.

"This is fun. Can I call you 'Steve,' too?" Christopher spoke up once he felt that peace had been made. He looked from his newly-acquired father to his impostor-mother and grinned. "I'm glad you're going with us. There's a lot we can do. When do you want to go for that walk on deck? Will you teach me how to play cards later?"

Sarah heard his excitement and tried to remember the last time he'd been happy. It pleased. her that he liked Steve, and she hoped that maybe some good would come out of their predicament after all.

"You'd better try 'Father' out for size, Christopher. 'Steve's' not going to work in public," he told him with a matching grin.

A knock at the door made Sarah jump; and, seeing her distress, Steve took the initiative. Defensively, he put himself between her and whoever was outside; but when he opened the door, he found only a porter with their luggage.

"Here you are Mr. Johnson," the man said, bringing their things inside.

When he'd gone, Steve locked the door again. He gave Sarah an easy smile as he picked up his bag.

"I'll take this bed," he announced. He set his things at its foot and stretched out upon it himself to test its softness. Folding his arms behind his head, he sighed.

Sarah stared at him, shocked by his careless demeanor. She'd never been with a man in such intimate surroundings and she wasn't sure how to act. As jittery as she was, though, Sarah believed it best to hide her nervousness. He thought her a widow, and as such she should be more at ease with men. No matter how embarrassing things became, she had to keep up that pretense.

"Please make yourself comfortable," she said graciously, averting her eyes demurely from his lean, muscular form.

Steve noticed that she was a bit uncomfortable and immediately felt ashamed of himself. Somehow, despite her hideously ugly dress, he'd forgotten that she was a recent widow. Suddenly conscious of the position he'd put her in and feeling a tad guilty over his scheme to use her and the boy to his advantage, he rose from the bed.

"I'm going out for a while. I'll be back," he told her as he started from the stateroom. Then, thinking of the men who might still be waiting outside, he paused to add, "If you need me, I'll be in the bar."

Sarah looked up, her expression proud and independent. "Christopher and I will be just fine."

"Well, in any case, lock the door." Then he was gone.

Sarah stared after him for only a moment and then followed his advice.

"How come Steve is pretending to be your husband, Aunt Sarah?" Christopher had been waiting for the chance to ask ever since the surprising scene in the shipping office. "You think it's because he likes us?"

His question was so hopeful that Sarah had to agree. "I'm sure that's it," she said. "And I have to admit I'm glad he's willing to help us. Those men at the office looked suspicious, and they did follow us onto the boat."

"I know, but Steve's with us now, so we'll be all right."

"Of course, sweetie. We're going to be fine." *For now . . .* Sarah added in her mind. She managed a smile as she gave him a hug. She wished she could believe as he did that everything would have a happy ending, but the terror of Elizabeth's death still preyed on her night and day. Her own innocence had been viciously stripped from her; and, adult that she was, there could be no pretending it had never happened.

If Sarah had met the handsome Steve Spencer a few weeks ago, she might have thought him wonderful. Now, she trusted no man. She was reasonably sure that Steve wasn't in Michael's employ. If he were, they would all be on their way back to Philadelphia by now. No, Steve had his own reasons—or demons—and they had to be important or he would never have saddled himself with a 'wife and son' for this trip. She thought again of his expertise with cards. Was he a gambler? He'd certainly taken a chance in the shipping office. Remembering that they'd agreed to respect each other's privacy, Sarah tried not to dwell on it, but she couldn't help but wonder at her newly-acquired 'husband's' past.

Sarah's gaze accidentally fell upon Steve's bed, and she felt her cheeks burn at the thought of his sleeping there. To travel this intimately with him was crazy, perhaps immoral. If anyone ever found out, her reputation would be destroyed, but—no matter what the cost to her personally—she would do whatever was necessary to protect Christopher.

Steve passed a few hours in the bar, having some drinks and watching the gambling. Several men he knew by reputation were working the tables, and he was hard put not to join in, rankled by the low profile he had to maintain. To those on board he was a family man. He was no longer Steve Spencer; he was Steve Johnson.

Steve stayed away from the cabin as long as he could to give Sarah time alone, but when dusk began to fall and the dinner hour neared, he went back to get them. He knocked once on the door, then tried the knob. He was pleased when he found that she'd locked it as he'd asked her to.

"Sarah, it's Steve." He knocked lightly again.

Christopher opened the door for him. "Better be quiet. Mother's still asleep," he advised in a low voice.

"She was tired?" he asked as he entered, glancing over to where she lay sleeping. His gaze traced the sweet curve of her cheek and the delicate line of her throat and then drifted lower to the swell of her breasts. Again he was struck by her delicate beauty. If it hadn't been for her mourning dress, she could have passed for a virginal princess in an age-old fairy tale. It took an effort to look away.

"Yes, we had to get up early because she needed to buy some clothes before we went to the depot. I think she was up late last night, too, talking with . . ." The boy stopped abruptly, realizing he was saying too much.

"Was St. Louis your home?" Steve questioned easily, trying to mask the extent of his interest.

"No." Christopher evaded the question.

"Where are you from? I grew up in Georgia."

He could see no harm in telling Steve that much. "We're from Philadelphia."

"And you're going to Kansas City? Do you have friends or family there?"

"No . . . uh . . . I think I'd better wake my mother up." Nervous, he hopped up next to her, startling her awake.

"Christopher? What is it?" For just an instant, there was a wild, hunted look in her eyes as she stared about the room trying to get her bearings.

"Steve's back."

"Oh," she breathed, relieved that there was no trouble. She sat quietly for a moment, thoughts

176

much we'd sink the boat. What do you think, Christopher?" Steve teased as the boy continued to eat.

"Uh-huh," he agreed, his mouth full.

"He must be growing," Sarah added, and the adults chuckled.

"I know what you mean," Edith sympathized. Her Rob was twelve already, and he was starting to grow quickly now.

Steve smiled, for it was the first time he'd heard Sarah laugh. He liked the sound a lot and wished he could get her out of mourning. She was young, beautiful, and very much alive, and he wanted to know more about her, much more. He was hard put not to ask the questions he'd promised earlier he wouldn't.

"Sarah, please forgive me if I'm being too inquisitive, but I was just wondering who you were in mourning for?"

"My father."

"I'm so sorry. Has it been long?"

Steve, listening idly to their conversation, realized this was his chance. He would force her hand. Certainly, he had nothing to lose and perhaps everything to gain. He spoke up quickly before Sarah could reply. "It's been nearly a full year since we buried him."

Sarah was stunned by Steve's interference. She managed not to let her surprise show, and remained quiet as he went on to tell the other woman how they'd sold the family home in Georgia and were heading west now to start a new life.

"But to mourn for a whole year?" Edith clucked to Sarah in a motherly fashion. "You're much too young and pretty for that. You have a wonderful husband and son, perhaps it's time you put the sorrow of the past behind you and started looking forward to the future you and Steve have together?"

"I know," Steve added, giving Sarah a loving look as he spoke. "I've been trying to convince her of that very same thing."

"But I loved him very much." Sarah focused demurely on a coffee stain on the table linen. "His death was tragic."

"I'm sure it was," the older woman said with empathy as she patted her hand. "But you mustn't allow yourself to be buried with the dead. As much as it sometimes pains us to admit it, life does go on. Think about it, dear. You have so much to live for."

"I suppose you're right," she agreed slowly.

"Of course I am," Edith declared good naturedly. "No doubt Mr. Spencer is longing to see you in something pretty again. How can you deny him that small pleasure?"

"It is difficult to deny him anything."

"There's a girl." Edith Langford patted her again. "You won't regret it, and I'm sure your father would understand."

The conversation drifted on to other topics. When Christopher had finally eaten his fill, they said good night to the Langfords and left the dining room. As Steve escorted them back to their cabin, he waited for Sarah to bring up the subject of her mourning, but she didn't. He'd expected anger and was surprised when she showed no sign of irritation.

When they reached the stateroom door, Steve unlocked it for them, but did not go in. He respected Sarah and wanted her to be as comfortable as possible with their arrangement. Since nighttime preparations would be awkward for her with him in the cabin, he gallantly offered to go.

"I'll leave you for now. I'm sure you'd like some privacy to get ready for bed."

"Thank you." His gesture was surprisingly kind and thoughtful, and Sarah's gratitude was heartfelt. She'd been worrying about the night to come and greatly appreciated his courtesy. It was going to be difficult enough getting any sleep with him in the same room, but if he'd insisted on accompanying them now into the cabin, she wasn't sure how she would have managed to undress and bathe. "You're very much a gentleman, you know."

"It's mostly because you, my dear wife, are very much a lady." Steve stared down at her in the semidarkness. She looked beautiful in the flickering, mellow light of the lanterns and he battled a compulsion to take her in his arms and kiss her. Instead, he gave himself a mental shake and held the door for her to enter.

Sarah was mesmerized by the intensity of his regard, his mouth so close to hers. All she had to do was . . . She started to sway against him then forced herself to draw back.

"My Aunt Blanche would be thrilled to hear you say so," she said lightly, needing to fight off the sensual mood that had swept over her. "She certainly tried her best to make me into one." Sarah moved passed him into the room, then turned to gaze at him. Again she was struck by his dark good looks.

Steve took a deliberate step backward to distance himself physically from her. "I'll be back. Oh. . . . and be sure to keep the door locked while I'm gone."

With that he strode down the deck, leaving Sarah behind, frowning as she watched him go. She couldn't imagine what had caused him to suddenly act so strange. Stepping back inside, she bolted the door. She got Christopher ready for bed first and then herself, but all the while her thoughts kept drifting to her counterfeit husband. He'd been nothing but courteous and kind to them since intruding on their lives that afternoon. He certainly was handsome, too. If she had to pretend to be married to anybody, Steve was an excellent choice.

When Sarah realized the fanciful turn her thoughts had taken, she sternly reprimanded herself. She had known Steve Spencer less than a day! They would part company when they reached Kansas City the day after tomorrow, and they would never see each other again. That was the way it had to be. She finished washing and changed into her nightgown behind a small screen. After turning down the lamp, she slid into the bed, taking the side nearest the wall so she would be the farthest away from Steve. Christopher was waiting sleepily for her.

"Good night, sweetie," Sarah murmured, giving him a soft kiss on his cheek.

"Night, Aunt Sarah," he said in a sleep-husky voice.

Sarah didn't correct him this time, but smiled at

him tenderly as he rolled over and promptly fell asleep. She settled back and pulled the covers up to her chin. Flimsy as they were, they were the only defense she had. But lying in the darkness, staring up at the ceiling, she thought about Steve and wondered how long he was going to stay away from the cabin.

Steve found a chair on the deserted deck and sat down to pass the time. The moon was lost behind a bank of clouds, and the night had grown dark. It was warm, and, for the first time since leaving St. Louis, he managed to relax. Leaning back and stretching his legs out before him, he stared across the river. He thought about the Dillons and what he would do if they did catch up with him. It wasn't a pretty thought. The faint sound of music drifted to him as the steamer's musicians struck up a melody for dancing, and he was glad for the distraction. He waited there for almost an hour, enjoying the distant melodies and the peace of the night, before starting back to the stateroom.

Steve had taken the key with him this time, and he let himself into the cabin. Not wanting to disturb anyone, he moved quietly, not bothering to light the lamp. He began to undress and had already shrugged out of his shirt and was starting to unfasten his belt, when he glanced toward the bed where the boy and his mother lay. Though he could barely see them in the dark, he was reminded of the Madonna and child, and it was then that he decided to sleep with his pants on. She deserved his respect. He sat down on the edge of the bed, took off his boots and lay down in the darkness.

Chapter Ten

When Sarah opened her eyes to the brightness of the new day, the first thing she saw was Steve. Naked to the waist, he was standing at the washstand shaving. Sarah had never seen a man so unclothed before, and she certainly had never seen one doing anything so personal as shaving. She lay in bed without speaking, fascinated by the play of his rugged muscles across the broad plane of his back. In the mirror's reflection she could see his chest and her eyes widened at the sight of the mat of fine black hair that covered it. She lifted her gaze upward and studied his face. The soap lather on his jaw and chin gave her an idea of what he'd look like with a beard, and she decided rather whimsically that he might look quite like a pirate should he ever decide to grow one—a black beard that is, not a white, foamy one.

The thought of Steve as a pirate struck a chord within her. Out of nowhere, he had swooped into their lives like an avenging corsair on the high seas.

Swept up by the whirlwind of his deception, she and Christopher had become pawns in whatever game he played. Yet, rather than resenting his interference, Sarah was almost grateful for it. Everything he'd done had coincided with her own needs. By brazenly claiming them as his family, he'd protected her from the two suspicious men, and last night his ploy before the Langfords had freed her from her mourning clothes. Sarah knew if the time ever came when they were at cross-purposes, she would stand up to him, but until then she would bide her time. Kansas City was two days and another night away. As she continued to watch him in the mirror, she acknowledged that, unlike a pirate, Steve had proven himself a gentleman. A strange twist of fate had brought them together—but why?

Christopher was already up and dressed, sitting on Steve's bed talking to him as he, too, watched him shave. "How soon do you think I can start shaving?"

"How old did you say you were?" Steve asked.

"Nine, but I'll be ten real soon," he responded proudly.

"Well, I started when I was twelve, but I have darker hair than you do. It really depends on what color your beard is. If it comes in dark, you could be shaving in another year or two."

"Oh, good!"

"You want to try it now? Just for practice?" he asked as he finished.

"Could I?"

"Here you are." Steve offered him his soap, brush,

and razor. "Put lots of soap on your cheeks so you don't cut yourself."

Christopher jumped off the bed and went to stand right before Steve at the washstand so he could see himself in the mirror. As his mentor had instructed, he lathered his face and then, after Steve had shown him how to hold the razor properly, he made the first swipe at his cheek.

"How'd I do?" he asked eagerly.

"No blood?" Steve took a close look at the young boy's pink cheek.

"Nope."

"Then you did fine," he complimented him. "Keep going, but remember to be careful. If you make a mistake, it's going to hurt."

"I'll be careful," Christopher promised solemnly, turning back to look in the mirror again. He noticed a movement within the reflection and saw that his Aunt Sarah was awake and watching them. "Good morning, Mother. Look what Steve's teaching me!"

"Good morning." She'd been deeply touched by the kindness and patience Steve was showing her nephew. Christopher had been traumatized badly and he needed to know a man could be gentle without losing his masculinity. If Michael had been more like Steve, they wouldn't be in this terrible position.

Steve had picked up a towel to wipe the remnants of soap from his face, and he turned toward Sarah. She looked so incredibly lovely with her sleep-flushed cheeks and early-morning innocence that he started to speak twice before he actually got the words out. "Good morning, Sarah. Did you rest well?"

"Yes, I did," she replied, trying not to stare at his hard-muscled, hair-roughened chest.

He saw her discomfort and realizing his state of undress, reached for his shirt. "Good. I'll be out of here as soon as I finish dressing. Then you can have the cabin to yourself."

"That's very considerate." Watching him put on his shirt, she pulled the covers up higher under her chin.

"If you'd like, Christopher can come with me."

Excited by the idea of spending more time with Steve, Christopher pleaded, "May I go with Steve? Please? I'll be good. I promise. May I?"

Sarah looked from confident man to eager young boy and was torn. She wanted Christopher to be happy, but she wondered if she dared trust Steve with him. Finally she realized that as long as the boat didn't make any stops during the time they were together, Christopher would be safe. "Go ahead. But Christopher?"

"Yes?"

"I think you'd better finish shaving first."

"Thanks, Mother." Christopher turned diligently back to the task and in a few minutes was done. Meanwhile, Steve put on a jacket and tie, and Sarah found her gaze lingering on him. She watched him move, admiring how well the jacket fit his broad shoulders. When he glanced up, she quickly looked away.

"Where would you like to meet for breakfast? They'll be serving in less than an hour."

"I'll meet you on deck near the entrance to the dining room."

"That'll be fine. You ready, Christopher? Let me take a look at you." He eyed the youth with an approving male air, noting his neatly combed hair, clean shirt, and pressed pants. "You look fine, and, by the way, for a first effort, you did a good job shaving. Let's go."

The boy glowed at his praise. "Bye, Mother. We'll see you in a little while."

"Bye, dear." She watched them go, noticing the way Steve put a gentle, guiding hand on the boy's shoulder as they walked out the door.

With no reason to hurry, Sarah decided to take her time and look her best. Half-way through her morning ablutions, she found she was smiling at the thought of not having to wear the hated mourning dress today. She took extra time with her hair and then moved to her traveling chest to select a day gown. The turquoise caught her eye. It wasn't a flashy dress. It was high-necked and long-sleeved, but the full-skirted style suited her. She donned it quickly. Sarah told herself she wasn't doing this to please Steve, but because she no longer had to play the part of a widow. A quick glance in the mirror told her she looked like a different woman; and, satisfied with the results of her efforts, she went out to meet her men.

On deck, Christopher and Steve strolled in companionable silence. When they passed other travelers, they offered cordial greetings; otherwise, they remained quiet, enjoying the cool freshness of the new day and each other's company.

"Steve?"

"Yes, Christopher?"

"Do you have any children of your own?" Wanting to know more about this man who fascinated him, Christopher could contain his curiosity no longer.

Wryly Steve replied, "Not that I know of. Why?"

"Oh, I was just wondering." Christopher smiled happily at the news.

"Well, that's one thing you don't have to worry about. I've never been married or fathered any children. You're my first son."

Christopher beamed at his answer. "I want to grow up to be just like you."

"What about your real father? You mustn't forget him." Steve was touched by his words, but urged him to think about the man who'd given him life. He didn't want the boy to transfer his love for his father to him out of loneliness or a sense of loss. He was surprised by the strange look Christopher gave him.

"I'll never forget him," was his answer.

His tone gave Steve pause. "Do you miss him a lot?"

He almost blurted out aloud "NO," but remembering his Aunt Sarah's admonitions to play his role, he answered cautiously, "Not as much as I thought I would." Christopher swallowed tightly at the memory of his father. He hated the man passionately.

"Death is a difficult thing to deal with. Time does

help, but the emptiness you feel never really goes away."

The boy thought then of his mother and the ache that sometimes threatened to tear him apart. He kept expecting to see her, expecting to hear her voice. He wanted to feel her arms around him and to put his arms around her. "It doesn't?" The prospect of feeling forever empty—with his sorrow still so raw and deep—frightened him.

"No, but that's good in a way, Christopher," Steve said gently. "If we miss them always, that means we loved them a lot; and no one can ask for more than that in this life." He hoped he wasn't talking over the boy's head, but somehow he believed Christopher understood. To cheer him, Steve made an offer. "You asked last night if I'd teach you how to play cards. Do you want to try now? We have enough time to get in a hand or two."

Christopher immediately brightened, glad to be drawn away from the memory of his mother lying dead at the bottom of the staircase. "I watched you play on the train, and I want to be as good as you are," he told him with honest admiration.

"Do you think your mother would approve?"

"Why wouldn't she?"

"Well, I take my card playing seriously."

"You do?" He was surprised. "You looked like you were having fun."

"There are times when it's fun," he granted. "And there are times when it's not." Steve looked down at Christopher. "But you and I," he went on, "will have a grand time!"

"Good. I won't tell Mother, if you won't."

"You got a deal. Let's play."

"Thanks!" Christopher's face lit up.

They sat down on two out-of-the-way deck chairs, and Steve pulled a deck of cards from his inner coatpocket and shuffled them. His quick, sure efforts earned him an admiring look.

"You do that great! May I try?"

Steve handed him the deck and the boy made a valiant attempt. His movements were slow and clumsy though, and he chewed on his lip in frustration as he fought to handle the cards as well as Steve.

"Don't worry. You'll get better with practice," Steve encouraged, and they shared a smile as Christopher handed the deck back. "Now, watch carefully. This is how you deal."

With practiced ease, Steve dealt the cards as his pupil observed intently. The boy watched in awe, amazed at the card tricks and quick to pick up the rudiments of poker.

"How did you get so good at this?" Christopher asked.

"Practice."

"Do you play a lot?" It was an innocent question.

"Every day. It's how I make my living."

"You're not a gambler." Christopher shook his head in disbelief. "I've seen pictures, and gamblers look slick. They wear big diamonds and are smooth talkers. You're not like that."

Steve grinned at the observations. "Oh, I've had my moments. There have been several times—especially lately—when I've had to do some fast talking."

"Like with Mother?"

"Like with your mother."

They turned back to their cards.

"What about bluffing?" Christopher asked a few minutes later as he studied the practice hand Steve had dealt him.

"It takes nerves of steel. You can't let any hint of emotion show. Look your opponent straight in the eye, and don't flinch," he explained. "I don't do it often. Only when the situation is desperate, and I have no choice but to win."

Christopher nodded. "You have to look serious?"

"Very."

They regarded each other, and Christopher experimented with his gravest expression.

"That's pretty good." Steve nodded in honest appreciation. "Keep working on it and you'll have it in no time." They finished their hand, then Steve gave Christopher the deck. "Go ahead," he said. "It's your turn to deal." Christopher held the cards almost reverently as he counted out their hands.

"I did it!" he cried exuberantly. "I did it. I'm a dealer."

"You sure are, son," Steve said proudly, and the game continued. They were having such a good time that they almost forgot about. meeting Sarah. Steve was the one who finally remembered.

"We'd better hurry. I don't want her to worry about me," Christopher told him earnestly.

They made it to the pre-arranged meeting place moments before Sarah appeared. She found Steve and Christopher standing at the rail, completely at ease together as they laughed and talked.

"Did you two enjoy yourselves?" she asked.

They turned to greet her, and Steve's expression clearly reflected both his surprise that she had worn something other than the mourning clothes and his full male appreciation for the change in her appearance. Wordlessly, he breathed in her loveliness. He'd thought her pretty in the drab clothes. In a colorful gown, he found her stunning. The blue-green set off her pale complexion to perfection, and the style— demure yet fashionable—fit her superbly, emphasizing the fullness of her breasts and the soft curve of her hips.

"We had a good time," Christopher was saying. He looked far happier than he had in days, and Sarah noted the change.

"I'm glad," Sarah said, approval in her voice.

To Steve she seemed aglow. He found himself wanting to make her smile. "You look beautiful this morning," he told her. "Turquoise is a wonderful color on you."

"Thank you." His compliment pleased her as much as the warmth of his gaze upon her.

Thinking of how much Christopher wanted to play cards and keeping up the pretense that they were a family, Steve put his arm around the boy's shoulders and said with a note of fatherly pride, "You know, Christopher's got a lot of his father in him. He's a regular chip off the old block."

At his words, so innocently put, Michael came raging into her thoughts. Sarah's smile faltered, then vanished completely. The idea, however remote, that Christopher might be like Michael made her ill. She understood Steve's intention and for the sake of their deception she knew she had to paste a happy look back on her face; but it took her a minute to pull herself together.

Seeing the change in her expression, Steve realized that he'd hurt her. He hadn't meant to, but he could tell that the reminder of her husband's death had cut deep. Obviously the memory was still a source of terrible pain for her, and he cursed himself for his insensitivity. He had enjoyed her light-heartedness and regretted that he could have been the cause of any heartache.

"Shall we go on in and eat?" she finally managed.

"Of course."

The delicious breakfast helped Sarah push Michael from her thoughts, and she began to enjoy herself again. But when they had finished eating and were leaving the room, Sarah noticed the two men from the shipping office seated near the door. They watched her leave, and she shivered in spite of the warmth of the day. They had, she was certain, noticed her change from mourning clothes and were eyeing her with overt interest.

Steve saw them, too, and having his hand at her waist to guide her from the dining room, he felt her tremble. The moment they were alone with no one close enough to hear, he asked, "Why do those men frighten you, Sarah?"

"They don't," she lied.

"Every time you see them, you panic," he pointed out.

"I thought we'd made a bargain not to ask each other questions."

They had agreed, he granted, but it didn't stop him from worrying about her. "Sarah, can I help?"

"Help? With what? Christopher and I are fine, but I think we'll go back to the cabin now," Sarah answered as they went on deck.

Steve stopped. "Wait a minute. I know I should mind my own business, but being your 'husband' for the duration of this trip is my business. If we're 'married,' then we should act married." They'd had such a good time at breakfast he didn't want to be parted from her. "You can't cower in the cabin. We should do what normal, married people do."

Sarah conceded his point. If those men suspected her, she had to meet the challenge. Hiding would only draw more attention to her situation. Abruptly, she changed her mind. "What do you want to do?"

"The same thing all river travelers do—watch the scenery," he replied promptly. They found three chairs in the shade on deck and sat down. Steve found her intelligent and witty as he engaged her in conversation. As time passed, she began to relax and seemed almost happy. He was glad.

Sarah, glad she had taken Steve's advice, found it far more pleasant to sit and talk with him than to hide in the cramped stateroom. He was kind and attentive and good with Christopher, who was full of energy.

The Langfords joined them a short time later. The

women sat together as the men moved to the railing for a "manly" talk.

"Sarah, you look radiant! Your gown is most becoming," Edith complimented her.

"Thank you. It does feel good to dress normally again."

"I'm sure your Steve is happy, too. Why, he can't take his eyes off you," Edith told her, atwitter over the way the handsome Steve Johnson was watching his wife. "If I didn't know better, I'd guess you two were newly married."

"Oh, really?" Sarah asked. Startled by the observation, she cast a covert peek at Steve and Stanley and met Steve's gaze. His hazel eyes glowed. The look touched her, and she thought of his offer of help as they'd left the dining room. If only she could trust him enough to say "yes"!

"Yes. The way you look at him gives you away, too. It's obvious you love each other very much."

"Is it?"

"It's easy to see how you feel about him. It's in your eyes." When Sarah blushed and looked away from Steve, Edith patted her hand reassuringly. "Don't be embarrassed, my dear," Edith went on. "It's a wonderful thing for a wife to love her husband. All too often, the love fades after a few years. But you two care very much for each other, and that's something to be proud of."

"Steve is a very special man," Sarah responded, glancing quickly at her "husband" once more. She discovered to her embarrassment that he'd heard her remark, and he gave her a strange half-smile that sent heat surging through her. She turned her attention back to Edith. "I don't know what I would have done without him. He's always there when I need him."

"Hopefully, my dear, it'll stay that way, and you'll be together always."

The two boys interrupted just then, and Sarah was glad. The other woman had meant to be kind, but the thought of her inevitable separation from Steve sent an unexpected shaft of pain through Sarah. Tomorrow, she would rediscover exactly what life would be like without Steve. When they docked in Kansas City the next morning, the game would end. They would part, and she would never see him again. Sarah lifted her gaze to Steve once more and found that he was still watching her. This time, though, his expression was unreadable.

Edith turned back to her once the boys were calmed, and the conversation drifted on to other things. Sarah was glad. She didn't want to think about tomorrow. She just wanted to enjoy this day while it lasted.

Supper that evening proved as sumptuous as the night before. They dined with the Langfords again and had a wonderful time. Sarah ate with particular relish for she knew good meals would be hard to come by very soon. She'd managed to learn a little about travel on wagon trains, and what she'd gleaned had convinced her that luxuries such as cleanliness, comfort, and good cuisine would soon become things of the past. The trip west would be hard, but they had no other choice.

After supper they returned to the cabin. Steve

paused after unlocking the cabin door. "Sarah, I'd like to speak with you privately for a minute after you've put Christopher to bed."

"All right," she answered, confused by his request.

"I'll wait out here on deck for you." She nodded and went inside with the boy.

"Aunt Sarah?" Christopher said her name once they were alone.

"Yes, dear?"

"What's going to happen when we get to Kansas City?" She could see the uncertainty in his eyes.

"We're going to find ourselves a wagon train and head for California so we can meet your Aunt Angel."

"But what about Steve?" He sounded earnest.

"What about him?"

"Is he going with us?"

"No, Christopher. He's not."

At his crestfallen expression, Sarah wished there was something she could say or do to cheer him, but she could think of nothing. It was just the two of them, and it would stay that way.

"I'm going to miss Steve. He's nice to me. He taught me how to play poker this morning. Did you know that's how he makes his living? Someday I'm going to be as good as he is!"

"He told you he was a gambler?"

"Yes. I sure wish he could stay with us longer so I could practice with him some more. I like him, Aunt Sarah. I like him a lot. Don't you?"

"Yes, Christopher. He seems a very nice man."

"Then why don't you ask him to go to California

with us? Nobody would bother us if Steve were with us."

Sarah had to admit that she felt safe and protected with Steve by her side, but she was an adult and realistic. It couldn't go on. They would part company in the morning.

"We're on our own."

"But why? If you like him, why don't you ask him?"

"Liking him has nothing to do with it, Christopher. Now, give me a kiss and go to sleep."

"All right, but I wish you'd figure out a way for Steve to stay with us," he mumbled as he kissed her and snuggled into the sheets.

"Good night, Christopher."

"G'night . . ." He started to say Aunt Sarah but heard her already turning the door knob and finished, ". . . Mother."

A sob choked him as he said the word. He was lonely, excruciatingly lonely, and soon he wouldn't even have Steve to talk to. He loved his Aunt Sarah, but she wasn't his mother. Tears burned his eyes, and he did not deny them. Tonight, he actually physically ached for his mother. He'd been thinking about her almost all day, and he longed with all his young heart to feel her arms around him again, to rest his head against her breasts, and to hear her tell him everything would be all right. His loneliness was agonizing, and it frightened him. He wanted his mother. Only she could make him feel better, only she would understand the terrors that haunted him.

The ugly realization that he would never again

know the sweetness of her kiss or the reassuring comfort of her embrace ripped at him with sharp, slashing claws. Curled in a ball, Christopher sobbed into the pillow. The logical part of him hoped his Aunt Sarah wouldn't hear him because he didn't want her to think he was a baby or a coward; the little boy deep in his heart just wanted a warm hug from his mother. He was slowly coming to accept that he would never experience that loving joy again, but acceptance didn't ease the pain.

Outside the stateroom, Sarah and Steve stood together at the rail of the deserted deck. It was growing late. The night breeze was cool and gentle, and the moon was a pale silver crescent low on the horizon.

"You know we're due to make port early tomorrow morning," Steve began, once he was certain they were alone on deck.

"I know. Is there a particular way you'd like to handle it when we disembark?" Sarah asked, directly facing the challenge the following day presented.

"I thought it would be best if I go with you to the hotel. Then, once I'm sure you're safely settled in, I'll move on."

"That'll be fine," she agreed.

Steve couldn't fight off the protective instinct he felt in her presence. In spite of the hardship she had suffered losing her husband, an incredible air of innocence still enveloped her. "I'm worried about you, Sarah. You'll be careful, won't you?"

The intensity in his voice sent a shiver through her. "Of course."

Lost in her dark, luminous eyes, Steve reveled in her beauty. Yet tomorrow she would be gone from his life forever. After they parted, he would not know where she was or what she was doing. He studied her lips. He wanted to kiss her, to have that one remembrance of this time. Desire stirred within him and he knew he could no more stop the emotions surging through him than he could alter the pattern of the stars that spangled the night sky. He wanted her.

The fierceness of his gaze caught and held Sarah. She'd thought him attractive, but now, here, alone with him on deck, she was spellbound. The night shadows cast his features into stark relief. He was strikingly masculine. She warned herself again that she didn't know him, that he was a stranger she would never see again after tomorrow. Sarah told herself that he had come into her life as quickly and mysteriously as he would leave it, but common sense and facts suddenly did not matter to her wayward heart. She couldn't look away. She told herself that Christopher was her one and only concern; but when Steve bent toward her she could no more resist him than she could have stopped the flow of the Missouri River.

It was a fleeting kiss, a soft, chaste kiss, and for an instant, Sarah forgot everything, enjoying the intimacy of Steve's embrace. Then reality intruded. She stiffened, drawing quickly away from that simple— yet electric—contact. She was supposed to be mourning a dead husband! She couldn't let Steve take such liberties with her, no matter how much she liked it! She had to maintain a protective deception—for Christopher's safety.

"Sarah?" Steve said her name softly, concerned. The kiss had jarred Steve to the depths of his soul. He wanted Sarah. He wanted to deepen the kiss, to part her lips and delve within the honeyed secrets of her mouth. He didn't understand why she was pulling away from him.

"No!" She took another step backwards, determined to break the powerful magnetic attraction he exerted on her. Her expression mirrored her misery at having to deny herself the kiss she desperately wanted. "No, I'm sorry . . ."

When Steve saw the pain in her eyes and heard it in her voice, he thought he understood. Where earlier he'd cursed himself for comparing Christopher to his "father," now he had invaded an even more sacred subject. Whether she was wearing the widow's weeds or not, she was still in mourning for the husband she'd loved, and he'd tried to take advantage of her. He smiled sadly as he lifted one hand to her cheek.

"No, Sarah. Don't be sorry. You've got nothing to apologize for. I'm the one who's sorry. You'd best go in now."

Her heart pounded as she lifted her eyes to his. Was this excitement from the wonder of his kiss or because she had almost betrayed Christopher? She nodded dumbly, not trusting herself to speak.

"I'll be back later." When she reached the door, he said, "Good night, Sarah."

"Good night," she answered softly. She had to get

away from him while she still had the strength to resist. She'd never known anyone like Steve; and if they'd met at another time under different circumstances, they might have come to care for one another. But at this time, in this place, it could never be.

Too upset to sleep, Sarah donned her nightgown and got in bed beside Christopher. As she lay there, she began to plan for the next day. After Steve left them, she would make inquiries about the fastest way to join up with a wagon train. She knew they left from the town near Kansas City called Independence, so finding transport there was another concern. She also had to get a wagon and all the supplies they'd need. It wasn't going to be easy, but she'd do it.

Several hours passed before sleep finally claimed her. She did not hear Steve come back into the cabin, and she never knew that he lay wide awake through the night, almost beside her in the bed so close to hers.

All too soon it was morning. Christopher was up at the crack of dawn, rousing Sarah in his enthusiasm. She sat up to find Steve gone. At first, she thought he hadn't returned at all, but then she saw that his bed was mussed. Where, she wondered had he gone so early? And why?

They dressed, then packed their things in anticipation of leaving the safe haven of the steamer. Ready, Sarah sat with Christopher on the edge of the bed.

"Today's the day," she began.

"What do you want me to do, Aunt Sarah?"

"Just stay right with me, and don't talk to anybody. After we get checked into a hotel, I'll have to go out for a while to see about joining a wagon train. It'll be safest if you wait in the room for me."

"All right."

"Good boy."

"What about Steve?"

"What about him?" she answered evasively.

"Did you ask him to go with us when you talked to him last night?"

"No, I didn't."

"Why not?" the boy pressed. "Why can't you just tell him the truth? He'd help us. I know he would."

"I wish it were that simple, Christopher, but it isn't."

Sarah ignored Christopher's glare. She didn't have the heart to tell him that not everyone was as noble as he believed them to be. Steve was a virtual stranger. A gambler! How could she trust him with their future? He'd forced his way into their lives, and in the process . . .

Sarah's thoughts and excuses conflicted. In the process of barging into their lives, what had Steve done? He'd managed to help them escape from any henchmen Michael might have sent after them. He'd entertained Christopher when the boy had been lonely and desperate for friendship. He'd played the part of her husband with more kindness and chivalry than she could ever have hoped for—and when he'd kissed her, he'd apologized. She could laugh or she could cry, but the parting was inevitable. The time had come.

"If things go well, we could be on the final part of

our trip to California in just a matter of days." She'd tried to cheer him, but he remained glum so she added, "The sooner we get to California, the sooner we'll see your Aunt Angel again."

"Good, I miss her. I hope she's all right."

"Me, too. Now, are you ready for breakfast? I'm sure we'll find Steve waiting for us."

Happier at the thought of seeing Steve, Christopher perked up. "I'm ready."

Sarah, however, was a little nervous at the prospect of facing her "husband" again. What would he expect after the kiss they'd shared last night? If he'd been there in the cabin this morning, as if nothing happened, she would have been fine. But his flight had troubled her. What would he say when they came face to face?

"There he is! There's Father!" Christopher cried, grabbing her arm excitedly when he caught sight of Steve walking with the Langfords. How he wished—with all his heart—that Steve really was his father.

Sarah watched the lean, handsome gambler striding toward her. She remembered all too clearly his kiss and felt shy. She wanted to look away, but she couldn't tear her gaze from him. Breathless, she waited for him to draw near and was completely surprised when Steve walked right up to her, smiled gently in morning welcome, and kissed her on the lips.

"Good morning, darling," he told her, the loving husband filled with devotion. "I'm sorry I had to leave the cabin so early, but there were a few things I had to take care of before we disembark. Then I ran into the Langfords and thought it would be pleasant to share our last breakfast together."

"Of course," was all she could say in her suddenly addled, suddenly sad state. *Our last breakfast together*. The words made her heart ache; but his kiss, so simple and so intimate, sent her senses soaring. Bewildered and perplexed, she almost forgot to greet the other family. "Good morning." She forced herself out of reverie and into awareness.

"Good morning," the Langfords returned.

"Are you ready to eat, Christopher?" Steve asked. He was, Sarah thought, too jovial when soon they would say good-bye.

"I'm starving!" At least Christopher, she noted, could stay in touch with the more mundane appetites that needed to—and could—be met.

"Then, let's go on in. We don't have a lot of time. The captain said we'll be docking within the hour."

As they breakfasted with the Langfords, Steve was attentive but casual. Sarah told herself and tried to believe that the morning's kiss had been merely for show before the Langfords. She was greatly relieved and deeply disappointed.

With the meal ended, good-byes were in order and the families returned to their staterooms. Kansas City lay before them, and it was time to get ready to leave the ship.

Chapter Eleven

This was where he would leave them. This was where they would say good-bye. Steve looked around the room they'd just rented under the name of the Johnson family and wondered how Sarah and Christopher were going to fare. He felt uneasy as he set their bags aside.

"Here you are," Steve announced. "I paid for two nights. If you need more time after that, just see the clerk at the front desk."

Sarah and Christopher had followed him inside and closed the door.

"Thanks," Sarah told him. "I appreciate your help."

"Don't mention it," Steve replied, hedging on leaving.

They'd hired a coach at the riverfront, and on the way to the family-oriented Mason Hotel, where they were now, he'd had the driver stop briefly at the Bartlett Hotel. He'd picked up a message from

George at the desk. The Dillon brothers, George said, were gone. It was safe for him to return to St. Louis.

Two days before, Steve would have been pleased by the news. Now, the only place he wanted to be was with Sarah and Christopher, protecting them. He was certain that they were being followed, but Sarah didn't want his help. She'd made it very plain that he was to go his own way.

"Well, I guess I'll leave you here," he said.

Christopher, unable to control his runaway emotions, protested. "Do you have to go, Steve? Can't you just stay with us?"

"You'll have to talk to your mother about it," the gambler replied gently. He looked at Sarah. "Be careful, Sarah." His voice was gruff.

"Good bye, Steve."

Steve gazed at her, committing to memory every detail of her face. Since he'd kissed her in the moonlight, he'd been torn by conflicting emotions. At first, guilt had assailed him, but as he'd lain awake through the long hours of the night, he'd slowly come to the conclusion that he hadn't done anything wrong. She was a woman—a living, breathing, beautiful woman—and he wanted her. There was nothing dishonorable in that. Her husband had died, but she had not. He had wanted to kiss her, and he was no longer sorry that he had.

Absolved of his guilt, Steve had been unable to resist the temptation to give her a husbandly kiss in front of everyone when he'd first seen her in the morning. He'd known their hours together were numbered, and he'd wanted to take advantage of every minute they had left. The chaste kiss had been far from the sensual embrace he longed to share with her, and it had only reinforced the gnawing hunger he felt for her already. He wanted her. He did not want to leave her; but, because it was what she wanted, he would go.

Steve cursed the nobility of soul that was sending him from their room and out of their lives. Lingering at the door, he hoped Sarah would call out to him, knowing she never would. She didn't want him to stay. Only the boy did.

"Steve. . . . wait!" Christopher's manly control shattered. He'd tried to be strong. He'd tried to do what his Aunt Sarah wanted, but he couldn't. Desperate, Christopher threw his arms around Steve's waist, hugging him tight.

Steve returned the embrace, lifting his troubled gaze to Sarah. Her face was pale and strained, but her expression was unyielding. He had his answer. "Christopher, I'm sorry, but this is the way it has to be." Gently, he pried the boy's arms from around him and with a tender hand cupped his chin so their eyes could meet. It surprised him to find he was crying.

"I'm going to miss you," Christopher choked. It seemed in that moment that everyone he cared about had left him—first, his mother; then, Aunt Angel; and now, Steve.

"I'll miss you, too, but you must promise me something."

"Anything," he snuffled, fighting his tears.

"Be strong for your mother." Steve patted his shoulder.

At the mention of his mother, a pang of longing struck Christopher, and his tears overflowed. "Yes," he agreed, "for my mother I'll be strong."

"Good boy," Steve told him, unaware of the poignant depth of meaning in those words. "I have to go, but I want you to have these." He dug in his pocket and pulled out the deck of cards they'd used the day before. Christopher's smile was watery as he took them, and he held the cards as if they were the finest treasure.

"Thanks."

Steve tousled the boy's blonde hair affectionately and then gave him a tight smile. It was all he could manage. He was going to miss him. "You're welcome, Christopher." Steve glanced at Sarah once more. "Good bye," he said, and taking his bag, he left.

"Bye."

After he'd gone, Christopher stared at the closed door. "I wish he could have stayed, Aunt Sarah."

"I know, sweetheart. I know." The boy's anguish had torn at Sarah's heart, but she could see no alternative. If she had given Steve any sign that she wanted him to remain, she would have had to explain. That was impossible. She would trust no one.

Steve's mood was foul as he strode down the hall to the main staircase that led down two flights to the lobby.

"Mr. Johnson?" The clerk at the counter saw Steve

and called out to him. "Did your friends find you, sir?"

"My friends? No. What friends?" Steve was instantly tense.

"Two men, sir. They asked for you just a few minutes ago."

"What did they want?"

"They didn't say. They didn't leave their names and there's no message except that they'll find you later."

"Did you give them the room number?"

"Yes, sir. I did. I'm sure you'll be hearing from them soon." The clerk leaned back, pleased with his efficiency.

Steve, furious that he'd given out so much information, restrained the impulse to yell. "I must have just missed them," he said, feigning puzzlement. "Is there another way upstairs? I came down this staircase, but I didn't see anyone."

"There's a small flight of steps that goes out through the kitchen, Mr. Johnson. It's restricted to the help, though. I'm sure they wouldn't use that one. Only employees are allowed in that area."

"I see." He took a quick look around the lobby, but recognized no one from the steamboat. He frowned. "The two men—was one tall, the other average?" The clerk nodded. "And they both had dark hair?"

"Yes, sir." The bad feeling that had been growing inside Steve grew worse.

"Could I leave this here?" Steve asked, indicating

his bag. At the clerk's assurance, he left it in his keeping and strolled from the lobby.

It was early in the day, and the streets were busy. Steve darted down the sidewalk and circled to the rear of the building. As he neared the alley that ran behind the hotel, he spotted one of the men from the steamer. His hunch had been right.

He surveyed the rest of the block. The man seemed to be alone. Cautious, but determined to get rid of these men once and for all, Steve walked nonchalantly toward the kitchen and the back staircase.

Steve was no stranger to a good fight, and he was more than ready for this one. It infuriated him that these men had been harassing Sarah. If there was one thing he could do for her before he left it would be to force them to leave her alone.

Steve came abreast of the man, who studiously ignored him; and, in a lightning move, Steve shoved him around the corner of the building into the alley and slammed him up against the brick wall. The man was caught off-guard, and that gave Steve the advantage. Though the stranger tried to fend him off, his blows were ineffectual against Steve's rage-driven savageness. Steve was brutal. His expression was fierce, and his eyes glowed with bloodlust as he gave Sarah's pursuer a violent shake and pinned him against the building.

"What the hell!" the man yelped.

"What's your name?" Steve ground out, glaring at him with death in his eyes.

"Slidell."

"Where's your partner?"

"James ain't here right now." Slidell was quaking in his boots. James wasn't going to be happy.

"Well, Mr. Slidell," Steve spat, "my name's Johnson, Steve Johnson, and I'm real sick of seeing your ugly face every time I turn around. What the hell do you want?" His hands tightened on him, promising more pain.

"Nothin'."

"Then why are you following us?"

"We thought your wife was a woman named Windsor, and we're searching for her, that's all! It was a mistake. Just a mistake! Your woman looks like the Windsor girl, and you got the kid with ya and all—"

"Look, I don't know anything about a woman named Windsor, and I don't care. If you and your partner value your miserable hides, you'll stay away from me and my family." Seething, he gave Slidell another shake.

"Sorry, Mr. Johnson," the other man groveled, truly frightened.

"You damned well better be. You got the wrong woman, my friend, and it'd be a real shame if you and your friend ended up dead over a case of mistaken identity, now, wouldn't it?" Steve growled, tightening his grip ominously.

"Yes." Slidell trembled. "Yes . . . sir."

"Now, stay the hell away from us. If I ever see you or your partner around us again, I won't be so nice." Steve gave him one last vicious shake. "Get out of here!"

Steve watched Slidell scramble away and disappear out onto the street. Still uneasy, Steve made his way to the rear of the hotel and the back staircase. Where was Slidell's partner? He had to make sure Sarah and Christopher were all right.

As Steve moved down the alleyway, the name Slidell had thrown at him hung in his mind. *Windsor.* He wondered if Windsor were Sarah's real name. If so, why she was calling herself Johnson? Angry and worried, he used the back entrance of the hotel so he could hurry up to Sarah's room as quickly as possible.

"Mister! Wait! You can't come in here!" the cook shouted at Steve as he boldly crossed the kitchen to the staircase the desk clerk had described.

"I'm a guest. I'm just passing through."

"But it's not allowed." By the time the cook had shouted it Steve had disappeared, taking the steps two at a time. Steve's strides were purposeful and furious, as he made his way down the second-floor hall. The more he thought about the danger Sarah was facing alone, the angrier he got. Christopher was a child, an innocent, and she was daring to put him in the middle of it! Steve was barely in control when he reached their door.

"Sarah, it's Steve. Open the door," he demanded, knocking loudly as he spoke.

"What's wrong? Why did you come back?" She heard the fury in his tone and opened the door right away. She had been about to leave, anxious to check on the Independence wagon train schedule.

He stalked passed her without an invitation, kicking the door shut behind him. "We're going to talk, and we're going to talk now," he announced tersely.

"About what?" she asked nervously, wondering what had happened in such a short time to make him so angry.

"About the men from the steamboat! About why they were asking about us at the desk and why one of them was outside watching this hotel when I started to leave!" He watched her expression as he spoke, and he saw how pale she went at his revelations.

"Good God!" She'd believed their deception as the Johnsons had worked. It stunned her to find that it hadn't. Panic welled up inside her. Michael's men were so close. They were just a breath away.

"A man named Slidell, if that means anything to you, was waiting outside the hotel for you. Don't you think it's time you told me the truth, *Mrs. Windsor?*"

Sarah had glanced away from him in her frantic effort to collect her thoughts, but when he said their family name, her head snapped up and her eyes widened in fear. She wondered how much more he knew and what he intended to do about it. Her reaction gave Steve his answer. "So your real name is Windsor, and you are the ones they're after." He paused, staring at her, waiting.

"Why did you come back? What do you want from me?" Sarah whispered, trying desperately to pull herself together. Had the men told him everything? Perhaps they'd offered him money to turn them over to Michael.

"What do I want?" he repeated, stunned by her attitude. *"I* don't want a damned thing. I came back here because I thought *you* might want something from me—*like my help."*

"We don't need any help. We'll be fine." The shaky note in her voice betrayed the firmness of her convictions as she tried to stand straight and tall before him.

"Sarah! Listen to me!" Steve was frustrated by her refusal. "Those men are not stupid. I may have warded them off for now, but they're not going to give up. The minute they realize I've left you alone, they'll be back. Tell me what's wrong. Let me help."

"I'll think of a way. We've made it this far." She put an arm around Christopher.

"You need my help!" he insisted furiously.

"No, I don't. This is our problem, not yours. Besides, you must be in trouble yourself. Why else would you have lied about your name in Jefferson City?"

"I can handle my problems," he told her confidently. "You're different. You're a woman with a small boy to protect, going up against two men who mean business. If you want my help, you're going to have to ask for it. I won't force myself on you again."

Sarah's pride warred with her sensibility, and reason won. "You win," she said grudgingly.

"Say it. Say, 'Steve, I need your help.' " Steve refused to make it easy for her. She had foolishly sent him away, knowing the danger. He wanted it plain, before they began again, that she did want him with her. She had to be willing to trust him this time.

Battered, Sarah almost hated him; but Christopher wasn't the least bit worried about pride. He knew they needed Steve with them. If his Aunt Sarah wouldn't say it, he would! "I'll say it! Stay with us, Steve, please? I need you." His terror was evident as he pleaded for Sarah.

"It has to come from your mother. If she doesn't want my help, I won't stay."

"Please, help us." Sarah finally got the words out. "We need you." Her humiliation was deep, but her desire to keep Christopher safe gave her the strength to utter the words. She wondered if she'd ever regret it.

"All right. I will." Steve held out an arm to Christopher and the boy left Sarah to run to his side.

"Thanks." Christopher's heartfelt reply was accompanied by a huge sigh of relief.

"Sarah, I want to know what's going on." Steve's tone indicated the importance of a straight answer. He would settle for no less.

"We have to get away." A shudder wracked her. The men had been so close to capturing them; and, if it hadn't been for Steve, they might have grabbed Christopher today and taken him back to Michael.

"Slidell is gone for now," Steve reminded her, "but I don't know if he believed my story. Where are you heading? Did you have a plan?"

"We've got to get to San Francisco. We'd planned to go by wagon train, but now that they've found us, we'd better take the stage. It's faster and—"

"And it'll be the first place they look." He finished the sentence for her. "There's got to be a better way." He paused to think, and then, still angry that the boy was caught in the middle of this dangerous intrigue, he demanded, "Why did you wait so long to ask me for help? Didn't you realize the danger you were putting Christopher in by trying to do this alone?"

"You think I'm not worried about Christopher?" She stared at him accusingly. "He's the reason we're going to California! I have to keep him safe."

"But why? What are you running from? Who are those men and why do they want Christopher?"

"I can't tell you that." She was tempted to tell him everything. Her instincts told her that Steve was a man she could rely on, but she'd lost faith in her own judgment. She'd been so terribly wrong about Michael. Though Steve had cared enough to come back and warn them about the men outside, she was still unsure. For her own peace of mind, she clung to the pretense of widowhood. "Just know that I'm doing this for Christopher."

Steve could see the fear and wariness in her eyes and decided not to force the issue right then. "What's it going to take to make you trust me?" he asked more gently.

"I learned not to trust in a very painful lesson. Blind trust leads to betrayal."

"Not always, Sarah. Not always." His expression softened. "But we'll take it one step at a time." She had admitted she needed his help, and that was a start.

Steve gazed down at her, his anger easing. Something terrible had happened to them, something so bad she still couldn't bring herself to talk about it. She'd left her home and family and run away with Christopher just to keep him safe, and that had taken courage. Brave and intelligent though she was, Steve also knew she was vulnerable, and it was because of that vulnerability that she needed him. He vowed to himself then and there that he would make sure no one ever harmed her or her son. He would keep them safe; and, perhaps with time, he would come to earn her trust and she would tell him the truth.

"What should we do?" Sarah asked.

"The wagon train still seems like the safest way to go, especially if we're going to keep up the the Johnson-family charade. Stay here, and don't answer the door for anyone else. Christopher?" He turned to the boy.

"Yes, sir?"

"Practice shuffling and dealing while I'm gone. When I get back, I'll play you another game of poker."

"All right!"

Steve left the room and waited in the hall until he heard her turn the lock. Assured for the moment that they were out of harm's way, he left the hotel. Sarah hurried to the front window. She watched the street below until she saw Steve emerge from the hotel, and she kept watch over him until he disappeared around a corner.

It was a strange act of fate, she thought, that had brought Steve Spencer into her life! Twice now, he'd saved her from disaster, and she was glad he'd returned. She would not let herself imagine what could have happened if he hadn't cared enough to help them. Sarah shivered, frightened.

Christopher sat on the edge of the bed, shuffling

the deck of cards with earnest intent. He obviously adored Steve, and it pleased Sarah that he had positive male companionship right now. He needed someone to show him how a real man was supposed to act and how a real man took care of his own.

Sarah stopped in mid-thought, startled by what had just slipped through her mind. *'His own'?* Where had that come from? Of course they were only pretending to be a family, but the fact remained that he'd cared enough to come back and warn them about Slidell. He was willing to help them; and, in return, all he asked was that she trust him.

Sarah frowned. She thought of his kiss and of her reaction. He could have pressed her. He could have forced himself upon her at any time on the steamer, but he hadn't. He'd been a gentleman in every way. He'd been kind and considerate. She knew nothing about him except through his actions, and yet, somehow, that was enough. Lost deep in thoughts of Steve, she sat down to await his return.

Slidell faced a furious James across a table in the back of the riverfront saloon.

"You fool! Didn't you see him coming?"

"Yeah, I saw him coming, but I didn't know he knew we was watching him! It don't matter anyway. I'm telling you we've been following the wrong damned woman."

"I don't believe it. She matches the description. She's even got the kid with her. The only thing that ain't right about it is that there's supposed to be two women."

"Don't you think that's strange? I mean, what if we tracked them all the way here, and it really ain't them? They didn't give no name in St. Louis when they bought train tickets, but this man says they're the Johnsons and it matches what they said when they bought the tickets for the steamer in Jeff City. We better send a wire to Harper and ask him what's going on. He was going to wait in St. Louis to hear from us, wasn't he?"

"Yeah."

"Then let's send the wire. If this is the wrong woman, then where the hell is the right one?"

"That's what we got to find out. There's a helluva lot of money riding on this, and I don't want to be wasting my time."

"It could take a while to get an answer back from him."

"So what? We'll keep watching the hotel to make sure they ain't going nowhere; and when we hear from Harper, we'll have our answer."

It was late in the afternoon when Steve returned. He picked up his bag at the front desk and went straight to the room. Christopher was quick to let him in.

"We're leaving here at midnight," Steve announced once he was inside. "Until then, we'll have supper and stay in the room."

"Where are we going?" Sarah asked. "Why do we have to leave in the middle of the night?"

"I've made arrangements for us to make the trip to

Independence tonight. Tomorrow, we'll buy what we need there, and the day after, we'll head for California. We happened to be lucky enough to arrive here just as a wagon train was forming up. The travel won't be fast, but it's as safe as we're going to get. I've signed us on under my name—Spencer. That should slow Slidell down if he's still after us."

"You don't think he is, do you?" Sarah glanced apprehensively toward the window. Christopher moved closer to her.

"I hope not," Steve said, "but don't count on it. We're going to have to keep watch and be careful."

Sarah and Christopher nodded. "What else can we do?" Sarah asked. "I mean, to get ready?"

"Nothing. When it's time to leave, we'll use the back entrance. We'll be riding to Independence with a shopkeeper who came into town today to pick up extra supplies. He has to get back right away; that's why he's making the trip at night. It won't be comfortable riding in his buckboard, but I guess we'd better get used to traveling by wagon."

"I'd walk it if I had to," Sarah admitted. At last they were taking some action! The long hours of waiting had unnerved her. She liked the idea of slipping out of town under cover of darkness. No one would see them. "Did you see any sign of the men?"

"No. Hopefully, they're gone forever. But if they're not, we'll have a good head start before they realize we've left the hotel."

They ate in the hotel's dining room, then returned to their own room to pass the evening. Steve kept his word to Christopher, and they played cards nonstop with Sarah as audience. When midnight neared, they gathered their things and stealthily left the hotel. With no staff on duty, they walked through the deserted kitchen without incident or notice. The trek to the rendezvous went well, and, to everyone's relief, their ride was waiting for them and ready to leave.

At the hotel in Independence, Sarah and Christopher slept while Steve laid in provisions for the trip to California. Sarah had given him money; and, although he hadn't liked the idea, he had found no argument that could stand up against her forceful insistence.

He returned mid-afternoon to take Sarah and Christopher to the staging area for a look at the prairie schooner they would call home over the next few months. Steve slipped an arm around Sarah's slender waist, not unaware that they looked very much the loving couple as he pointed out their covered wagon.

"We've got everything we need," he explained. "Our six oxen are grazing with the others right now, but they'll be hitched up and ready to go when we pull out at four tomorrow morning. What do you think?"

Christopher let out a whoop and immediately climbed aboard to get a look. Covered by a waterproofed canvas top, the wagon was ten feet long and three-and-a-half feet wide. Steve had stocked it with everything they could possibly need for the trip.

"This is great!" Christopher cried as he scrambled from one end of the cramped wagon to the other.

Perching on the bench seat, he asked, "Can I sit up here all the time? Can I drive?"

"If you can handle the reins," Steve assured him, and Christopher tugged on the leather straps in anticipation.

"It's wonderful," Sarah finally replied. She was very much aware of his arm around her waist, and she was trying to force her thoughts away from the realization that she was going to have to spend the next few months with Steve in the close, intimate confines of that small wagon. And she'd thought the stateroom on the steamer had been too intimate! "But it's not very big, is it?"

"No, it's not," he answered, his eyes darkening at the thought of sleeping so close to Sarah night after night.

Sarah fought against the blush that threatened, but when he smiled down at her, she could only gaze up at him, all rational thought struck from her mind. Steve was kind and considerate. His protective nearness offered her shelter in what was the storm of her life. It would have been easy to turn all her troubles over to him, but she had to maintain her independence.

"Don't worry," he went on, sensing her distress and wanting to calm her. "From what I understand, the sleeping arrangements depend on the weather. Most men spend the nights outside under the wagons. Women and children stay inside."

"Oh." He heard the relief in her voice.

"We spend tonight here, so we need to move our bags out of the room. Are you ready to go?"

Christopher climbed down from his post on the driver's seat, and as they started back to the hotel Steve kept his hand possessively at Sarah's waist. He cast one last look over his shoulder at the covered wagon, hoping for rain.

Chapter Twelve

New Orleans

"Are you crazy?" Lucky blurted out as he stared at Angel, unbelieving. They had been up only a few minutes, but she had already announced a change in travel plans. Now, she'd said, this very morning they would be leaving for California on horseback.

"Crazy, no. In a hurry to get to Christopher, yes," Angel answered calmly with a smile.

Lucky, however, saw nothing worth smiling about. "The deal was we were sailing. There ain't no reason for us to have to ride across country," he argued stubbornly.

"The deal was you would accompany me to California, period," she reminded him.

"I thought we were going by boat," the boy persisted.

"What difference does it make how we go as long as we get there? We should make much better time this way." She couldn't understand why he seemed so upset.

"And get ourselves lost or killed or worse doing it!"

"We will not. Do you remember the man we saw at dinner last night?"

"Yeah."

"He's Blade Masters, and he's an experienced guide. I've hired him to accompany us." When Lucky shot her a skeptical scowl, she added, "He knows the land. Everything's going to be fine."

So now Lucky knew what last night's meeting had been about, but he didn't feel any better. If anything, he felt cornered. "This is stupid! I ain't goin'," he declared. "You can forget the deal. Just pay me what you owe me for the time I've been with you, and I'll clear out."

His demand brought Angel up short. She'd prided herself on having come to understand him quite well. She hadn't expected this reaction. Her gaze met his then, and she could see the tinge of fear behind his bluff and bravado. "Why don't you tell me what's really bothering you, Lucky?"

"There ain't nothin' bothering me," he answered, defiantly. "I just quit. That's all."

"Well, in that case, I have bad news for you."

"Oh, yeah?"

"Yeah," she rejoined. "Our deal stands only if you accompany me all the way to California. If you walk out on me now, you get nothing. We agreed to the terms that I would pay you when we got there and not before."

He glowered sullenly. He remembered the conversation.

"Now," Angel went on, "do you want to tell me the truth? What's the matter? Don't you know how to ride?"

"I know how to ride all right," he blustered. He couldn't lose face by admitting that he'd had little experience with horses.

"Then, what is it?" she urged, her voice quiet and encouraging.

Lucky sulked. He was caught. If he walked away now without telling her the truth, he'd be penniless in a strange town. If he told her the truth . . .

"I know how to ride," he mumbled reluctantly. "I just ain't no good at it."

Angel knew how hard it had to be for him to tell her that he couldn't do something. "You want to know something?"

"What?"

"I'm no good, either," she confided.

"You're not?"

"No. In fact, I'm terrible; but that doesn't matter. By the end of today, I plan to be riding with the best of them."

"Think I can learn that fast, too?" He was buoyed by her confession.

"I'm sure of it. It's really simple. All you have to do is hold on with your knees and point the horse in the right direction."

"What if I don't do it right? What if—"

"How difficult can it be? You'll get the feel of it."

"You're sure?" He was still doubtful.

"Just pull on the reins whichever direction you want to go. . . . and remember to always mount from the left side." Angel simplified what little she knew. *A right turn here, a left turn there. It couldn't be that much different from driving a carriage, could it?*

"If you know so much about it, how come you're no good at it?" Lucky asked.

"I don't like horses." She started to giggle, and after a moment Lucky joined in.

"You're going to have to start liking them real fast," he chortled, and Angel nodded.

"Real fast. We don't want Masters to think that we can't make the trip. We've got to convince him we can ride. All right?"

"I won't tell him a thing," Lucky promised. If Angel couldn't ride, his own embarrassment no longer mattered. "All I have to do is hold on tight. That's what you said, right?"

"Right. Now, let's see what we've got to wear."

Angel dug out her boots and the blue riding habit with its matching hat. Fortunately, her purchases for Lucky had included practical clothes. While the boy dressed, she brushed her hair, braiding it in a single, thick plait before going downstairs for a quick breakfast. They'd gotten up early, so it was barely nine when they returned to their room to wait for Blade.

Minutes, then hours, passed. As noon neared, Angel grew more and more anxious. Had the gunfighter taken her money and run? When the knock finally came, Angel almost threw the door wide open without caution. She stopped only at the last minute.

231

"Who is it?" she demanded, her hand on the door-knob.

"Masters." Only one word, but she recognized his voice. "I've come with your gear."

"Good morning, Mr. Masters," Angel greeted him as she came face to face with him for the first time that day. She stared up at him in fascination, struck again by the incredible maleness of him. From the powerful set of shoulders to his lean waist, he seemed to fill the entire doorway. He was dressed in dark western garb, and it made him seem even more intriguing. His dark shirt was open at the neck, revealing the strong, tanned column of his throat, and he wore tight dark pants. A black hat was pulled low over his eyes. His gun rode low on his hip. Angel realized then that he really was half-Indian for there was an untamed aura about him. She felt no fear. She'd wanted a man capable of dealing with threats and the unexpected, and Blade Masters was her man.

"Mornin', Miss Roberts." Blade spoke politely, but his gaze swept over her. Their relationship was strictly business, but he was a man who appreciated beauty when he saw it. She wore a tiny ridiculous hat that was far from practical but was somehow endearing. Her hair, pulled back but not pinned up, was styled into a long, golden braid that hung nearly to her waist. The blueness of her riding habit complemented her fair complexion, and its style, nipped in as it was at her tiny waist, emphasized the full curve of her bosom. She was, he acknowledged, one good-looking woman.

"Come in."

"Thank you, ma'am." He removed his hat and turned his concentration to his job, pushing all thoughts of her attractiveness from his mind. She was the boss. Picking up the parcels he'd brought with him, he stepped inside the room.

"This is my brother, Lucas, but everyone calls him Lucky. Lucky, this is Mr. Masters, our guide."

"Hello." Lucky got his first up-close look at the man he'd thought imposing the night before and found him even more impressive. This was someone you didn't mess with.

Blade nodded to the young boy, appraising him. Though he, too, was wearing clothes more suited to a Sunday outing than a cross-country trip, Blade quickly judged him healthy and able to handle the rigors of the trek they were about to embark on. He wished he was as sure about the woman.

"We're ready to leave, if you are," Angel announced, pleased with herself. Everything was coming together.

"I'm ready, but you two aren't," Blade stated.

"What do you mean?" she countered defensively.

"I told you last night, this wasn't going to be a church picnic or ride in the park, Miss Roberts. What you're wearing wouldn't last a day, let alone weeks and months." He thrust one of the big, bulky, paper-and-string-wrapped parcels at her. "Here."

She took the bundle from him, confused. "What is it?"

"I had a feeling you might need some cross-country traveling clothes. This one's for you, Lucky. I

233

guessed at the sizes, but I think everything should fit." He handed the second parcel to the boy.

"Thank you, sir."

"My name's Blade, son. Use it. And don't thank me. Your sister told me to buy what you needed for the trip, so I did."

Angel ripped open her package and found a leather riding skirt, two practical, long-sleeved white blouses, a pair of leather gloves, walking boots, and a hat. The hat was western style, nothing like the prim little small-brimmed bonnet she'd been wearing. "You expect me to change?"

"If you've got any sense you will." His gray eyes challenged her. "The sun gets mighty hot in the afternoon, and that little thing you're wearing isn't going to help a bit."

She gave him a tight nod. She'd hired him for his expertise, and she'd be foolish to disregard anything he said. Lucky, tearing open his package, discovered a pair of boots, denim pants, two shirts, and a hat. He smiled with childish delight. Since meeting Angel, he had acquired more clothes than he'd ever owned before. He immediately set about changing.

"I've bought horses for us: three mounts and two pack animals. They're saddled and ready to go down at the livery. We can leave immediately." He walked to the door. "I'll wait outside." The door swung shut in Blade's wake, and Angel hurried behind the small screen to undress. Lucky changed by the bed.

"Everything fits," he announced rather proudly as he stared down his new clothes.

"Mine do, too. Even the boots." Angel was

amazed at Masters' ability to judge their sizes. He was, she realized, remarkably observant. She stepped out from behind the partition. "What do you think?" she asked hesitantly.

Lucky studied her carefully. "You look nice. Different, but nice," he concluded.

"What does that mean?" Angel moved to the mirror over the washstand and peered at herself in trepidation. She found the reflection reassuring. The leather split-skirt fit her perfectly, clinging to her hips as if it had been made for her and her alone. It was a little shorter than her usual length, hitting her at mid-calf, but with the higher boots no expanse of leg showed. The white blouse fit well, and she pulled on the gloves with ease. Satisfied, she examined Lucky. In his denims he looked like a miniature cowboy. "You look nice, too," she assured him with a quick hug. "Now, we'd better hurry and get our things together. Mr. Masters is waiting."

"He asked us to call him Blade, Angel," Lucky reminded her as he stuffed the "Sunday-picnic" clothes into his bag.

"Blade." She tried it out and decided she liked the name. It suited him. Had his Indian mother chosen it? Or his father? She would probably never know. "Yes. Well, *Blade* is waiting."

"We're ready, Blade." Lucky opened the door.

Blade surveyed Angel, admiring the way the leather skirt fit her rounded hips. He adjusted the boy's hat, satisfied. He nodded in approval. "Where are your bags?"

Angel indicated the luggage—three ample suitcases. The guide scowled. "We've only got room enough for two."

"But—" Angel began and then thought better of it. It made sense to travel light and fast. When they reached California, she could buy more. She decided quickly what to discard. Then, armed with only the most basic wardrobe, money, and Lucky's new possessions, they left the room and civilization behind.

"Oh, boy." Lucky gazed up—way up—at the horse he was expected to mount. Big was an understatement. The red-brown creature towered over him, massive in height and girth. Lucky wondered how he was supposed to get on the damned thing, let alone control it.

The horse, sensing his clumsiness, swung its neck around to size him up. It wheezed, exhaling loudly, and its breath blew puffs of hot air on Lucky's skin. The boy felt clammy—and sick.

"All right, horsey, let's see how we're going to do this," Lucky muttered with false affection, trying to remember everything Angel had told him about horsemanship. *Mount from the left side* rang in his thoughts, so he made a grab for the pummel but was too short to grasp it. He was looking for something to stand on when Blade appeared.

"Let me give you a hand," Blade offered, helping Lucky into the saddle. He'd deliberately bought the biggest, sturdiest horses he could find. The trip would be long, and he wanted the best mounts available. He'd assigned the boy the quietest of the three saddle horses, a strong roan gelding named Blue.

"Thanks," Lucky told him as he settled in astride the huge horse. He sat easily, his features schooled into a feigned calm that gave Blade the impression that he was confident and knew exactly what he was doing.

"You comfortable?" Blade checked the stirrups to make sure they were the right length.

"Yeah, I'm fine."

"Good boy." Blade handed him the reins and went on to see about the pack horses.

Lucky cast a glance down at the ground and swallowed nervously. His hands tightened unconsciously on the reins, and Blue sidestepped skittishly. At that unexpected move, the boy grabbed on the pommel and hung on. When the horse calmed, he let out his breath and noticed that Angel had already mounted up. She seemed at home on horseback.

Shifting uneasily, Lucky tried to get used to the feel of the wide, powerful animal beneath him. It was a strange sensation. He remembered what Angel had told him about hanging on with his legs, so he tightened his knees. Again the horse moved restlessly, and it impressed him to know that he really did have influence over the big animal's behavior. His confidence grew—a little.

"Ready?" Blade asked as he picked up his own reins and swung up onto his mount in a fluid, easy motion.

"Ready," they echoed in unison.

Oblivious to their inexperience, Blade turned his horse and started out of town, the pack animals in tow. Angel, determined not to let Blade know she was a novice rider, had already made up her mind that she would match him mile for mile. She locked her gaze on Blade, confident that she could learn by watching and imitating him. When he used his heels against his mount's sides, she did likewise, and her mount moved easily after Blade's. Lucky urged his horse on, too, and Angel let the boy in front of her so she could keep an eye on him. Then, with little fanfare, they were on their way.

Her shaken confidence returned as they headed north out of New Orleans. Soon, they would be far away and safe from Michael.

Blade had seen their initial awkwardness in the saddle, but had assumed that it was because they had not ridden recently. He kept the pace slow as they made their way out of the city, his plan for the trip simple. They would follow the river road as far north as the Red River, then take the northwest cutoff. No matter which way they traveled overland, the terrain would be rough. Louisiana roads were notoriously bad, and when it rained—as it often did this time of year—they were non-existent. The woman's refusal to sail suggested that there was more behind this trip than she had admitted. But all he was concerned about was the money. If his boss had insisted they ride, they would ride.

Blade continued at a moderate rate until they were away from the city. It was only then, when he urged his mount to go faster, that the truth became apparent. Miss Angela Roberts bounced in the saddle, and her brother, hands wrapped in the reins, looked to be holding on for dear life. Blade slowed until they all were riding abreast.

"Something wrong?" Blade asked, as amused as he was annoyed.

"No. Why do you ask?" Angel parried his question, trying to avoid the inevitable.

"How much riding experience did you say you had?" Blade asked, a mocking gleam in his gray eyes.

"Enough," Angel answered tersely, uncomfortable in the face of his scrutiny. "If I look a little awkward, it's because I always rode sidesaddle before. That's all." *It was not a real lie,* she told herself. *The three times she'd ridden in Philadelphia, she had ridden sidesaddle.* "I'll be fine in a little while. Riding astride takes some getting used to."

"What about your brother? Why is he having such a hard time?" Blade transferred his assessing gaze to the boy, whose face was grim and resolute.

"No, Blade. I'm doing fine. Honest." Lucky gave a smile, but when Blue side stepped, he quickly grabbed the pommel.

"You're holding the reins too tight, Lucky. Ease up on them, and he'll handle better," Blade instructed without censure, knowing the importance of a young boy's pride.

Lucky did as he was told, and Blue immediately calmed.

"Is there anything else we should know, Mr. Masters?" Angel asked for the sake of expediency. If she were doing something wrong, she wanted to hear about it now. She was proud, but she wasn't stupid.

"The name's Blade."

"All right," she agreed. "My name's Angela." She refused to tell him her nickname, wanting to keep some degree of formality between them.

"It's a pretty name." His gaze was warm upon her.

She flushed. "Thank you. Now, about our riding . . ."

"We'll keep it at an even clip until you two get the feel of it."

"No. Don't slow down for us. The faster we move, the better," Angel insisted.

"We've got a long way to go," he cautioned. "If you wear yourself out the first day, you'll only lose ground later." He wondered at her need to hurry. Ignoring his warning, Angel dug her heels into her horse's sides, and her mare ran on ahead of the other two.

"You doing all right, boy?" Blade asked Lucky, one eye on the boy, the other on his demanding 'boss.'

"Yes, sir."

"Guess we'd better catch up with your sister, then." Blade, too, spurred his horse to action.

Lucky saw how Blade sat in the saddle and copied him. He saw how Blade held the reins with ease, and he did the same. He saw how Blade moved as one with the horse, and he tried too. It was much harder than it looked, but Lucky wasn't about to give up. Blade Masters was a man who knew what he was doing, and Lucky wanted to be just like him.

The miles unfolded endlessly as the day progressed, but Angel didn't change her mind. Doggedly, she kept herself upright in the saddle even though her body screamed for relief from the incessant pounding of the horse's pace. The afternoon heat was sweltering, but she focused solely on the mud and the rutted road in front of her. She'd had no idea that the roads were this bad, but she said nothing. Blade had warned her, and she'd look the fool if she said anything now after only a few hours. Angel thought she understood why the natives traveled mainly by boat.

No one spoke. Blade because he preferred not to; Angel and Lucky because every jarring movement of their mounts knocked the wind out of them. They passed endless fields of sugar cane and cotton. In the distance they could see the plantation estates of the owners of those fields, and Angel found herself duly impressed by their elegance. Most of the mansions were at least two stories tall with massive columns supporting the verandas that encircled them. Lush, green lawns spread out in manicured splendor before the southern palaces, and huge oaks draped with Spanish moss offered cooling shade and added beauty and a romantic mystique.

"Are you hungry?" Blade asked, finally breaking the silence as the sun climbed above them. "There's a tavern a few miles ahead." They'd been on the road for nearly three hours, and he was certain they were both in need of a rest.

"I am!" Lucky spoke up without waiting for Angel to answer. The small breakfast, eaten hurriedly that morning, hadn't been nearly enough; but that was not his real motivation. He'd had enough and would have volunteered to take a bath just to get off Blue for a while. He glanced at Angel hoping she wanted down as much as he did.

"All right, let's stop." Angel answered, unaware that Lucky let out a whoop of joy at her decision. She was too busy wondering if she was going to be able to dismount, let alone stand up, once they reached the tavern.

The Cypress Inn was a ramshackle building. It had seen better days, but Angel didn't give it a thought. She was grateful to come to a stop at the hitching rail and sat quietly, too tired to move.

Blade swung down from his horse and looped his reins, along with the reins of the pack horses, around the rail. He had started inside when he noticed Angel's strained expression.

"Something wrong?" he asked with a straight face.

"No." Her retort was instantaneous. She refused to let him see her in a state of weakness. With every ounce of strength she had left, she swung her leg over her horse's back and slid, less than gracefully, to the ground. She leaned heavily against her mare, her legs like mush. After a moment, she took a few tentative steps, but she kept a supportive hand on her horse, just in case. She was relieved when feeling returned to her legs, and she was able to walk normally.

Lucky, too, was having trouble. He had managed to get down all right but could barely stand. His knees felt like water, and he was slow to follow Blade. He watched with admiration as Blade walked ahead of them with his usual easy stride. The long hours in the saddle had had no effect on him. In a valiant attempt, Lucky mimicked his swagger, but his wobbly legs turned it into a stagger.

In a move that both surprised and pleased Angel, Blade waited and held the door for them. She entered the cool, dark interior of the inn first and was glad to see that it wasn't crowded.

The menu was sparse, but nourishing, and after they'd ordered, Angel went to freshen up. Crude though the facilities were, she did manage to wash her face and hands and she felt a little better when she returned to the table. As she crossed the room to rejoin them, she noticed how intently Lucky was listening to Blade. Her first reaction was negative for she feared the boy might accidentally reveal their secrets, but then she realized how starved Lucky was for male companionship and how good being with Blade was for him. Certainly, she could help him a lot, but there was no dismissing the influence a man had on a young boy. She hoped that the boy would not reveal any of their private dealings to the gunfighter. It was essential that her story remain intact.

The food was plentiful, if not particularly good, and as far as Angel and Lucky were concerned their time at the inn was too short. It seemed the moment they began to feel normal, it was time to mount up once more. Blade appeared behind Angel and helped her mount. His big, strong hands encircled her waist, and he lifted her with relative ease into the saddle. Their eyes met as he handed her the reins, but she could read nothing in the dark gray depths. He helped Lucky up, too, and they headed north.

"I'm glad you came back!" Cyril exclaimed as the man approached the desk.

"You saw her?"

"I think I did. Of course, at the time I didn't realize why she looked so familiar. Let me look at that portrait again," the clerk suggested.

"Here." Brad Watkins held out Angel's picture, and Cyril smiled widely.

"That's her, all right. She was in here last night."

"She was?" Watkins was excited. At last, a break!

"Yes, sir. It was the strangest thing, too. A lady like her . . ." He gave a disapproving shake of his head. "I would have never thought—"

"You would have never thought, what?" he prodded.

"Why, her asking for Blade Masters, that's what. She said her name was Angela Roberts and that she wanted to see Masters. When he wouldn't come out of the bar to see her, she went traipsing right on in there looking for him!"

Watkins cursed. A day late! "What happened?"

"I don't rightly know. She and Masters sat in the back of the bar talking for a while, and then they left here together. I never did see her after that. He came back, though."

"Where's this Masters now? What room's he in? I have to talk to him."

"He checked out this morning first thing."

"Damn!"

"Do I get the reward money you were offering?"

"First, tell me this. Did she have a boy with her? Or another woman?"

"No. She was alone."

The man paused thoughtfully, then told the desk clerk. "If you find out where they went after they left here, I'll double this." He handed over the promised twenty dollars.

"Where are you staying again?"

The man gave him the name of his hotel, and Cyril nodded.

"If I find out anything more, I'll send word right away."

Chapter Thirteen

Night. At last, it was night. Angel lay in her bedroll near the small campfire, staring up at the star-spangled sky with unseeing eyes. She'd thought herself a strong person. She'd thought she could handle anything. She'd thought she felt as bad as she was going to feel when she'd gotten off her horse; but as the hours had passed, her body had tightened up on her, and she'd found out just how wrong she'd been.

She ached everywhere. Blade had watched her throughout the evening, gauging her resilience. Steeped in pride, she'd refused to let him know her agony. She'd pretended she was fine and had almost convinced herself—until now. Lying flat on her back on the lumpy, unyielding ground, she'd discovered to her mortification that she was stuck. She couldn't move.

Angel grimaced in the darkness as she tried unsuccessfully to shift positions. She'd never known the ground could be so hard! She wanted to be quiet because Lucky and Blade were sleeping nearby and she didn't want them to wake up and find out how badly she was hurting. Angel slowly tried to lever herself up on one elbow so she could roll over.

Angel hadn't meant to groan. The sound involuntarily escaped from her as she moved and unexpected pain exploded through her body. The groan surprised Angel as much as the way Blade, in the blink of an eye, was on his feet, his gun drawn and ready, peering into the darkness that surrounded them.

"Angela?" he said her name quietly, not wanting to cause alarm, yet ready for trouble.

Angel had been holding her breath, not only from the pain, but from the lightning way Blade had moved to protect them. He hadn't made a sound, but had been ready to defend them almost instantly. It unnerved her a little to know that he was that good, and she trembled. "I'm fine. I didn't mean to disturb you. It's nothing."

It was a bald lie. The truth was Angel was caught in mid-roll and couldn't move one way or the other. She gave a desperate shove, and another grunt escaped her as she managed to roll onto her stomach.

Blade, aware of her stiff, awkward movements, had admired her pluck. She was not a complainer. Now, however, he knew it was time to step in. Stiff-necked, proud woman that she was, his "boss" would suffer all night rather than ask for his help. Knowing at least that much about her personality, Blade holstered his gun, reached in his saddlebags, and hunkered down beside her.

"Lie still," he commanded.

"What do you think I'm trying to do?" she asked, annoyed. She looked at him over her shoulder, a movement that caused her untold pain. "What do you want?"

"I want to help you."

"Just go away. I'll be fine." Forcing a bravado she didn't feel, Angela tried to hide the extent of her helplessness.

"If you think you're sore tonight, wait until tomorrow," Blade chuckled. "Now, take off your shirt." He delivered the order in a deliberately gruff voice. If she wouldn't accept it gracefully, he would force her to yield to the help she needed.

"Why?"

"Because I'm going to use this liniment on you." He held up a bottle for her inspection and waited as she read the label by the firelight. "If I don't, you'll be so sore in the morning that we'll have to move at a snail's pace and we won't make any time at all." When she still hesitated, he chided, "I thought you were in a hurry to get to your fiancé. You'll be the one holding us back if you can't stay on your horse." He sat on his heels, waiting for her response.

Although irritated by his impeccable logic, Angel could not deny the truth in his words. If she felt bad now, how would she feel after lying in one position for the rest of the night? She regarded Blade frankly. "The liniment will really help?"

"I promise you'll feel better."

"All right. Use it," she told him. But as her eyes met his, she felt a disturbing response to his presence. "Just be careful where you put it."

"Don't worry. I'll be *very* careful," he said slowly. "This is strictly an employer/employee relationship—unless you want to change our agreement?"

"No!" she protested quickly, and when he answered she could hear the laughter in his voice.

"I didn't think so. Now, sit up—let me help you—and take your blouse off. You'll notice a change by morning."

With Blade's assistance Angel managed to rise to a sitting position and awkwardly began to unbutton her blouse. Blade watched her free the top button, then the second one. His gaze was fixed on her slender fingers as she worked the third button where it fastened over her breasts. His throat tightened, and his concentration grew fierce as he waited for the pearl restraint to slip through the buttonhole. Suddenly, he wanted to be the one freeing that button. He wanted to be the one baring the treasure hidden beneath the protective layer of cloth. When she loosed the button, he caught a glimpse of the creamy slope of her breasts above the lacy edge of her camisole, and his heart slammed against his ribs. Quickly, he swung his gaze away. Over and over in his mind, he repeated, *She's the boss. She's the boss.*

Angel finished the last button and attempted to shrug out of the blouse, but the movement was excruciatingly painful.

"Here, let me," Blade offered. Without giving her opportunity to protest, he slipped the garment gently from her shoulders. Laying the blouse aside, he opened the bottle of liniment and poured some into the palm of his hand to warm it.

"This will go on better if you lie back down."

Angel managed to stretch out once again on her blanket.

Blade stared down at her as she lay quietly before him. Burnished by the flickering light of the campfire, she was a golden goddess, and another kind of heat began to burn low in his body. He traced the graceful line of her neck and shoulders with his eyes and his unbidden stirrings of desire grew even stronger.

Blade told himself this was business. He was always in control, and he meant to stay that way. He was going to get his ranch, and she was going to California to get married. It didn't matter that one of the thin straps from the delicate web of her camisole had slipped down her shoulder. All that mattered was that he massage the liniment into her soft, satiny flesh and be done with it.

Giving himself a stern mental shake, Blade forced his errant thoughts back under tight control. She was his boss. A man didn't kiss his boss, but then he'd never had a boss like Angela Roberts before. The thought brought a wry smile to his lips.

"This may feel a little cold at first," he said finally, warning her that he was about to begin.

"I'm ready. Go ahead." Angel had her head turned to one side and her eyes closed. Whatever he was going to do to her, she couldn't feel any worse than she did right now.

Blade brushed her thick, golden braid aside and then nudged the other camisole strap down to give him unhampered access to her neck, shoulders, and back. When he reached out to begin his massage, it startled him to find that his hands were shaking. By sheer force of will, he stilled them and then spread the lotion evenly over her shoulders. He rubbed it in, marveling at the silken softness of her. Beneath the satin of her skin, though, Blade could feel the terrible tightness of strained muscles, and he kneaded her neck and shoulders, easing her misery.

As his big hands worked their magic, Angel drew a ragged breath. She was surprised he could be so gentle. His massage felt more like a caress than a curative. He knew exactly where she was having the most pain and exactly the right amount of pressure to use to relieve it. His sure expertise lulled her. When he started to work down her spine, spreading his hands across the width of her back, it felt so good she couldn't suppress a moan.

At the sound, Blade stopped immediately. "Did I hurt you?"

"Yes," she managed in a husky, lethargic whisper, "but it hurt good, if that makes any sense."

"It does," Blade told her, and he resumed working his way down her spine, stopping only when he came to the top of the dangerously low camisole. He stared down at his hands upon her back, noticing how dark they seemed against her pale skin. Another surge of desire shot through him. Blade wanted to press a kiss to the nape of her neck. He wanted to take her in his arms and strip away the swathe of silk that separated her flesh from his. Angela was lovely. Angela was beautiful. Angela was lying quiet and expectant. He wanted to . . . *Angela was his boss.* The thought screamed through his senses, jolting him back to reality. He stopped cold, not trusting himself any further, and withdrew from contact with her.

"Are you done?" Angel asked, jarred by the cessation of his hynotic touch. She couldn't imagine why he'd suddenly stopped and then realized that the sharp-edged pain had dulled to a throb.

"For tonight," Blade answered a little more curtly than he'd meant to as he picked up her blouse. "Do you feel any better?"

"Much."

"Let's get your blouse back on."

He watched as she started to sit up, greatly relieved when she repositioned the camisole straps. He wrenched his gaze away from the smooth arc of her throat and the softly sculptured line of her bosom beneath the clinging undergarment. She was a temptation, and Blade gritted his teeth against the baser urges that filled him. When she was ready, he held her blouse so she could slip her arms into the sleeves.

"You'll need the liniment again tomorrow night," he advised her, and Angel grunted a reply as she lay back down. She was so exhausted and finally relaxed, now that the pain was gone, that she was already drifting into blessed oblivion.

"Well, good night." He got to his feet.

Angel was almost asleep when she murmured. "Blade . . . thanks."

Blade scowled, annoyed that his body responded to the soft sound of her voice. He tightened the lid on the liniment a little too tightly and stuffed it back into his saddlebag. As he lay down on his own bedroll, Blade was ready to swear out loud. Before, Angela had been the one who couldn't sleep; now, he was going to be the one desperate for rest. This time it was his body that was aching, but for a very different reason.

He stared up at the starry sky. She would need another massage tomorrow. Was he dreading or looking forward to it? Then he remembered the reason for her desperate trip to California—her beloved fiancé. With an animal-like growl, Blade rolled onto his stomach in search of sleep.

Angel awoke before daybreak. As she sat up in her bedroll, she was pleased to discover that she felt reasonably good. The liniment had worked wonders, and she threw off her blanket. But when she tried to stand, the deadness she'd felt in her legs yesterday had transformed into raw agony. She bit her lip to keep from crying out loud as she struggled to her feet.

"Good morning, Angel!" Lucky was exceedingly cheerful as he brought her a cup full of fresh, hot coffee.

"Good morning," she returned, wondering how he could be so happy. Surely, he had to be aching as much as she was. "How do you feel this morning?"

"Fine, why?"

"I'm a little sore, and I thought you might be, too."

"No. I don't hurt at all."

"It must be because you're young," she sighed with a smile, envious of his youth and vigor.

"Well, I've been up for over an hour helping Blade.

He's teaching me how to take care of the horses," he told her proudly.

"And you're a fast learner," the gunfighter said as he came to see how Angel was doing. "How are you?"

"Half of me is fine, but the other half. . . . How long will it be before all parts of me are working in harmony again?"

"About a week. But when we start across Texas, it's going to be a much harder ride. At least here we've got some roads, bad as they are. Once we leave Louisiana, we'll be riding cross-country."

Angel gave a lift of her chin as she replied, "Then I'll just have to work that much harder at getting in shape, won't I?"

"You're doing well, but you can expect today to be the roughest of the whole trip."

"Then let's get started and get it over with."

"You're not intimidated by much, are you?" he asked, his respect for her growing.

"I miss Christopher. It's worth any price to me to get to him as fast as I can."

"In that case, we'd better get going." Blade bristled at the mention of her fiancé. He didn't have any use for a man who would let his woman travel this way unprotected. Had he been in love with a woman who lived back East, he would have gone for her himself. He would never have left her to fend for herself so that she ended up at the mercy of a man like him. Blade kept his opinion to himself, though, for as she'd aptly pointed out during their first meeting, he was working for her.

"Good."

They cleared camp, and Blade and Lucky saddled the horses. Angel watched as Lucky worked side-by-side with him. It was only their second day together, and she could see a change in the boy already. While he'd been quick to pick up what she could teach him, he was even more avid to learn from Blade. Whatever Blade told him to do, he willingly made an earnest attempt. And if he had any trouble, the gunfighter was immediately there, explaining what he'd done wrong and showing him how to avoid the problem in the future.

It was exactly what Lucky needed—a man's guiding hand. She was glad Blade was so kind to him. How, she wondered, could he be so nice, so gentle, and yet make his living as a hired gun?

Lucky had just finished saddling his own horse and had his foot in the stirrup when it happened. Blue gave a sideways leap, startled by a movement in the grass near his hooves, and sent the boy tumbling to the ground. Lucky thought it was his own clumsiness that had caused him to fall. Embarrassed, he started to get up when Blade's voice rang out cold and clear.

"Don't move."

The boy froze in place, and the shot that immediately followed accurately parted the eighteen-inch distance between the boy and the nervous horse's legs. It hit the poisonous snake as it was about to strike Lucky. The bullet smashed into the slithering, deadly creature with such force that it tossed the three-foot reptile into the air.

"Oh God!" Any thought of her own discomfort

was struck from Angel's mind as she raced to Lucky. She dragged him into her arms and clutched him to her. "Are you all right?"

"I'm fine," Lucky managed, shivering uncontrollably in the aftermath of such a close call, but feeling completely safe in Angel's arms.

Angel lifted her frantic blue-eyed gaze up to the gunfighter, and Blade saw how frightened she was. "How did you know?"

"I was lucky enough to see it in time. That's all," he answered, checking the body. It was unquestionably dead.

"That was some shot!" Lucky blurted out. From the haven of Angel's arms, he could see the snake that Blade held up for his inspection. He was in awe of Blade's perfect aim. "You're good!"

"Sometimes it pays to be fast." Blade slid his gun back in his holster; and, tossing the snake aside, he gave the boy an affectionate pat on the shoulder.

"Will you teach me how to shoot like that?" Lucky asked excitedly, moving away from Angel to follow him as he went to settle Blue down. "I want to learn how to shoot just like you. Where did you learn? You must have been using a gun for a long time to be that fast and that good. How old were you when you first—"

"Whoa!" Blade stopped him, not at all happy with the rosy picture the boy was painting of gunplay. "Knowing how to shoot a gun is important out where I come from, but a sidearm is not a toy. It can kill more than snakes, you know."

Lucky looked up at him with great respect. "When did you get your first gun?"

"I was a little older than you. I needed it for hunting."

Angel remembered the story she'd heard the two gossips relate and she wondered what it was he'd been hunting at such a young age—food or revenge?

"Could you show me how to shoot just a little?" Lucky toned down his excitement, trying to convince Blade that he wouldn't be wild with a gun.

"There's no such thing as shooting 'just a little.' You either know how to handle a gun or you don't." Blade eyed the boy, seeing his excitement and his intelligence. "Once we're out in the wild, away from people, we'll see."

"I'll be careful, Blade. I promise."

"Being careful is important, but you also have to be smart."

"I can be smart," Lucky wheedled.

"You have to think before you pull the trigger."

"I'll try."

Blade and Lucky regarded each other seriously, brown eyes meeting gray without guile. Blade saw in the boy the eager innocence he'd possessed at that age, and he felt an even closer affinity. Lucky saw in Blade the caring male authority-figure he'd lacked for so many years. This was a man deserving of his respect. He was brave and had just saved his life. Lucky thought he was wonderful and intended to do everything he could to learn to be just like him.

Blade broke the spell by handing Lucky the reins to his horse. "Your sister's going to be after us if we don't get on our way. Want to try mounting up again?"

Lucky flashed him a wide grin and almost vaulted into the saddle. "Was that better?"

"Much." Blade patted Blue on the rump and went to Angela, who waited and watched.

"That was close," she commented in a strained voice.

"Everything's all right. The snake's dead, and Lucky's fine."

"Thank you."

For a moment they just looked at each other, then Blade answered her. "You're welcome. He's a good boy. I wouldn't want anything to happen to him."

"Neither would I. I love him very much." Angel realized as she said it that it was the truth. Lucky had claimed a place in her heart.

"Need some help mounting?" Blade offered, gesturing toward her waiting horse.

Angel grimaced as she tested her legs and found that her thighs were still stiff and sore. "I'm afraid so," she admitted, glad for his help.

They walked to her horse and he lifted her onto its back. The feel of his hands at her waist was familiar now and reminded her of his soothing touch the night before. Heat shot through her, yet perversely, she shivered.

"Thank you," Angel said. Avoiding eye contact, she forced away the memory of his gentle massage.

Blade handed her the reins, then swung up on his own horse. After gathering up the leads to the pack animals they headed north along the river again.

"Blade? Were you very good at shooting when you got your first gun?" Lucky asked. They rode side by side.

"No. I was terrible."

"You must've practiced a lot to get this good, huh?"

"I did."

"Do you still have to practice?"

"Yes. But being a quick draw is no measure of a man's worth, Lucky."

The boy frowned as he considered his words. "You don't like being quick with a gun?"

"I've made my living by the gun. There is no glory or honor in it," Blade said. "Remember, don't draw on a man unless you're prepared to kill him. As ugly as it is, if you're using a gun, that's the only way you can survive."

"Can't you just scare 'em off?"

"There's always someone trying to beat you whether you want to fight or not. They won't let you walk away."

"You can't just quit?"

"That's what I'm planning to do just as soon as we get to California," Blade answered, not wanting to disillusion the boy by telling him the ugly truth about his life.

"What are you going to do?"

"I'm buying a ranch in Texas and settling down. It's a place where a man can put the past behind him and start over again new."

"Do you like it there?"

Blade nodded. "It's where I belong. My mother's

people live there. The sky is as clear and blue as the land is beautiful—lots of rolling hills and sweet grass."

"Where do they live? Have you still got family there? Do they own a ranch, too?"

Blade smiled at the boy's naivete. "My mother's people are the Wichita Indians," he answered with pride.

"You're an Indian?" Lucky was impressed. "I never met an Indian before. You sure don't look like one."

"My father was white, and I was raised as a white man."

Lucky's curiosity was running rampant. "What's your mother like?"

"Lucky, maybe you shouldn't ask so many personal questions," Angel interrupted. She remembered the gossip she'd heard and wasn't sure how Blade was going to react.

"No, it's all right." Blade put her fears to rest. "My mother's dead. She died when I was just a few years older than you, but I still remember everything about her. In English her name meant Summer Dawn, and she was a very beautiful woman." He paused, thoughtful. "My father passed away at the same time."

Talking with Lucky stirred memories of his childhood, and Blade recalled clearly how pretty his mother had been and how her loving touch and kind words could cure any hurt. He remembered the sweetness of her song and how it felt just to be with her. He had adored her and her gentle ways. Suddenly remembering too much, Blade's mouth twisted in bitterness, but Lucky didn't notice the change in him.

"My parents are dead, too," he told the older man.

"It's been almost a year now," Angel hurriedly added, hoping Blade wouldn't think it odd that he said "my" instead of "our."

Blade noticed, though, and wondered at it. "So you have no family left?" He addressed the question to Lucky; and, when he saw how the boy deferred to Angel to answer, his suspicion that there was more to their background than he'd been told was revived.

"Just our Aunt Blanche in Philadelphia," she supplied.

"Is that where you're from originally?"

"Yes." Angel could see no reason to lie. It was far easier to tell the truth whenever she could.

"You've come a long way."

"And we've still a long way to go."

"Well, considering where you started, when we reach Texas you'll be better than half-way there."

"I'm going to like Texas," Lucky spoke up, thinking of what Blade had said about settling there and starting over. He'd been wondering about what he would do once he and Angel parted in California—and they would part, he knew, because she'd told him she was only hiring him for the trip. It was a reality he had to face eventually, and now he knew what he would do when the time came. He would go to Texas, just like Blade. He'd have the money she'd promised to pay him, and he'd start a new life on his own. The idea gave him something to hold onto, for the thought of being parted from Angel was too much to bear right now.

Chapter Fourteen

Blade knew Angel was still sore, and he had intended not to push her too hard that day. To his surprise, she actually seemed to be sitting a little easier in the saddle. Once his initial concern about her faded, he set a steady pace. They paused only long enough at midday to eat a cold meal and let the horses rest, and then they were riding again. Near sundown, Blade found a secluded spot on the riverbank for them to make camp.

"How far did we go today, Blade?" Lucky asked as he struggled to pull his heavy saddle from Blue's back.

"Nearly forty miles."

"No wonder I'm so tired," he said with a grunt as he gave another fierce tug and the saddle came sliding off. The weight of the leather padding nearly knocked him to the ground, and it was a strain for him to heft the contraption out of the way. That done, he finished tending to Blue's needs.

Angel was busy setting up the campsite as they worked with the horses, but she could hear them talking. It pleased her to learn they had covered so much territory in just one day—the more distance between them and New Orleans, the happier she was.

Though she was thrilled at the number of miles they'd traveled, she was paying the price for it physically. The numbness that had claimed her earlier in the day had worn off, and now every inch of her body felt like it was on fire. Blade had warned her that today would be her worst, and he'd been right. At this particular moment, she honestly believed death would have been a blessed relief. At least when you were dead, she reasoned, you couldn't feel anything.

Certain that if she stood still in one place too long she would never walk again, Angel kept moving. They needed firewood, so she limped from the clearing in search of kindling. She spied some good-sized sticks and was bending down to pick them up when a vicious cramp pinched the back of her leg and she nearly fell. The aches and pains of the night before seemed relatively minor compared to the raging muscle-seizure that attacked her calf and rendered her immobile.

Dropping to the ground, Angel began to rub the painful area, but touching it made it worse. She was tempted to call Blade, but decided against asking for help. She would handle this herself.

Blade had looked out for Angel all day. He hadn't deliberately meant to, but for some reason he hadn't been able to take his eyes off her. He'd tried to convince himself that he was watching her only to make sure she wasn't in any trouble. But, in truth, she was beautiful, and he hadn't wanted to look away. The memory of the massage—of his hands upon her—had made it nearly impossible for him to think about anything else. Now, as he was seeing to the horses with Lucky, he glanced up just she stumbled. Instantly dropping everything, he raced to her side.

"Blade? What's wrong?"

"Your sister's fallen," he called back to Lucky as he ran, and the boy came running, too.

"What happened? Are you all right?" Blade reached her first.

"It's a cramp," she admitted, her plan to remain stoic failing miserably as the muscle tightened even more and she grimaced.

Without a word, Blade scooped her in his arms and cradled her against him.

"What are you doing?" she demanded.

"I'm going to carry you back to camp," he explained patiently, as if he were talking to a small child.

"No. . . . don't. I can walk," she protested a little too frantically, for her body reacted instantly to the intimate contact with the solid wall of his hard-muscled chest. Her pulse quickened, and her breath caught in her throat. His massage the night before had been enthralling; but, until this moment, she'd managed to convince herself that she'd only liked it because it had eased her pain. She realized now that she'd been fooling herself. This man's nearness affected her like no other's. There was something elemental and powerful about him that threatened her composure. Angel wanted to defend against it, but she'd never known anything like it before and wasn't sure how.

"On one leg?" Blade asked, giving her a derisive look. "Relax, I'm not going to hurt you."

"I didn't think you were," she countered, not wanting him to think she was afraid.

"Good. Then put your arms around my neck and hold on so I don't drop you."

As ordered, Angel linked her arms around Blade's neck to ease his burden, and the motion brought her even more fully against him. Her heart jolted as one breast was crushed against him. She lifted her gaze to his to find him staring down at her. His eyes burned with an intensity she'd never seen before, and she was captured easily.

Angel's world suddenly narrowed to the two of them. She was aware of the day's growth of black beard on his lean jaw and how it added a rakishness to his appearance. She had a great desire to touch his cheek and feel the rasp of the dark coarseness against her fingers. The heat of his chest burned against her breast. Her body longed to get closer to him. Her mind shouted for her to beware. A war waged within her, and she wasn't sure which side would win.

Blade stood unmoving with Angel in his arms. The moment their eyes had met, he'd been lost. He'd intended only to help her back to camp, but the moment she'd willingly put her arms around him logical thought had vanished. All he could think of was how soft the mound of her breast was as it seared his chest and how he'd seen the beginning slope of that sweet orb the night before. In his mind, he lay her down upon the lush grass, stripped the blouse and camisole from her and bared that silken flesh to his avid caresses. He was on the verge of indulging his fantasy and doing just that, when Lucky's voice rang out in fear and jarred him back to his senses.

"What's the matter? Is Angel hurt bad?" Lucky ran to them.

Blade recovered his wits and answered, silently lecturing himself as he did so, "The boss has got a bad cramp in her leg. It's nothing serious, but I'm going to need the bottle of liniment that's in my saddlebag. Will you get it for me?"

"Sure." He raced off.

When Blade reached the campsite, Lucky was waiting for him by Angel's bedroll. He lay her down—a fragile, precious treasure—and then, without bothering to ask permission, he pulled off her boots and socks.

Angel was upset. She didn't understand the wild emotions that wreaked havoc on her senses. Blade Masters was a gunfighter she'd hired to guide and protect them. He was there because she paid him. If a better offer came along, he'd be gone in a minute. He accompanied them for money, not for any great moral purpose like helping or liking them. The memory of his attitude in the saloon before she'd explained the business she had with him, still stung. Reminding herself of the facts of their relationship helped a bit, and she managed to regain some mastery over herself.

Blade had imagined that Angela's legs were lovely

and seeing them now reaffirmed his guess. Long, slender and shapely, they were a man's dream. As uncontrollable as his thoughts had been, Blade found himself wondering how it would feel to lie between them.

"What are you going to do?" Lucky asked, breaking into Blade's reverie again as he held out the liniment to him.

"I'm going to rub some of this on her legs to help take the ache out," Blade explained as he took the bottle from him.

"Oh." Lucky plopped down on the ground beside Angel to watch, unaware that they found his tension-breaking presence both a blessing and a curse.

Angel glanced up at Blade from beneath lowered lashes and was surprised to find his gaze still upon her. She quickly looked away, afraid that he might see too much of her confusion revealed in her eyes. She shifted her position, wanting to distance herself from him so she could think more clearly, but it was a mistake. Wrenching pain jolted through her leg and left her gasping.

"Sit still," Blade commanded as he sat down next to her. In a bold move, without even bothering to ask, he lifted Angel's legs across his lap and pushed her riding-skirt above her knees. It was an intimate position, and he felt her tense as he began massaging the lotion into her taut calf with the same precision he'd used on her neck and shoulders the night before. "Easy," he said. "It'll only hurt for another minute."

His voice was soothing and calming, but there was nothing soothing or calming about the way her body responded to his touch. When his fingers slipped to the sensitive area behind her knee, Angel almost threw herself out of his reach. It took enormous self-control to withstand his continuing assault on her senses.

Angel tried to look anywhere but at Blade. She stared first at the forest around them and then out at the river nearby, but again and again her gaze was drawn back to him. Studying his profile, she committed to memory the strength and ruggedness of his features.

"Is it gone?" Blade asked, interrupting her thoughts as he stopped his massage. He glanced up at her, but she'd already forced herself to look away.

"I think so," she answered, cautiously rotating her ankle to test it, "but it's still sore."

"It'll probably feel almost like a bruise for a while," Blade advised. Gently, starting with her foot, he gave her entire leg a slow, thorough rubdown.

Angel had never thought of her legs as a particularly sensual part of her body before. As Blade's practiced touch inched ever higher to her knee and above, shivers of delight coursed through her. When he brushed her skirt out of the way so he could have access to her thigh, her blood quickened. She told herself he was doing this only so they could continue on schedule to California, but logic didn't stop the uncontrollable feelings flooding through her.

Blade had worked on her leg without looking up, but when his hands skimmed the firm flesh of her slender thigh, he could not resist a cautious glimpse. Angel's attention was focused on him, her eyes darkened with the turmoil of emotion, her cheeks flushed, and her lips moist and slightly parted. Only Lucky's presence kept Blade from embracing her. Abruptly, he lowered her skirt and switched his ministrations to her other leg.

"Lucky, hand me the bottle again, will you?"

"Sure, Blade. Aren't you almost done? I'm awful hungry." Young and innocent, the boy remained unaware of the sensual tension between Blade and Angel.

"We'll be done here in no time."

"You can stop now if you want," Angel spoke, but could find no semblance of intelligent thought in her mind. All she could think of was how wonderful his hands felt. She warned herself that Blade was a man who sold himself to the highest bidder and that it might prove a fatal mistake for her to trust him too much.

"I always finish what I start," Blade stated firmly, kneading her other leg. This time, however, he stopped just above the knee. "That should take care of you for tonight."

"Thanks." Angel quickly slipped her legs from his lap and pushed her skirt back down.

"Why don't you stand up and see how you feel? If your legs are still too sore, we can camp here an extra day."

"No," she answered quickly, not willing to lose a full day of travel. "I'm sure I'm all right."

Lucky gave Angel a hand, and she accepted his help gratefully. She moved gingerly, testing and stretching. Though she still ached, she could walk.

"See, I'm fine. There's no need for us to fall behind schedule. I'll be ready to ride in the morning." She looked straight at Blade and added in a measure that was pure self-defense, "Christopher's waiting for me. I have to get to him."

Blade's expression hardened at the mention of her fiancé. "Whatever you say, ma'am," he responded tightly. "You're the boss." He turned away from the tempting sight of her as she stood before him barefoot and beautiful.

Blade awoke suddenly in the middle of the night and reached instinctively for his gun. Something—he didn't know what—had disturbed his rest. Rolling to his side, he checked Angela and Lucky's rolls. The fire had burned low, but he could still see well enough to determine immediately that, while the boy lay curled in a tight ball and sound asleep, Angela was missing.

Rising soundlessly, Blade peered into the darkness. Tracking and hunting lessons learned in his youth quickly revealed her trail. He paused. With no sign of a struggle or trouble, perhaps she was tending to personal needs and required privacy. But when Angel hadn't returned after a reasonable time, Blade followed her down to the riverbank. Whatever her reason for wandering alone late at night, he intended to make certain she would never do it again. Danger could be lurking anywhere, and it always paid to be cautious.

Angel had not been able to sleep. After several

hours haunted by her reaction to Blade, she'd given up and left camp to get away from the sight of the handsome gunman across the fire from her.

Aided by moonlight, Angel made her way to the river's edge and found a small cleared place to sit. Confusion filled her. She'd only known Blade for three days—three days!—and yet his very presence affected her, addled her. He was attractive, but she knew other equally attractive men. Michael, as much as she hated him, was good looking, but the thought of his hands upon her filled Angel with revulsion. Thoughts of Blade, however, stirred a deep and primitive hunger in her soul. It was that untamed appetite that had left her tossing and turning through the night.

Angel cast a small twig into the river. As the current caught it and spun it downstream with ever increasing speed, she felt an affinity with the broken bough. She was separated from her roots and her home, adrift on a perilous journey.

In the darkness, Angel's legendary courage deserted her. Her eyes filled with tears, and she felt sorry for herself. She wanted someone to trust, someone she could lean on, someone who would take her weighty troubles from her shoulders and resolve them for her. But there was no one. Blade's loyalty was purchased. If Michael's men caught up with them, he might switch sides if they offered him a better deal. She was alone.

In that bleak moment, Angel felt a kinship with Elizabeth; and, with that understanding, her spirit returned. Scared though she was, she would prevail.

She would foil Michael at every turn and keep Christopher safe from harm.

"Angela?"

Blade's voice startled Angel, and she jumped up to find him only a few feet behind her. How could he have come so close without her hearing him?

"What are you doing here?" she demanded, fighting the physical attraction between them. Her heart pounded in her breast because he was near. It was ridiculous; she was no better than an animal in heat, but it didn't quell the excitement that filled her.

"It's not safe out here at night, Angela. You're vulnerable alone."

"But there's no one around." She spoke softly, mesmerized by the way the moonlight softened his features.

"Things can happen in the wilderness." Blade thought her the most lovely woman he'd ever seen. She was as innocent and beautiful as she was fiery and defiant. Desire flamed within him, and he lifted one hand to stroke her cheek.

Angel longed to lean into his caress, to step closer to him. She savored the sweetness of his touch, imagining herself in his arms again. She wanted to know the ecstasy of his kiss.

"Ah, Angel!" Blade's voice was barely a whisper as he used her nickname for the first time. Touching her was heavenly for him. He saw the bewildered surrender in her eyes and knew she wanted him as much as he wanted her. There was no turning back. He bent to her, seeking her lips with his own in a tentative encounter. The soft exploration unexpectedly exploded into something far more powerful and wonderful than either of them had ever imagined possible. Wrapping her in his arms, he brought her fully against him as his mouth burned over hers. His embrace was powerful and potent. From breast to hip, they were molded as one—she, infinitely soft; he, hard and male.

Angel was enraptured. She'd been kissed before, but not by Blade Masters. Never like this. She wanted to stay in his arms forever. She wanted to kiss him again and again.

Fortunately, what little sense she had left, held. A distant warning rang through her. Perplexed by the potent effect he had on her and frustrated by her inability to defend against it, Angel stiffened and broke off the kiss. She retreated a step backward.

"Angel?"

"You're right about it being dangerous out here, Blade. Lucky's alone. We'd better get back." She didn't trust herself to look at him again.

"It wasn't Lucky I was thinking of," he told her in a deep, velvet voice that sent shivers down her spine.

"I know." Angel stopped and glanced back at him, her expression cautious and wary.

"What are you running from, Angel?"

"It's not what I'm running from. It's whom I'm running to," she told him, drawing on her pride for the strength to deny her desire for him. She had to keep it strictly business between them. There was too much at stake. "I have to go back." She walked away. It was one of the most difficult things she'd ever done.

This time Blade didn't try to stop her. He watched her go, and in that moment he both hated and envied her Christopher. After a while, he followed her back to camp.

The days that followed developed into a quiet routine as Angel strove to keep a polite but firm distance between her and Blade. As he'd predicted, her aches and pains had peaked that second night, and she was glad. The last thing she wanted was any further physical contact with Blade Masters. They passed the hours, cordial but cool, while Lucky kept things from getting too awkward with his constant, inquisitive conversation.

They crossed the Mississippi by ferry and began to head northwest toward Texas along the Red River. The roads went from bad to worse to nonexistent, and they progressed accordingly. Thankfully the weather cooperated. Roads that would have been little more than swamps in times of rain were passable. By the end of the first week, Angel and Lucky had adapted to the long hours in the saddle and were growing more adept at handling their mounts.

The eighth day out was particularly hot, humid, and miserable. The road, a gracious description for the narrow, overgrown path, proved difficult and took its toll on man and beast alike. Even though it was only mid-afternoon when they came upon the small, inviting lake, they decided to stop for the day.

"Me and Blade's going swimming!" Lucky announced with glee as he ran to speak to Angel once his work was done.

"Blade and I are," Angel corrected.

"You're going, too?" Lucky completely missed her reference. "Oh, good. We'll have fun!"

"No, I can't go swimming with you," she laughed. "I was correcting your English."

"Oh." He looked crestfallen. "Why can't you? We'd have lots of fun."

"I can't because it wouldn't be proper."

"Who cares about proper when it's this hot?"

Angel smiled at his disregard for convention. "I might get in after you and Blade are done. It would feel good to take a bath."

"A bath?" He pulled a face.

"Yes, and, come to think of it, it wouldn't hurt you to come in close contact with some soap while you're out there having fun."

"I don't see what difference it makes. We're only going to get hot again tomorrow."

"Do it for me," she coaxed with a grin as she dug through one of their bags for the cake of soap she'd brought along. She held it out to him. "Have fun."

"Won't you at least come down to the lake and watch us?" he invited as he took the soap.

"All right. I'll be along in a minute."

He flashed her a big, light-hearted grin and dashed off to join Blade, who was already sitting on the bank pulling off his boots.

Angel waited until they were both in the water and then made her way to the bank and sat down to watch. Lucky was floating on his back relatively close in. She spotted Blade farther out where it was deep, treading water. When he saw her, he started to swim back to the shore with long, powerful strokes. Angel watched him come, his body boldly slicing through the water.

"Hey Angel! Watch this!"

Lucky's call distracted her, and she glanced in his direction to watch him at play in the shallows. His childish antics captured her attention and had her laughing in delight.

"Sure you don't want to come in?" the boy invited.

"No thanks."

"Are you sure?"

Blade's voice vibrated through her, and Angel looked over in surprise to find him standing just a few feet from shore in waist deep water. His naked chest was tanned to a deep bronze, lightly furred with hair. She'd been aware of his strong shoulders, but seeing them now, water-sleeked and corded with thick muscle, sent ripples of excitement through her. Angel wanted to run her hands across the sculpted hardness of his chest and arms. The memory of their kiss singed her thoughts and she quickly extinguished the teasing recollection. That kiss had been a mistake, and staring at him now was a mistake, too.

"No. No, I don't think I should," she refused.

"We promise not to splash you too much," Blade teased taking a step in her direction and moving into shallower water.

"No. You two go ahead and have your fun," she answered, tearing her eyes away from him for fear of what his next step would reveal. "I'll stay here and watch."

Blade saw her nervousness and chuckled softly as he took another step. "That's no fun."

"Oh, yes. It is." Angel's gaze was frantic as she tried to avoid looking at him. It was only then that she saw his pile of discarded clothing nearby and noted, to her relief, that he had left no pants on the bank. She fought to regain her composure as she turned back to him, thinking it safe to look. He stood in thigh-deep water now, but his trousers, wet and clinging, rode seductively low on his hips. "I'm quite comfortable," she told him, trying not to gape. She hadn't seen any men dressed—or rather undressed— this way, but she was certain that Blade had to be a magnificent specimen of manhood.

"You look awfully hot," Blade went on, giving her no peace. "Don't you think she looks hot, Lucky?"

"Very!" The boy immediately began to splash in her direction, deliberately trying to get her wet.

Angel had not really expected them to splash her, and she let out a girlish squeal of dismay and surprise as the cold water hit her.

"Come on, Blade, help me!" Lucky cried out, and he was thrilled when Blade joined in, dousing her. "Angel, come swimming! You're already wet! You might as well get in!"

"Two on one's no fair! I'm going to get even with both of you! Little boy, you'd better hope your name holds true!!" Soaked, Angel threw off her boots and socks as fast as she could and, forgetting her leather skirt, charged into the water to claim her revenge.

It had been years since Angel had played in water. As children, they'd often gone to a friend's farm in the country and played in a creek there. Elizabeth and Sarah had always ganged up on her, so she'd learned early how to fight. She was used to being outnumbered, and she attacked her assailants now with the same fierce resolve that had left her victorious with her sisters.

Thrashing her arms in the water, Angel sent up a defensive shield that caught them both full in the face. This was war, and she was going to win! Fighting her way through the water, she went after Lucky first. She let out a whoop of triumphant glee when in his laughing effort to escape her, he lost his footing and fell, dunking himself.

"Gotcha!!" Angel exclaimed.

He came up sputtering to find that Angel had already turned her attention to Blade who'd wisely moved out to deeper water.

"Now, it's your turn," she threatened in mock anger as she made her way toward him, the weight of her skirt hindering her movements.

"You'd better quit while you're ahead, Angel," Blade warned, backing still farther away. Though his words were meant to discourage her, they had no such effect; and he couldn't help but smile at her feisty refusal to give up gracefully.

"You're the one who's afraid! You're the one in retreat," she pointed out with smug superiority as she continued her pursuit, ignoring the ever-threatening drag of her clothes. She realized as she trudged through the water that Blade and Lucky had had the right idea, stripping down to next to nothing as they had. She thought it a shame that girls were always forced to go swimming with practically all their clothes on.

"I'm not retreating. I'm being smart. You can't splash me if you have to swim to get to me," he told her as he reached the drop off in the lake's bottom and started to swim away.

"You can't get away from me. I'm going to get you just like I did Lucky." Angel knew he was bigger and stronger than she was and that an outright chase would leave her the obvious loser. She was going to have to rely on deviousness to outmaneuver him. Slowing her pace, she felt along the muddy bottom searching for the place where the lake bottom dropped away. When she reached it, she deliberately went under, throwing her arms up as if she were in trouble.

"Blade! Angel disappeared!" Lucky shouted, suddenly afraid.

Blade watched for a minute, expecting her to surface right away. When she didn't, his amusement turned to concern.

"Stay where you are," he ordered Lucky. "I'll find her." He broke into a fast stroke and knifed through the water to the area where she'd gone under.

Angel had been holding her breath as she stayed close to the bottom waiting for Blade to come looking for her. It wasn't easy to see in the murky water, but when he dived, she was ready. Pushing off, she broke the surface, took a deep breath, and then, with an exultant laugh, dived after him. She grabbed his ankle as he felt his way along the bottom.

Blade had been terrified that their play had turned deadly. When he felt someone grab his ankle, he thought it was Lucky disobeying his order to stay put. He reached back to grab him, not wanting him in danger, too. He found when he dragged the boy up to him and clasped an arm around his waist to hold him that he'd caught not the boy but Angel. With a powerful kick, he sent her upward.

"What the—?" he growled, glaring at his water-logged captive.

Angel sputtered and laughed. "Fooled you!"

"You did more than fool me, you just about scared us to death," he said sternly, keeping an arm tightly around her as he treaded water.

"Hah! All's fair in love and war!" She was laughing as she made her declaration, but she instantly sobered when their eyes met and she saw the intensity of his gaze.

Angel became conscious of the cool, sensuous caress of the water around them and the contrasting heat of his strong arm clasping her to his hot, bare chest. The steady motion of his legs as he kept them afloat aroused her. Instinctively, she wanted to wrap her arms and legs around him. She wanted to trust him with her life and almost felt she could. Her eyes widened at the thought.

Blade's gray eyes were stormy. One moment Angel was his cool and haughty employer; the next, she was a light-hearted vixen taunting and teasing him with her innocent ways. She couldn't know that he lay awake at night, remembering the single kiss they'd shared at the river's edge. At the memory of that kiss, heat seared his loins, and his gaze fell from her eyes to her mouth. He wanted to kiss her again. And more. He wanted to carry her up on the bank and make love to her. He wished they were alone! He was very glad they weren't.

"Is Angel all right?" The sound of Lucky's splashing as he attempted to swim out to them interrupted Blade's erotic reverie.

"She's fine," Blade answered, fighting desire. In irritation, he realized he'd better not swim in too close to the shore; he wouldn't be able to stand up in the shallows for a while. He was glad the water was cold.

"Yes, I'm all right," Angel confirmed. Then, trying to lighten the mood, she added, "But I did get even with you both!"

"Yeah, but we were wet already," Lucky argued as he thrashed back to safety.

Blade reached the area where they could touch bottom and quickly released her. He moved away, staying in water up to his chest as Angel got her footing and stood up. Blade had thought his torment was over. He'd thought himself safe now that she was out of his arms. He'd been wrong. She rose before him like an ancient water goddess. His eyes darkened as his gaze dropped to her breasts. Her wet blouse and camisole were nearly transparent, molded to her body like a second skin. Every enticing detail of her breasts was revealed to him beneath the pale veil of soaked fabric.

Angel saw his reaction, and she glanced down. She gasped and turned away, crossing her arms across her chest, and started for the bank.

"Angel, you want to play some more?" Lucky asked as she sloshed past him on her way to dry ground.

"I may take a bath later, but I think I need to dry out right now. Remember to wash while you're here, all right?"

"I will," he promised.

Blade stayed in the lake with Lucky for some time after Angel left them. He gave him a few tips on how to improve his swimming and then played and rough-housed with him in the age-old way of males until it was almost dusk. Only then did they pause to wash before returning to the campsite, Lucky leading the way.

Angel had changed into her riding habit and was sitting by the fire. As Lucky approached, it occurred to her how completely he'd changed. The sullen, hostile little boy she'd caught stealing from her was gone. In his place was a happy, robust child who looked as if he hadn't a care in the world. It filled her with joy to know that he was so much better off.

"That was fun, huh, Blade?"

"Yes, and once you practice your swimming a little more, I'll race you."

"You're on!"

Blade was clad only in his pants and boots when he and Lucky joined Angel. He'd heard her tell the boy earlier that she'd wanted to bathe, so he told her, "If you want to go wash before it gets too dark, we'll stay here so you can be alone."

"It would feel good to be clean again," she admitted, oh-so-aware of him standing nearby.

"Here's the soap, Angel." Lucky tossed it to her.

"Thanks, sweetie. You look much nicer now that you're cleaned up."

"I don't know how you can tell the difference."

"I can tell." She stood up and gathered her things, then went down to the lake. "I won't be long."

Angel was a bit hesitant about undressing completely, but a glance back at the camp showed Blade to be a man of his word. He'd sat down with his back to the lake, Lucky beside him. No one would see her. Quickly, she unfastened the tie that held her hair in a braid, then stripped off her riding habit, grabbed up the soap, and dashed into the lake.

Angel let out a long, delighted sigh as she sank down into the chilly water. She was in ecstasy. A sensuous laugh escaped her as she wet her hair and then washed and rinsed it thoroughly. It felt delicious to be clean. She hummed a soft melody as she continued to scrub. Angel could not remember when she'd enjoyed a bath so much. It didn't matter that she was in the middle of a lake in the wilds with only a cake of crude soap. If cleanliness were next to godliness, she was in heaven. She floated on her back until total darkness threatened and then made her way back to the bank.

On impulse Angel put on the one and only daygown she'd brought with her. She felt the need to look like a woman again for at least a little while. She buttoned the sedate dark blue dress, noticing that without petticoats it seemed even plainer. But Angel felt good. She wrapped her towel around her hair turban-style and strolled back.

Blade had told himself he was a man of honor. He'd promised Angel would have privacy for her bath, and he'd meant it—at the time. But from the moment he'd heard her first splash into the lake and the realization had hit him that she'd shed all or at least most of her clothes, he'd been fighting a raging battle with his less-than-chivalrous side.

It took all of Blade's considerable self-control to remain where he was talking idly with her brother, and he silently cursed his self-inflicted gallantry. Minutes passed. His active imagination did not rest. He wondered in short-tempered irritation why it was taking her so damned long to wash. She wasn't a big woman. He could have washed her himself in about two minutes flat.

Blade shifted positions. He tried to distract himself, tried to think of other things, but there was no mental escape. Her soft melody was a whisper on the wind and it was weaving a spell around him like a siren's song. Blade knew if she didn't get done soon, he was going to have to get up and move. There was only so much a man could be expected to take.

"I'm done," Angel called, coming into view.

The minute Blade saw her in the dress, he almost groaned his appreciation. Without underskirts the gown fit closely, outlining the feminine curves of her hips to perfection.

"Good, now we can eat!" Lucky said, serving up the food he'd been anxiously awaiting.

Angel took her plate from Lucky and sat down across the fire from them. After eating the plain but nourishing fare of beans and meat, she set the dish aside and unwrapped the towel from her hair. Shaking out her tangled mane, she began to work her comb through it until she realized that Blade was watching her. "Is something wrong?" she asked.

Blade wanted to tell her how incredibly lovely she looked with her hair down. The firelight added a red-gold cast, and the silken strands looked like molten gold. He wanted to run his hands through the shimmering cascade.

But he was there to protect, not ravish, her. Blade denied himself again. When he answered, his tone was harsh. "You aren't planning to wear that dress to ride tomorrow, are you?"

"No. The leather skirt should be dry enough to wear by then."

"Good." He scowled, his voice curt and brusque as he stood up. "You wouldn't last an hour in that thing."

"I know, I—" Angel got no further. Blade had stalked into the darkness. Puzzled, she stared after him. What had she said? What had she done?

Chapter Fifteen

Lonely, since Angel was already asleep, Lucky went in search of company.

"Blade?" he called softly at the edge of the lake.

"Yeah, Lucky. What do you want?" Blade's answer came to him through the darkness.

"I was just wondering where you went, is all. You swimming again?" he replied drawing closer to the water.

"Thought I'd take advantage of it while I had the chance. Stay where you are, I'll come out now." Blade had needed to douse the fire in his body and had swum vigorously until the exercise eased the ache in his loins. But the vision of Angel in his mind was harder to banish.

"Why aren't you asleep?" Blade asked as he pulled on his pants and sat down on the bank beside Lucky.

"I couldn't sleep. Angel fell asleep right away, though."

A vision of her crept disturbingly into Blade's

thoughts. "Damn, but I could use a smoke right now," he muttered in exasperation.

"Don't go anywhere," Lucky told him. "I'll be right back."

Before Blade could say a word, the boy jumped up and darted back toward camp. Lucky was excited. He hadn't had the chance to smoke since that night in town. Taking care not to disturb Angel, he dug through his pack, then—his prize tightly in hand—he raced back to the lake.

"Here." He held out the cigarette makings he'd bought from Eli and Joss.

"Where'd you get this?" Blade was amazed.

The quick-witted Lucky wove his reply into Angel's story of their background. "From my father's things. He smoked, and I wanted to try as soon as I could get away from Angel. Promise you won't tell her? She'd be mad." To the boy's great dismay and frustration, Blade took all the tobacco and papers from his outstretched hand.

"Thanks."

Lucky watched with a sinking feeling in the pit of his stomach as Blade rolled two cigarettes, pocketed one and lit the other. Lucky had wanted to smoke. He'd wanted to sit there with Blade and be men together. He almost cussed.

"Can I have the other one?" he ventured in one last desperate hope.

Blade glanced at him, his expression stern. "Your sister would be mad for good reason. You're too young. Wait a few years until you're a man on your own."

Lucky wanted to blurt out that he was a 'man on his own' and that he had been for some time now, but he didn't. He wanted to earn his money from Angel more than he wanted that one cigarette. "Yes, sir," he replied miserably.

"You won't be sorry. You'll have a lot of time to smoke when you're older." Blade fell silent for a moment. He understood the boy's rush to manhood. "By tomorrow night we should be far enough out to take some target practice. What do you think? Do you want to try?"

"Oh, boy, do I!" Lucky's excitement was real, his disappointment over not sharing the cigarettes almost forgotten. "Which one are you going to teach me to use? Your rifle or your gun?"

"We'll start with the handgun. The rifle's heavier and harder to handle. I'll show you how to use that later, after you've mastered the gun."

"Thanks!"

"The most important thing to remember is that a gun is a tool—a dangerous tool. If used right, it can be for good; but if it's used wrong, people die." There was a tension in his words, and Blade took a last, long drag on the cigarette before putting it out.

Lucky listened intently. "Who taught you how to shoot so good?"

"My father."

"Was it hard for you to learn?"

"Very. There's a lot more to marksmanship than aiming and firing. It takes a steady hand and a good eye."

"I hope I do good," Lucky said earnestly, wanting to please Blade.

"You'll do fine," he assured him.

"You gonna teach Angel too?"

His question took Blade by surprise. He hadn't considered that she'd want to learn. "That'll be up to her. If she wants to, I will."

"You really like Angel, don't you?" he pried.

"Your sister's a nice lady, and she is my boss."

"No, I mean, you really *like* her. You know."

Blade was glad it was dark so Lucky couldn't see the consternation in his expression. "Lucky, you don't really understand the way things are between a man and a woman." He tried to avoid the topic as gracefully as generations of men before him had tried with inquisitive young boys; and, as with past generations, it didn't work.

"You sure looked like you liked her a lot when we were swimming. She's awful pretty, isn't she?"

"Your sister's a very lovely woman."

"Why don't you tell her you like her?"

"Things just aren't that way between us. Like I said, she hired me to do a job, and she expects me to do it. Besides, she's going to California to marry her Christopher."

"Yeah," Lucky agreed, remembering her marriage plans and wondering how she could think any man could be better than Blade. That Christopher of hers had to be real special.

"What do you say we turn in for the night," Blade suggested, and they returned to camp. Everything was peaceful. Everything, that is, except Blade's thoughts. He paused near Angel to watch her rest.

The boy was right, Blade admitted painfully to himself. He did care for her. He desired her, but— even more—he would protect her and keep her safe, no matter what the cost.

Love. The word entered his consciousness unbidden. *Did he love her?* Blade considered the revelation, remembering her words *All was fair in love and war.* He wondered which it was going to be. He knew that decision was up to Angel, but if it came to war, he was ready to fight and win.

The next day they made good progress, and late in the afternoon Blade started looking for a place to stop where they could take target practice. He found a large clearing about an hour before sunset. Blade was ready to show Lucky the mechanics of loading a sidearm, and since Lucky had mentioned that Angel might want to learn how to shoot, too, he decided to ask her.

"I'm ready to give Lucky his first shooting lesson tonight, if you want to watch."

"Thanks, I'd like that. I don't know the first thing about guns, and considering where we're heading, it certainly couldn't hurt to learn." Angel's words sounded forthright, but she had an ulterior motive. When the day came when she would have to defend Christopher from Michael, she wanted to be ready.

Angel and Lucky listened to Blade's comments about safety and preparation. They each practiced loading until they became reasonably proficient, and then it was time for their introduction to marksmanship.

"Can I go first?" Lucky asked eagerly, his dark eyes aglow.

"Just remember what I told you," Blade cautioned, wanting to temper enthusiasm with respect. "Take your time and aim carefully."

The gun felt awkward and heavy in Lucky's hand, but he was determined to learn. He closed one eye and bit down on his tongue as he concentrated on the target Blade had fixed for them—a piece of sackcloth tacked to a tree some thirty feet away. To the best of his novice ability, Lucky aimed and fired. The brush stirred several feet to the side of the tree. "I missed," he groaned.

"Try again. Up a little and to the left this time, and don't hold your breath," Blade advised.

Lucky nodded. Focusing solely on the square of material, he aimed. This time his shot was closer, but still fell short of accurate. The target was unscathed and could be used another day. At the boy's crestfallen expression, Blade tried to cheer him.

"Don't worry. I told you it takes a lot of practice. For your first time shooting, you're doing well. Angel? Are you ready?" Blade took the gun from Lucky and handed it to Angel.

"I'm as ready as I'll ever be," she admitted.

Angel lifted the revolver with one hand, but discovered immediately how heavy it was. She squeezed one shot that went high and wide, then tried to aim again. Her second shot was off the mark, too, and the gun felt leaden.

"Are you having trouble holding it?"

"It's heavier than I thought."

"Let me show you a different grip," Blade offered, positioning himself behind her. "Hold the gun with two hands."

He put his arms around her to steady the weapon. The fire within him that he'd kept carefully banked all day raged to life anew. He wanted to draw her back to him and kiss the side of her neck. He wanted to fit the softness of her hips fully against his. He wanted to make love to her until they were both exhausted.

"Now, sight down the barrel." He had to lean closer to show her the proper way to aim, and he was tempted to press a soft kiss on her ear.

Angel was having trouble thinking straight. She was acutely conscious of the heat of his body against hers, of his lips so close to her ear, and of his strong arms around her. Her breasts tightened in response, and an ache gnawed at her heart. She had to force her voice to be firm as she asked, "Like this?"

"Right. Now, just squeeze the trigger slowly. Almost like you're caressing it."

Angel did as she was told; and, with Blade steadying her, her shot nicked the edge of the cloth.

"We did it!!" She was thrilled, and she twisted in his arms to look up at him. Her movement brought them face-to-face, a mere breath apart. Their eyes met, and she saw something flicker in the now stormy gray depths of his gaze that both frightened and excited her.

Blade almost gave in to the urge to tighten his arms

around her, pull her to him, and kiss her, but he controlled his passion. This was not the time. He dropped his arms. "Try again, but be careful."

Angel felt bereft when he let her go and moved away from her. She turned back to the target so he couldn't see the confusion in her eyes. Her thoughts bewildered her. Had she really wanted him to kiss her again? In that one breathless moment when their eyes had met, she'd felt. . . . unnerved.

"Blade, can I try one more time after Angel's done?" Lucky spoke up. "Will you help me like you did her? I bet I can shoot better if I use two hands."

"Sure."

Angel tried the two-handed grip on her own; and, while she came closer than she had on her first try, the target suffered no further damage.

"We sure need a lot more practice, don't we, Angel?" Lucky asked as he took the gun from her and got ready for his second attempt.

"I think I need a shotgun," she laughed a little nervously, still feeling unsettled about what had passed between her and Blade.

"All right, Lucky, show me if you learned anything watching your sister." Lucky tried Angel's way. Still far from accurate, he was closer than before. "Good."

"How can you say that was good, when I didn't even come close? I want to hit the target right in the middle like you. I want to be able to draw fast."

Blade pinned him with a silencing look. "A gun is important, not because you use it but because you know how to use it. I'm willing to teach you how to shoot so you can defend yourself, not so you can go looking for fights. Do you understand that?"

"Yes."

"Good. It's going to take a lot of patience on your part to learn. If you're serious, you're going to have to keep at it and not get frustrated and give up."

"I won't."

Blade nodded his approval. "We'll try again tomorrow night."

"Are you going to keep practicing, too, Angel?" Lucky asked.

"As long as Blade has no objection." She looked to him for an answer and found his eyes upon her, his expression inscrutable. The intriguing emotion she'd seen mirrored there earlier, was masked now.

"That'll be fine." Blade took the gun from Lucky, checked it, then slid it into his holster.

They ate their evening meal and got ready to bed down. The ground seemed particularly hard to Angel tonight. She had trouble getting comfortable, let alone falling asleep. As she tossed and turned, Blade kept intruding on her thoughts. She remembered the feel of his arms and the sound of his deep voice in her ear as he'd curved himself around her to help her with her aim. She reminded herself again that he was a mercenary. There had been nothing tender or devoted in his actions. Everything he did was calculated, with his eye fixed on the money she would pay him once they reached California. The memory of his kiss in the moonlight would not be dismissed, though. Nor the feelings his kiss had aroused.

In her search for comfort, Angel rolled over again

and this time noticed that Blade was not in his bedroll. He often went to check on the horses and take a look around the campsite before going to sleep, so she wasn't unduly concerned until she heard the sound of riders approaching the camp.

"Blade?" She called his name in a strangled, nervous voice as she sat up.

"Angel, what is it?" Lucky was the only one who replied to her call.

"There are horses coming. Do you know where Blade went?"

"No. I didn't even see him go. Who do you think is coming?"

"I don't know." Angel felt a surge of panic as the sound of the horses' hooves grew ever louder.

She and Lucky were alone. Blade might be nearby, but that wouldn't be good enough if the mystery riders were Michael's men and they were coming into camp armed.

"Why are you so scared?" Lucky could see how pale she'd become. He wasn't especially worried himself because he was certain Blade was somewhere close by.

"We don't know who it is."

Her gaze darted back to Blade's bedroll, and she was relieved to see his gun and holster there. Without hesitation, she scrambled to snatch up Blade's revolver. Her desperation transferred itself to the boy, and he jumped up and ran to her side just as the two strangers appeared within the circle of the fire's light. Angel put an arm around him in a sheltering gesture as she faced their unwanted company.

"Hello." The heavy-set, dirty man riding the lead horse reined in as soon as he caught sight of Angel. His eyes feasted upon her from her hair to her bosom—and lower.

"Who are you and what do you want?" Angel demanded in a firm voice as she lifted the gun and aimed it at them. She had to fight to keep both her voice and the gun steady. She didn't want to reveal the deep, bone-chilling fear that held her in its icy grip. She studied their faces in the flickering firelight, trying to see if she recognized either man as the one she'd seen in New Orleans.

"Whoa there, little lady," the man protested quickly, his eyes widening a bit at the sight of the gun in her hand. It didn't matter that her hand was shaking a little. At this distance, he didn't think she'd miss no matter how bad her aim. "We didn't mean no harm."

"We heard the shots earlier and thought there might be trouble here. We headed this way, and when saw the light from your campfire we thought we'd come see if you was needin' any help," the second one added.

"We don't need any help, thank you. You can be on your way now."

"Now that ain't so neighborly of you, ma'am. Name's McGraw. Hank McGraw, and this here is Lou Jones."

"Ma'am." Lou Jones openly leered at Angel. It had been a long time since he'd had a woman. "There really ain't no need for a gun now, ya know."

"Your man hereabouts?" Hank asked, casting a quick look around but seeing no one.

Angel stood her ground without flinching. Though neither man was the one she'd seen in New Orleans, she realized that didn't mean they were in any lesser danger. Blade had warned her, and she was ready. She tightened her grip on the revolver and was about to answer when Blade's voice cut through the night.

"Evening, gentlemen. There a good reason why you stopped for a visit?" Blade's words were cordial enough, but his tone left no doubt that he considered their presence an intrusion and a threat.

He stepped forward into the light, his rifle at ready, and the strangers immediately tensed. They'd thought the camp might be easy prey, and when they'd seen the woman they'd anticipated more. The boy they dismissed as unimportant. That perception was now shattered as they faced a mean and angry Blade. His silvered gaze was fixed upon them with lethal resolve. They sensed the savagery in him and knew this was no man to mess with. Their instincts screamed to get out, and McGraw and Jones always obeyed their gut reactions.

"We was just bein' neighborly, is all," McGraw whined.

"We'll head on now. You folks take care."

They turned their horses slowly and plodded off into the night, knowing they were lucky to get away unscathed. They didn't stop to wipe the cold sweat from their brows until they were out of sight. When they'd disappeared into the darkness, Blade followed after them on foot to make sure they really left the area.

"Angel, you can put the gun down now," Lucky urged as she remained standing stock-still, gun in hand, staring into the darkness in the direction they'd gone.

"No, Lucky, not yet." Her voice was a hushed, tense whisper as she waited. Her hand was shaking, but she didn't once let her guard down. There was still a chance that they were from Michael. She knew they might come back. She had to be ready. She waited.

Blade tracked the strangers. Once he was sure that they were not doubling back to cause more trouble, he returned to camp. The sight of Angel, gun in hand, shocked him.

"Angela, it's all right now. You can give me the gun." Blade took the weapon from her and handed it to Lucky to put away.

"They're really gone?"

Angel looked up at Blade, and he saw for the first time the look of terror on her face. She was pale, her eyes wide and filled with unspeakable fear. When he realized how badly she was shaking, he swept her in his arms and held her close.

"Yes, they're gone," he said quietly.

"You're sure?" she asked hoarsely, unable to stop shivering.

"Positive. You're safe. I'll protect you."

Angel went limp as he held her. That had been close—too close. The strength and emotion that had sustained her during the confrontation drained from her. Tears threatened, and she felt ashamed and cowardly. *She had managed this time, but what about next time? Would she be as ready, or would they catch her unawares?*

Angel bit down on her lip trying to force her runaway fears back under control, but the warmth and strength of Blade's embrace made that harder to do. She wanted to confide in him. Her heart urged her to trust him. Logic reminded her he was a gunfighter, a gambler, and a stranger. She was on her own.

"Angel, it's all right now." Blade's deep voice was a velvet caress as he held her protectively against him. "I will keep you safe," he promised, and her breathing slowed to a more regular pace. "Go back to sleep. I'll stand guard the rest of the night."

More in control, Angel drew a ragged breath and pushed slightly away from the haven of Blade's arms. "No. I'm all right." She lifted her chin, drawing on what little pride and strength she had left. "They surprised me. I hadn't expected. . . . not this late. . . . and then you were gone . . ."

"Don't you think it's time you leveled with me?" Blade asked, his tone serious. "It's time to tell me the truth."

"I don't know what you're talking about," she lied.

"I'm talking about your rush to get out of New Orleans. I'm talking about the kind of fear that just left you paralyzed. Now is the time to tell me. If you're in trouble, I can help."

Angel wrenched against his grasp, but his hands

tightened on her arms. He held her captive within his embrace. "I'm not in trouble," she denied.

"It's my job to keep you and Lucky safe until we reach California. How can I do that if you don't tell me what I'm up against? Who's looking for you? What are they after? How many of them are there? What should I be watching for?"

"You're wrong. Nobody's after me. I was just scared because you weren't here. That's all."

In frustration, he released her. Angel immediately moved away from his overwhelming presence.

"I guess we'd better get to bed. Morning's going to come early tomorrow," she said, going quickly to Lucky who'd been observing the two of them in silence. She tucked him in and gave him a kiss, then made her way to her own bed.

For Blade there would be no sleep. He didn't believe one word of her denial. He was going to stay up and keep watch. Something elemental and primitive in him wouldn't let him rest as long as he thought she was in danger. Taking his rifle, Blade settled just out of the circle of light. His lonely vigil would see them safely through the long night.

Chapter Sixteen

Tense and tired, Blade had awaited the first light of dawn, but instead of brightening his mood, dawn had revealed dark storm clouds to the west. His already edgy mood blackened.

"Angel, it's sunup. We'd better get an early start today," he told her as he built up the fire to boil water for coffee. He was in dire need of some of the hot, bracing brew.

"Why?" Angel asked wearily as she came awake. She'd been restless all night, worrying about Michael's men catching up to her, and had only just fallen asleep.

"It's going to storm before noon. We need to make as much time as we can while it's clear."

Weary but determined to keep going, she dragged herself out of her bedroll and woke Lucky. Within a short time, they were mounted and on their way.

The mist began late in the morning and turned from a light drizzle to a full-fledged downpour by afternoon. Blade had known that there would be bad weather on the trek, so he'd bought them rain gear. But with the onset of the gusts and squalls, nothing could keep them dry.

"We'd better stop early," Blade advised as the pelting rain continued. The roads would only get worse, and the river could overflow.

"No," Angel objected. "We haven't gone far enough today. We have to go on."

"Yes, ma'am. You're the boss, ma'am." Rigid, Blade deferred to her wishes.

Much later, Blade spotted a grove of trees on high ground that would offer protection from the elements for the night. Soaked, exhausted, and generally miserable, they sought the shelter of the trees. Blade set up makeshift tents and then sought solitary rest while Angel and Lucky huddled together.

"Angel?" Lucky said her name softly as he snuggled close beside her in their tent.

"Hmm?" she responded sleepily.

"Do you think it'll ever stop raining?"

"No. We're probably going to have to start swimming tomorrow."

He knew she was teasing. "Shoulda taken a boat, huh?"

"And miss all this fun and togetherness?"

There was a long pause as Lucky thought about the cold and rainy nights he'd spent alone, wet and hungry on the streets of St. Louis. This was heaven in comparison. He answered quietly, "You're right."

"I am?"

"I've slept out in the rain a lot before, but I was

always by myself then." He spoke in a whisper so only she could hear.

Angel was deeply touched. Love for him filled her heart, and she pulled him to her and wrapped her blanket around them both for extra warmth. "Sleep now. You won't be by yourself ever again."

"G'night, Angel." Lucky wanted to believe her, but he could not forget that they would separate once they reached California. For now, though, he would enjoy what happiness he had. He sighed and drifted off to sleep.

"G'night, sweetheart." Angel could barely make out his features in the gloom of the rainy night. He looked young and innocent, a far cry from the defiant, angry little boy she'd cornered less than a month before. Her heart warmed.

As she settled in for the night herself, Angel wondered how Christopher and Sarah were faring. She prayed they were safe and well on their way to California. It would be weeks before she would see either of them again, and it worried her not to know how they were.

What, she wondered, would Christopher think of Lucky? She decided her nephew would like him. He was brash and wild but, underneath it all, a good boy.

In the darkness, listening to the unceasing rain, Angel began to plan a future that included both Christopher and Lucky. Somehow, she was going to make certain that both boys were healthy and happy and grew to manhood knowing they were loved.

* * *

Dawn the next day was equally wet and dismal. Black clouds hung low in the sky, promising another day of unrelenting rain. They'd gotten little rest, and Blade's mood was as black as the clouds. He could see the exhaustion in Angel's and Lucky's faces, and he knew it would be best if they stayed put until the weather let up. Convincing her was the problem. Only one other person he knew could compare to her for sheer grit and determination once set on a goal, and that was himself.

"I think we should camp here until it clears," he told them as he ducked low to enter their small shelter. The ground was little more than ooze, and rain continued unabated.

"We're going to ride today," she insisted. "We can't wait it out. There isn't a break in the clouds, and it might be another whole day before the weather lets up."

"All the more reason not to travel," he said. "The roads are nothing but mud. Footing is bad, and the creeks are running wild. It's dangerous."

"That's why I hired you." Angel stiffened, obstinate.

"What about the boy?"

"I'll be fine, don't worry," Lucky put in. He hadn't slept well and was worn out, but he had to please Angel. If she wanted to go, he would go.

"Well?" Angel turned to Blade. The memory of the terror she had felt when she'd thought Michael's men had found her wouldn't let her rest.

"Let's ride." Blade turned to the horses in surrender.

Hour after hour, they plodded through the drenching rain.

"Is it dry in Texas?" Lucky asked hopefully, breaking the silence.

In spite of the cold rain trickling down the back of his neck, Blade smiled. "In the summer."

Lucky groaned. "It's still spring, isn't it?"

"It's still spring," he confirmed.

"How soon will we get there? We should be leaving Louisiana soon, shouldn't we?"

"If the rain hadn't slowed us down, we would have made the border today. As it is, depending on the weather, we should make it some time tomorrow."

"Good. I know when we get to Texas, the sun's going to come out again."

"I hope you're right," Angel joined in.

"If you could be anywhere else right now, where would you be?" Lucky asked.

"Let's see." The memory of home as it had been drifted warmly in her thoughts, but she instantly remembered that the home of her childhood no longer existed. "How about on a steamboat in their best stateroom, sleeping in a big soft bed?"

"With lots of hot food and dry clothes?"

"And no horses," she concluded with a smile.

"Yeah."

When Angel mentioned the stateroom and the bed, Blade immediately saw her lying upon it. He imagined himself walking into the cabin to find her waiting, eager and ready for him. Quickly he checked the image.

Angel's cozy daydream lasted no longer than Blade's, interrupted by the specter of Christopher's frightened face. Guiltily, she pushed the self-indulgent fantasy from her mind. Her discomfort was nothing compared to what Elizabeth had suffered.

Cold rain water trickled down Angel's neck and along her spine, but she balked at giving in to weakness. She would not let her own misery be the reason to stop.

The road was a treacherous quagmire. Creeks had backed up, and they sloshed through the overflow.

Blade frowned at the telltale dark smudges beneath Angel's eyes. Her features were gaunt and drawn, and her hands shook. He wished she trusted him enough to tell him the terrible secret that held her in its grip. But until she chose to confide in him, he could only wait and watch and try to keep her from harm.

Blade's patience came to an abrupt end. They were crossing a swiftly-flowing creek and had to climb a muddy bank on the opposite side. Angel had gone first and made it safely to the top, then Lucky was to follow on Blue. Starting up the incline, the horse lost his footing and stumbled. Lucky, numb from exhaustion, had been almost asleep in the saddle. When Blue started to go down, he was caught by surprise.

"Angel, help!!" The boy was halfway in the water, clinging to the pommel and in danger of being swept away.

"Lucky!!" Angel shouted. She threw herself from

the saddle and staggered through the mud toward him, but Blade was beside Lucky in an instant. Charging across the rushing waters, he hauled him to safety across the front of his own saddle only to spy Angel sliding down the bank in an effort to help.

"Dammit, woman! Get back up there before I have to rescue you, too," he snapped, fearing that she would slip into the fast-moving current. She responded immediately, scrambling up the bank. Guiding his mount to the higher ground, Blade stopped a safe distance from the stream and let Lucky down.

"Thanks, Blade," the boy gasped. He was wet and chilled and frightened.

Angel ran to them and hugged the half-drowned child. "Are you all right?"

"I guess." Lucky shivered violently, and his voice trembled.

Even Blade was shaken. Both Lucky and Angel could have been killed! Furious, he swung down from the saddle and turned on Angel. His face was set like stone and his eyes blazed.

"We're making camp for the night. Here. Now!"

Awash with fear and filled with respect for Blade's decisive handling of the emergency, Angel nodded assent.

The clouds began to lift in the late afternoon, and by sundown the rain had stopped. Lucky recovered quickly from his scare, but he was still worn out. Blade managed to get a fire going for a hot meal. Lucky, too tired to eat, went to bed early. The long, miserable hours of riding in the rain had taken their toll on him.

Blade and Angel sat on opposite sides of the fire. Neither had much to say. Blade was still too angry, and Angel knew the accident today had indirectly been her fault.

"I guess I'll lie down," she announced, uncomfortable under his gaze.

"It's time you and I had a talk," he said, his tone imperative. He had acceded to her wishes for too long, nearly costing two lives.

"Talk?" Angel was defensive.

"Let's get away from here. I don't want to wake Lucky." He led her toward the creek.

"All right." Angel followed him to the trees near the bank and remained standing a short distance from him. Tension etched every line of his powerful body, and she grew nervous as she waited for him to speak.

"From now on my better judgment will be followed without question. Do you understand?" His words were a command.

"Yes."

"Good." But he couldn't let it go at that. "Do you realize how close you came to losing your brother today? Not to mention your own life."

"I know," she confessed in a tight voice.

"Knowing is easy after the fact, Angel." He paused, then plunged forward. "Tell me what you're afraid of. What's so important in California that you're risking your life to get there? What is it,

Angel? Tell me. Trust me." Blade waited for the truth.

Angel was torn. Everything Blade had said was right. But could she confide in him? Could she trust him with her life? "I can't."

"Angel, you had enough confidence in me to hire me, didn't you? You entrusted me with your lives for the trip. Trust me now." Curbing his anger, he tried to reason with her. "You should know by now that I'd never let anything harm you."

"I'm paying you to take us to California, Blade. Don't try to convince me that you're doing this for any more noble reason than money." She hurled the words at him, but then felt her guard drop as she remembered how he'd saved Lucky from the snake and chased off the two men who might have harmed them. He'd rescued them from danger again today, danger that she was responsible for.

Blade took a step closer, stung by her words. "Yes," he admitted. "I did take the job for the money. I wanted that ranch, and you made it easy for me to get it. But now . . ."

"If money's so important to you, what's to stop you from selling yourself to the highest bidder now?" Angel challenged, her green eyes darkening as she imagined the worst: Michael paying Blade to return her to Philadelphia.

"I told you I'd take you to California, and I will— if that's what you really want." He waited for her reply.

"What if someone came along and offered you

twice what I paid you to betray me, would you do it?"

"Betray you?" His gaze hardened as he realized she thought him capable of such treachery. "You think I'm that low that I'd turn on you for money?" He could see the uncertainty in her expression, and he lifted one hand to caress her cheek. His smile was bittersweet. "You don't know me very well, love. I'd lay down my life for you if it would take away the terror I see in your eyes. Trust me."

"It's not that simple," she insisted, trembling at the touch of his hand.

"It is that simple," Blade countered. He took her by the shoulders and pulled her to him. His eyes were burning with an inner fire. He wanted her. He loved her as he'd never loved before, and yet he could feel her slipping away from him. How could he prove to her that he cared? That he would never hurt her? "Look at me, Angel! Look in my eyes! Can't you tell how I feel about you? Don't you know that there isn't anything I wouldn't do for you?"

"Blade, . . . I . . ." She lifted shimmering emerald eyes to stormy gray ones that revealed the depth of his feelings for her. Another of her carefully constructed defenses shattered. He was battering them down one by one and leaving her vulnerable and unprotected. She wanted to keep resisting him; she didn't know how.

"Angel." Blade groaned her name as his mouth sought hers with unerring accuracy. Although a kiss right now might destroy what little existed between them, he could think of no other way to reach her.

With firm, but gentle persuasion, his lips moved over hers. He showed no force or passion that might frighten her in his embrace, only a coaxing, tenderness that awakened the desire she'd been trying so frantically to deny. As his tongue parted her lips and sought the honeyed sweetness within, her passion erupted in explosive wonder, and another of her shields against him was vanquished.

Her defenses were devastated—not by his power, but by his gentleness. Angel clung to Blade, matching him kiss for heated kiss. The truth of her desire was revealed, not only to him, but to her; and it frightened her even as it thrilled her.

"Blade, don't do this to me," Angel begged when she broke away from him. She was breathing hard. High color stained her cheeks, and her eyes were clouded with conflicting emotions. She had to clench her hands into fists to still their shaking.

"Don't shut me out, love. Tell me that you're feeling what I feel when I kiss you." He reached for her again, but she eluded him.

"I don't know how I feel!" she insisted.

"I love you, Angel," Blade said softly.

She stared at him, bewildered. "Don't say that! I can't love you!"

"Why not?" Blade stiffened as, at her last words, a terrible possibility reared its head and he faced it squarely. Angel might desire him, true, but he was a half-breed. She might think him good enough to work for her, but that was all. It wouldn't be the first time he'd encountered prejudice.

"There are . . . obligations I have that . . ." The shadow of worry crossed her features.

"Christopher." Though her words eased his one fear, he practically spat out the name of his despised rival.

"Yes, Christopher!"

"Don't you realize that Christopher doesn't give a damn about you?!" Blade attacked the unseen man who stood between them. "He doesn't love you! If he did, he would have come for you, not left you to fend for yourself! You deserve someone who will take care of you." His voice deepened with intensity as he gambled one more time to win her. "Forget Christopher, Angel. Be honest with yourself. You want me just as much as I want you. Let me show you what love really is."

"It doesn't matter what I want." She dropped her gaze from his with a defeated shake of her head.

"You would deny what we feel for each other? Why does this man have such a powerful hold over you? Why are you so afraid? Let me fight your battles." He pulled her into his arms again and kissed her passionately. "Tell me the truth, Angel," he demanded harshly.

She tore herself away from him. "You know the truth!" she cried. "I love Christopher!" It was a meager defense against the overwhelming power of his love.

"How can you say that when you respond to me the way you do?" Reduced to begging, he cast his pride aside and reached for her, drawing her to him once again. She was fragile. He tried to cradle her against him to comfort her, but she resisted. Pain stabbed him. It would always be that way. He loved her, but she didn't want him.

A sadness filled Blade, dulling the furious edge of his frustration and coloring it with sorrow and loss. She would never be his. As before, the complete baring of his soul had only led to rejection. He began to harden himself so he could face what was coming next without revealing the pain he knew would be his.

"You don't understand," Angel said with great weariness.

"You're right. I don't understand, and I never will," he replied in defeat. He cupped her face with his hands and pressed a final, tender-soft kiss to her lips. It was over. Ended. He would never touch her again.

Angel had fought her love for him. She had denied it at every turn, but Blade's last loving kiss proved the killing blow to her battle. All resistance went out of her, and a sob caught in her throat. When his lips brushed hers, she relaxed against him, craving the haven of his embrace. Blade was safety. Blade was protection.

When the kiss ended, Angel wrapped her arms around him and rested her head against his chest, hoping to draw strength from him. The heavy, steady beat of his heart eased her, and the relief that swept through her was immense. Tears filled her eyes. She would trust him. He'd proven himself to her over and over. No one could have given more. The struggle against him had been so hard and so senseless; the defeat so simple and so wonderful.

Unaware of her turmoil, Blade felt he had to get away from her. He couldn't hold her this way and remain unaffected. He grasped her arms and held her from him so he could see her face. Crystalline tears coursed down her cheeks and touched his heart.

"Angel?" Her name was a choked, husky whisper that revealed the hope and confusion roiling within him.

Angel looked up at Blade and saw revealed in his strong, handsome features a passion so intense and so raw that it frightened her even as it reassured her. Her heart swelled with love for him. She'd been a fool not to believe in him.

"Christopher has no hold over me—no power over me except love," Angel explained, her voice thick with emotion. The words couldn't come fast enough, and she saw pain flicker in Blade's eyes. When he suddenly released her and stepped back, she realized what he'd thought and rushed on. "Blade! Wait!" In desperation, she grabbed his arm. She couldn't let him go, not now. She took the last, irreversible step and confessed, "I love Christopher, true, but not the way I love you. Christopher is my nephew, and he's only nine years old."

Blade had believed it was over. He'd believed that the next four weeks would be pure, unadulterated hell. He'd believed that he would have to eat, sleep, and breathe next to the woman he loved but could never have. And if that weren't difficult enough, he was going to have the torture of delivering her into the hands of a man who didn't deserve her and then walk away and never look back. It had been a painful prospect, but one he knew he would do no matter what the cost. He stared at her, repeating in his mind the words she'd just said. *I love Christopher, true, but not the way I love you.*

"Angel?"

"I love you, Blade." The barriers were down, and Angel smiled at him. Her eyes still shimmered with tears, but now they were tears of happiness instead of sorrow. When she saw the look of joyous disbelief on Blade's face, she boldly crossed the short distance between them and looped her arms about his neck. "I love you."

"I never thought I'd hear you say that," he murmured, crushing her to him. He buried his face in her neck, savoring the feel and the scent of her. *She loved him. It wasn't over.*

Angel drew him to her and kissed him freely. It was a rapturous exchange, and her heartbeat quickened as he held her close. She pressed against him, no longer wanting to deny her feelings. She wanted to be near him.

Blade reveled in the change in her. There was nothing he wanted more than to make love to her, but the need to know the full truth still tormented him. He ended the kiss.

"Talk to me, Angel," he murmured softly, drawing her beside him on the lush grass in the protection of the trees.

"Where should I start?" she asked, turning her troubled gaze to him.

Blade couldn't resist another kiss. His lips brushed hers in a sensuous yet controlled caress. There were questions he needed answered; a truth he needed revealed. "Start at the beginning," he urged.

"In Philadelphia," she told him, setting the scene, and the horror of the past weeks came tumbling out. She told him of Elizabeth's death and their fearful flight from Michael. She explained how she, Sarah, and Christopher had parted in St. Louis to make it tougher on Michael and how she'd met Lucky strictly by accident. She explained her bargain with the boy.

Blade smiled at this news. He'd been curious about the boy. "He's a good little actor."

"He's smart as a whip. Clever, too." Angel praised him, then added, "You know, I really do love Lucky. He's come to mean a lot to me."

"He doesn't know about Christopher?"

"No. I didn't want to tell anyone. All I wanted to do was try to draw Michael's men away from Sarah and Christopher. I did, too!" She told him of her close encounter in New Orleans, and suddenly he understood why she hadn't wanted to sail.

"You're some woman, you know that?" he told her, his eyes aglow as he looked at her. He was proud of what she'd done. "There aren't many people around who would do what you did."

She shrugged away his compliment. "He's a sweet little boy, and I love him. How could I not help him? I just wish I'd known what my sister was going through so I could have helped her before it was too late."

He heard the very real regret in her voice and tried to comfort her. "You couldn't have known if she didn't tell you."

"I know," she sighed. "But it doesn't make it any easier."

"Well, you're not alone anymore." There was a steel edge to his words. "You'll never have to deal with Michael again. I'll do everything in my power to help you, your sister, and your nephew."

Her heart was in her eyes as she gazed at him in the muted moonlight. "Thank you."

"There's no need to thank me. There's nothing I wouldn't do for you."

He reached for her then, and Angel went to him. There was no longer a need for words. They had breached the barrier of Angel's fears and there would be no more half-truths and deceptions between them. They trusted. They loved.

Chapter Seventeen

Sheltered by a canopy of low-hanging branches, Blade and Angel came together. The ugliness of the past and the danger of the future faded for the moment in the glory of their newfound love.

"I love you," Blade whispered in wonder, still not believing Angel was his. Moments before he'd thought her lost to him forever.

Joy filled him and it was so intense it was almost painful. His mouth claimed hers and her response told him that she felt the same way. She parted her lips in invitation and he eagerly accepted. Blade deepened the kiss, his tongue delving into the dark sweetness of her mouth to challenge hers in a sensual duel that left them both breathless.

When they broke apart, Angel's emerald eyes were shining and a passionate blush stained her cheeks. She gazed up at him, seeing for the first time a softness in his features. No longer was he the arrogant, hard gunfighter. She knew him now. He was the man who loved her, the man who would go to hell and back for her, the man who had won her heart by being as stubborn as she was. She framed his face with her hands and stood on tiptoe to press a gentle kiss on his lips.

"I love you, Blade Masters. You're the most wonderful man I know."

Reverently, Blade accepted her precious kiss. He hugged her close never wanting to let go. He buried his face against her neck and kissed her. Lovingly, he turned her in his arms so her back was to him.

"What are you going to do?" Angel asked.

"I'm going to fulfill a fantasy of mine," he told her huskily as he unfastened the clasp that held her hair in captive restraint.

"I've wanted to do that since the first night you walked into the hotel bar," he admitted in a hoarse voice, combing his hands through the golden tresses, freeing them from the braid's twining prison.

"You like it down?" Her eyes drifted shut. His fingers sleeked through her hair in an unexpectedly erotic caress.

"I love it down," Blade growled.

Her hair was as soft as he'd imagined, and he took great pleasure in feeling it slip between his fingers in a silken caress. The curls cascaded down her back, and Blade marvelled. Brushing her hair aside, he kissed the nape of her neck, and when she shivered and leaned back, he boldly slid his arms around her, his hands coming to rest just beneath her breasts.

Angel's breath caught in her throat, and she arched instinctively back against him. Blade wanted to go slow, but she was nearly making it impossible for him when she responded so freely to his caress. Withdrawing from that near intimacy, he let his hands skim over her, retracing the same paths he'd taken that first night when he'd massaged her neck and shoulders. Desire, hot and demanding, began to pulse through her slender body. She turned to him and wrapped her arms about his neck, kissing him passionately.

Fired by emotion, Blade laid her down upon the soft grass to make love to her, but held himself back. She was innocent, and he needed to take his time. He pulled slightly away to cool his blazing ardor.

"Blade? What is it?" Angel asked softly, her emerald eyes wide and questioning.

"Nothing, love. I just wanted to look at you . . . You're so beautiful." His mouth settled over hers again in a possessive brand. Blade was in heaven. His dream had come true. Angel loved him. His lips left hers to plant kisses along the sensitive line of her jaw. One hand settled at her waist, holding her tightly against him, while the other sought the soft mound of her breast.

The bold, intimate touch left Angel gasping with pleasure. Excitement coursed through her and her legs grew weak.

Blade could wait no longer to see her. He began to unbutton her blouse, and Angel did not resist. When the buttons were freed at last, she quickly took off the blouse and cast it aside. He started to slip the delicate straps of her camisole from her shoulders, but Angel anticipated his wish. In a very sensuous, womanly gesture, she reached up and gently pushed them down.

Blade's mouth went dry and passion's flame glowed in his eyes. His gaze was riveted on her as he stared at the enticing silken undergarment, caught and held up now only by the swell of her breasts. Unable to resist the temptation, Blade lowered his head to press hot kisses along the top of the camisole.

She tightened her arms around him, afraid he would slip from her grasp. Her eyes closed in ecstasy as his hands slid upward to cup her breasts. When he kissed them through the soft fabric, she moaned.

Blade raised his head to look at her. "You can't imagine how many times I've yearned to touch you and hold you like this."

"Perhaps as many times as I've wanted you to," Angel replied.

His gaze dropped from the sweet curve of her mouth to the camisole that still shielded her bosom from his questing gaze. "I want you, Angel. I have from that very first night."

"Oh, yes," she sighed.

Blade tugged gently at the camisole, and it settled at her waist. His breathing was labored as he stared at the beauty of her creamy, pink-tipped flesh.

Angel felt shy. She feared that she might not be pretty enough for him and that he wouldn't find her attractive. But one look at his smoldering expression eased her concern.

"You're lovely."

Made bold by his words, she reached for him. At

his questioning look, she told him, "I want to see you, too."

Blade found Angel's innocent gesture arousing. He didn't wait for her to undo his buttons, but tore at them himself in desperation. He threw the offending garment down, and he clasped her to his naked chest. Desire ruled his every action. Her satiny flesh was cool against the heat of his body, and he groaned in exquisite agony at the feel of her hard-tipped breasts crushed against him. They sank to the ground, their bodies straining together. Kissing her in wild abandon, he moved over her, and settled himself between her thighs.

Blade's lips sought her breasts and he suckled, giving her pleasure with the hot, wet touch of his mouth. The feel of his lips upon her breast flooded Angel with desire. Yearning for him, she instinctively moved her hips in search of release. Angel was mindless with pleasure.

When Blade broke away, she called out to him, begging him not to go. He silenced her with a searing kiss, exploring the slender length of her legs. Tentatively, he eased the soft undergarments from her body and at last allowed himself to gaze upon her natural beauty. Her full hips invited his touch. Her waist was tiny, her breasts full and round. Ready for her, he dropped his own clothes onto the grass.

That night at the lake, Angel had seen that he was beautiful, but she was amazed now by the perfection of his lean form. Blade was handsome. Where she was soft and round, he was hard and solid. He was tanned. His legs were long and straight; his chest wide and powerful. When she saw the hard strength of him for the first time, she did not draw away, but held out her arms in invitation.

Blade had been worried that seeing him naked would disturb her, and he was glad when she did not turn away from him. He lay down beside her again. Bracing himself up on his elbows, he gazed down upon her. The expression in his eyes was one of gentle understanding. He would still stop if she wanted him to. It wasn't too late.

"Angel, are you sure you want to do this? Are you sure you want to make love?"

"Yes, Blade. I want to love you," Angel's voice was throaty with desire as she lifted her hands to frame his face and drew him to her for a soft kiss.

At Angel's response, Blade moved over her. She wanted him as much as he wanted her. His passion became a raging torrent that swept any remaining doubts from his mind.

Blade wanted only to please Angel, to give her love's full pleasure. His hands searched out her most sensitive places. His every touch was designed to show her more of what loving really was. He was careful and gentle as he stirred the fire of her need to a fever pitch equal to his own.

Angel had never known excitement so intense. She moved restlessly beneath Blade's pleasure-giving touch, driven by the need to know him more fully. When he shifted over her, positioning himself between her legs, she lifted glowing eyes to his.

"I love you, Blade," Angel whispered.

He dipped his head, kissing her softly. There could

be no turning back the floodtide of his love, and the softness soon gave way to passion. His mouth moved over hers, coaxing and at the same time demanding, as he pressed his hips forward. That first entry into the depths of her womanhood gained, he thrust deeply into the heart of her innocence, piercing that proof of her virginity.

Angel bit down on her bottom lip at the sharp, stabbing pain of his possession.

"I'm sorry I hurt you." Blade could almost feel her pain. He began to caress her again, wanting her to know he loved her, needing to let her know he'd never intended to hurt her.

The discomfort subsided quickly. She felt the heat and power of him deep within her and hugged him close. "It's all right. I wanted this . . . I wanted you. Love me, Blade. . . ."

Her words brought him a surge of joy. His lips met hers. When he felt the tension begin to dissipate, he moved within her. His rhythm was slow at first. He wanted only to please Angel, to show her just how wonderful love could be. His hands sculpted her body, exploring her satiny curves.

As her passion grew, Angel instinctively began to move with Blade. Her hands clutched at his back as the coiling knot of desire grew ever tighter within her. His steady, powerful rhythm took her higher and higher, edging her ever closer to the moment of Elysian ecstasy when nothing mattered but the glory of his body deep within hers and the splendor of holding him in her arms.

It happened then—paradise. In a moment of exquisite beauty they reached that pinnacle of rapture together. Their bodies locked in love's fulfilling embrace, each giving to the other, each taking from the other in a perfect unending circle of love.

When at last the heavenly, heart-stirring excitement passed, Blade rolled to his side, taking her with him. Their bodies were still one, and they rested in each other's arms, their legs entwined in a sensuous tangle.

Blade held her near, one hand gently stroking her hair. He could not remember a time in his life when he'd been so content, so happy. He savored the moment, wishing he could stop time and stay right there in her arms for all eternity. She was his heaven. In her embrace, he'd found that which he'd always sought and never hoped to find. Peace and love.

Angel lay in Blade's arms, treasuring the incredible poignancy of being one with him. Dazed, she wondered how she'd managed to resist him for so long. Only with Blade was she loved. Only with Blade was she safe. How difficult it must have been for him to listen to her talk of Christopher. She smiled into the darkness, glad that he'd loved her enough to fight for her. Blade would own her heart forever. He had given her the gift of himself, and she would cherish that gift always.

They lay together in the darkness, sharing tender kisses and gentle touches. Reality would not stay at bay, though, and eventually they knew they would have to return to the campsite. With regret, Blade drew her to him for one, last lingering kiss.

"We'd better go back," Blade said sadly, yet he made no move to let her go.

"I know," Angel agreed with a sigh, not wanting to leave his embrace. "I wouldn't want Lucky to come looking for us right now."

They remained quietly together for a little longer, then slowly moved apart. Blade helped her dress, kissing and caressing her as he did so.

"I liked taking them off of you much more than I like putting them back on," he told her with a wry smile.

She kissed him then and almost made him forget his good intentions. Once they were both fully clothed, Angel linked her arms around his waist and rested her head against his chest.

"I'll talk to Lucky in the morning."

"What are you going to tell him?" Blade asked, wrapping his arms around her and holding her to his heart.

"The truth. It's time," Angel answered simply. "Now that you know everything, there's no reason to keep it from him any longer."

"That's good. He deserves to know what's going on." Blade hesitated, then took her gently by the shoulders and held her slightly away from him as he asked, "What will you tell him about us?"

Angel looked up at this magnificent man. "I'll tell him that I love you," she whispered.

His eyes darkened with emotion. He bent to kiss her. "Tell him we love each other."

Blade took her hand in his, and they walked slowly back to the campsite. They paused just outside the ring of the firelight to kiss once more, then he walked with her to her bedroll and waited until she'd lain down. He wanted to stay with her, to hold her in his arms and make love to her again, but he didn't. He moved off to his own separate bed, content for the moment with the joy of knowing she loved him.

Angel curled in her bedroll; her heart filled with wonder, her body alive in the aftermath of passion. She fell asleep, reliving Blade's declaration of love, and for the first time in days, she slept soundly.

Blade lay down across the fire from Angel, wishing she were beside him. Far from diminishing his need for her, making love had increased his desire. He wanted to hold her and kiss her and keep her with him every minute of every day. As he lay there staring sleeplessly up into the night sky, he went over every detail of their intimacy. He had taken her innocence and had claimed her. She was everything he'd ever wanted in a woman, and she was his. He smiled to himself at the thought.

The smile faded, though, when he let his thoughts drift back over their conversation. He'd been right from the beginning. She was running from someone, a man who'd murdered his wife and would harm his son if he got the chance. Michael Marsden. The name was a curse in his mind, and Blade vowed to make certain the man never hurt anyone again—not Angel or her sister or her nephew.

Blade closed his eyes and tried to sleep, but the image of Angel, naked in his arms stirred too many feelings for him to rest. He sighed, but decided that it had been worth another sleepless night.

* * *

The eastern horizon was already brightening when Lucky finally woke up. It startled him to have slept so late, and he jumped up nervously, thinking Blade and Angel would be annoyed with him. To his surprise, he found Blade sitting by the campfire, looking quite relaxed, drinking coffee.

"G'morning," Lucky said slowly, frowning. Every day since they'd been on the trail, Blade had been up and moving before dawn—even on days when it had rained. Today, however, the sun was shining, things were dry, and yet Blade was sitting there acting as if he were enjoying himself. It didn't make sense.

"Good morning." Blade smiled.

"You want me to wake Angel?" he asked urgently. "I know it's late and we—"

"No," Blade answered. "Let her sleep."

"You sure? She's going to be awful mad if we're not riding soon," Lucky cautioned.

"Don't worry. I'll handle it if she gets mad," he assured the boy confidently. "I want to rest the horses. The last few days were rough on them and they need to take it easy for a while."

"All right," the boy agreed, puzzled. Something must have happened last night after he had gone to sleep. He'd known Blade was angry, and from the way things looked now, he supposed the two of them must have had it out with Blade the victor. Still, he was curious about what had happened, and he couldn't wait for Angel to wake up so he could find out. To his dismay, it was almost an hour before she stirred.

Sunshine finally penetrated Angel's sleep, and she opened her eyes to find the new day well under way. She threw off her blanket.

"Good morning, Angel!" Lucky called out cheerfully. He and Blade were tending the horses.

"Morning."

Blade heard the boy's call and her answer and looked up to see Angel sitting on her blanket. Her hair was free and tumbling about her in glorious disarray, and she looked as though she'd awakened from a night of passionate lovemaking. A current of desire shot straight through Blade, and he couldn't look away. He'd thought her hair lovely in the moonlight, but that dim, unearthly glow hadn't done it justice. In the sunlight, her tresses shone—a myriad of shades blended together by nature's hand. He longed to touch her curls.

Angel felt wonderful. She saw Lucky where he stood by the horses, but she had not yet seen Blade and she wondered where he was. *Blade*. Just the thought of him brought a soft smile to her lips and, as if sensing his gaze upon her, Angel glanced in his direction. Their gazes locked. Neither one could forget the intimacy of the night before.

Blade had to admit he was a little nervous about facing Angel this morning. He wasn't sure just how she was going to react to him. He'd been awake for most of the night, but the dreadful fear that she might harbor some regrets hadn't occured to him until a short time before. As he watched for her reaction, he was careful to keep his expression inscrutable. It wouldn't do to appear too eager if she had awoken this morning with a change of heart.

Angel saw Blade standing near the horses, looking much like the serious gunfighter she'd seen that very first morning in New Orleans when she'd overheard the two women talking about him. She'd found him intimidating before, but now that she had held him in her arms, she could only love him. They had touched souls, and she'd found a gentleness in him. She could not keep her love for him hidden, and a bright, silly smile spread over her face. He was the man she loved, and she wanted him to know it.

Blade saw her smile and all the dread that had haunted him vanished. He hadn't realized he was so tense. Helpless to do anything else, he smiled back at her. Nothing had changed overnight. Everything was wonderful. Drawn magnetically to her, he walked away from what he was doing and went straight to her.

Angel's heart lightened at his answering smile, and when he came toward her she rose from her bed to greet him.

"How are you this morning?" Blade asked as he joined her.

"Fine," she said, her eyes sparkling as she gazed up at him. "In fact, I can't remember ever feeling better." She wanted to hug him, but knew she couldn't. Lucky was only a short distance away and would have been able to see them had she decided to be so delightfully brazen.

"Good." Blade was smiling down at her and

couldn't seem to help himself. He realized he probably looked like a damned idiot, but he didn't care. She was absolutely breathtaking in the morning, and he imagined what it would be like to wake up with her in his arms. It was an appealing daydream. He wondered how soon he could make it come true.

"How are you?" She took a step closer to him, a small concession to her desire to launch herself into his arms.

"I'm fine. Real fine."

"How soon did you want to leave?" They could not speak freely in front of Lucky, and she felt awkward.

"If we ride out before noon, we can still make good time today. I'm going to change our direction a little bit."

"Why?"

"There's a special place I want to take you."

"Where?"

"I want you to meet my mother's people."

Angel was stunned. He'd revealed little of himself to her, and this new openness touched her. "I'd like that. Is it far?"

"If the weather stays clear, it's less than a week's ride and it's on the way."

"What is?" Lucky asked, joining them.

"I thought you might like to pay a visit to an Indian village," Blade explained.

"Can we go, Angel?" Lucky turned imploring eyes to her.

"Yes. Blade says it's safe."

"My mother's people are peaceful. We'll be welcome."

"When do we leave?" Lucky asked, unable to contain his excitement.

Angel grinned. "Later this morning," she replied. "First, though, come sit with me while I have some breakfast. There are a few things I need to tell you." Angel poured herself a mug of coffee and helped herself to some of the food Blade had prepared earlier.

After taking a deep, bracing drink of the strong, hot brew, Angel lifted troubled eyes to Lucky as she started to speak of her horror for the second time in less than a day. "It's time I told you the truth about why I'm going to California."

"You aren't going there to get married?"

"No. I'm not. In fact, most of what I told you, I made up."

"Why?"

Angel explained everything from her sister's violent death to their flight with Christopher to the moment when she'd caught Lucky trying to steal from her in St. Louis. "You needed someone to care for you, and I knew I could do it. I thought if we traveled together, we might draw any of Michael's men who were following us away from Sarah and Christopher and give them time to escape."

"Why didn't we take the steamboat out of New Orleans like you'd planned?"

"There was a man named Watkins already in New Orleans looking for me. I overheard him talking to some men in the steamship office that day I went to check on our passage."

"So that's why you hired Blade. . . ."

"Yes. I still had to get to California so I could meet with my sister and nephew, and overland was the only way left. If Michael's men had caught up with me that soon, there would have been no way Sarah could have gotten far enough away to guarantee Christopher's safety."

"Does Blade know the truth now?"

"Yes. We talked last night and I told him everything."

Lucky stared at her, trying to grasp what it all meant—and where it left him. "You used me," he accused.

"No. Never that," Angel denied. "I wanted to help you, but I knew you were much too proud to accept any offer of help and I knew you didn't trust me. That's why I made you the job offer. I was sure you'd be better off with me anywhere, than you would be staying all alone on the streets."

"So there are men still chasing you?"

"Yes."

"Why did you suddenly decide to tell us the truth?"

Angel looked a bit shame-faced. "Because I finally came to trust Blade. He's very special."

Lucky agreed. He thought of that day at the lake when he'd first realized that Angel and Blade were attracted to each other, and he asked, "Do you love him?"

Angel gave him a quick, surprised look and then

answered with a resigned smile, "Yes. I love him, and I trust him completely."

Lucky was glad that everything was straightened out between them, but he grew defensive as he thought about his own predicament. It was good that they were happy, but what was going to happen to him? "What about me now?"

"What about you?"

"Is our deal off? 'Cause if it is, I still want the whole amount. You said in New Orleans that I wouldn't get paid if I quit, but you didn't say nothing about what would happen if you did," he demanded angrily. The strong emotion hid the panic that gripped him at the thought of losing Blade and Angel.

"Lucky," she said gently, wanting to ease his fear. "Nothing's changed. We're still going to California. The only thing that's different is that you and Blade now know the truth."

"You still want me to go with you?" He covered his pleasure with caution.

"Of course I want you with me! I love you, Lucky. I don't want to lose you." Angel held out her arms to him; and, for the very first time, Lucky went to her and hugged her. She held him tight. Lucky cherished her embrace.

Later, when they were getting ready to saddle up and ride out, Blade approached him. "We're going to have to take care of Angel, you and me," Blade told Lucky as he rested a warm, affectionate hand on his shoulder. "She needs us, you know. We have to keep her safe."

Lucky was pleased by this unexpected man-to-man confidence, and he felt proud as he answered him, "I know. I don't want those bad men to hurt her. I may not be her real brother, but I wish I were. I love her."

"Good." Blade smiled down at him with genuine respect, liking him, knowing he had the makings of a fine man despite his rough beginnings. "That makes two of us, son."

The boy gazed with open affection at the man who had become his hero. They shared a manly look of mutual regard, and then mounted their horses to escort Angel to safety. They rode westward again.

Chapter Eighteen

"I'll take your horse," Blade offered as he helped Angel dismount. His hands lingered at her waist as he set her on her feet before him. He longed to take her in his arms and kiss her, but he held himself in check. Lucky was nearby, and he didn't want to do anything untoward.

"Thank you," Angel replied, smiling up at him. She had no idea that Blade thought her smile seductive. She just knew that she loved him and wished she could kiss him right that minute.

Reluctantly, they moved apart. Angel began to set up camp, while Blade took their horses and joined Lucky.

"You gonna marry Angel?" Lucky asked as Blade approached. He'd been watching them and had noticed their closeness, but Blade was caught completely off-guard by the question. "What?"

"You said you loved Angel. Are you gonna marry her?"

"I don't know."

"If you love her, you should marry her." Lucky's logic had a straightforward simplicity Blade liked.

"I wish it were that simple," Blade hedged. He'd been thinking of little else. Being near her and not being able to touch her frustrated him. They'd shared a short, sweet kiss every chance they could; but, with the boy along, they'd both decided it would be best if they remained apart. He dreamed of proposing and taking her with him to the ranch, but reality intruded on his dreams and shattered them. He could not ignore his past and reputation.

"Why isn't it that simple?" Lucky persisted. "You love each other. Right?"

"Right," Blade agreed. "But sometimes things don't turn out the way we hope they will."

"Aren't you even going to ask her?"

"When the time is right," he answered evasively.

"Good." Satisfied for the moment, Lucky returned to his work.

Blade, however, could not turn his thoughts away from Angel. Since their night of loving, she had been foremost in his mind. He wanted her for his own, but he held back. There was so much about him she didn't know, so much he never talked about to anyone.

She believed she loved him, but would she still feel that way once she'd learned everything about him? He had to be certain. When they stopped at the Wichita village, her reaction to his mother's people would show him if she could accept his heritage. Though he'd been raised as a white man, he came face to face with prejudice every day. And there was the violence of his lifestyle. No matter how much he wanted to retire to the ranch, there was always the danger that some young gun might come looking for him. He had to be sure Angel understood everything. He never wanted her to regret her decision, should she agree to be his wife.

A few hours later when Blade was finally ready to turn in, Angel was still awake. He felt her gaze upon him, but turned and walked away from the camp. He wanted to lose himself in the night.

Angel had noticed that Blade had been unusually quiet all night, his expression guarded. She'd watched him, trying to gauge his mood, but couldn't figure out what had upset him. When she realized that he'd left the camp because of her, she knew she had to go after him.

"Blade? Is something wrong?" Angel asked, coming up behind him in the darkness.

"No, why?" Blade answered, turning to her in the moonlight. To be this close to her and not be able to make love was torture.

"I don't know," she said softly. "You looked preoccupied all evening, and I thought something was bothering you."

He smiled wryly. "The only thing bothering me is you, love." He couldn't resist the urge to lift his hand and brush his knuckles along the soft curve of her cheek. "You're beautiful, and I want you so badly."

His light caress left her feeling cherished and loved. She sighed and slipped her arms around his neck, rising on tiptoe to kiss him. That he loved her enough to deny himself increased her respect for him. "Once this is over, things will be different for us."

"I hope so," he said, kissing her again. He'd meant to keep the kiss chaste, but the control he so prided himself on deserted him the moment he held her close. Her lips were honeyed; her flesh a sweet, alluring invitation. His hands dropped to her hips and he brought her tight against him. His body responded instinctively to hers, and he was a breath away from heaven when he ended the embrace. He managed a weak smile as he pressed his fingertips against her lips to ease the pain of breaking apart.

"You'd better go on to bed now."

"I don't want to."

"Me neither." Why was the right thing always the hardest thing to do? "Tomorrow's going to be a long day."

"Aren't they all?"

"Yes, but tomorrow, we'll reach the Wichita village."

"Are you sure they won't mind our just riding in like this?"

"We'll be welcomed," he assured her. It had been a while since he'd last visited his grandparents, but they always greeted him with open arms and this time would be no exception.

"You haven't said much about your mother's family. Do you have a lot of relatives?"

"Just my grandmother, Soaring Dove, and my grandfather, Night Wolf."

"Do you see them often?" Angel asked. Blade was

still a mystery to her. Loving him as she did, she was eager to find out all she could.

"Not as often as I should. But don't worry, they'll be glad to see us."

"Tell me about them. I don't know anything about Indians except . . . well . . . what people say."

"What do they say?" he asked, but he already knew.

"That Indians are blood-thirsty savages who kill for no reason," she told him.

"Do you believe that?"

"Is it true?"

"Some tribes are more hostile than others, as some white men are more vicious than others. The Wichita are peaceful unless they're defending their own."

In the moonlight she could see the Indian heritage etched clearly in his features. She could see strength and pride. It was easy to imagine him as a warrior for his tribe, and the thought sent a shiver through her. "Blade?"

"What?"

"How did your parents meet?"

"My father was a trader. He was injured, and the Wichita found him and nursed him back to health," he revealed. "While he was in the village, he fell in love with my mother. She loved him, too, so they married. When he left, she went with him."

"Was it hard for her, leaving her home that way and going to live in a whole different world?"

Terrible memories flooded through Blade. His mother had been a gentle, loving woman, but he remembered all too clearly how she'd been looked down upon by the whites whenever they'd gone into town for supplies. They'd thought her less than human and treated her that way.

"It was very difficult for her, but she was happy with my father. Only death could have separated them." His answer was terse as he remembered the depth of their devotion.

"If two people love each other, then even the hardest of trials are bearable," Angel remarked softly, gazing up at him. "It must have been very difficult for you when they died."

"I was fourteen. The fever took them." His expression turned bleak.

"What did you do all alone so young?" Angel put her arms around him as she saw the despair in his eyes.

He shrugged as he tried to force the turmoil of his emotions back under control. "It wasn't easy, but I handled it." *Yes*, he thought, *he'd handled it all right. He'd practiced with his gun until he'd been fast and accurate, and then he'd gone looking for the three men who'd kept him from getting the help that would have saved his mother.* "It wasn't too much after that that I started hiring my gun out."

"But you were just a child."

"By then I was a man."

She heard the hardness in his voice and knew that that had been the terrible turning point in his life. "I heard the talk about you when I was in New Orleans." She paused as she felt him stiffen. "What really happened, Blade?"

It was so painful that Blade almost couldn't tell

her. She had been honest with him, though, and now it was his turn. She needed to know what she would have to face if she married him. The rigidity left him as he began to explain. "My father caught the fever first, and my mother tried to cure him in her own way, but nothing worked. The same day he died, my mother was struck down. I went into town for help, even though she begged me not to go." He stopped and drew a deep, shuddering breath.

She urged, "Go on." Her arms tightened around him as she saw him in her mind's eye—a terrified boy racing to save his mother's life.

"I was scared, but I went anyway. She'd been right, though. The doctor wouldn't come. He didn't have time to waste on a squaw."

Pain stabbed at Angel's heart as she listened.

"I tried to hurry home, but three drunks who didn't want half-breeds or Indians in their town stopped me. I begged them to let me go." The terror and helplessness that had gripped him then filled him now. His tone went flat as he continued, "I wasn't much of a challenge for them. I don't remember what happened. When I came to, I was tied on my horse, out in the countryside somewhere. By the time I got home, my mother was . . . really bad." Blade remembered how, even in her weakened state, she'd reached out with tender hands to smooth the tears from his bruised cheeks and to tell him she loved him. Those had been the last words she'd ever said to him. His jaw tensed at the recollection. "She died a little later."

"I'm sorry," Angel whispered huskily as a rush of tender emotion filled her.

Blade moved out of her embrace. "The next day I wasn't scared any more." His words were harsh and deadly, but the look in his eyes was haunted as he remembered the pain and sorrow that had filled him as he'd stood over their barren graves. "I buried them both by myself. Then I got my gun. When I got good enough, I went looking for the three drunks." His eyes locked on hers as he tried to see into her soul. He needed to know how she felt about his thirst for revenge. Did she understand—or was she repulsed? "I made sure it was a fair fight in front of witnesses. Then I left town, and I've never gone back, not even to the ranch."

"I can understand why," she told him, her love for him growing ever stronger.

"I've lived by the gun ever since, Angel."

Angel was too much in love to worry about that. She trusted him. Blade had deliberately distanced himself from her as he'd talked, and she now took a step toward him, wanting a return to their intimacy. "I love you, Blade. Nothing will ever change that." She saw a flicker of something in his troubled gray eyes. *Doubt? Or was it hope?* She pressed a soft kiss to his mouth. "Thank you for telling me. I know it wasn't easy for you, and I'm glad you confided in me."

"It's something I don't think about very often."

"I understand," she said gently. "I try not to think about the night before Elizabeth's funeral when I found the marks on her arm. It hurts too much."

Blade kissed her once more, this time with poignant tenderness. He held her to his heart. "I wish I could hold you like this forever."

"And ever."

They clung to each other in silence, enjoying the serenity of their embrace. Reluctantly, they moved apart.

"We'd better get some rest."

Blade walked her to her pallet, kissed her once more, and then sought his own solitary bedroll. He hadn't dredged up those painful memories in many years, but now, having faced them with Angel, he didn't feel the same depth of pain he usually experienced. Angel cared. A deep, abiding sense of peace filled him. She had heard him out and had offered only acceptance and love. She had not condemned him or otherwise passed judgment on anything he'd done. She'd said that she loved him and that nothing would change that. He wanted to believe, but he had to be sure. Tomorrow when they reached the village, he would have his answer.

Across the campfire, her heart filled with love for Blade, Angel curled in her blankets and slept.

As Blade, Angel, and Lucky approached the village late that afternoon, the word spread among the Wichita people that visitors were coming and they left what they were doing to see who was riding in. When one of the men, a short, dark-skinned man of stocky build, recognized Blade, he called out a greeting to him in the native tongue. Blade smiled broadly, lifted a hand to wave, and responded in kind.

Angel and Lucky stared in fascination tinged with fear as Blade led their way slowly into the village. It was much larger than Angel and Lucky had expected, with over thirty homes in the camp. To their surprise, however, the abodes were not tepees, but round buildings constructed of sturdy supporting poles with grass coverings.

The people who'd gathered to watch their entrance stared at them with open interest. The weather was warm, and the men wore only loincloths and mocassins. The women were dressed in far less revealing attire; their deerskin gowns, decorated with elks' teeth, hung below their knees. Angel could tell they were talking about her, for they whispered and laughed, pointing at her. Not wanting to betray her nervousness, Angel clutched her reins a little tighter and tried to smile. It was not easy.

"My grandfather's home is just ahead," Blade told them as he angled his horse toward a hut a short distance away.

"Are you sure we're welcome here?" Lucky asked.

Blade flashed him a quick smile. "Scared?"

"A little," he admitted, but then added with a surge of bravado, "but only 'cause I don't know what they're saying."

"There's no need to be afraid. They've been talking about Angel's hair. One woman said it was the color of dead grass." He chuckled at the remark as he glanced over at Angel, thinking her golden mane glorious. "But another insisted it was the color of the summer sun—vivid, glowing, and bright. I think the summer sun is closest."

"Thanks," she returned, managing a real smile at last. "I wondered why they were laughing."

"We're here," Blade said, reining in his horse and dismounting before an elderly couple who watched him with great pride. "Come and meet my grandparents, Soaring Dove and Night Wolf."

Night Wolf was of average height and had coal black hair and black eyes. He tended to the heavy side and looked ferocious until he smiled at Blade. He called to him in his native tongue and went to embrace him as soon as he'd dismounted.

"It has been a long time, my grandson," Night Wolf scolded, his dark eyes dancing with joy at the sight of his daughter's child. "What has kept you from us?"

"Many things, Night Wolf, but none matter now that I am back with you."

"You're right," he decided with a big smile. "Come see your grandmother."

Soaring Dove, a short, thin woman with gentle eyes and a gentle smile, enveloped him in a warm hug. For just a moment, Blade let himself enjoy her embrace. As always, her touch reminded him of his mother and filled him with a painful mixture of sorrow and happiness.

"Hello, Grandmother," he told her, smiling down at her with open love and affection when they broke apart. "I've missed you."

"And I've missed you," Soaring Dove said, tears of happiness shining in her eyes. "It has been too long, much too long." She glanced at Angel and Lucky, who'd dismounted and stood awkwardly to one side. "She is a beautiful woman, this one. Have you finally taken a wife?"

Blade was glad that they spoke in the Wichita language. He looked at Angel and the boy, then back at his grandmother. "No, I have not married—yet."

She gave him a sharp look. "What does that mean? When you look at her there is love in your eyes, yet you have not taken her for your wife?"

Blade recovered and flashed her a wide grin. "I said 'yet,' Grandmother. As usual you are far too wise and know me much too well."

Soaring Dove looked pleased. "What is her name?"

"Her name is Angela, but we call her Angel. The boy is Lucky." He pronounced both their names in English. "Come, I will introduce you."

He made the introductions quickly in English. Although his grandparents could speak the language, for they'd learned it from his father, they preferred their own tongue. But as a courtesy to Angel and Lucky, they spoke English.

"It is good to meet two friends of my grandson," Night Wolf welcomed them. "Come into our home and be comfortable. We will eat soon and you can rest."

Soaring Dove ushered them inside, and Angel was amazed at how spacious the lodge was. The fire pit was in the center of the floor, vented through the peak of the roof. There were raised sleeping platforms along the side walls with buffalo hide curtains hung to afford some privacy. The curtains had been decorated with paintings and added much color to the inside of the home.

After they'd eaten, the men and women separated. Blade took Lucky with him, and they joined Night Wolf in visiting with the other men of the village. Lucky was round-eyed as he listened to them talking in the foreign tongue; but soon he grew bored and when Blade urged him play with the other boys in the village, he was glad to go.

Soaring Dove, meanwhile, had taken Angel under her wing and had introduced her to her friends in the village. The old woman's warmth and good humor quickly put Angel at ease, and Angel found herself eager to learn all she could about the Wichita and Blade's family. As they walked through the village, Angel occasionally caught sight of Blade with his grandfather and the other men. When she did, she found herself gazing at him raptly. For the first time since she'd met him, he seemed completely at ease, his guard down. He was laughing with these men more than she'd ever heard him laugh before. It was good. Blade glanced in Angel's direction to find her eyes upon him. He smiled at her, and she couldn't help but smile back.

"Do you care for my grandson?" the old woman asked perceptively. She'd never been one to mince words. She believed in telling the truth always.

"I love him, Soaring Dove," she answered her honestly.

"I thought so." She nodded knowingly as she gave

her an assessing look. "But can you bear the heartache?"

Angel was confused. "I don't understand."

"Blade is a fine man, a good man, and you say you love him now, but will your love for him be strong enough? Will you stand by him when all others hate him for his Indian blood?"

Angel's expression grew serious, and her eyes shone with the truth of her next words. "I will love him more, Soaring Dove. I will stay with him always."

Again the old woman's eyes assessed her. "We will see," she said cryptically, then changed the subject. "Tonight, there will be much excitement in the village."

"Why?"

"Little Crow is going to offer for Laughing Waters. He is a brave warrior and has a rich family, but she has not shown him any preference. His uncle visited her family last night, and it was agreed that Little Crow should come tonight for a visit. It will be interesting to see if she wants him. If she does, there will be a big marriage feast tomorrow night."

"And if she doesn't?"

"Tomorrow night will not be a happy one for Little Crow." Soaring Dove smothered a chuckle at the thought of the vain warrior being refused.

"There will be a marriage feast," Blade said confidently as he and Night Wolf joined them. He knew Little Crow, and he knew no maiden would turn him down.

"Only if Laughing Waters agrees," his grandmother countered. "We will find out tonight."

"She would be a fool to refuse him," Night Wolf said.

"And Laughing Waters is no fool," Soaring Dove agreed.

As darkness fell, the news came that Laughing Waters had indeed agreed to marry Little Crow. Everyone in the village was happy that there would be a great celebration the next night.

"Angel, would you like to stay here an extra night? The horses could rest, and we could join in the party."

"I'd like that," she agreed quickly. Soaring Dove had put her at ease among the people, translating for her and helping her fit in. It hadn't been long before her fears had disappeared. She enjoyed the company of these genuine friendly women.

"Good." Blade bid her good night and left her at the hut with his grandmother while he went to join the men to talk and tell stories.

Angel was given a bed all to herself with a curtain to give her privacy from the men. She slept soundly that night despite the foreignness of her surroundings.

Lucky had been having fun playing with the boys, and he regretted having to go to bed when Blade called him late that night. When Blade told him they would be staying an extra day, he was thrilled. He looked forward to another day with his newfound friends.

When Blade finally retired for the night, he lay on

his sleeping platform across the lodge from Angel, contemplating his future. She had fit in far more perfectly than he'd ever hoped. There had been no disdain or hatred in her eyes when she'd met his family and mingled with his grandmother's people. She had been open and curious and honestly interested. Soaring Dove had even taken him aside and told him that she was a woman worth having. That coming from his grandmother. who would have preferred him to marry an Indian girl and live in the village, was high praise. The wedding feast tomorrow night would give him the opportunity he sought, and he determined with a firm resolve to ask Angel to marry him then.

Chapter Nineteen

The wedding celebration began just after sundown the next day. Little Crow and his family came to Laughing Waters' home with presents suitable for the woman he was taking to be his bride. The gifts were extravagant. Her family was given four horses and three buffalo robes, and it was obvious to all that he loved her very much. The feast followed, and all were welcomed, for Little Crow was a very rich, very important man in the tribe. The food was delicious and more than plentiful. The Wichita were a farming people, and the bounty from their gardens was prepared in many different ways. Buffalo meat was served along with other Wichita staples. The bride glowed under the attentions of her handsome warrior-husband, and all present wished them many healthy children together. It was a celebration the village would long remember and relive.

Lucky had been with his friends all day, learning to use a bow and arrow, swimming in the small creek nearby, and racing their horses. He'd never known such a carefree life, and he regretted that they had to leave so soon. When his friend, Sitting Dog, invited him to spend the night with him at his lodge, Lucky went in search of Blade and Angel to ask permission. He found them sitting with Blade's grandparents amidst the revelers. Dropping down on the ground beside them, he watched the dancing rituals with interest.

"Angel, Sitting Dog has asked me to stay the night in his lodge. Can I?"

Angel deferred to Blade because he knew the customs of the people, and he thought the idea a wonderful one.

"That'll be fine, but just remember we do have to leave in the morning." Blade had an ulterior motive. If Lucky were occupied elsewhere, he'd have Angel to himself. That would give him the time he needed to propose.

"We can't stay any longer?" It was as close as Lucky would let himself come to begging.

"I'm sorry, Lucky. I know you're having a good time and you've made many friends here, but I have to get to California." She was truly sorry that she had to put an end to his good times so soon.

Lucky understood, though, and felt ashamed for having so easily forgotten the danger to her nephew. He reminded himself that staying with Angel was the important thing. She needed him, and he was determined to help Blade protect her. Thinking of Blade, then, he slanted a look at him, wondering if he'd thought any more about proposing. Blade had said he was waiting for the right moment, and tonight certainly seemed like the right time to Lucky.

"This getting married looks like fun," the boy prodded, hoping to urge Blade on. He was surprised when Angel looked a bit sad.

"With the right person, marriage can be a wonderful thing, but it's a lifetime obligation and not one to be taken lightly," Angel told him, her thoughts on Elizabeth and Michael and how he'd blinded her sister with his smooth ways. "It's important that two people know each other very well before they get married."

"If I were older I'd marry you tonight, right this minute, Angel," Lucky vowed, giving Blade a look that spoke volumes.

Blade saw the challenge in his gaze, but pretended to ignore it.

"If you were older, I just might accept," she replied, oblivious to the undercurrents between the two men in her life.

"Just?" He pretended outrage.

"I like to keep my beaux guessing, like Laughing Waters did Little Crow," she teased, happy and light-hearted again. Glancing up, she saw Sitting Dog waiting for him. She smiled as she urged, "Go on. Have fun. Your friend is waiting. There's no need to sweet talk me any more; you know I love you."

"G'night." Lucky raced off with his friends.

The boy's goading worked, and it wasn't much later that Blade suggested to Angel that they take a walk. She was more than willing to leave the crowd of celebrants and spend some time alone with him.

Since they'd come to the village, he'd spent most of his time with his grandfather and, while she understood, she'd missed his company.

The moon provided all the light they needed to escape from the noise and confusion. As they walked farther away from the brightness of the village's fires, the sky came into focus and Angel could see the thousands of stars that sparkled in the heavens.

"It's a beautiful night," she breathed as they stopped near the creek.

The gentle sound of the water rushing by, coupled with the soft, cool night breeze, made the moment idyllic. It was almost as if they were truly in paradise.

"Did you like the wedding feast?" Blade asked as he slipped an arm about her waist and drew her to him. He thought she looked absolutely breathtaking tonight. Her hair shimmered, cascading down her shoulders, and she'd worn her one dress.

Angel wrapped her arms about him and rested her head against his chest. He felt warm and solid, and she felt safe in his arms. "It was much like most parties, I think—a lot of food, drink, dancing, and laughing. Weddings should be happy times, but when Elizabeth got married, I wasn't happy."

"You weren't? Why?"

"I was young, but I knew even then that Michael was no good. I'd seen him kissing a maid in the front hall of our home while he was waiting for Elizabeth. I tried to tell her, but neither she nor my aunt would listen. They thought Michael was perfect, and I was the one who was punished." Angel sighed. "If only I could have convinced them that night—if only they'd believed me, none of this would have happened."

"But Angel, if they had listened, you wouldn't be here with me right now," he murmured, holding her close and loving the feel of her slender body in his arms. "Good has come out of it. There's Christopher, and you saved Lucky, and you saved me."

She looked up at him in surprise at his last words. "I saved you?"

"Hmm," he said softly. "I was alone in the world, and you made me whole again."

Blade gazed down at her, his soul aching with the depth of love he felt for her. He knew now what Little Crow must have gone through the night before when he was awaiting Laughing Waters' answer, and he sympathized greatly with the brave warrior. He'd faced down many a gunfighter in his time, but he'd never known a greater fear of failure than he did now.

Blade knew he would have no better opportunity to ask her to be his wife. Everything was perfect. The moon had cooperated, lighting the night with its soft, romantic glow. The breeze was just light enough to cool them. A night bird called out its lilting song, adding a exquisite touch of serenity to the moment. He was in heaven, and she was his guardian Angel.

"Angel, I love you. If I could, I'd ask my grandfather to go to your home right now with gifts of horses and robes." He watched her expression carefully. He was hoping to see joy there, but he was prepared for rejection. "Angel . . . Love. . . . Marry me."

Angel's heart ached with happiness as she gazed up

at the man who would be her husband. "I love you, too, Blade, but there's one more thing I need to know before I can give you my answer."

Blade's throat tightened. He'd told her everything. She knew the truth of his life. He couldn't imagine what else it was that she needed to know. "What is it?"

Angel was having a hard time trying to keep a straight face as she asked with great seriousness, "How many horses would your grandfather bring?"

Blade was so intent on the moment that it took him a second to realize she was teasing. When it finally dawned on him, a slow, sensuous smile curved its way across his handsome lips. "You are worth every horse I own on the ranch. I'd gladly walk the rest of my days just to claim you for my own."

Joy surged through Angel, and her tears fell unheeded. "Yes, Blade. Oh, yes! I'll marry you." Her mouth found his and she told him with her kiss, everything he'd ever wanted to know. She loved him. They would be together always.

Alone in the night, they shared a heated embrace. Blade's lips moved hungrily over hers, starving for a full taste of her love. Angel couldn't stop the moan that escaped her when his hands cupped her breasts. Excitement coursed through her. She wanted him as much as he wanted her. She drew back, her eyes glowing.

"Love me, Blade."

Blade needed no further invitation. He was filled with desire. They sank down on the soft grass, and he moved over her.

"You're so beautiful, Angel. I can never get enough of you."

"I don't want you to," she whispered, pulling him down for a flaming kiss that left no doubt in his mind what she wanted.

Her hands moved over him, unbuttoning his shirt and pushing it from his shoulders, then slipping back to caress the hard muscles of his chest and to twine her fingers through the mat of dark chest-hair that covered him. As she trailed her hands lower, wanting to please him, hoping to arouse him as he aroused her, he groaned in animal enjoyment.

"Easy, love, or we'll be done before we start." He caught her wrist and drew her hand to his lips, pressing a kiss to her palm.

"Hurry, Blade. I want you now," Angel encouraged, eager to be one with him again. She longed to feel her breasts naked against his hair-roughened chest and to feel the power of his manly pride deep within her.

Blade worked to free her from the gown, and she helped him, slipping quickly from her clothes. She came back to him, wanton. This was Blade. She loved him, and he loved her. She would give him the gift of her love tonight. To seal her acceptance of his proposal with the brand of her body. They were one, and would be one, now and always.

Angel lifted her arms and clasped him to her. The heat of his body seared hers. She moved beneath him restlessly for her body felt empty and unfulfilled. He had shown her love's full joy, and she wanted to share that wonderful intimacy with him again.

Blade was in exquisite agony. He wanted to hold back, to make their lovemaking last, but tonight Angel was the aggressor. Her movements beneath him were enticing, and her bold caresses stirred his already smoldering passion to an inferno. When, at last, he could bear it no more, he fit himself to her and sought the center of her desire.

Angel hugged him tightly as he thrust forward and made her his own once more. It was ecstasy to be one with him. She kissed him wildly, urgently moving her lips against his.

There could be no resisting. Blade willingly surrendered. He began to move, seeking the tempo that would bring them both the greatest excitement. Their bodies were joined, and so were their spirits. His hands traced fiery paths over her silken limbs. He explored the fullness of her breasts and then moved lower to grasp her hips and lift them tighter against him. As his need grew, he moved quicker and harder. Angel did not resist the power of his desire. It filled her with soul-stirring excitement to know that she could rouse such frenzied passion in him. She wanted only to please him.

They strained together, seeking that pinnacle of passion that would free them both from the bondage of their desire. Ecstasy burst upon Angel in an explosion of rapture.

"Blade!" she cried out his name as she clung to his wide shoulders, breathless before the enthralling pulse of pleasure that pounded through her.

At her abandoned cry, Blade knew he'd satisfied her and he gave in to his own frenzied need. His body shuddered as he poured the proof of his love deep within her. In that moment, it almost seemed they could reach up and touch the heavens. Sated, they lay together, their bodies molded as one, their hearts beating in unison, their minds focused on the future they both believed in.

Later, when the sounds of the wedding feast drifted to them on the night wind, Angel asked, "When will you tell Lucky?"

Blade smiled into the darkness. "First thing in the morning."

"Blade?" Angel rose up on one elbow to gaze down at him. "What will we do about him?"

"I love him, too, Angel. He's a part of us already. I'd like to keep him with us and raise him ourselves."

"I was hoping you'd say that," she confessed as she bent over him to kiss him, her bare breasts teasing his chest.

"When do you want to get married?" he ventured, knowing it was something they should settle before they talked to the boy.

"As soon as we can. I'd like to have a wedding with my family, but there's no telling when I'll ever get to go home again."

He heard the sadness in her words and cuddled her close. "I'll make it up to you."

"You don't have to make anything up to me," Angel refused. "The dreams of a fancy wedding are just that—girlish dreams. I'm a woman now—your woman. No matter where we marry, we'll be happy." Elizabeth had had a fairy-tale wedding, and her life had been a living hell. It was the love that counted, not the outward trappings.

"I'm glad you think so," he murmured as he kissed her.

"I know so."

Sorry that this wasn't their wedding night, they rose and dressed. In the morning, they would seek out Lucky and tell him of their plans. They would be a family, and they would be happy.

Lucky played hard with his friends for hours after leaving Angel and Blade. When the boys were ready to go to bed, Lucky left the village and wandered onto the range to be alone for a little while.

Thoughts of Angel had been with him all evening, and he was desperately hoping that Blade had asked her to marry him tonight. He knew they would be happy together, and he hoped, against hope, that if they did marry they would ask him to stay with them. He knew it was selfish of him to want happiness for others only so he would benefit, but he loved Angel and Blade both and never wanted to be separated from them.

It had been years since he'd prayed. For a long time Lucky had felt that God had abandoned him, but tonight he would try one more time. He had done everything he could, and now he would ask God for help. There was no one else to turn to.

Sitting down on a low rise that gave him a wide view of the earth and sky, Lucky gazed up at the stars and silently began to plead with God for this one special favor. He promised to be good for the rest of his life if God would let him stay with Angel and Blade. Tears burned in his dark eyes as he made the solemn pledge, and he continued to sit there for some time, quietly waiting and hoping for a sign that his prayer would be answered.

Brad Watkins along with his partner, Shawn Darnell, and the tracker he hired named Payson couldn't believe their good fortune. After their maddening pursuit of gunfighter, woman, and boy across Louisiana, they'd finally caught up with the kid and, miracle of miracles, he'd practically come to them. Fate had smiled upon them.

"You sure it's him?" Darnell asked warily. It seemed too easy.

"Who else would it be? You know damned well that that's him!" Watkins snarled. Foiled at every turn in trying to locate the Windsor woman and her nephew, he had nearly given up back in New Orleans, and then the little desk clerk had come through with the information he'd needed and he'd been back on their trail again. He had the boy in sight, and he was going to grab him tonight. The celebration in the village was so loud and boisterous that even if the kid did get the chance to cry out, it was doubtful anyone would hear him. By the time anyone noticed he was missing, they would be well on their way back to Philadelphia—and a great big reward. He thought it a pity that the woman wasn't with the boy. Marsden had promised an extra bonus to whoever brought in the woman named Angel, and Watkins could have used the money. Still, the reward for the boy was the biggest, and that was all that mattered now.

"I hope you're right, 'cause if that ain't him—" Darnell worried.

"Shut up." Watkins looked over at Payson. "You got an idea how we can get him out of here without bringing that whole village down on us?"

"Don't worry about a thing. I'll grab him. You two get the horses ready. We're going to have to travel hard and fast. We need to put as many miles between us and the camp as we can just in case he's found out missing right away."

"All right," he agreed. "You sure you can handle the kid alone?"

"What's one little kid?" Payson sneered as he crept toward the silent boy. He thought it unusual that a kid would be sitting alone this time of night, but he didn't worry about it. It was a break for them, and they desperately needed one.

Lucky had his eyes closed and was praying so fervently that he completely missed seeing Payson crawling toward him. When the man struck, pouncing on him and clamping a big, dirty hand over his mouth, Lucky was completely unprepared. He fought as hard as he could, but a brutal cuff to the side of his head dazed him, stilling any resistance he might have mustered.

The next thing Lucky knew he was gagged, his wrists bound before him, and he was being dragged down to a grove of trees where two other men waited with horses. Within minutes, he was thrown on the back of a horse and his mount was led away from the Wichita camp.

Frightened, Lucky tried to keep up a brave front. His realized that unless Sitting Dog decided to look for him, no one would know he was missing until morning. Trying to be rational in the face of his fear, he told himself that if he were going to escape, he would have to do it on his own. With that in mind, he waited for the opportunity to break away.

The men set a breakneck pace, and it took all of Lucky's concentration not to slip off. He tried several times to make his horse balk by using his knees, hoping that he would then be able to wrench the reins free from his captor and get away; but his efforts were in vain. The other man kept tight control over his mount.

Terrified though he was, Lucky refused to let it show. He told himself to stay calm and bide his time. Angel and Blade would come after him the minute they found out he was gone. So even if he couldn't get away on his own, he would eventually be rescued.

Watkins, Darnell, and Payson did not stop through the night. They rode eastward by the light of the moon. Briefly, at dawn, they rested the horses, then they put more miles between themselves and the village.

Blade was up first, joined by Angel a short time later. She was dressed in her regular riding clothes, her hair once more restrained in a sensible braid, and he mourned the loss to practicality.

"Where's Lucky?" she asked, glancing around. She'd expected him to be helping Blade as he always did.

"I haven't seen him yet this morning. I guess he and Sitting Dog stayed up too late last night. I'll check on him in a minute," he offered.

"Thanks." Angel went in search of something to eat, leaving Blade to rouse the boy. Within minutes, Blade was back with Angel, his expression troubled.

"What is it?" Fear edged her voice.

"According to Sitting Dog, Lucky didn't spend the night with him. Lucky took a walk and never returned, so Sitting Dog went to bed thinking Lucky had come back to our lodge to sleep with us."

"Oh my God!" Angel's face went white. Her heart skipped a beat as her hands clenched into fists at her sides. She lifted agonized eyes to Blade. "They think he's Christopher. They've taken him!" The words came out in a strangled, horrified whisper.

"We don't know that yet." He tried to calm her as he took her in his arms. "Let me take a look around camp and see what I can find."

"I'm going with you," she declared.

Blade returned to Sitting Dog and with his help located Lucky's tracks leading out of camp. He discovered the place where the boy had been sitting and saw immediately the signs of the struggle where he'd been overpowered. Angel was right.

"Well?" Angel had noticed the close attention Blade was paying to the ground. She had to know what he'd found.

"He was sitting here, and someone came up to

him. It looks like there was a fight of some kind, and then both of them walked off down this way." Blade followed the tracks and discovered the place where the other men had hidden with the horses.

Near violent emotions churned through Blade. He'd thought they were safe in the village. He'd let his guard down just this once; and, in that moment of weakness, the boy had been captured. He cursed himself for not believing these men could achieve their goal.

"Someone took him," he announced tersely. "From the tracks, I'd say there were three grown men. They had four horses, so they were expecting to have another rider with them."

"I knew it." Her words were choked; and she, too, was overwhelmed with guilt and worry. "It's all my fault. I should never have brought him into this. I knew it might be dangerous for him, but I deliberately ignored it."

Blade embraced her. "Don't blame yourself. If you hadn't taken Lucky in, he'd still be living on the streets. At least we know they're not going to hurt him. They think he's Christopher, and they're taking him back to his father."

"I know," she breathed, terror filling her so badly that she started to shake.

"I'll go after them. You can wait here for me."

"I'm going with you."

"All right." He led the way back to camp, his thoughts deep and worried. "Michael doesn't want Christopher dead, does he?"

"No, he wouldn't dare harm him until after his tenth birthday, and that's some months away."

"What about when he finds out that it's Lucky they brought back and not Christopher?"

"He'll be furious when he finds out I tricked him again. There's no telling what he'll do, and there's no telling what price Lucky might have to pay for being a party to my deceptions."

Blade paused and held her for a moment wanting to give her strength. "Don't worry, love. We'll find them."

"Blade, I hope you're right."

Chapter Twenty

On the wagon train

The days on the trail were long and arduous. Every morning, just after sunup, the oxen-led wagons rumbled off, heading westward at their slow, methodical pace. The wagon train, thirty wagons in all, stopped at midday for the noon meal and to rest the animals, then moved out again and kept going until just before dark. At night, the wagons were circled and fires built for cooking and for light.

One night, two weeks into the journey, Steve was just returning from tending to their stock when he found Sarah waiting for him a short distance from their wagon. His gaze upon her was warm with definite male approval as he approached. The days in the sunshine had agreed with her, bleaching golden streaks into her brown hair and adding a becoming flush of color to her fair complexion. He'd thought her lovely before, but after all these days and nights of close contact, he was entranced.

Steve had been hard put to only "play" his part of husband. The intimacy of their arrangement frustrated him, especially since his competition for her affections was a dead man. How could he compete with a ghost? Still, as he watched her waiting for him in the flickering firelight, he vowed he would never give up. Sarah was a prize worth any effort to attain.

As he drew closer he saw her troubled expression. "Sarah? What's wrong?" he asked.

"I'm not sure anything is, really," she ventured hesitantly, "but Christopher's complaining of a headache and he feels a little warm."

"I'll take a look at him," he offered.

Sarah was grateful. Although her role was that of experienced wife and mother, she actually knew little about childhood illnesses. She was glad for Steve's support. Somehow, she'd known she would have it when she'd sought him out.

They hurried back to find that Christopher had already bedded down under the wagon, where he'd been sleeping with Steve. He'd liked sleeping outside like one of the men, and Sarah had voiced no objection.

"Your mother tells me you're not feeling well," Steve said as he knelt beside the boy.

"My head hurts," Christopher mumbled, turning fever-bright eyes to Steve.

Steve rested a big hand across the boy's forehead. "Sarah, he's burning up!"

"Oh." It was a small sound from a usually noisy boy.

"Rest, son. Your mother and I will be here. We'll take care of you."

Christopher managed a weak smile, then closed his eyes in weariness. There was a drawn tightness to the boy's usually cheerful features. Steve stood up.

"I'll get some fresh water so we can bathe him and keep him cool. With any luck, the fever will pass as quickly as it came."

Sarah stayed with Christopher while Steve drew the water from the stream nearby. He was back within minutes, and Sarah immediately dampened a cloth and began to stroke her nephew's fevered brow, neck, and chest with a slow, cooling motion. Though Christopher shivered under her ministrations, he did not protest, and eventually he fell asleep.

Relieved, Sarah and Steve wandered to the campfire for coffee. Without hunger, they ate leftover biscuits from breakfast and a few pieces of cold meat.

Keith Collier, a lanky blond man of thirty, and his short, plump, dark-haired wife, Myrtle, owned the wagon that followed theirs. Seeing Steve and Sarah by the fire, they came over to visit with them for a few minutes before turning in for the night.

"Where's Christopher? I haven't seen him all evening," Myrtle asked. She liked the cute little boy and wondered where he was.

"He's not feeling well tonight. He's got a touch of fever, so he went on to bed early," Sarah told her.

"He should be fine by morning," Steve added.

"Well, if he's not, be sure you bundle him up real good and sweat that fever right out of him."

Steve thought her advice was outrageous. He knew sweating a fever did more harm than good, but he wasn't about to argue with the well-meaning woman. "We're going to do everything we can to make him better," he told her.

"Good. He's a sweet child. We certainly don't need him getting real sick," Myrtle responded.

To which Sarah added a silent *'Amen'* in her heart. Angel had entrusted Christopher to her care. She had to keep him safe and healthy.

"Tell him we hope he's feeling better right away," Keith said as they returned to their own wagon.

Steve and Sarah checked on Christopher once more to find that he was still hot but sleeping quietly.

"Do you want me to take him inside?" Steve offered.

"It's cooler out here, and I hate to disturb him."

"All right. You go on to bed, and I'll keep watch."

"I can't leave him when he's this sick."

Steve admired her motherly devotion, and they sat down beside the wagon near the sleeping boy to watch over him.

"Steve?" Sarah said his name quietly, not wanting to wake Christopher.

"What?"

"Thanks." She was grateful for his help. Steve seemed to know instinctively what to do to help her, and she wanted to let him know how much she appreciated him. Leaning toward him, she intended to press a kiss to his tanned cheek, but to her surprise, he turned his head and met her lips fully with his own. It was a quick, tender exchange because she drew quickly away, but it left her staring up at him in wonder.

"Sarah." His eyes met hers, but his expression was carefully masked, revealing nothing of his inner thoughts—of how much he wanted to clasp her to him.

Unnerved by her response to Steve's kiss, Sarah shifted away, trying to put a safe distance between them. It would have been easy to go into his arms and stay there, and she tried not to look at him for fear that he would read her feelings in her face. Even as she pretended to ignore him, though, she could not push him from her mind. Since they'd been together, he'd proven to her that he was a man of his word, and her respect for him had grown enormously. He was no stranger to hard work and was always ready to help others. When wagons had gotten stuck in the mud, he'd volunteered to help free them; and when it had been time to cross the river, he'd done more than his share in keeping everyone safe. He'd taught both her and Christopher how to handle their team, and he'd shown the boy how to make repairs to the wagon.

Sarah realized now just how foolish her plan to make the trek west alone had been. She wouldn't have lasted a day on the wagon train without Steve, and with every passing sunset, she appreciated him more and more.

"Mother." Christopher's pitiful cry jerked Sarah back to reality. Sarah and Steve both moved under the wagon to check on the boy, and Steve knew almost immediately that he was worse, not better.

"He's worse?" she repeated after him, putting her hand to Christopher's forehead. A terrible, dry heat emanated from him. His cheeks were reddened from his burning illness, and his usual color had faded to a dull grayish tone.

"Yes." Steve was already reaching for the bucket and rags.

"Let's take him inside now. He'll be a little more comfortable on the bed, and we can strip him down completely."

Steve did as she'd asked, quickly moving out from under the wagon to lift Christopher into his arms. Sarah hurried on ahead to hold the flap while he climbed inside with the boy.

"You can put him on my bed," Sarah told him. "It'll be easier to get to him there."

Steve laid the boy carefully on the larger of the two beds, and Christopher opened his eyes. "I want my mother," he murmured.

"She's right here," Steve assured him, and he stepped out of Sarah's way so she could be at his bedside.

Steve didn't see the hope that lit the boy's face. Christopher wanted Elizabeth to hold him and soothe him and love him. He thought Elizabeth was coming to him.

"I'm here, sweetheart," Sarah said softly as she sat down on the edge of the bed. She could see the confused look in the boy's eyes and prayed that he wouldn't blurt out anything in his delirium that would reveal their true identity.

Before Christopher could say anything, though, Steve spoke up, "Do you want the water bucket?"

"Yes, please," she responded, then turned back to her nephew.

"Mother." Christopher sighed, seeing in Sarah's lovely face the resemblance to Elizabeth and believing the illusion. "I missed you, Mother. I missed you a lot."

Sarah's heart was breaking as she listened to him ramble. It was all she could do not to burst into tears, touched by the depth of his pain and loneliness. "I'll take care of you, sweetheart. I promise. Here, drink this." She pressed a cup of water to his lips.

He sipped listlessly. "I don't feel good, Mother. I don't feel good at all."

"I know, and I'll try to make it better."

Christopher took a deep breath and closed his eyes wearily. When Steve returned with the bucket and rags, Sarah sponged the boy, fighting the fever with the chilling water.

"Let me help," Steve offered, placing his hand over hers.

"All right."

Sarah gave him another rag. She was glad that Steve was with her. When he was gone, she felt vulnerable and exposed, alone against the world. In his presence, she felt secure and safe.

For the rest of the night, they remained by Christopher's side, changing the cooling compresses on his brow and bathing him to bring the raging fever down. The hours wore on. Sarah's hope faded with the dawn. Christopher grew worse. Tossing restlessly, he called out to his mother. One minute he was sweating, and the next he was shivering with cold.

"What am I going to do, Steve?" she asked, close to panic.

"There's not much else we can do right now," Steve said, wiping the boy's forehead.

"But he's so sick. What if something happens to him?" Sarah stared at Christopher, feeling inadequate. "What if he dies?" she whispered, fear catching in her throat.

"He's strong, Sarah." Steve reassured her. "He'll be fine in a day or two. You'll see."

"I hope you're right."

Steve put his hands on her shoulders and turned her to face him. "Have I been wrong yet?"

Sarah's gaze was troubled as she looked up at him, and she was touched when she saw mirrored in Steve's eyes all the love and unquestioning support she would ever need. In that moment, Sarah longed to confide in him. She wanted to go into his arms and draw upon his wondrous strength, but she turned quickly back to the ill child.

"It's dawn and the wagons will be pulling out within the hour," Steve reminded her. "Would you rather stay here another day and try to catch up with the train later when he's well?"

Staying in one place appealed to her, but the terror of Michael's men was never far from her mind. Steve saw the conflicting play of emotions in her expression, and he knew her answer even before she gave it.

"No. We can't stop. We have to keep moving."

Steve wondered again at the terrible secret that held her in its grip. "Sarah." He reached out and took her hand. "Don't you know by now that I care about you and Christopher? Don't you realize that I'd do anything for you? Let me help you."

"We have to go on."

He studied her for a long, quiet moment, then said, "I'll get the team ready, and I'll bring you some breakfast before we go."

"Thank you."

Sarah remained with Christopher, never leaving through the interminable hours that followed. At noon, Steve spelled her, insisting she rest before they moved on. She hadn't thought she'd be able to sleep; but, curled on the small bed that was Christopher's, she found she was exhausted.

Steve watched Sarah as she slept. He noticed that dark circles marred the pale flesh beneath her eyes. He realized the trauma of the boy's illness was taking its toll on her as well, and a surge of protectiveness filled him. He had to make sure Christopher recovered.

With a start, Steve realized he no longer felt he was playing the role of husband and father. Sarah and Christopher were the closest thing to family he had, and he wanted to make it permanent. He loved Sarah and wanted her to be his wife. He wanted to cherish her and build a future with her, and he wanted to raise Christopher as his own.

The revelation shouldn't have surprised him. A gambler, he hadn't given much thought to settling down, but now it seemed the only possible course. He wanted the best for Sarah and Christopher, and he would do whatever was necessary to provide it for them. Steve reluctantly woke Sarah.

"Is something wrong?" she asked, coming awake quickly, instantly afraid.

"No, nothing's changed. It's just time to roll the wagons again. Did the rest help?"

Sarah stifled a yawn as she sat up. "Yes, thanks. I guess was I more tired than I thought."

Steve saw to the team, then climbed back up in the driver's seat to take up the reins. They moved on again, and Sarah returned to her vigil at Christopher's side.

By the time they made camp that night, Sarah was growing terrified. As if patterning itself after the heat of the day, Christopher's fever had grown hotter with each passing hour. He'd become completely delirious, and she feared each breath would be his last. Steve came to help her, and they tried to make him drink but met with little success. Steve was frustrated by the boy's worsening condition. His heart was heavy as he sat with Sarah. Christopher had grown very quiet, and his stillness worried them even more than his delirium. The fever had sapped his strength, draining away his will to live.

Sarah's hands twisted nervously in her lap. "Steve, what will I do if anything happens to Christopher?" she asked, choking as the tears she'd fought against for so long finally began to fall.

Steve could see her desperation, and he reached out to wipe away her tears. "We're not going to give up," he told her firmly. "We'll pull him through this. He's going to live, Sarah. Christopher is going to live."

"He's so little."

"He's young, but he's strong. He'll make it." Steve tried to sound confident.

"I can't lose Christopher, too," she told him frantically. The boy was the only living connection to the sister she had loved.

Steve saw the anguish in her eyes and believed she was thinking of her dead husband. How he loved her! If he could have, he would have traded his own life for the boy's just to make her happy. He wanted her to smile again.

"I understand, Sarah. You've lost so much already." He tightened his grip on her hands. "I know how much your husband must have meant to you and how much you miss him."

"I can't lose Christopher, too, Steve. I couldn't bear it."

"I know how much you've suffered, but I'm here now. Trust me. Lean on me. Together, we'll save him."

Her eyes met his, and Sarah saw concern in his gaze. She knew then that she not only trusted him completely but loved him as well. If it were possible to will someone to get well, Sarah knew Steve would do it. She said nothing but went into his arms, resting her head against his broad shoulder. His arms went around her, protecting her, strengthening her, shielding her from all harm. She could hear the powerful thudding of Steve's heart and drew comfort from it.

Together, they remained at Christopher's side through the long dark hours. Steve knew Christopher's life was in God's hands; and, though he hadn't prayed in many years, he prayed for the fever to break. When at long last exhaustion claimed them, Sarah dozed in Steve's arms as he sat with her, holding her against him.

"Mother." Christopher spoke the word hoarsely for his throat was parched and dry.

Their eyes flew open at the sound of his voice, and Sarah threw herself from Steve's arms when she realized her nephew was awake and alert. She touched his cheek and found it cool. Tears fell freely—tears of happiness, not sorrow.

"What happened? Why are you crying?"

"You were sick, son," Steve told him, "but it's over now."

"Oh," he responded dreamily. "Can I have a drink?" he asked. "I'm thirsty." Rejoicing, they poured him a fresh glass of cool water. Steve helped him sit up while Sarah held the glass to his lips. "Thank you." He lay back, smiling as he muttered, "I'm tired. I'm going to sleep for a while."

They kept watch until he drifted into a relaxed, normal sleep, then they looked at each other in joyous wonder. The lines and shadows of fatigue showed plainly in their faces, but happiness and relief lit them with a peace-filled inner glow. The trauma was over. Christopher's fever had broken. He would pull through.

Steve climbed down from the wagon then waited to help Sarah. His hands firmly holding her at her waist, he lifted her lightly to the ground. He expected her to move away from him the moment he released her, but Sarah didn't. She remained next to him, her hands resting on his shoulders as she gazed up into his eyes.

"You said you'd do it, and you did," she whispered, the true love she felt for him shining in her misty eyes. "Thank you, Steve Spencer. I don't know what I would have done without you. I would never have had the courage to face this alone."

"Of course you would have. You have more courage than most men, Sarah," Steve told her.

"Well, I thank you."

"I don't want your gratitude."

"It's not gratitude I'm offering, Steve." Without saying anything more, Sarah pulled him down to her. Her mouth sought and found his. Although her experience was limited, her desire was great. Steve gathered her to him.

"I love you, Sarah." The words were finally spoken.

"And I love you, Steve."

Steve could hold back no longer. He clasped her to his chest, unleashing the love and devotion he'd kept locked inside. His lips were firm as they moved over hers, evoking a passionate response. He believed her to be experienced. He believed she knew what she was doing. When they broke apart, he took her by the hand and drew her to the privacy of his bed beneath the wagon. The fires were banked and gave off only the faintest glow. They were alone in a joyful world of their own. Man and woman. Together.

Chapter Twenty-One

Her weariness vanished as Sarah lay down with Steve under the wagon. It was cave-like there, dark and warm and protected; and, as they came together on the softness of his bed, the world and its ugliness disappeared. Sarah knew she belonged in Steve's arms. It was right that they were together.

Steve's mouth claimed hers in a wondrous kiss, and Sarah responded eagerly. She had never been held so intimately by a man before, and she gloried in how perfectly they fit together. The hard planes of his body seemed made for the soft contours of her own. Sarah gave a sigh as his lips moved persuasively over hers, coaxing, then becoming more demanding as his hunger for her grew. She clung to him, offering herself completely.

Steve held Sarah close, his head spinning. He'd longed for this moment from the first time he'd seen her on the train. She'd been beautiful then, despite her mourning clothes; but now, he thought her even more lovely. Sarah was everything he'd ever wanted in a woman. She was beauty and gentleness and courage. Her very touch could arouse him.

There were still many things about her he didn't know—many mysteries about her past that were as yet unsolved, but they no longer seemed important. All that mattered was that she had come to him willingly. She loved him. Tonight, at long last, he would make love to her. He would show her with his body how much she meant to him, and he would try to replace the thoughts she had of her dead husband with newer, happier ones of them together. He hoped this night of love would give them the foundation they needed to build a future together, for he no longer wanted to play at being her husband and Christopher's father. He wanted the role in real life.

"I love you," he whispered once more in a love-husky voice.

Steve's lips left hers to explore the soft sweetness of her throat, and Sarah arched against him as he pressed heated kisses to the sensitive skin near her ear. The thrust of her breasts against his chest urged him on, and he could no longer resist the driving urge to caress her. His hands skimmed over her womanly curves, tracing patterns of fire wherever he touched her.

Sarah had never been touched so boldly before, and when his hands cupped her breasts, she stiffened in surprise. She was frightened by the power of the feelings he created within her. Steve sensed her resistance and kissed her again, more gently this time, urging a response from her, warming her with his tenderness.

Sarah relaxed at his tenderness. This was Steve, who had rescued her so many times and asked nothing in return but her trust. She had come to love him against her will, and she wanted to share that love with him now. She wanted to hold him, kiss him, and never let him go. Snaking her arms about his neck, she kissed him with abandon.

Steve had been worried when he'd felt Sarah tense beneath his caress, afraid that she would balk at loving another man. Not wanting to force her, only wanting to please her, he slowed his pace. Only when she put her arms around him and told him with her kiss that she wanted him, did he finally believe she was his. Joy filled his heart, and he removed his shirt and began to unbutton her dress.

When Steve slipped her gown from her shoulders, Sarah felt shy but did not protest. Instead, she reached for him, eager to run her hands across his chest and recalling the stirrings of desire on that first day when she'd watched him shaving.

"Sarah." He groaned her name at her display of boldness. He wanted her to desire him, and it thrilled him that she did. Steve slipped her undergarments from her with her help. When at last she lay before him, he couldn't take his eyes off her. She was perfect. She was his dream.

"You're beautiful, Sarah," he spoke in a husky voice as his gaze seared her.

Sarah trembled. She wanted him as much as he wanted her, yet she hesitated to tell him. Steve saw her tremble. Was she having second thoughts? He had to ask. "Is something wrong?"

"No," Sarah answered with a soft smile as she lifted her arms to him in invitation. "I'm just a little afraid."

"Don't be, love. I'd never hurt you."

"I know."

When he came to her, Sarah opened to him like a blossom to the sun. When his hands sought her breasts, she reveled in the excitement that pulsed through her. His mouth covered hers and then Sarah moaned as his lips moved to her taut breast. The sensation was new. A longing began to grow deep in the womanly core of her body. It urged her to move against him, to seek out the hardness of him. She caressed Steve as he'd caressed her, her fingers exploring the strength of his shoulders and his back before moving up to tangle in his hair. A cry escaped her as he turned his loving attentions to her other breast and his hand moved between her thighs with intimate knowledge.

Sarah should have been shocked by his touch, so intimate, so exciting, but in her eagerness she could not deny him anything. His touch was gentle, and the heated kisses left her ecstatic. She believed he would never hurt her. She knew he would be kind. She trusted him.

His skin was hot to the touch and as he moved over her again, she celebrated the erotic excitement. She caressed him, and when he groaned in pleasure at her daring, she was pleased. It excited her to know that she could arouse him, too.

Steve kissed deeply, his tongue seeking and finding hers in the sweetness of her mouth. She moved restlessly beneath him, and he knew she was ready for him. Once more he caressed her hips and thighs and then sought her most piercing pleasure point. He wanted to please her.

Sarah was aflame with desire. Steve's intoxicating kiss and touch were taking her higher and higher, coiling to near-painful excitement the aching need within her. She needed him. She needed what he could give her. She needed . . .

Sarah wasn't sure exactly what it was she needed to ease the frenzied ache in her heart. She only knew that it could be found in Steve's embrace. Wrapping her arms around him, she held him tightly to her, loving the feel of his weight upon her.

Steve moved away to shed the rest of his clothes, and, feeling the loss, she begged him to come back. When he did, his lips reclaimed hers in a hungry kiss. Sarah clung to him, returning his kiss with willing ecstasy. His mouth left hers to trace a fiery path down the side of her neck to her shoulder and then lower once more to her breast. Sarah moaned as desire mounted to an ever-heightening peak within her. As his mouth worked wonders on her supple flesh, his hands continued their maddening foray.

Steve wanted to know that he'd satisfied her. His caresses grew more and more intense until she cried out in rapture as the thrilling peak burst upon her. Sarah clasped him to her as the first waves crashed through her, leaving her breathless with a mixture of explosive need and wonder. It passed all too quickly, and in the blissful aftermath of the thrilling pleasure he'd given her, she felt limp, almost exhausted, yet oddly exhilarated.

Steve was elated that he'd pleased her, but he was not about to let her rest. He wanted to show her love's fullest joy. Fitting himself to the perfection of her body, he slid his hands beneath her hips and positioned himself to take her.

Sarah's eyes flew open and she gazed up at him. As he rose above her, she thought him the most handsome man in the world. His features were passion-hardened, and his eyes were dark with the emotions that filled him. She'd never dreamed that this moment could be so poignant, so perfect. She thought she should be a little afraid, but she wasn't. This was Steve. This was what she wanted.

Steve watched her, thinking her the most breath-taking woman he'd ever seen. As his gaze met hers, he saw a flicker of caution. Or was it fear? Slowly, he thrust himself into her, mesmerized by her sweetness until—abruptly—Steve realized that Sarah was a virgin. He was stunned. *Sarah . . . how? Why? What about Christopher?* Steve froze and began to pull away.

"Sarah? What—?"

"Don't stop, Steve, please. Love me. Please love me." She urged him to hold her, her dark eyes wide with passion as her arms reached for him.

"But I don't want to hurt you."

"You won't. Please."

"But Sarah . . ." His confusion was real, but the tight heat of his body wiped out rationality. She was untouched, yet she wanted him. When she silenced him with a passionate kiss, there was no way he could stop. Her fire enflamed him. With utmost care and gentleness, he penetrated that fragile proof of her untouched state and made her his in all ways.

Sarah gasped in sweet agony. He was big and powerful, and she ached with the perfection of his love-making. This was what was meant to be. They were one.

Steve was consumed by passion as he slid fully within her. Sheathed in her body, there was no way he could remain still. He wanted her. The questions would have to wait. For now, they would love. All that existed was Sarah and him and the unity that was theirs as one body.

Steve's rhythm built as he strained to take her again. His hands continued to caress her, tracing over her satiny skin with a knowing touch.

They soared higher and higher together. Each thrust brought them closer to pure bliss. When Sarah reached the pinnacle of her release, Steve could no longer hold himself back. He lost himself completely in the enchantment of union.

They lay quietly together for a time, sated. Their joy was a mutual, giving, living thing. They loved.

Steve had to find out the truth. There could be no more secrets between them.

"Sarah," Steve began, needing answers to ease his bewilderment. He gazed down at her, seeing her with different eyes now, knowing that everything he'd believed about her had been a lie. It wasn't that he was disappointed in finding her a virgin. There wasn't a man alive who didn't want to be the first to make love to the woman of his dreams. He would make Sarah his wife as soon as she would agree to marry him. But first, he had to know.

"I know." Sarah gave him a small, apologetic smile. "I wanted to tell you sooner." She lifted a hand to caress his cheek, and he seized it firmly, pressing an ardent kiss to her palm.

"Talk to me, love. Tell me the truth now. There's no need for any secrets between us."

Sarah couldn't resist the temptation to kiss him, and she pulled him down to her for a soft, emotional kiss. "You already know my real name is Windsor. What you don't know is that Christopher isn't my son. He's my nephew. His name is Christopher Marsden, and it's his father, Michael, who's chasing us."

"Christopher's your nephew? Where's his real mother?"

"Elizabeth, my sister, is dead . . . Murdered by her own husband," Sarah confided. Steve held her close, listening to the pain and sorrow in her voice and marveling at her courage.

"And your sister Angel is traveling to California, too?"

Sarah nodded. "We parted in St. Louis the same day you and I met. Angel is smart and brave, and I'm sure she's all right; but I can't help but worry about her."

Steve stopped her. "Sarah, I'm sure your sister Angel is a wonderful woman, but don't think you're not as strong or as brave as she is. You left a comfortable life to save your nephew. You gave up everything to take him to California, and you dared to travel unescorted, just the two of you, using only the widow's weeds as a disguise. I've never known another woman who was as strong and courageous as you are." He spoke with such fervor that she smiled, relieved.

"Are you sorry I'm not who I said I was?" she asked.

Steve chuckled. "I love you, Sarah. Nothing will ever come between us."

"Nothing," she agreed, kissing him.

"Do you think Christopher's father will give up?" Steve asked, curious.

"Never. That's why I didn't fight you that day in the shipping office. I suspected that those two men were working for Michael, and I was right. They're probably still looking for us, although I doubt if they can find us now."

"Let's hope not." He held her close.

"Michael will never let Christopher go, Steve, never." She explained to Steve about the will and that the boy was due to inherit within the year.

"Do you really think you'll be able to hide in California until it's safe to bring him back?"

"That was our plan."

"But that could mean you'd be in hiding for years . . ."

"Angel and I knew that, but what choice did we have? We had to protect Christopher. If you'd seen Elizabeth's arm that night, you'd understand."

Steve gathered Sarah to him, holding her to his

heart, thinking her the most wonderful woman he'd ever known. "Most women would have been defeated by what you've faced."

Sarah felt safe and secure in his embrace. "Angel and I love Christopher. We couldn't let anyone harm him."

He heard the staunch determination and knew for all of her sweet outward appearance what a fighter she really was. "I understand," he told her, kissing her again.

Sarah sighed when the kiss ended. "I'm glad you forced me to ask you for help in Kansas City. I still hadn't recovered from finding out the truth about Michael. All those years I thought he was the most wonderful man in the world." She paused and frowned. "Angel didn't, though. She hated Michael from almost the first time she met him. I didn't believe her then, but I do now. That's what made me doubt my own judgment. I don't know how I could have been so wrong, and that's why I was so afraid to trust you. I was afraid you might betray us."

"I'm not like Michael, Sarah," Steve declared fiercely.

"I know that. Now." She smiled up at him tenderly. "But in the beginning, how could I be sure?"

He bent to kiss her again. "I'll never hurt you, Sarah. I love you. You mean more to me than life itself."

"Thank you." Tears stung her eyes at his tender declaration. She knew he was speaking the truth and it made her heart swell with emotion. Steve loved her. He was a man worth loving. "I've told you the truth, now it's your turn to tell me. Why did you say you were my husband at the shipping office?"

"I'd like you to believe that I'd fallen in love with you already and couldn't bear the thought of being parted from you, but it isn't that nice." He drew a deep breath. "I was gambling in St. Louis . . ."

Sarah listened intently and saw the sorrow in his eyes at the memory of the other man's death. "I'm sorry that man died, but I'm not sorry you had to pretend to be my husband."

"Neither am I. It was one of the most daring bets I've ever placed, but I won the best hand ever. I won yours. Marry me, Sarah. Now, right away. Let's end this charade and make it real," he proposed in a hoarse voice.

"Yes, Steve, I'll marry you. But I think we have a little problem."

"What?"

"Everybody already thinks we're married."

Steve gave a short laugh. "You're right. I guess we'll have to wait until we get to California."

"I'm sorry."

"So am I, but it doesn't matter, as long as you know I love you."

"I know, and I love you, too."

They embraced once more, secure. As Steve's mouth took hers in a cherishing kiss, desire grew within them again. This time they came together more quickly in a burst of passion.

As they held each-other through the long, dark night, Sarah and Steve thought of the weeks remaining on the trail and knew they would be long and difficult. Knowing they had each other eased the strain, and they knew that no obstacle would be too difficult for them to overcome. As dawn lightened the eastern sky, Sarah dressed and left Steve to check on Christopher. She was pleased to find that he was still sleeping peacefully, the fever that had threatened his life gone. As Sarah watched the sunrise, she felt content for the first time in weeks, and she began to believe that perhaps everything truly would work out for the best.

"This has to be the right one!"

"That's what you said about the other wagon train!" his partner snarled.

"This is the only one left."

"And we don't know for sure if they're on it!"

"We've tried everything else. This has to be the one."

"I'm glad you're so sure."

"I'm not giving up. We were that close and we let them slip away. I don't know who that mean bastard is, but I'll take great pleasure in stealing the kid right out from under his nose."

"First, we've got to find them."

"We will. They aren't that much farther ahead of us now. You know how slow oxen are. We should catch up with them by tomorrow at the latest."

"And how do you intend to get the kid away from them?"

"Let me worry about that."

He gave his partner a strained look. "I left you in charge in Kansas City and look where it got us."

"Don't worry. This time I'm not going to fail. There's a lot of money riding on this. If you're not interested, you can leave now. I'll handle this myself."

"I ain't leaving now. I've been in on this too long to quit when we're this close."

"Good. Within a few weeks, we're going to have some money."

"I'm holding you to that."

The two men rode on, following in the direction of the wagon train.

Chapter Twenty-Two

The days that followed were some of the happiest Sarah had ever known. Christopher recovered quickly from the fever, and she told him that she'd confided in Steve. The affection Christopher had for Steve grew even more with the knowledge that his "father" would stay with them. He wanted to be just like Steve.

The wagon train continued west. Steve made the long, hard days wonderful with his gentle attentiveness and little kindnesses. One day he picked a bouquet of wildflowers for her, and the gallant gesture left her feeling like a school girl. The nights, after Christopher went to sleep and Steve came to her in the privacy of the wagon, were bliss-filled and ecstasy-bound. Steve was a tender, devoted lover, and Sarah eagerly looked forward to the day when she would be his wife and their future would be bound together.

Four nights later, after Christopher recovered

from his illness, the wagon train made camp a short distance from a tree-lined creek. Christopher had had few opportunities for play since they'd been on the run, so while Steve tended their stock and Sarah made dinner, Christopher and his friends explored the stream.

"Hey Christopher! Watch this!" eleven-year-old Tommy Webster shouted. He threw off his shirt and shoes, then grabbed a low-hanging tree branch and swung out over the water that ran about three-feet deep. With a whoop of excitement, he let go midstream, and he fell with a resounding splash into the cold current. He screeched as he hit the chilled water, scrambling back to the safety of the bank.

"Come on, Christopher! You try it!" ten-year-old Ricky Moran urged as he copied the older boy's stunt and fell with screaming glee into the bracing water. He emerged, a drowned-but-smiling rat, moments later.

"All right! I'll do it!" Unable to resist, Christopher followed their lead. Shedding his shirt and shoes, he grasped the branch with equal daring and swung out as far as he could. He dropped into the creek and managed not to shriek as the cold water closed over him. He came up laughing and struggled to the bank to join the others. They played until the sun dropped low in the sky and darkness threatened.

"You want to play hide-and-seek?" Christopher asked. It had been his favorite game at home, and he missed playing it.

"No, it's late. I'm going back," Tommy told him as he gathered up his clothes.

"Me, too," Ricky said, following the older boy. "You coming with us?"

"Not yet. I'm going to stay here a little longer," Christopher said, disappointed that they wouldn't play his game. He was having so much fun being a kid again that he was in no hurry to return. "I'll be back before it's gets too dark."

The two boys headed back to the train while Christopher, putting on his clothes, lingered near the water's edge, throwing rocks into the creek and enjoying the solitude.

Concealed in the foliage nearby, James and Slidell watched and waited. They had the Windsor boy in their sights, and they were ready to make their move. For a minute they feared their prey would elude them again, but their confidence returned when Christopher decided to stay behind by himself. He wasn't going to slip away from them this time! They would snatch him and head back east to claim their reward.

The two men plotted while Christopher sat idly on the bank. Ready with their plan, James circled through the trees and foliage to a hidden place where he could watch. Slidell situated himself on the same side of the bank a short distance away from the boy and threw a small rock into the stream where he could see it. He hoped to draw his attention and bring him down to explore.

Daydreaming, Christopher paid little attention to what was going on around him. When he heard the splash of another rock hitting the water close by, he thought Ricky or Tommy had come back to surprise him and play hide-and-seek.

"So, you decided to play after all! I'll find you!" he called out happily. Life had been so good lately that he'd managed to put the ugliness of the past from him. It did not occur to him to be afraid, and he leaped to his feet in search of his friends, charging through the bushes and trees. For once he was having fun.

The powerful hand that clamped down on his shoulder and spun him around startled Christopher, and then he recognized one of the men from the steamer. They'd found him!! Christopher started to scream for Steve and Sarah, but the gun pressed against his spine stopped him.

"Don't make a sound," the deep voice snarled. "I'd hate to have to shut you up permanently."

Christopher nodded, terrified.

"You ain't as dumb as you look," Slidell chortled in a low voice. "Let's go. We ain't got much time."

With James' help, he gagged the boy. They were dragging him to the horses when the the woman approached.

"Christopher?" Sarah shouted. She'd finished preparing dinner and had seen the other two boys come back without him. Though she had no reason to feel uneasy tonight, something told her to check on him. Taking the dish towel, she dried her hands as she ran to the creek.

"Damn!" James and Slidell swore angrily, exchanging nervous looks. "We'll have to take her, too."

The idea didn't sit well. She would slow them down, and they didn't want another run-in with the man. But no matter what, they would not admit defeat now that victory was in their grasp.

Sarah stared around the creek's banks, frowning. There was no sign of Christopher anywhere. "Christopher?" Her call was a little more tentative this time, as worry engulfed her.

Sarah walked farther along the bank, and when she heard the splash of a rock being thrown she was almost relieved. She and Angel had often indulged him in games of hide-and-seek at home, and she grinned at the thought that he was merely hiding from her.

"I talked to the boys and they told me you wanted to play hide-and-seek," she continued, "but it's time to come back now. It's dark and dinner's ready. Steve will be wanting to eat soon."

She paused at the water's edge, and something struck her from behind. Pain. Blackness. She pitched forward, falling unconscious to the ground.

"Now I know she ain't gonna yell," Slidell said with satisfaction.

"Hurry up, we've got to get out of here," James snapped back, irritated by the extra aggravation the woman presented.

They wrestled Christopher into the saddle and dragged Sarah's limp form onto Slidell's horse. They walked their horses quietly from the campsite before giving them free rein.

No one from the camp noticed. Steve was repairing a wagon wheel, and over an hour passed before he returned to their campsite.

"Sarah?"

When she didn't reply, he threw back the canvas flap on the wagon, but found it deserted. Puzzled, he sought out families in wagons nearby, but no one had seen them go. Finally, he found Tommy.

"Have you seen Christopher?"

"Not since we were playing at the creek. Me and Ricky came back, but he wanted to stay longer. I didn't see him after that, 'cause we got busy eating supper, but your wife came lookin' for him about an hour ago. I told her where he was, so I guess she went to get him."

Worried, Steve peered sharply around the clearing but could see no sign of Sarah or Christopher. "Where were you at the creek? Could you show me if we walk down there?"

"Sure." Tommy quickly agreed to help, and his father, Joe, grabbed up his rifle and went along.

Steve got a burning log from the fire to use for a torch, then followed Tommy's lead to the stream. Their search proved more than difficult, but the torchlight helped, and they spotted Sarah's white towel. Steve saw the footprints and understood with clarity what had happened.

"Oh, my God," he groaned.

"What is it?" Joe Webster asked nervously.

"They've been taken."

"Taken? Taken by Indians?" Tommy asked, suddenly scared.

"No." He left it at that. "I've got to go after them."

"You can't go tonight," Joe Webster pointed out.

"It's too dark. There's no way you can follow their trail until morning."

Steve knew Webster was right, and the frustration left him enraged and hopeless. They returned to the circle of wagons, and Steve sought out the wagon-master. After telling him of his plan to leave the train at first light and making arrangements for another family to tend their wagon, he methodically began to gather together everything he would need in his rescue attempt. The last thing he took out of his own bag was his gun. Steve didn't like violence and strove to avoid it at all costs, but in the morning he would strap it on. If necessary to save Sarah and Christopher, he would use it.

"Steve?" Joe Webster hesitated at the back of the wagon.

"Yes?"

"Listen, there are a few of us who'll be glad to ride with you in the morning if you want. There were at least two of them. You'll need the help."

"Thanks, Joe. I'd appreciate it."

"We can't let this kind of thing happen to our womenfolk and children. We've got to protect them and keep them safe."

His words slashed at Steve. "I know."

"I was wondering . . ." Joe had never been known for minding his own business. "What's going on? Why would anybody want to take Sarah and Christopher?"

Steve's grateful expression turned stony at the inquisition. "It's personal." There was no warmth in his tone, and his answer silenced the nosey Webster.

"Well, no matter." He was embarrassed. "What time do you want to leave?"

"I'll be riding out as soon as it's light."

"We'll be with you." Joe backed away from the wagon, still curious, and Steve drew a ragged breath, glad that the man was gone. He returned to his packing. He had never before invaded Sarah's privacy by going through her belongings, but now he had no choice.

Sarah had told him the details of her life in Philadelphia, but Steve did not know exactly where she'd lived. The men who'd taken her and the boy no doubt had been hired by Marsden to bring them back. For that reason he sorted through their bags for clues to their past.

As he dug through Sarah's clothes, Steve found the widow's dress she'd worn to mislead Marsden's men. His hands tightened on the garment. He remembered the kiss he'd given her on the boat and the guilt that had followed. He'd loved her even then, he realized, and his feelings had only strengthened in the time since.

The emotions that flooded through Steve were so fierce that he found himself crushing the black fabric in his hands. He felt impotent before the battering winds of fate. He was at the mercy of the night, and he knew his rage and frustration would continue until Sarah and Christopher were safe.

Steve's mouth twisted bitterly. It hadn't done them any good to be in his protection tonight. He'd been in camp the whole time and hadn't even known that they were in trouble until it was too late.

The need to resort to violence grew strong within Steve. He'd never considered himself savage, but he'd never had his loved ones threatened before. A vicious curse exploded from him, and he vowed that he would save Sarah and the boy from the evil Marsden—no matter what it took.

With an effort, Steve drew upon his years as a gambler to formulate a plan. He had to think, to use his head.

He laid the widow's dress aside and, with methodical precision, sorted through Sarah's personal belongings until he found some correspondence that gave him an address in Philadelphia. He pocketed the letter but kept searching until he'd located the rest of her important papers and her money. Wrapping them carefully, he stowed them in his bag. Once he rode away from the wagon train, he might never come back, so Steve took all essentials with him.

As he started to close Sarah's bag, Steve noticed a small oil portrait partially concealed at the bottom. He carefully pulled it out and stared down at three lovely women. It was an old picture, and Sarah looked barely fourteen years old, but there was no mistaking her expressive dark eyes and gentle beauty. She was in the center of the picture, flanked by two distinctive blondes. One was a child—Angel, he assumed. The other had to be Christopher's mother, Elizabeth. They looked so happy and contented in the picture that it only increased Steve's pain. He tucked the portrait into his bag for Christopher.

Steve left the haunting, lonely confines of the wagon to wait outside. Though he and Sarah had

403

been lovers for only a few days, she'd branded his soul with her love, and he could not sit inside without thinking of her. They had shared nights of bliss on that small bed, and he couldn't bear the anguish of reliving those moments of loving while she was in danger.

Sitting down before the low-banked campfire, Steve waited for dawn. His nights in Sarah's arms had passed too quickly, but tonight each minute lasted an eternity.

Slidell and James rode steadily all night. With the coming of daylight, the woman and child had to be released from their bonds. James rode double with Sarah, but Christopher was astride a horse of his own. Freed from the shackles of ropes and gag, he weighed the odds of escape. James, one step ahead of him, kept his prisoners separated, suspecting correctly that one would not flee without the other.

"Don't even think about trying to get away, kid. I've got your aunt right here. Your daddy doesn't care much if she comes back or not. You're the only one he wants, so it ain't gonna matter if she lives through the trip."

Christopher's eyes narrowed at the threat, and he wished he were older and stronger and had a gun. He longed to take on these two the way Steve had in Kansas City. He ached to free Sarah from that vile man's hold, but he had no chance of success.

His helplessness riled Christopher, but he remembered Steve's poker lesson on bluffing. With an effort, he composed his expression, taking care to reveal nothing of the fury and hatred that filled him. They knew who he was and understood him enough to guess his thoughts and intentions. From now on, he would have to be very careful. *Besides,* Christopher tried to cheer himself, *Steve would save them soon, and everything would be all right again.*

"Hurry it up a little," Slidell insisted. "That man she was travelling with is a mean one. I don't want to meet up with him again."

"All right," James agreed, putting his heels to his horse's flanks.

They continued at a rapid pace for most of the day and kept careful watch for any sign that they were being followed. They pushed the horses with no concern for their welfare, anxious to get far enough away so no one could catch them. Kansas City was close, and they would be there in less than two days.

Sarah and Christopher had no chance to speak to one another during the bone-jarring ride, but they both kept praying for Steve to appear and rescue them. As mile after mile passed and there was no sign of him, their spirits began to sink. Sarah realized what awaited them at the end of their journey, and as they rode farther from Steve and closer to Michael, she prepared herself for the confrontation. A few months ago, she would have felt powerless before Michael's charismatic personality, but not any more. She would be ready to deal with him.

They did not stop until late, and even then they did not light a fire. Both men were determined to get to Kansas City and make connections with a steamer heading for St. Louis quickly. The faster they delivered the kid and his aunt, the sooner they received their reward money.

Slidell made sure that Sarah's and Christopher's hands were bound in front of them again as soon as they made camp. He handed them a canteen to drink from and thrust plates of cold food at them.

"Eat it," he told them. "That's all you're gonna get tonight."

They ate in silence.

"I'll sit first watch," James offered, standing beside his partner. "You go ahead and get some sleep. I'll wake you after midnight."

"All right, but keep a sharp eye out. I don't trust 'em."

"Don't worry. We got 'em now. The only place they're goin' is back East with us."

Sarah and Christopher ignored them, and when Slidell bedded down and James went to keep watch, Sarah and Christopher huddled together under the one thin blanket they'd been given between them.

"Aunt Sarah, what are we going to do?" Christopher worried.

She hugged him with a reassurance she did not feel. "I don't know. It doesn't look like Steve is going to get here in time."

"I'm scared." They'd fought a hard battle, and they'd lost. "Aunt Sarah?"

"What is it, sweetie?"

"I'm sorry. I shouldn't have stayed down at the creek so long. I should have remembered." Christopher was miserable.

"Oh, Christopher, don't blame yourself," Sarah said softly. "It's not your fault. None of this is. Besides, Steve can't be far behind. It may take him a while to find us, but he'll get here. I know he will."

The boy's mood improved at her encouraging words. "Steve will come. He won't let them take us back."

"But while we're waiting for Steve, let's try to figure out a way to escape on our own." Sarah knew that they had little chance to get away. Still, it didn't hurt to be prepared.

"I'll do anything."

"Good boy."

They hunched together against the cold. And prayed.

It was just barely dawn, the second day out. Steve was up and dressed and ready to ride even though darkness still claimed the land. He faced this second day with grim determination as he tightened the cinch on his saddle. He had to find Sarah and Christopher. He had to! Steve wasn't surprised when Joe Webster and the other men from the train who'd accompanied him joined him by his horse.

"We hate to do this, Spencer, but we've got to turn back. Our own women and children are defenseless back with the wagon train."

"I know," he told them, understanding. "I appreciate your coming with me this far."

"I wish we'd caught up with them."

"So do I."

"What are you going to do now?"

"I have to keep going. There's nothing else I can do," he told them flatly.

"What about your wagon?"

"Take it on with you. If I manage to find them, we'll join you within a week, ten days at the most. If we're not there by then, use what you need, but save the personal things."

"But Steve—" Joe protested.

"Take it. If I don't have my family, I don't need to think about settling down in California."

The men still longed to find out why his wife and child had been taken, but they did not force the issue. Spencer was a private man; and after spending a full day riding with him, they knew he was a dangerous man, too. If he hadn't told them his story by now, he never would.

"We'll plan on seeing you and your family in a week," Joe told him, trying to sound positive.

Steve nodded and watched as they mounted up and prepared to head back to the wagon train. As they rode off, Steve answered Joe's statement in his heart. *In a week. God, I hope so.*

He turned to the east, into the rising sun. Somewhere, Sarah and Christopher were being held against their will, but Steve vowed to find them. If he had to, he would go straight to Michael Marsden. Nothing was going to separate him from his family. Nothing.

Chapter Twenty-Three

"What the hell are you two trying to pull?" Michael exploded in anger as Watkins and Darnell deposited Lucky in front of his desk.

"What are you talking about?" Watkins stared at him in confusion.

"You said you had Christopher. Where is he?" Michael demanded, jumping to his feet. He eyed the defiant boy.

"This is." Watkins indicated the boy, who looked smug and amused. Michael, however, was unquestionably irritated. A sudden sickening feeling settled in his stomach, and Watkins looked at his partner.

"Your son?" Darnell finished cautiously as he, too, glanced from the boy to Michael.

"I've never seen this boy before in my life." Michael spat indignantly as he glared at Lucky. "Where did you get him?"

"He was traveling with the blonde woman in the

portrait. We followed them all the way to Texas before we managed to catch up with them."

"You fools! Don't you realize Angel led you on a wild goose chase?!" While he was raging at the two for their incompetence, he couldn't help but feel a pang of admiration for Angel and her daring. "I don't know who this boy is, but he's not my son."

"I tried to tell 'em, but they wouldn't listen," Lucky finally spoke up. When the men had first kidnapped him, he'd been scared, but after he realized they weren't going to hurt him, his fear had turned to anger. During the course of their travels to Philadelphia, he'd tried several times to escape. He was sure Angel and Blade were right behind them, and he wanted to do everything he could so they could catch up. It hadn't worked, though, and now he was facing the man Angel had told him about. He could understand why Angel and her sister had taken their nephew and run. This Michael Marsden had the same cold, unfeeling look in his eyes as the people who'd run the orphanage.

"Shut up!" Watkins snarled, backhanding him. He'd restrained himself from laying a hand on this obnoxious kid. He'd tolerated his wild escape attempts and wretched pranks, but now there was nothing to hold him back. If he wasn't Christopher Marsden, it didn't matter. Lucky barely flinched at the man's brutal blow. He stood before him, his lip bloody and swelling, glaring at him with hate-filled eyes.

"I get a turn after you," Darnell put in with pleasure, his hands itching to punish the boy who'd put burrs under his saddle.

"Enough!" Michael raged. "Get out of my sight, both of you!"

"But what about our money?"

"The reward money was for the return of Christopher Marsden."

Watkins and Darnell were livid. Darnell grabbed Lucky by the collar, hauling him from the room. He intended to beat the boy senseless. It was bad enough that they'd had to put up with him for the entire trip, but now to find out that they'd made a mistake and grabbed the wrong kid, he wanted to take his anger and frustration out on him.

"Hold it!" Michael commanded. "Leave the boy."

"He's not your son. You said you didn't want him, so he's ours now."

"Here's a hundred dollars for each of you. Now get out!" Disgusted, Michael threw the money at the thugs.

It took Watkins and Darnell only a few seconds to realize the money would ease their frustration more than hitting Lucky would. They snatched it and rushed from the room, glad to leave the little trouble-maker behind.

Michael circled around from behind his desk, never letting his icy-blue regard shift from the boy. Angel's ploy had been brilliant. The boy was of the same size and weight as Christopher and had the same brown eyes. His hair color was darker and his features bore little resemblance to his son's, but that didn't matter. Assuming he was Christopher would be an easy mistake for anyone to make who hadn't met the Marsden heir face-to-face. Michael smiled wryly at her ingenious plan.

A tremor of apprehension went down Lucky's spine. He'd made it this far with little trouble, but now came the real test. He was alone in Philadelphia and at the mercy of this man—a man Angel knew to be a killer. Girding himself, Lucky faced him with all the courage he could muster.

"Tell me, young man. What is your name?" Michael asked, keeping his tone conversational and civil. It was a tone that didn't match the look in his eyes.

"My name's Lucky."

"Well, Lucky," Michael said slowly. "I think you and I can come to some kind of 'gentleman's' agreement here, don't you?"

"What d'ya mean?" He was alert for trickery and did not trust Michael Marsden.

"I mean, you tell me where my son Christopher is, and I'll see what I can do about your future."

"I never met your son. I don't know anything about him."

"You were with Angel and yet you say you never met Christopher?" The tension rose in his voice as he took a threatening step toward him. "I don't believe you."

Lucky tried to look indifferent. He was being stalked, and the street wisdom told him not to back away.

"Why were you with Angel, and where were the two of you heading when those men caught you?"

Lucky stayed silent. He would not reveal anything to this man. He realized that Christopher was safe for the moment, but if he told Marsden what he knew, he could endanger the other boy.

"Well? I'm waiting?" Michael's patience was nearly at an end.

"I told ya. I don't know anything about it."

Michael erupted in anger. He grabbed Lucky by the arm and gave him a bone-rattling shake. "Listen to me. I don't know who you are, and I don't care. All I care about is finding my son! I could kill you right now, and no one would know the difference! No one would care!" His eyes glazed with a terrifying coldness.

"Angel would!"

"Oh, she would, would she?" Michael shook him again.

"She's coming after me! Blade is, too! They won't let anything happen to me!"

Michael gave a triumphant laugh. "So! The lovely Angel is coming after you. Good. Very good."

He eased his grip on the boy. It wouldn't do for Angel to return and find this boy, whomever he was, bruised and battered. He would not give his meddling sister-in-law any ammunition that she could use against him. She couldn't prove a thing and he wanted to keep it that way. "Who's Blade?"

"He's Angel's friend." Lucky offered no more.

The news that Angel had a "friend" didn't sit well with Michael. She was his. She just didn't know it yet. "Well, in that case, we'll have to be waiting for both of them when they come looking for you, won't we? I offer you the comfort of my home until Angel arrives."

Michael kept his hold on the boy as he pulled him from the study and dragged him up the steps to the third floor. Lucky fought but was no match for him. Michael opened the door to the windowless, empty room at the far end of the hall and shoved him forcefully inside. Lucky sprawled on the dirty floor.

"There's no way out of here except through this door. No one will hear you if you scream, so you can forget about trying to escape." He could see the fear in the boy's eyes and felt a surge of power. "Perhaps I'll let you out once Angel returns and tells me where she's hidden Christopher. Until then, I suggest you relax and enjoy your accommodations."

Lucky stared at Michael as he backed from the room and slammed the door. The sound of the key in the lock had a finality to it, but Lucky charged to his feet anyway. He tried the door—which was securely locked from the other side.

Lucky began to search the room for something he could use to pick the lock. If Marsden thought he could lock him in here and forget about him, he was mistaken. The lock hadn't been invented that could keep him out or, as the case may be, in.

It was late that same afternoon when the hired carriage stopped before the Marsden house. Inside, Sarah sat beside Christopher in silence. They were both tense, and she held his hand tightly in hers.

When he glanced up at her nervously, she gave him a reassuring smile.

"We're going to be fine."

Christopher did not reply but turned his gaze on the house that loomed ahead. The memory of his mother's death assailed him, and he trembled as he prepared himself to face his father again.

"Of course you're going to be all right," Matthew Harper cut in uninvited. "Your father misses you. Why else would he have gone to all this trouble to get you back? You should have never run off, you know."

Sarah didn't bother to respond to the heavy-set, balding man with obsidian eyes. She'd made it a point to ignore him since he'd appeared on the scene in St. Louis and made it known that he was James' and Slidell's boss. He'd taken charge of the rest of their trip home.

Home. Bitterness welled up within Sarah at the thought of it. Philadelphia was no longer their home. Only heartaches and sorrow existed here. The only home they had now was with Steve.

The driver came around and opened the carriage door.

"Looks like we're here," Harper announced with open pleasure, glad that the chase was at an end. He was going to be rich. He climbed out first, then reached in to help her.

"I can get down myself, thank you." Sarah rebuffed his offer of help and climbed out on her own. Harper rankled at her superior attitude, but let it pass. He'd have his money soon and would never have to see the pair again. Christopher reluctantly hopped down and quickly grabbed Sarah's hand. She could feel the tension in his grip and knew he was frightened.

"Aunt Sarah, will you promise me something?"

"Anything," she answered firmly.

"Don't leave me here."

"I'll do everything I can to stay with you."

Christopher nodded and gave her a small smile, but the look in his brown eyes was troubled. Any good memories he'd ever had of the place were gone now, replaced by haunting visions of his mother lying dead at the foot of the staircase. He did not want to go back inside. He did not want to see his father again. He wished Steve were there with them. Angel, too.

"Let's go," Harper ordered, taking her by the arm as they started up the walk.

Sarah would have jerked free, but there was nothing to be gained in making a scene. They had been caught and returned. Her worst nightmare had come to pass. All that was left to do was to deal with Michael as best she could.

Sarah lifted her head in proud dignity as they mounted the steps. She would not let Michael know she was afraid. She would face him as boldly as Angel would—unflinching.

They were admitted to the house and directed to Michael's study. The door was closed, but Harper opened it with familiarity and strode in, bringing them along with him.

"I told you I'd find them," Harper announced with

pride as he presented himself to Michael, one hand still firmly holding Sarah's arm. He wasn't about to let her go until he had his money in hand.

Sarah stared at Michael as he sat behind his desk. He appeared the cultured gentleman, and no one would have ever guessed that he was a murderer. The thought chilled her, but gave her nerve.

"So you did." The surprise that had shown first in his handsome features changed, and his gaze hardened as he glanced at Sarah and the boy. He unlocked his desk drawer and took out a thick envelope. Getting slowly to his feet in a predatory move, he said, "And I told you I would pay you well if you did." Michael moved around the desk and handed the cash-stuffed envelope to Harper. "I thank you for your help."

"Any time, Mr. Marsden. Any time."

With that, Harper was gone, and Sarah and Christopher faced Michael.

"Well, well, well," he said with a triumphant smile. "It's good to see that my son suffered no ill affects from his kidnapping."

"Aunt Sarah didn't kidnap—" Christopher started to argue.

"Shut up!" Michael snarled, and the boy, seeing the barely controlled rage in his steely eyes, fell silent. "Now, as I was saying. I'm glad Christopher's all right."

"I'm sure you are." Sarah's temper blazed through her sneer. "But you and I both know Christopher was far safer with me than he ever was or will be with you."

Michael was startled by the change in her and more than a little angered. "I wouldn't get too confident if I were you, my dear. Kidnapping is illegal; and though I haven't gone to the law yet, I will if you give me any trouble."

Sarah stiffened. She remembered what Mr. Hayden had said. She knew they had no case against Michael. Christopher was his child and without proof that Marsden had killed Elizabeth, the boy was doomed to remain with him.

Frantic, she glared at her smug brother-in-law. Michael had won.

"You killed Elizabeth," she accused hotly.

"I did?" he mocked. "What proof do you have?"

Sarah fell stubbornly silent.

"You see? The law is on my side. According to the authorities, you're the one who broke the law—not me. You kidnapped my son."

"To save his life!"

Michael's expression turned black, his tone threatening. "I'd be very careful if I were you, Sarah. It wouldn't pain me in the least to see you in jail for what you've done. Of course, we can avoid all that unpleasantness if you'll leave my house right now and never attempt to see Christopher again."

"I'm staying. Christopher needs me."

"I'm the only one Christopher needs! Get out before I change my mind and send for the authorities." Michael grabbed Christopher by the arm and pulled him to his side.

Christopher fought down the terror that welled up inside of him. There was nothing his Aunt Sarah could do but leave. If he cried out to her and begged her to stay, it would only make matters worse. He stood beside his father, his face ashen, and faced his future alone.

"Christopher, I've got to go for now," Sarah said calmly, her resolve to protect him growing more fierce. "But I'll be back."

"Aunt Sarah." He tried to run to her to hug her, but Michael's heavy hand restrained him.

"Good-bye, Sarah." Michael gloated. Now all he needed was to see Angel again.

Sarah was desperate when she left Michael's house. She started back to her childhood home in search of Aunt Blanche. She was frantic to help Christopher, but she wasn't sure what else she could do. As Michael had said, and as Mr. Hayden had previously warned them, Christopher was his son. They had no claim on the child except one of love. Sarah reached her home and was reunited with her distraught aunt. Sarah had to get word to Angel, but she also sent a message to John Hayden right away.

Michael waited until Sarah had gone from the house before he turned on his son. He saw that Christopher feared him, and he was glad. "You're right to be afraid of me. Running away from home wasn't a smart thing to do."

"This isn't my home. Not anymore. Not without my mother."

"Don't be ridiculous. I am your father, and this is your home."

"You're no father of mine! You killed my mother!" Christopher threw the accusation at him in defiance. The worst had already happened. He had nothing left to lose.

"Your mother's death was an accident." Michael's jaw clinched in fury. He longed to strike him, but did not. There would be time for that later, once Christopher had turned ten and the money was in Michael's control. For now, he would bide his time.

"Everybody knows you did it!"

"Ah, but no one can prove it, can they? Perhaps a few days locked in your room with nothing to eat will teach you respect for your father."

"I'll never respect you! Never!"

Without another word, Michael led the boy from the study up the stairs to his bedroom on the second floor. He locked him in and pocketed the key.

Michael was more than satisfied with the way everything had turned out. All that remained was to face Angel, and he was looking forward to the confrontation. He was glad that Lucky had told him she'd be coming for him, for he had a few things he wanted to propose to her when he saw her again. He imagined she would be most responsive to what he had to offer now that Christopher was where he belonged.

Eagerly anticipating Angel's return, Michael went back to his study to wait. As he sat down at his desk once more, he began to think about what Sarah had said, and he realized he probably hadn't heard the last of her. Scribbling a short message, he called for one of his servants.

"I wish John Hayden would send word that he got my note," Sarah worried as she paced the parlor in the family home. "I can't stand this waiting and not knowing."

"What else can we do?" Aunt Blanche asked nervously from her seat on the sofa. She felt they were beaten.

"That's the problem. I don't know. Do I have to give up or—"

"We'll never give up!" Angel's voice surprised them both as she appeared in the parlor doorway with Blade at her side. "We're going to keep fighting Michael forever if we have to!"

"Angel! You're back!" Sarah flew to her sister and launched herself into her arms.

"Angel." Aunt Blanche was there, too, hugging and kissing her.

"Everyone, I want you to meet Blade Masters . . . my fiancé."

The women surveyed the tall, handsome man and smiled their approval. "Hello."

"Blade, this is my Aunt Blanche and my sister Sarah." Angel made the introductions as she took his arm.

"It's wonderful to meet you, Aunt Blanche." He turned his gaze to Sarah and smiled warmly. "So, you're Sarah. . . . I think we're going to be good friends."

"I hope so," she replied, liking him instantly.

Aunt Blanche beamed at him, impressed by his

extraordinary good looks. "Where did you two meet? How?"

"Later. First, tell me about Christopher. Where is he?" Angel turned on Sarah.

"Michael has him."

"Michael? I didn't know. Blade and I came back because Michael's men kidnapped Lucky, thinking he was Christopher."

"Who's Lucky?" Sarah and Aunt Blanche exchanged confused glances, and Angel quickly detailed all that had happened to her since she'd last seen Sarah boarding the train in St. Louis. "So you've already been to Michael's house?"

Sarah picked up the narrative. "Harper, Michael's hireling, took us straight there. But if I ever go back, Michael'll have me arrested for kidnapping."

"We'll just see about that!" Angel stood up in agitation, ready to go after Michael.

"Wait a minute, Angel." Blade tried to calm her. "Let's think about this."

"He can't keep us away from Christopher."

"We have to be careful. We have to make sure what we do will work."

"He does have the law on his side," Sarah pointed out reluctantly.

"Damn that man!" Angel's hatred was alive with fury.

Blade chuckled at her words, but Aunt Blanche gasped at the obscenity. "Angel!"

"I hate him, Aunt Blanche. He's torn this family apart, and I hope he burns for it." Angel spoke fiercely. Turning to her sister, she asked, "Was Christopher all right when you left him?"

"He was scared, but fine."

"Thank heaven." Elizabeth's son was well, but Angel's concern for Lucky was mounting. "Michael didn't say anything about another boy?"

"Not a word."

Angel and Blade exchanged troubled looks. What might Marsden have done with a boy who wasn't important to him? "He must have Lucky somewhere."

"But where?"

"That's what we have to find out. I have to see Michael."

"I'm going with you," Blade said firmly. "I have a few things of my own I'd like to say to this man."

Angel saw the deadly fury in Blade's eyes and sensed it would be better if she spoke with Michael alone. "No, Blade," Angel said quickly, putting a hand on his arm. "Let me try on my own. If I talk to Michael myself, maybe I can get through to him."

"The man's a killer! I don't want you facing him alone."

"I'll go with you," Sarah spoke up.

"It's too dangerous for the two of you," Blade argued.

"No, it's not," Angel returned. "You and Aunt Blanche will know where we are. We're going in broad daylight, and we'll be together."

"Besides," Sarah added. "I sent word to John Hayden that we needed to talk to him, and someone has to stay here at the house in case he comes by."

Blade still wasn't convinced. "Angel, this man knows no mercy. He'll hurt you if he gets the chance. He's already killed your sister. We have to fight him on his own terms."

"We're not facing a man who fights fair, Blade. Michael's as low as they come. He's a snake. He'd never face you man-to-man, and if something did happen and Michael died, we'd still lose in the long run. No matter how wrong it is, he does have the law on his side." Angel gazed up at him, grateful for his devotion. "Trust me," she pleaded.

Blade didn't like to have them go unprotected, but he gave in to Angel. "All right. But I'll be waiting right here with your aunt. If you're not back within the hour, I'm coming after you."

Angel kissed him softly. "Thank you."

Chapter Twenty-Four

When the butler announced to Michael and his guest that Angel and Sarah had arrived, Michael smiled in complete satisfaction. Things were going perfectly according to his plan.

"Thank you. I'll be right out." He turned to his guest. "They've arrived."

"Would you like me to come with you?"

"No, that's not necessary. I'll bring them in here to meet you."

Feeling completely in control and more confident than ever, Michael left the room to greet the two women. He wondered how long it would take to bend Angel to his will.

"Angel. Sarah. I've been expecting you," Michael welcomed them as his gaze fell hungrily upon Angel. It was obvious she'd been out in the sun for her hair was now gold-kissed and her skin tanned to a warm blush. His eyes travelled over her, approving of the daygown she wore that emphasized the lush curves of

her breasts and tiny waist. He imagined her unclothed, upstairs waiting for him in his bed. He was
going to enjoy the coming weeks of slaking his desire
for her. He'd grown weary of pretending Mary Anne
was Angel when he bedded her. Now he had the
means to force Angel to agree to his terms, and he
could hardly wait. That night, he would sink deep
within her body. He hardened at the thought.

"I'm sure you have," Angel retorted, her flesh
crawling under his avaricious regard. "Where are
Christopher and Lucky? I want to see them."

"The boys are fine, but before we discuss them,
there's someone I want you and Sarah to meet."

Angel and Sarah exchanged skeptical looks.

"This is hardly the time for pleasantries, Michael,"
Sarah stated firmly. "You know why we're here."

"Indeed, I do, and that's precisely why I think you
should meet my guest. This will only take a moment," Michael motioned them toward the study.
"Ladies?"

They followed him into the room and tensed when
they saw the constable who rose at their entrance.

"Officer Davenport, I'd like you to meet my wife's
sisters, Angel and Sarah Windsor." They exchanged
cautious greetings, and at Michael's direction they
sat as he stood behind his desk. "I asked Officer
Davenport here this afternoon because I had a feeling I'd be hearing from you again." He looked pointedly at Sarah.

"I see," Angel managed tersely.

"Mr. Marsden has been telling me that you have
some concerns about his son's welfare. However I

can assure you the boy is in good health and appears quite happy."

"That's a matter of opinion," Angel spoke up disdainfully. "I'd like to see Christopher myself. It's important that I talk to him, and I also demand that you bring Lucky to me."

"Lucky's fine. There's no need to concern yourself there. As far as seeing Christopher goes, I'm afraid I can't let you see him. He's resting, and I don't want to disturb him."

"What have you done with him, Michael!" Sarah broke in. "Where is he? I want to see him right now!"

"Miss Windsor, while you are the boy's aunt, Mr. Marsden is his father and well within his rights not to allow you to visit him," the constable stated firmly.

"Officer Davenport, do you know—"

"Mr. Marsden has told me of your accusations, and I must inform you that if you decide to press this issue, he'll be entirely within his rights to bar you from the premises. He could have you arrested for trespassing if he so chose."

Angel and Sarah paled at his statement.

"I want to see Christopher, and I want to see him now," Angel repeated, her emerald gaze defiant.

"Perhaps if Angel and I could have a moment of privacy, we could come to an understanding," Michael suggested. He gave the officer and Sarah a telling look. Sarah glanced at her sister, wondering if it were safe to leave her alone.

"It's all right, Sarah," Angel replied. What was Michael up to?

"I'll wait right outside," Sarah declared staunchly.

Her expression was filled with loathing as she glared at Michael.

"You do that," Michael remarked with casual indifference, and he waited to speak until they'd left the room and closed the door behind them.

Blade's nerves were stretched taut as he waited with Blanche in the parlor of the Windsor home for Angel's and Sarah's return. Letting Angel take the risk of facing Marsden by herself unsettled him. Everything she'd said made sense, but he'd still wanted to go with her. He wanted to protect her and to confront the cause of her misery. Since they'd left, Blanche had distracted him with small talk, but nothing helped to ease the agony of the wait.

More than half an hour had passed and Blade was getting ready to take action, when a knock came at the front door, bringing them both to their feet. Blanche reached the door before the maid and threw it open. A stranger stood before her.

"Is this the Windsor residence? Are Sarah and Christopher here?" Steve asked intently as he faced the diminutive, gray-haired woman. At a movement in the background, he looked up to see a tall, dark-haired man step into the hallway.

Blanche blinked in confusion at the stranger's questions, but Blade recognized him immediately from Sarah's description and came forward to greet him.

"You must be Steve." Blade offered his hand in

friendship. "I'm Blade Masters, and this is Blanche Windsor, Sarah and Angel's aunt."

Steve's dark eyes lit up with hope. If this man knew who he was, Sarah had to be there. He smiled at the old lady as he shook hands with Blade.

"Come in," Blanche welcomed. "We're waiting for Sarah and Angel."

"You mean, Angel's here too?"

Blade nodded.

"What about Christopher? Is he all right?"

"Angel and Sarah have gone to Marsden to get Christopher and Lucky back."

"You let them go alone?!" Steve exploded at the news.

Blade's silver gaze hardened at his reaction. "I gave them an hour alone with Marsden."

Steve saw the deadliness in Blade's eyes. "One hour, and then I'm after him."

They shared a look of understanding and were about to sit down when a carriage drew up and John Hayden strode up the front walk with another man.

"It's the lawyer Sarah sent for," Blanche told Blade as she hurried to the door. She opened the portal before Hayden had time to knock. "Mr. Hayden, please, come in. I'm glad you're here. So much has happened."

"Indeed, it has. I have news for you and Sarah."

"You do?" Her eyes widened in fearful expectation.

"Yes, let me introduce you to Lee Jackson. Mr. Jackson has some information that might prove helpful to us."

They settled in the parlor once more. Blanche brought the lawyer up to date, ending with how the women had gone to face Michael.

Hayden looked uncomfortable. "They're there now?"

"Yes," Blade answered. "Is there something more we should be concerned about?"

The lawyer glanced at Lee Jackson and then told Blanche, Steve, and Blade how he'd begun checking into Michael's past right after the girls had run away with Christopher. "To my horror, I discovered that his marriage to Elizabeth was not his first. When he lived in Richmond, he was married to a young woman named Helene Jackson."

"What?" Blanche was clearly shocked.

Hayden nodded, then let Jackson tell the heart-breaking story of his sister's death. When Jackson had finished, Blade, Steve, and Blanche were all silent. Their expressions mirrored a grim hatred.

"If this Michael Marsden is the same one I know, he's a cold-blooded murderer. I could never prove it, but I know in my heart that my sister died at his hand," Lee told them.

Suspecting Marsden only of Elizabeth's tragic accident was one thing. Finding out that he'd murdered another woman before her was something else. Blade and Steve both came to their feet as outrage filled them. The two women they loved most in all the world were alone with a killer. They had to get to them right away.

"I've been looking for Marsden for years," Lee went on. "I'd almost given up hope of ever finding him when I heard from Mr. Hayden. I want to get a look at this man to make sure it's him."

"What can we do if Michael is the same man?" Blanche asked. "We still have no real proof."

"The authorities believed one accident could happen, but the two timely accidental deaths of his wives might convince them to take a closer look," the attorney explained.

"How long have Angel and Sarah been gone?" Lee asked. The weight of the gun he wore strapped to his waist comforted him as he anticipated confronting the man who'd killed his sister all those years ago.

"Too long," Blade declared, his hand reaching for his sidearm, making sure it was ready just in case it was needed.

"Let's go after them." As much pain as Marsden had caused Sarah and Christopher, Steve was more than anxious to face him down. He, too, wore a gun.

They left the Windsor house and climbed into Hayden's carriage for the ride to Michael's house.

Lucky had picked many a difficult lock in his time, but this one tested his abilities. Hours had passed since Marsden had left him there, and he had had enough of being caged like an animal. He hadn't liked it when he'd been shut in the closet at the orphanage for imagined infractions of the rules, and he didn't like it now. He knew Angel and Blade would be coming for him as soon as they could, but that didn't mean he had to wait to be rescued. He'd taken charge of his fate before, and he would do it again.

He was determined to get out of Marsden's house as quickly and as quietly as he could.

For what seemed like the hundredth time, Lucky tackled the stubborn lock. His concentration was fierce as he once again worked at freeing himself. When at long last he heard the bolt click and he was freed, his excitement was immense. He opened the door and peeked into the hallway. To his relief, it was deserted, and without so much as a look backward, he charged down the hall toward the staircase that led to freedom.

Creeping down the steps, Lucky kept a close eye out for trouble. The second-floor hallway was wide and carpeted and he made his way down it, wondering how he was going to get out of the house without being seen if this were the only way downstairs. He moved passed several bedrooms with doors standing open and had just passed one that had the door closed, when he heard someone inside turning the doorknob.

Lucky flattened himself against the wall, waiting and listening. After a moment the doorknob stopped jiggling, and he heard a resounding curse from inside. Lucky could not imagine why anyone else would be locked in a room here, so he decided to investigate. It was far easier to pick the lock from the outside. Done, he turned the knob and cautiously pushed the door open, slipping inside.

"Who are you?" Christopher demanded in surprise as he whirled to find himself facing a boy of about his own age.

"Are you Christopher?" Lucky asked.

"Yes, but who are you?"

"My name's Lucky. Your father thought I was you."

"What?"

"I was traveling with your Aunt Angel—"

"Aunt Angel's here?" Christopher was suddenly excited. His Aunt Angel could help him.

"Not yet. But she will be. You know the rest of the house. Can we sneak out of here without anybody catching us?"

"We can try. I want to get as far away from him as I can," Christopher said, hatred in his voice.

"Is there another way downstairs?"

"No. There's only the front steps. Do we risk it?"

Lucky nodded and followed Christopher's lead.

Michael faced Angel from across the room. He smiled smugly. His goal was within reach. It was only a matter of minutes.

"Your ploy was clever, Angel."

"Too bad it didn't work," she countered. She felt uncomfortable being alone there with Michael, but she was not about to let it show. She knew she couldn't reveal any weakness before him.

"You always were a challenge," he murmured, closing the distance between them. "But then I love challenges."

"Get to the point, Michael. What was so important that you had to talk to me in private?"

"The point is this," he shot back, suddenly serious. "If you think for one moment that I'm going to let you take my son away from me, you've greatly misjudged me."

"If there's one thing I've never done, Michael, it's misjudge you. From the very beginning, I was the only one who saw through you and knew what you really were."

Angel's eyes were flashing emerald fire as they boldly met Michael's. What she saw in the depths of his cold, blue-eyed gaze sent a chill through her confirming everything she'd ever believed about him. He was amoral. A man without a soul or conscience. The devil incarnate. He took what he wanted and gave no thought to the consequences. He cared only for his own gratification and nothing more.

"That's what's always intrigued me about you, Angel." His voice was mesmerizing as he moved within arm's reach of her. He raised one hand to caress her cheek and smiled when she flinched from his touch. No other woman had ever dared treat him as she had, and he looked forward to breaking her to his will.

"The fact that I find you repulsive intrigues you?"

"You have a sharp tongue. If you were smart, you'd be careful not to abuse my good nature right now. You see, I determine whether or not you'll ever see Christopher or Lucky again. It would behoove you to be kind to me."

Angel had no intention of groveling before him. "What was it you wanted to talk about?" She changed the topic back to their original reason for being alone together.

"I have an offer I'd like to make to you. One I think you might find to your liking."

"Oh?"

Michael let his gaze wander over her again, taking in every lovely detail of her body. "Yes, I will allow you full access to Christopher, if . . ."

"If?"

"If you move into the house with us."

"You want me to marry you?" The thought set her stomach churning and made her want to retch.

Michael threw back his head and laughed out loud. "Hardly, my dear. I never intend to marry again. I thought perhaps we could come to an agreement between us, a barter of sorts."

"Such as?" she ground out, her temper rising.

"You come to my bed willingly and openly as my mistress, and I'll let the boy named Lucky go and allow you to have a hand in raising Christopher. If you refuse, I will make certain that you never see either of them again. Well? What do you say?" He was confident and smug, leering at her. He was certain he had her cornered and that she would accept his offer without question. He stepped closer, meaning to take her in his arms and kiss her. He did not expect her reaction.

Angel was livid. This man was even lower than she'd ever imagined. Her rage knew no bounds as she pulled herself together. "I would rather be dead than go to bed with you!" she seethed. She slapped him as hard as she could, then turned for the door. She managed to get one hand on the knob and started to open the door before he caught up with her.

"You little slut! Who the hell do you think you are?" Snaring her by the arm, he jerked her around to him, dragged her to his chest, and kissed her violently.

Angel bit down on his lip as hard as she could, drawing blood. When he yelped in pain, she tore herself from him and ran into the hallway. Michael lunged for her and caught her by the arm, unaware that Blade, Steve, and the others had just been admitted to the house by the butler and were standing in the foyer with Sarah and the officer just a short distance away.

"I'll never be your mistress, Michael! Never!" Angel swore as she fought to be free of him.

"You'll pay for this!" Michael was in a rage as his hands tightened upon her.

"Why you!!!" Blade had been talking quietly with Sarah and Steve when Angel came running out of the study. The sight of Michael's hands upon her and his vile threat shattered his calm. "Let her go!" Blade charged down the hall ready to throttle Michael with his bare hands.

"Blade!" Angel cried his name, thrilled that he was there.

Michael looked up to see the big, angry man coming at him with a lethal look on his face. With all the strength he could muster, he shoved Angel straight at him and ran for the steps.

"Hold it, Marsden!!"

At the sound of that voice from his past, Michael looked into the deadly eyes of Lee Jackson, who looked up at him gun in hand. All color drained from

Michael's face. He knew he was trapped, caught with no way to escape. His world was crashing down around him. A minute ago his life had been nearly perfect. Now, things were happening so fast, he had no time to think. He was desperate as he barged up the steps, but he stopped as voices from below called out to him.

"Mr. Marsden, wait." Officer Davenport didn't get to say another word as Lucky and Christopher came running down the steps heading straight for Michael.

Michael took advantage of the one chance he had. Grabbing Lucky because he was the closest to him, Michael drew the small derringer he was carrying in his pocket and pointed it at Lucky's head.

"If you want this boy to live, you'll all get out of here right now."

"Michael. Please, no. Don't hurt him." Angel begged.

"Let Lucky go," Blade demanded as he set Angel from him and moved toward the bottom of the stairs. His own heart was pounding as he approached the madman. He could see the terror in Lucky's expression as Marsden held him captive and deeply feared what might happen if they weren't careful.

Lee edged closer, too, his gun still aimed straight at Michael's heart. "I've finally found you, and you're hiding behind a child. Somehow that fits, Marsden, that truly fits."

"I think you both should put the guns away." Davenport tried to take control of the situation.

"Never," Michael hissed.

"Mr. Marsden, there's really no need for this." Again, the officer tried to make peace, but things had gone too far.

"This is about murder, officer," Hayden told the lawman.

"That's right," Lee added. "This man killed his first wife, my sister, in Richmond, just as he murdered his second wife, Elizabeth Windsor, here. I'm not taking this gun off of him until you've arrested him and charged him with their murders."

"Marsden?" Davenport glanced up at the man who, moments before, he'd believed to be innocent of any wrongdoing.

"I'll never put my gun down! Never!" Michael seethed. "You can't put me in jail! They deserved exactly what they got!!"

Michael's hands tightened on Lucky as his own hysteria grew, and Lucky knew he was going to have to act fast if he was going to save himself. He swung back with his elbow as hard as he could, striking his captor in a vulnerable spot just as Christopher jumped on his father from behind.

In a desperate attempt to throw off Christopher, Michael loosened his hold on Lucky just enough so the boy managed to break free. Twisting sideways, Lucky jerked away just as Michael's gun went off wildly. Lee fired back at his hated prey, but missed as Michael dove for cover.

Blade and Steve were racing for the stairs to give chase when Michael stood again and lunged for the boys. The look on his face changed from ugly determination to sudden confusion and horror as he lost his footing on the steep staircase and started to fall over backward. The last thing he saw as he lost his balance completely and tumbled out of control down the steps to his death was Elizabeth's smiling face in her portrait on the wall.

Silence held everyone in its grip. Blade and Steve reached Michael first, but both men knew right away that he was dead.

"Dear God," Blanche breathed, and her words broke the paralysis that held everyone.

"Aunt Angel! Aunt Sarah!" Christopher ran for the comfort and safety of their loving embraces, ignoring his father's fallen form and the officer who was now hovering over him.

Steve rose and followed the boy. He took Sarah into his arms and kissed her, then hugged Christopher to him once the boy had finished greeting Angel.

Lucky, alone, remained standing on the staircase, looking down on the scene below. He saw Angel hugging Christopher and felt a pang of unbidden jealousy. His gaze shifted to Blade just as Blade looked up at him. Without a word, the gunfighter rose from the dead man's side and walked toward the steps, opening his arms to the boy. Lucky flew down the staircase and Blade's arms closed around Lucky in a hug.

"Lucky!" Angel ran to Blade and the boy. The three of them stood together, wrapped in the warmth and protection of their love.

Epilogue

The sound of the wedding march swelled through the church, and Blade and Steve waited for their brides as the procession began. Seated in the front row with Aunt Blanche, Christopher and Lucky craned their necks to see Sarah and Angel.

"There she is." Christopher whispered to Lucky as Sarah drew near.

The boys watched in awe as Sarah glided gracefully past them. She wore an ivory-satin gown trimmed in lace and pearls. Her veil trailed the floor. When she reached the altar, Steve stepped forward and she took his arm.

"Isn't she beautiful?" Spellbound, Lucky stared, enchanted, at Angel. Off-the-shoulder and full-skirted, her white gown was trimmed in ribbon and matching satin rosettes. She joined Blade at the altar and put her hand in his.

The ceremony began.

Lucky could never in his wildest dreams have

imagined his new life. Angel and Blade had already taken the steps necessary to legally adopt him. For the first time in years, he knew he was loved and wanted. He had a ready-made family. He had Aunt Blanche, Aunt Sarah and Uncle Steve, not to mention Christopher, who would be his cousin.

Christopher watched the wedding with equal joy. Steve and Sarah had asked him to come and live with them; and, once they returned to Philadelphia from their honeymoon trip, they would become a family. Until then, he had Aunt Blanche and Lucky to keep him company, so he knew he would be all right.

As Christopher listened to the marriage ceremony, he thought of Elizabeth and tears misted his eyes. He'd loved his mother dearly and felt as he sat there in church that she was watching over him. Christopher smiled. Things would be better now, for they were all surrounded by love.

Steve took Sarah's hand and led her to the bed in their stateroom on the steamboat. They had slipped away from the wedding reception to take their honeymoon trip, and they were at last alone.

"I love you, Sarah," he told her as he drew her close and kissed her with sweet passion. She murmured softly and met his lips with equal fervor. She'd been waiting for this moment all her life, and now, at last, it was hers. She was married to the man she loved, and they were going to live happily ever after.

Steve scooped Sarah into his arms and lay her upon the wide bed. Shedding their clothes, they came

441

together in a rapturous mating. There was no shyness tonight, no need to hold back. Each gave to the other; and, in the aftermath of ecstasy's storm, they lay together, not talking, only feeling. It was perfection, and they would treasure this bliss forever.

"What are you thinking about?" Blade asked Angel. She stood at the window of the hotel room, and he wrapped his arms about her and drew her to his chest.

"Nothing and everything," Angel sighed, leaning against him. His arms were strong, and she cherished the moment.

Blade brushed the golden veil of her hair aside and pressed a heated kiss to her neck. He was rewarded by her shiver of desire. "Thinking back, I still can't believe you walked right into that bar to hire me, but I'm glad you did."

She turned in his arms, pressing herself against him. "Blade, have you decided what you want to do about the ranch? Do you want to live in Texas or do you want to stay here?"

"I love Texas, but I love you more," he told her, kissing her, parting her lips and tasting of her honeyed sweetness.

As his hands skimmed over her slender figure, Angel gave herself up to his expertise. She reveled in the excitement his kiss and touch aroused. She returned caress for caress, brazenly trying to give him the same pleasure he was giving her. Blade broke away from her.

"I wanted to take my time loving you tonight, but I won't be able to if you keep that up," he growled in a low voice.

"We've got the rest of our lives to take our time. I want you, Blade. I want you now."

They came together in a frenzied joining that spoke of passion and desire. Each strove to give to the other the perfect ecstasy, and in seeking to please each other, they gave more joy to themselves. When Blade moved over her and possessed her, he shuddered at the intensity of emotion that surged through him. There was something so tender and so precious about their lovemaking that he knew they would never be apart, that they would always be together. Moving as one, Blade and Angel sought love's pinnacle and reached it together. They drifted in heavenly peace, savoring the happiness that was theirs and knowing that nothing would ever separate them.

"I think Lucky would be happier in Texas," she whispered as she curled against Blade's side some time later, her head resting on his shoulder, her hand softly exploring his hard-muscled, lightly-furred chest.

"What about you?" Blade was determined not to pressure her into anything she didn't want. If she wanted to remain in Philadelphia, he would stay.

"I think I'd like to go to Texas with you and Lucky. If it's as special as you say it is, I know I'll be happy there."

"I promise I'll make you happy, Angel—as happy as you've made me." Blade kissed her deeply. "I love you."

"And I love you."

They blended together again in the dance of love, secure in the knowledge that their future days would be filled with love and laughter and their nights would be filled with passionate ecstasy.

"Aunt Blanche, what are we going to do tonight?" Christopher asked as he settled in at the Windsor house with her and Lucky late that night after the reception. He and Lucky would be staying there with the spinster until the newlyweds returned from their honeymoons.

"I don't know, sweetheart. What would you like to do?" she asked, a wee bit tired from all the excitement of the day, but not unwilling to spend some time with the boys.

"Want to play some cards?" Christopher asked, taking care to keep his expression blank. He knew it wouldn't do to let her and Lucky know just how good he'd become since Steve had taught him so many tricks.

"All right," she agreed.

Christopher turned to Lucky and asked, "Do you want to play, too?"

"Sure," Lucky answered easily. "What are we playing? Five card stud or seven card draw?"

Christopher regarded him with a spark of respect, wondering if he'd made a mistake in thinking Lucky would be an easy mark.

Lucky smiled to himself. He was an experienced

card player, and fully intended to win some of Christopher's money. Lucky followed them into the dining room, ready to test his skill. Like his name said, he was lucky.

GREAT BOOKS, GREAT SAVINGS!

When You Visit Our Website:
www.kensingtonbooks.com
You Can Save Money Off The Retail Price
Of Any Book You Purchase!

Visit Us Today To Start Saving!
www.kensingtonbooks.com

Romantic Suspense from
Lisa Jackson

See How She Dies	0-8217-7605-3	$6.99US/$9.99CAN
Final Scream	0-8217-7712-2	$7.99US/$10.99CAN
Wishes	0-8217-6309-1	$5.99US/$7.99CAN
Whispers	0-8217-7603-7	$6.99US/$9.99CAN
Twice Kissed	0-8217-6038-6	$5.99US/$7.99CAN
Unspoken	0-8217-6402-0	$6.50US/$8.50CAN
If She Only Knew	0-8217-6708-9	$6.50US/$8.50CAN
Hot Blooded	0-8217-6841-7	$6.99US/$9.99CAN
Cold Blooded	0-8217-6934-0	$6.99US/$9.99CAN
The Night Before	0-8217-6936-7	$6.99US/$9.99CAN
The Morning After	0-8217-7295-3	$6.99US/$9.99CAN
Deep Freeze	0-8217-7296-1	$7.99US/$10.99CAN
Fatal Burn	0-8217-7577-4	$7.99US/$10.99CAN
Shiver	0-8217-7578-2	$7.99US/$10.99CAN
Most Likely to Die	0-8217-7576-6	$7.99US/$10.99CAN
Absolute Fear	0-8217-7936-2	$7.99US/$9.49CAN
Almost Dead	0-8217-7579-0	$7.99US/$10.99CAN
Lost Souls	0-8217-7938-9	$7.99US/$10.99CAN
Left to Die	1-4201-0276-1	$7.99US/$10.99CAN
Wicked Game	1-4201-0338-5	$7.99US/$9.99CAN
Malice	0-8217-7940-0	$7.99US/$9.49CAN

Available Wherever Books Are Sold!
Visit our website at **www.kensingtonbooks.com**